SCRIBER

BEN S. DOBSON

Cover art by Ronnell D. Porter

ISBN: 1468085387
ISBN-13: 978-1468085389

DEDICATION

For my parents, John and Janice Dobson, who badgered me relentlessly until I wrote this book, in a very supportive way.

And for Morgan, who taught me how to gallop.

PROLOGUE

Scriber Elyse tapped at the stone with her chisel, shaving just the slightest bit off the statue's cheek, and then climbed down from the ladder to consider her work. After a moment, she set aside her tools and sat before the open journal at her desk.

She had read this one more than once; it had been written by Dennon Lark during the most famous period of his life. There was no better way to become familiar with her subject. Learning Scriber Dennon's voice—the way the man wrote and thought—allowed her to better visualize what form the statue would take. She could almost hear him telling the story as she read his journals, though it had happened well over a hundred years before.

The desk was strewn with books—every journal and history by Dennon Lark that the Academy had to offer. That she had been chosen to sculpt such an historic figure was an honor, and she took her research seriously. But this particular journal was her favorite, and not only because it offered the best insight into her subject. No, she liked this one because of the small note Scriber Dennon had scrawled on the inside cover. She liked what the words said about the man:

In my life, I have been called many things: prodigy and madman, traitor and visionary, blasphemer and failure and fool. In the end, most people seem to have settled on hero.

People are idiots.

It is not me they should revere. I am only an historian, and I deserve to be remembered as nothing more. But I have known *heroes, those whose deeds saved the Kingsland from destruction. So to all who read these journals, I say this:*

If you would remember anyone, remember them.

Smiling, Elyse turned the page and began to read.

CHAPTER ONE

I disliked Bryndine Errynson the moment I first saw her. She must be the most irritating person I've ever known.

— From the personal journals of Dennon Lark

The letter was a torment, as they always were. My untouched meal slowly cooled on the table as I unfolded, read, and refolded the small parchment again and again. But no matter how many times I looked, the words remained the same.

I was alone in the Prince's Rest that night; there were no customers but myself most nights, really. Waymark was a small, isolated village, not a place that had much use for an inn. Even in a larger town Josia Kellen's cooking would not have attracted a great deal of business—leaving it uneaten might still have been the proper choice without the distraction of the letter. But on that particular night, the night I met Bryndine Errynson for the first time, I would have ignored a feast cooked in the King's own kitchens. It was the same every time Illias wrote me.

Josia Kellen bustled out of the kitchen, kettle in hand, to refresh my tea. "Important news from the city, Scriber Dennon? You've barely touched your food." She was beside me in two steps—the Rest was little more than a converted family residence, and the common room had space for only two tables, uncomfortably close to one another.

I raised a hand to my temple. "It's a personal letter, Josia. I'd prefer not to talk about it." Not for the first time, I made a silent vow to start preparing my own meals at home. Josia was an impossibly chatty woman, and she fretted over me relentlessly. She had it in her head that I must be terribly lonely, living by myself with no wife or family. I had all my meals at the inn, and not one of them went by that she didn't try to engage me in conversation. I hated it.

But for once she respected my desire for solitude. "I'll leave you be, then," she said. "Call me if you need anything."

She hurried from the room, and I turned my attention back to Illias' letter.

It had come that evening, delivered by a Scriber-pinned courier shortly before my usual late dinner at the Rest. Far from the Saltroad that ran between Three Rivers and the Salt Mountains, Waymark was not a place the couriers serviced regularly. Illias would have personally asked the man to take the detour; it was not the first time he had done so.

Waymark should have been a distant enough place to escape my past, nestled against the Salt Mountain foothills in the north-western corner of the Three Rivers barony. The villagers thought it an important historical site—a mark on the path of Prince Willyn the Lost, on the journey that had given him his name almost two centuries ago—but the rest of the kingdom ignored the village despite those dubious claims.

Unfortunately, Illias was undaunted by my isolation. He wrote without fail, once every few months at least. The message was always the same: though he rarely came out and said it directly, what he wanted of me was the one thing I would not give, not even for him. And every time, I would fret for days before I finally shoved down my guilt, stowed the letter in a drawer with all the rest, and neglected to write back.

It was always the same, but even knowing that, it was a cycle I was helpless to break. With a heavy sigh, I unfolded the paper and looked it over again.

Denn,

I hope this letter finds you well—but not too well. I need you back at the Academy, and the sooner you tire of that backwater you've exiled yourself to, the better.

The School of Arts is reconstructing more of Adello's songs every day, and you are the only one who has ever appreciated the true historical relevance of his work. Legends and children's tales, they say, as though that discounts their worth. Damn it to the Dragon, they're all we have left. We can't expect to just stumble across the truth if we ignore the clues we're given. The Scribers have become indolent, waiting for discoveries to be brought to us for research and cataloguing.

The Council is no help of course. Pig-headed idiots, the whole lot. I wish I'd never taken a seat among them. They argue over money and appearances, and oaths be damned. I have no intention of sitting idle, hoping some farmer will miraculously uncover a hidden cache of history books in his basement. The Forgetting was almost five hundred years ago now, and what have we found since then? Nothing.

I'm surrounded by fools, Denn. I need you here. You saw the value in this pursuit before anyone. Come back, and help an old man accomplish something before he dies.

Your friend,
Illias

He had never so overtly begged me to return before. Usually he preferred to disguise his intentions, speaking of current affairs in the Kingsland or the latest decisions of the Council, while the subtext of every word screamed at me that I was wasting my life. This was different, though; there was nothing veiled about this.

Help an old man accomplish something before he dies. That was not an easy thing for me to refuse, even knowing he had likely chosen the phrase with just that intention. My mother had died before I could remember, and my father when I was just a boy—Master Illias Bront had as good as raised me. I would never have earned my Scriber's pin without him.

When I was young, nothing had seemed more noble or exciting than becoming a Scriber. Other boys dreamed of becoming warriors, joining the King's Army and upholding Erryn's Promise; all I had ever wanted was to swear the Scriber's oath, to wear that golden pin, to pledge myself to the preservation of knowledge and the recovery of the Kingsland's lost past. It was not an ambition that met with much approval from my father, a practical man of the Army—as far as Trestan Lark was concerned, reading and writing were pursuits for the weak. And besides that, enrolment in the Academy was as near to impossible as anything could be for the son of a low-ranking soldier, with neither the money to pay tuition nor the connections to seek the sponsorship of a Master Scriber.

And then one day, Master Illias caught me—a ten-year-old soldier's son with no money and no connections—sneaking about the Academy campus looking for a glimpse of my impossible dream. Instead of throwing me out, he offered me a job running errands for him, and fostered my desire for knowledge by lending me his books and answering my constant questions. When my father was killed patrolling the Highpass cliffs that same year, Illias found me room and board with the Academy staff, and on my sixteenth birthday, he sponsored my entry into the Academy. As Master of the School of History, he oversaw my education for eight long years. When I graduated, it was Illias Bront who finally placed the golden quill-in-inkwell pin of the Scribers onto my collar with his own hands.

But when a dream becomes a reality, it is not always a good thing. I could not go back to the Academy, not even for Illias. Too many memories of failure lived there, and a Scriber never forgets.

Josia's voice interrupted my thoughts once again. "Are you sure you don't want to talk, Scriber Dennon?" Very little time had passed since she last refilled my tea, and the cup was more than half full, but she poured anyway—an obvious excuse to bother me.

"I'm fine, Josia."

"It's only that you seem upset," she said. "It helps to talk about these things. I'm always here to listen."

She meant that sincerely, I knew. Josia was one of the few truly kind people I had met in my life. She was not particularly quick-witted and her constant nattering annoyed me, but it was comforting to know there was at least one good person left in the world. Most people in Waymark—most people anywhere—only cared about other people's problems to the extent that they made good gossip.

But for all of that, I still wished she would leave me be. "Not tonight, Josia. Please."

She was about to reply when the creak of the front door

stopped her. It was not a common sound at the Prince's Rest, and I was grateful for the distraction.

"Excuse me, Scriber," Josia said, and hurried over to greet the new guests. I glanced towards the door with mild curiosity as she ushered two women inside.

That was the first time I laid eyes on Bryndine Errynson.

CHAPTER TWO

Though few records remain from before the Forgetting, there is little doubt that the Errynson line began approximately one thousand years ago with Erryn the Burner and his wife Aliana, the last princess of Elovia. Erryn forged his kingdom with fire, bringing his people up the Conqueror's River and burning back the First Forest to clear the land. The Burning is considered by most historians to mark the beginning of Erryn's reign, and the calendar of the Kingsland is measured in years After the Burning, or AB.

The family took the surname Errynson, after the barbarian tradition, and the burning tree, crimson on a brown field, became their sigil. To this day, the Errynson family is associated with fire and rebirth, and on the eve of each new year the Festival of Burning is held in their honor, during which symbols of the year gone by are burned and prayers are made for the prosperity of the Kingsland, the King, and the Errynson family.

— From Dennon Lark's *Royal Blood: the Errynson Family*

I knew who she was almost immediately, by reputation and rumor. Broad-shouldered and muscular, she was larger than any woman I'd ever seen. Larger than any man, for that matter. She stood well over seven feet tall, maybe closer to eight—nearly two feet taller than the woman with her, and almost double that over the small, matronly Josia. Though we were both near thirty years of age, I would have looked a child standing next to her, and at a lanky six feet, three inches, I am by no means a short man.

Despite her size, though, it was her apparel that truly identified her. She carried a heavy-looking greatsword in a scabbard at her back, and a big round shield of plain steel strapped over that. The brown tabard of the King's Army covered her boiled leather jerkin, with the crimson burning tree of the Errynsons emblazoned full across the chest and a silver Captain's cord draped over the shoulder. No woman wore that tabard save those of Bryndine Errynson's company, and only one wore the Army's colors with the royal arms full-sized instead of in miniature over the heart.

I couldn't imagine why, but the King's niece—the woman they called the Bloody Bride—had just walked through the door of the only inn in Waymark.

Josia noted the coat of arms as well, and she hardly knew what to do with herself. "My lady… it is such an honor. An Errynson in the Prince's Rest! Why, not since Prince Willyn—"

Josia was prepared to go on, but Bryndine's companion interjected. "We are not here to stay. The Captain requires a Scriber."

I could have said something then, but I had come to Waymark to avoid attention, and attending the King's infamous niece was counter to that goal. I chose to stay quiet and keep my eyes on the table, but not before sparing a quick glance at the second woman. She was lean and trim, with the deep olive skin of the Southern Islanders. Her black hair framed sharp features, dark brown eyes, and a heavy scowl. She too wore the brown of the King's Army, with the burning tree insignia over her heart, like most Army soldiers. Pledged to the service of the King, but not of royal blood.

Bryndine shot her a disapproving look. "Courtesies, Sylla. We represent the King's Army." She inclined her head towards Josia. "I apologize for my companion, matron. But she speaks truly—we do not intend to stay. We saw a Scriber's shingle hanging just down the road, but there was no answer at the door. If you'll see that our horses are fed and watered and tell us where to find the Scriber, you will have a silver for your trouble."

Josia's eyes widened; a silver mark was more than the Rest would make in a month. "My lady, I… I can't accept… My husband takes care of the stables, and he is late coming back from Barleyfield, I…" The woman was too honest for her own good. The Kellens needed that silver badly and everyone in town knew it. Running an inn in Waymark was not a profitable venture.

Bryndine took the innkeeper's trembling hand and pressed the coin into it. "Sylla will see to them, then, if you will only provide the feed. Now, where might I find your Scriber?"

Josia gestured weakly towards me, still gaping at the coin in her hand. I had never seen her so speechless—it was rather delightful. Less so was the sudden attention of Bryndine and her companion.

Reluctantly, I stood and gave a shallow bow. Keeping my head down, I muttered, "An honor, Lady Bryndine."

"You know who I am." It was a statement, not a question.

An answer passed my lips before I had time to think. "Considering all that they say about you, how could I not?" I meant it in jest, but as soon as I said it I realized how the words could sound to a woman of Bryndine's repute. I might have been referring to any of a thousand ugly rumors.

"Mind your tongue, Scriber!" Sylla strode towards me with startling intensity. I felt the blood leave my face, and cursed myself for a fool. The Islander woman was smaller than her Captain, but at that moment—marching towards me with her hand on her sword—she looked far more dangerous. I am not a religious man, but I praised the Mother and the Father when Bryndine raised her right hand to block the other woman's advance. Her left arm, I noticed, she kept held tightly to her side, and I thought I saw a bandage wrapped about it, but I could not get a clear look.

"I am sure he meant nothing by it, Sylla. Please, go see to the horses."

"Bryn, he can't—"

"Sylla. The horses. Please."

Sylla glared at me for a moment longer, then turned on her heel and marched out the door, pulling Josia with her. When she was gone, Bryndine pulled out a chair and sat down across from me. I tried to catch a glimpse of the arm that might have been wounded, but she held it out of sight beneath the table.

I examined her as she settled herself in her chair. Sheer size aside, her appearance did not entirely live up to the tales. I had heard that she shaved her head bald to look like a man, but her hair—the golden-blond common among the Errynsons—was simply cut short above the ears in a somewhat masculine style. Her face was solemn and plain, perhaps slightly square-jawed, but not hideous or mannish as it was so often described. Frankly, she was quite dull to look at if one ignored her imposing bulk. Even her eyes were a colorless grey.

I needed to make amends before anything else. "Lady Bryndine, I didn't mean to insult you. I apologize if my words caused any distress." The last thing I wanted was to make an enemy of this woman. Even if she had not been armed, she looked as though she could pick me up and swing me one-handed. And as the King's niece and daughter of the Lord Chancellor, there were things far worse than simple violence that she could do to me.

It was often said that Bryndine's blood was flawed, that her mother's low birth drove her to follow the soldier's path, but she spoke with the ice-cold arrogance of a trueborn noble. "I know what you meant, Scriber. And I would appreciate it if you addressed me by my proper rank. I am a Captain in the King's Army." Though her unnaturally solemn face made it difficult to judge, she seemed to have taken my earlier jest in the worst possible spirit. But I was used to people thinking poorly of me—if she was not going to give me a fair chance, at least it meant I could give up playing so polite.

"As you wish, *Captain*. What would you have of me?" My tone made the title an insult, and I pointedly lowered my eyes to the burning tree at her chest, where a gold-stitched numeral would have indicated the company of a true soldier of the King's Army. There was nothing there. Though Bryndine and her women wore the uniform, they lacked any kind of formal authority. But if my intended slight struck home, she gave no sign, which only frustrated me more.

"Might I see your pin first?" She glanced at the Scriber's

pin on my collar. It was wise of her to be careful—I might easily have been a backwoods charlatan—but it did not sit well with me. Not coming from a woman who herself was pretending at being a soldier.

I unfastened the small gold pin and slid it across the table. "Sworn and pinned at the Academy, Captain Bryndine. Six years ago now." The pin was slightly over an inch high, a quill-and-inkwell of gilded bronze, engraved with the Old Elovian phrase that encompassed everything about the Scribers: *Voia Rae*—"Never Forget". Like most Scribers, my livelihood depended on my pin. Without one, the practice of medicine is illegal, and it is extremely difficult for the unpinned to find work in other Scriber dominated fields.

Bryndine took the pin with large, surprisingly deft fingers, flipping it over to check the other side, where my name was engraved. She knew that much at least—barring obviously poor gilding, the most reliable way to identify a fake pin is to check the back, and not only to see if the name matches. A genuine pin is gilt only on the front; on the back, the exposed Scriber-made bronze has a brilliant red-gold shine. Fakes tend to be dull and lusterless, or simply gilded entirely, hiding the metal beneath.

"Dennon Lark?" She made a question out of my name, and I nodded in response. Satisfied, she handed the pin back and I fastened it to my collar, dreading the reaction that was sure to follow. But if she recognized my name, she chose not to comment. I gave silent thanks to the Mother and the Father for that. The worst thing that could happen to my life in Waymark was for word to spread about my past.

"I hope you'll forgive me, Scriber. When impostors of your order crop up, it tends to be in out of the way villages like this one."

"Of course, Captain Bryndine." But forgiveness was far from my mind. It was galling that the Bloody Bride herself would think me an imposter—from everything I had heard, the woman was only allowed to bear arms and armor because her father was the King's brother.

"Well, then. I have an injury that requires treatment." She stretched her left arm out on the table, finally allowing me the glimpse I had been seeking. I saw immediately that it was no minor complaint; I was surprised she could speak without wincing. Her sleeve was torn up to the elbow, and beneath it her wrist and forearm were badly swollen, messily wrapped in a bloody piece of fabric. Through gaps in the makeshift bandage, an ugly gash was visible, splitting the flesh from the back of her wrist to a few inches beneath the elbow.

"How did you come by a wound like that out here, Captain?" I asked, genuinely intrigued. That something had brought the King's niece this far out into the back roads of the Kingsland was a curiosity by itself, but the wound added an entirely new level of strangeness to the story.

"Perhaps we could move this to your home, Scriber," Bryndine said, evading my question. "I would prefer to have this dealt with quickly, if possible. I must rejoin my company by morning—I would not have delayed here if Sylla had not insisted on taking me to a Scriber."

I fancied that she was struggling to hide her impatience under that composed veneer. The thought made me smile. "I am here to serve, Captain," I said, getting to my feet and tucking Illias' letter into my belt. "You saw my shingle, you know the way."

All of Waymark was visible from the front stoop of the Prince's Rest. A single street divided the village in half, with a makeshift town square in the middle where the dirt road split to circle a crumbling stone well and the large fireleaf tree that grew beside it. There were seven homes on the east side of the street, nine on the west, and that was the entirety of Waymark. The Rest sat on the east side, directly before the square, and my own cottage with its badly painted Scriber shingle was across the road and just a few homes down to the south.

It was a brisk autumn evening outside, and a cool breeze blew from the northeast, down from the Salt Mountains. I wrapped my arms tight around my chest for warmth as a gust blew through the boughs of the large fireleaf in the square, making the bright red leaves dance like flame.

Bryndine jogged around the side of the building to let Sylla know where we were going. She was apparently unaffected by the cold, and I was embarrassed by my own reaction. I unfolded my arms briefly, but decided that my pride wasn't worth the effort as another chill wind wound its way down the street, raising gooseflesh on my skin. When Bryndine returned moments later, I was hunched once more against the cold, and more annoyed than ever at her seeming immunity to it.

"You needn't have waited, Scriber. I know where your home is." Bryndine seemed surprised that I was still there, which bothered me—she apparently didn't think me capable of even a simple courtesy.

"I've been told it's not proper to let a member of the royal family wander the streets alone, Lady Bryndine," I replied. I hoped that something in that would sting, either the failure to use her rank or the implication that she needed an escort, but I was disappointed in both cases. I can't say why, but her perfect composure irritated me as much as anything ever has. It was childish, and very likely unwise, but as I hurried down the street towards my home, trying to keep pace with Bryndine's long strides, I made a vow to myself that I would get a reaction out of her before the night was over.

The warmth as we entered my small cottage was a wondrous thing, bringing life tingling back into my fingers and toes. I gestured Bryndine towards a chair at my work table and began to gather my supplies as she sat and unwrapped her wound, laying her arm across the table. When I had what I needed, I sat down across from her, taking her arm and probing it with my fingertips.

"Well, it isn't broken, but from the swelling at the wrist I'd guess you've sprained it in addition to the cut. It may be important for me to know how you came by such a wound, Lady Bryndine." I continued to eschew her military rank in the hopes of prompting a scowl, but she seemed to have given up that battle already. As I spoke I doused the gash with alcohol to clean it, but even that failed to make her flinch.

"It was nothing exciting, Scriber. My company is spread across the area doing routine scouting. I was tending my horse when something startled her and made her kick. I was lucky it was only my arm she caught."

"Last I checked, the King's Army doesn't routinely do anything in these parts, Lady Bryndine." I passed a thread through the eye of my needle, and pressed the point against her skin. "This will hurt," I warned as I pushed the needle through flesh.

"We do not normally come this far, it is true, but these are difficult times, Scriber. Has news of the unrest in the baronies reached you here?" She did not so much as gasp as I sewed up her wound, though I made a point of being rougher than necessary. Nothing affected the woman; it was infuriating.

"A little, m'Lady. There is talk of rebels putting villages to the torch around Three Rivers." Illias' letters had touched on the subject in the past. Moments later, I realized what she was saying, and my stitching came to an abrupt stop. "Are you saying that the Army expects them to strike here? What statement could they possibly make by attacking Waymark?" I forgot briefly about trying to anger Bryndine; the thought of the village burning was a sobering one.

"We believe that they seek to prove the royal family has failed to uphold Erryn's Promise. Striking at areas the Army is not actively protecting would be the easiest way to make their point." Her face betrayed no emotion, but she looked away as she spoke. "Each time the Army fails to stop one of these attacks, more people begin to talk about how the Promise has been broken."

She was silent for a long while as I finished stitching her wound and tied off the thread. I opened my mouth to fill the silence, but just then something snapped her out of her reverie.

"But you have nothing to worry about, Scriber," she said. "We found no sign of these so-called 'Burners'. Sylla and I are rejoining the rest of my company in Barleyfield to return to Three Rivers."

Relieved, I began to wrap her arm with cotton bandage. "You'll want to replace the bandage quite often," I said. "And clean the wound when you do, to make sure it doesn't fester."

"I have a Scriber in my company. I will have her see to it when we regroup."

"Fine. Just be sure to rest the arm until the swelling goes down and the wound heals."

Bryndine shook her head. "Just bind it tightly, Scriber. If I should need my shield arm, I will tolerate some pain."

"And risk injuring it further? Don't be foolish, Lady Bryndine."

"I will try to follow your advice, Scriber, but if the need arises, my duty takes precedence. Please, bind it tightly; it will be fine."

"I'm sure you know best, m'Lady," I muttered, wrapping the bandage as tightly as I could. *Sky and Earth, she thinks I'm a complete fool.* She had no intention of following my advice, I was sure; she had formed an opinion of me after my hasty words at the inn, and couldn't be bothered to listen to me now. Why should she? She was Bryndine Errynson, daughter to Elarryd Errynson, who was King Syrid's brother and Lord Chancellor of the realm. Royal blood ran in her veins. *Why should she listen to me? I'm only a trained, educated Scriber.*

"You likely won't find any need to use the arm anyway," I said as I tied off the bandage and stood up from the table. "Not on tame patrols like this one. It is very kind of the King to make sure his niece is kept safe."

She stared at me silently for a moment, and I thought for certain that I had gotten to her, but she only stood and took a silver coin from her purse, dropping it on the table.

"Goodbye, Scriber Dennon," was all she said as she strode swiftly to the door; she left without waiting for a reply. I had never managed to make her so much as blink, and it rankled me. She left as assured of her superiority as when she came.

It was late by then, but before I retired for the night I made an entry of the day's events in my journal. A Scriber's habit, that; deeply ingrained in me by Master Illias over eight years at the Academy. My record of the meeting with Bryndine was not kind to her, but it was unlikely that anyone would ever read it—I simply needed a way to release my frustration. In truth, I expected that I would never see Bryndine Errynson again.

CHAPTER THREE

Sometimes I need to remind myself that a Scriber swears his oath to the people of the Kingsland, not to the King. We swear to pursue the advancement of all knowledge and the rediscovery of all that which has been lost, and to serve the people in whatever way is needed—anything from teaching children to providing medical treatment. I swore that oath, and I truly believe in it.

But by the Father above and the Mother below, I loathe *serving the people.*

— From the personal journals of Dennon Lark

It did not take long to put Bryndine out of my mind the next morning—I had little peace from the moment I woke until I retired that night. Before I had even made it to the Prince's Rest for breakfast I had to see to Darlia Ginnis' little boy, crying over a scraped knee that made me wonder if he had been playing in a bed of nails.

At breakfast, Josia harangued me into writing a letter to her husband Hareld, two days late returning from Barleyfield. The messenger who had delivered Illias' letter late the previous day had stayed the night and would be heading back that way shortly.

No doubt Hareld had lost track of time while enjoying the company of a cheap prostitute or gambling away their savings.

Only Josia believed him when he said the monthly trips were to "check in with friends in the business". For all that her constant chatter bothered me, she was still a decent woman, and she deserved better than her ass of a husband. But there wasn't a suspicious bone in Josia Kellen's body, and I did not want to get involved, so I kept my mouth shut.

When I was done with Josia, Penni Harynson showed up at my door for her weekly lesson. She ostensibly wanted to learn her letters, but never absorbed a thing; the girl was an idiot. She only came because at seventeen, she was of an age to be married, and she had decided the local Scriber would make a better husband than Logan Underbridge's fat son Jason. Compared to that pimple-faced adolescent I was positively dashing, I suppose, despite being almost thirteen years Penni's senior.

I have never been an overly handsome man, but Penni chose to focus her flattery on my black hair and apparently "soulful" green eyes, ignoring my scrawny frame, narrow face, and over-long nose. After a fruitless hour trying to get her to write even one word correctly, I threw her out until she was ready to stop acting like a lovesick child. She left petulantly, telling me not to expect her back the next week.

On the way to the Rest for lunch, I was accosted by Ashton Norgand. His wife Carine was heavy with child and ready to give birth any day, and they called for me every time she so much as felt a chill. This time she was certain the baby was coming because she had a headache; it was not, of course, and I was forced to spend an hour pretending to examine her in order to convince her of that. I preferred that to actually having to deliver a babe, though—I can't abide the mess, or all of the shrieking that tends to come with childbirth.

After lunch came the worst part of my day: teaching the local children. I have no fondness for children, nor they for me, and every lesson went much the same. I would try to teach them of King Erryn and the Burning; they would demand stories about the tree spirits called the Wyddin, the jealous first children of the Mother and Father who sought vengeance on mankind for stealing away their parents. I would explain that the Wyddin were only legends, religious allegories; they would ask who it was, then, that Erryn fought with a sword of fire to conquer the Kingsland. I would move on to the Forgetting and King Ullyd; they would scream and rub snot in each other's hair.

Getting the children to remember anything I taught them was an impossible battle—yet if I asked any one of them about Waymark's history, they would offer up a wholly false story about the Lost Prince without hesitation. The hours I spent teaching them were never less than excruciating, and it was no different that day.

I ate a late dinner at the Prince's Rest, as always. Logan Underbridge and several other men chose that evening to stop by for drinks, and I was forced to listen to them gossip about the other villagers and give superstitious explanations for the sickly crops and poor harvests of the last year. Given the size of the Rest, I could not avoid being pulled into the conversation, though I tried to stay silent. Night had long since fallen by the time I extracted myself. It was then, on my way home, that I noticed something extremely curious.

The fireleaf tree in the village square was shedding leaves.

This would not have seemed such a momentous thing to most, but a Scriber knows things most do not. And one of those things is that a fireleaf—unique among all trees—*never* sheds its foliage, not throughout the autumn and winter months, not in the most violent of winds. Those flame-red leaves leave their branches only when they are torn off by human hands. Most of those leaves would have grown there for hundreds of years; some of them might even have budded nearly a thousand years ago, when the first trees began to grow back after the Burning. And yet, a thin circle of a dozen or so now littered the ground in the middle of Waymark.

I wondered when they had begun to fall. I had not noticed it before that moment, but I might easily have missed one or two, hidden behind the thick trunk of the massive tree—it was unlikely that they had all fallen while I was eating dinner. I picked a leaf from the ground and peered at it closely. Bright crimson at the center faded to a lighter orange-red around the edges; a wide base narrowed into a sharp, slightly curled point at the top. It truly looked like a lick of flame sitting in the palm of my hand, which of course was where the name came from.

In the First Forest south of Timberhold the fireleafs budded green, but throughout the rest of the realm they grew red, and it was tradition among the Plains barbarians who had founded the Kingsland to name a thing by its most familiar traits.

Were the leaves falling all over the Kingsland, or just in Waymark? Was it natural, or the result of some sickness or infestation? The questions flitted through my head, but I had no answers. This was a matter for the School of Sciences, and my primary discipline was History. I didn't have the expertise to pursue the matter.

I thought I heard a voice then, a faint whisper floating past my ears. There was something terribly sad in the sound, though I could not make out the words. When I looked around for the speaker, no one was there. But I could not shed the sense of unease that had taken hold of me, and I hurried towards the safety of my home.

It was a long while before I fell asleep.

* * *

The dream began as it always did, every night for the last five years.

The only light was dim and flickering, thrown by two handheld lanterns near the east wall where the men were working. The air was thick with the dust of centuries of neglect, and the sounds of digging echoed off the walls—the sharp ring of tools against rock, the rough scrape of stone on stone. I surveyed the chamber with growing dread. Long ago the sight had given me great satisfaction, even joy, but here in the dream, I knew what was coming. I shouted for the men to stop, but they didn't listen, couldn't hear me over the sounds of their work. And then there was another sound, a deep groaning, a terrible rumble and crack, and the roof was falling.

The screams of the workers assaulted my ears as debris crashed down from above, crushing the men as they tried to escape. A torrent of brightly colored glass rained down upon me, shards of blue and green and yellow and orange slicing into my flesh, tracing deep red lines where they cut. But no rocks fell where I stood—I could only watch while the others died.

And when the noise stopped, and the dust cleared, the worst part began.

The dead men began to claw themselves out from beneath the stone, bleeding and broken, staring at me with accusation in their milky eyes, and they began to chant.

"*In books of power, writ in blood...*" I covered my ears and screamed, trying to drown out the words, but snippets drifted through, scraps of old rhymes, of ancient songs. The men lurched closer and closer, circling me as they continued their terrible litany. "*The doom of Old Elov—*"

But abruptly the chanting stopped. The men were still there, still staring at me with condemnation in their eyes, but something was different—this was no longer the dream I knew.

Moonlit night surrounded me in place of lamp-lit darkness, and there was grass under my feet rather than stone. There was something against my back, and when I looked I saw that it was a mighty, ancient fireleaf, its rustling leaves as bright as fire even in the darkness. But no, they were not leaves; the tree was truly aflame, casting red light across the faces of the men surrounding me. And I no longer knew those men.

They were naked, all of them, and there were women among them now. All bore terrible wounds, but not like the men that had come before. These were the wounds of battle, the deep cuts of swords and axes, yet none of them bled. Their mouths were not moving, but there was a low whisper in my ears—their voices, I realized. Dozens, no, hundreds of voices, all whispering at once. And growing louder.

I could make out perhaps one word in a hundred, but all of them were terrible. "*Death,*" I heard, and "*Pain,*" and "*Vengeance,*" and over and over, "*We are the Burnt.*" But the worst was not the words themselves, it was the torment and the rage behind them. I could feel their anger as if it was my own.

I clapped my hands over my ears, but it did no good. The voices grew louder and louder, rising to a screaming fervor. Then, when I thought I could take no more, they united as one terrible voice, speaking a single undeniable command:

"*BURN,*" the voice demanded. And I did.

The flames of the burning fireleaf licked downwards, engulfing my body in a torrent of fire. I shrieked in agony as my skin melted and bubbled and sloughed from my bones; I felt my eyeballs burst and drip from their sockets. I was half mad with pain, screaming for mercy, begging the Mother and the Father and even the Dragon for respite from this torture.

And then, inexplicably, I heard a loud rapping noise: knuckles on wood. A pause, and then again, louder, and a shout.

"Scriber Dennon!"

I woke with a start to the sound of knocking at my door and Sylla's voice shouting my name.

CHAPTER FOUR

Erryn's Promise is the ideal the Kingsland was founded upon. The exact events that led to it are lost, but an idea of the true story can be found in the legends that survive to this day.

Erryn's tribe offered protection to Princess Aliana and the survivors of Elovia after the cataclysm drove them from their home. The other tribes demanded blood, for Elovia had warred with the barbarians for centuries. But Erryn wanted peace, and sought to find it beyond the Wasted Plains.

He made a pledge to his tribe, to Aliana's people, and to all those who would follow him: he would forge a new kingdom, founded on the simple tenet that he and all Kings after him would not demand service, but give it. If a King failed to provide protection, freedom, and equality to his people, he was no King at all; he would lose his right to the crown.

This came to be known as Erryn's Promise, and from far and wide people came, swearing to follow the man who had made it wherever he led.

— From Dennon Lark's *The Promise of a Kingdom*

"One moment!" I shouted, leaping out of bed and struggling to pull on my trousers before Sylla battered her way inside. When I finally opened the door to greet her, her expression was murderous—though in my brief meeting with her two days prior, she had given me no reason to believe she ever looked particularly pleased.

"The Captain wishes to speak with you, Scriber. Now."

"Now? It's the middle of the night!" Over Sylla's shoulder I could see other women knocking at other doors, and other villagers stumbling bleary-eyed out of their homes. A low commotion of whinnying horses and confused voices disrupted what should have been a peaceful midnight silence. "What is this? If it's so important, where is she?"

Faster than I could follow, Sylla's hand snapped forward, seizing my forearm with painfully strong fingers and twisting it violently. "Scriber, I swear by the Divide I will break your arm if you don't come with me right now," she growled. I let out a pained squeak and tried to pull away, but Sylla only squeezed tighter. "You can ask questions later," she said. "Let's go."

"Yes! Of course, I'm coming!" I bobbed my head in vigorous assent, terrified she would make good on her threat. To my relief, she relaxed her grip, though she did not release me fully until I had stepped out the door and closed it behind me.

"This way." She gestured towards the village square and waited for me to move first, staying slightly behind and to my left, clearly ready to grab me again if I tried to go anywhere but towards her Captain.

Around a dozen people had already gathered in the square, and Bryndine's company was still moving from door to door, rousing others from their sleep. Those that were already awake stood apart from the women who had woken them, muttering unhappily amongst themselves. A dozen or so horses were hitched to the rail outside the Prince's Rest; the Kellens' stable had no room for the mounts of an entire company of soldiers.

Bryndine stood beside the fireleaf in the center of the village, speaking in hushed tones with some of her women. A large, empty wagon sat in the street nearby. It must have come with them, because it did not belong to anyone in Waymark.

Bryndine glanced up and saw Sylla and me approaching, favoring me with a small nod in greeting. The dressing on her left arm had already been replaced with clean bandages—at least she had taken my warning seriously in that regard.

Sylla grabbed me from behind just outside Bryndine's earshot and whispered, "Listen to me, Scriber: if you don't do exactly what the Captain asks, I'll make you wish you had." She released me and shoved me forward, and I stumbled towards Bryndine, dreading whatever she intended to ask of me.

Bryndine was giving orders to a tall brown-haired woman whose back was to me as I approached. "Lieutenant, have the women set up a guard around the village. Selvi and Elene have the best eyes; send Elene with Genna, Nalla, and Janelyn to watch the west—the Burners will most likely come that way. Selvi, Orya, and Wynne can take the east, and put Deanyn and Ivyla on the north and south entrances. I doubt they will come by the road, but better to not take the chance."

"Right away, Captain." The woman gave a formal salute—right fist over the heart, left hand held upright with fingers splayed like the branches of the burning tree—then turned towards me. I recognized her stern, sun-browned face immediately, though her brown hair was streaked with grey that had not been there when I had last seen her. I shifted my eyes to check her collar, and sure enough, found a golden Scriber's pin.

"Tenille?" She had briefly been at the Academy while I was. Six or seven years my senior, she had been in her next-to-last year of study as I began my first. Though she had ostensibly been pinned in History like myself, she had chosen to focus primarily on military history, and used it as an excuse to stand in on Warfare classes as research. They called her the first woman pinned in Warfare, even though it wasn't officially true, and few outside the Scribers knew her story. I had vaguely known that she was Bryndine's second-in-command, or at least had heard some rumors, but it had not occurred to me until that moment that I might see her. My heart sank into my stomach. Having another Scriber in Waymark—and one who knew me by name—was the last thing I wanted.

"Dennon. Good to see you," Tenille said politely, almost certainly lying. She was a Scriber, and the Scribers never forget. Save for Illias, I doubted I would ever again meet one of my brethren who was truly pleased to see me. "We'll have to speak later. I have work to do."

Tenille strode briskly away to carry out Bryndine's commands, leaving me alone with her Captain. That she was too busy to speak at that moment was a blessing, but now that she had seen me she might tell Bryndine or the others of me at any time. There was little I could do to stop it.

"Scriber Dennon." Bryndine greeted me politely, glancing over my shoulder at Sylla, who still stood sentinel behind me as though I might try to bolt at any time. "Sylla, give us a moment, please."

Sylla reluctantly stepped away—but only a short distance, keeping her wary gaze fixed on me.

Bryndine gestured for me to come closer and lowered her voice. "I apologize for Sylla, Scriber. She is… protective of me. I want you to know that you are in no danger from us. I need your help."

"You have a funny way of asking for help, my La—Captain Bryndine." I glanced over my shoulder at Sylla, hoping she hadn't heard my near-failure to address her Captain by her proper rank.

"As I said, I apologize. There is no time to quarrel about this." Bryndine glanced up at the growing crowd of villagers, making sure they were not eavesdropping. "The Burners are closing on this village as we speak. They will attack in a few hours, if not sooner. We are here to evacuate Waymark and bring all of you with us to Three Rivers. The First Company is on its way; the High Commander sent us ahead to begin preparations."

I stared at her for a moment, unable to speak. "I… Three Rivers?" That was the last place I wished to go.

"Refugees from the attacks are being gathered at the capital, under King Syrid's protection. The King wishes to show his people that Erryn's Promise still stands, even if the Burners seek to disprove it." She placed a hand on my shoulder as she continued. "Scriber Dennon, I need your support. These people will not leave their homes at my word alone. As you mentioned when last we met, my reputation precedes me. I will not be trusted, but they may listen to you."

"I can't! I—"

"I am not asking you to tell them yourself, only to help convince them if they are resistant after I explain," Bryndine interjected. "If you do not, many of these people may die. The First Company is coming, but I do not know if they will arrive in time. My women will do all they can, but we are too few to defend the village ourselves."

"So you're putting it on my shoulders?" Responsibility for the people of Waymark was too much; I had come to Waymark to *avoid* ever having lives placed in my hands again. Though they were proud to have a Scriber where most villages their size had none, I was far from beloved in the community. There was no guarantee they would listen to me at all. But Bryndine had put me in a position where I could not refuse, and it made me furious. "Is that what this is, Captain? If I can't convince them, this is my fault, not yours?"

"Think what you will of me, Scriber, as long as you agree to do this."

"You know I have to," I answered bitterly. "I swore an oath." I was not about to let her see me flinch from the task—it would only give her another opportunity to judge me.

"Good. Go then, join them. I will address them shortly; be prepared to lend me your support."

I was about to turn away when a thought blossomed in my mind: *her arm.* With a sour certainty, I eyed her cleanly wrapped wound.

"A horse kicked you, you said."

She nodded but said nothing. Her face remained an expressionless mask, but I thought I saw a hint of something flicker in her steel-grey eyes.

"It wasn't your horse. You had already found the rebels. You *knew* they were coming!"

"Yes, Scriber Dennon," she admitted with a sigh. "I did."

"Why didn't you say anything? We could have been safely away yesterday!"

"My company was sent out as scouts, and Sylla and I only encountered a small party. Three men, likely scouts themselves," Bryndine explained. "They surprised us and wounded me, but they were not skilled; we dispatched them quickly. I had orders to report to the First Company outside Barleyfield before spreading word of anything we found, to avoid starting a panic."

"You had *orders*? You just told me that the First Company likely won't arrive in time, and that we have only hours to evacuate! How good could those orders have been?"

"I am sorry, Scriber, I truly am." Bryndine lowered her eyes, either ashamed or simply unwilling to meet my glare. "But it is not my place to question the High Commander's orders. It is already done, in any case; we are wasting time. Please, go join the other villagers."

I opened my mouth to say more, but Sylla stepped up quickly and pulled me away from her Captain.

"Not another word, Scriber. Just do what she told you." She pushed me again, this time towards the crowd of villagers, now composed of nearly the entire population of Waymark.

The crowd buzzed with curiosity. I heard Logan Underbridge's son, Jason, telling Penni Harynson the story of the Bloody Bride—that each time Bryndine's father tried to marry her to someone, she slew the intended husband. It was obviously untrue, and I couldn't imagine how anyone believed it. Even the King's niece could not commit such a blatant crime and remain free. Bryndine had been betrothed only one time that I knew of, to the son of Baron Hurryd Rafynson of the Bridgefort, many years ago. The boy had died when they were accosted by bandits on an outing in the countryside, not at Bryndine's hand, but the rumors persisted.

There were other muttered tales as well: that Bryndine's impure blood had driven her mad; that she was cursed by the Mother for her impropriety; that her very presence was like to bring divine vengeance down on the entire village. I let them talk, and took some pleasure in hearing the awful woman maligned, even if it was for the wrong reasons. Nothing I could have said would make them trust Bryndine even had I been willing to try; defending the infamous Bloody Bride would only have hurt any chance that they would heed my own advice.

Logan Underbridge spotted me through the crowd and waved me over to where he and many of the men of Waymark stood. He was something of an unofficial village chief; Waymark was too small to bother choosing a true mayor, but Logan's opinions tended to guide the rest. Unfortunately, he was a profoundly ignorant man, prone to superstition and easily taken in by rumor. I wouldn't have been surprised if it had been Logan himself who had filled his son's head with those stories about Bryndine.

Logan's usual collection of followers stood closest to him: Ashton Norgand; the tanner Iayn Gerynson, a big bear of a man; long-haired Brother Randal Ginnis in his sky-blue robe. The rest of the men crowded around the core group, listening raptly.

Logan eyed me somewhat suspiciously. "Scriber Dennon! I seen you speakin' to the Bloody Bride. What were you sayin'?" He had always been wary of me, worried I might try to use my "book learning" to oppose his often outlandish assertions. To Logan Underbridge, education was something to be feared and mistrusted.

"You ain't workin' with her, are you Scriber?" Ashton Norgand asked. Logan's closest friend, his role in village discussion tended to be reinforcing everything Logan said by saying it again, slightly rephrased. "Josia tole me you seen her t'other day."

"I can't stand the woman," I assured them. "She only wanted to know if there was anyone missing. She won't be satisfied until they've disturbed every man, woman, and child, it seems." If being hard on Bryndine would improve my chances of getting everyone out of the village alive, I was all too happy to do it.

Logan clapped me on the shoulder. "That she won't, Scriber. Yer a smart man, I always said so; glad we're thinkin' the same on this." Some of the others followed Logan's example, slapping me on the back. "We need 'er gone; you all heard the stories," Logan continued. "The Lord Chancellor shouldn't never've married low. King Eddyl would've put a stop to it if he'd been alive, Father keep him. Erryn's blood weren't meant to mix with common stock. She's cursed by the Gods, everyone says it."

The other men nodded and harrumphed judgementally, casting sour looks at Bryndine. It was blatant hypocrisy—Branwyn Errynson was no more lowborn than any of the villagers. Her daughter's flaws were not a matter of blood. But I said nothing to contradict Logan.

"She has sinned against the Mother," Brother Randal asserted, while Ashton nodded stupidly at his side. "Women were made to nurture, not to slay; the Father made men for battle."

"You know what she wants, Scriber?" Logan asked.

"I've no idea, but she said she'd let us know shortly." It seemed unwise to tell them too much; better to let the news come as a surprise and hope the shock made them pliable. "Look, here she comes."

Bryndine approached the villagers, and Sylla followed behind, her dark eyes daring anyone to speak out against her Captain. The rest of Bryndine's company—those she had not sent out to guard the perimeter of the village—fell into formation behind her, though with only eight of them remaining, it was a less than impressive sight. It caught the people's attention though, and the low murmur of conversation stopped abruptly as they waited to see what the Bloody Bride had to say.

"I have grave news," she began, and a worried murmur rippled through the crowd. "A rebel group known as the Burners is approaching Waymark as we speak. They will be here in no more than two hours." She stood before the huge fireleaf in the village center, and as she spoke I saw a leaf fall from the branches above her and drift slowly to the ground. After the dream I had woken from earlier, it felt like a sign. I normally put no stock in such things, but my heart began to beat faster in my chest.

More than a murmur answered Bryndine's declaration. "*She's lying!*" I heard someone shout, and "*Leave us alone!*" Those that didn't react with anger chose scepticism; I recognized Carine Norgand's voice, asking "What could they possibly want here?"

Bryndine simply raised her voice, cutting through the commotion. "We are here to relocate the people of Waymark to Three Rivers, where you will all be under the King's protection. King Syrid intends to see Erryn's Promise upheld, and provide refuge for all of his people. Please, return to your homes, and gather what you can. We have a wagon for any items too heavy to carry, but space is limited; only bring what you need. And please, move quickly. We have little time to waste."

"We'll do nothin' of the kind, woman," Logan Underbridge answered as he pushed his way to the front of the crowd. I could barely see him anymore from where I stood; only the top of his head was visible, a shiny bald patch surrounded by thinning orange hair. "I don't see as how we ought to up and leave just because a woman in a soldier costume says so. Most like you just saw a shadow in the trees and got scared."

Ashton Norgand let out a donkey-like laugh, and many others followed his example. Sylla looked as though she might draw her sword at any moment, but Bryndine laid a hand on her arm, and she restrained herself.

"You are a sinner in the eyes of the Mother," Sister Joslyn declared, holding two fingers upright and slicing them horizontally through the air in the sign of the Divide. "If we go with you, her wrath will fall on us all!" There was much gasping at that, and many panicked hands sweeping through the air in an effort to ward of the evil of Bryndine's presence.

Things were getting out of hand, and there was little chance now of Bryndine getting the crowd back under control. Clearly the people of Waymark could not be counted on to do the wise thing without prompting. I breathed in deeply, preparing to do something I had fervently hoped I would not have to.

"*Enough!*" I bellowed at the top of my lungs. In moments, all eyes in the crowd were focused on me. "Are you all fools?"

"Now, Scriber—" Logan began, but I barrelled onwards, the words tumbling out of my mouth.

"I don't like this woman any more than you do, but do you really believe that she travelled almost a hundred leagues just to amuse herself at our expense? Are any of you lackwitted enough to *really* believe that? Or are you just scared to believe that she might be telling the truth?" Dead silence answered, occasionally broken by my own panting; I had used all my breath shouting.

Finally, Logan spoke up again. "Yer sayin' we should leave our homes, Scriber?" he asked, uncertainty creeping into his voice.

"Father in the Sky, yes!" I almost had them; I could see it in their faces. "Don't you see? If we leave and it is nothing, we can come back. If we stay and the danger is real…" I spread my arms. “They don’t teach us how to bring back the dead at the Academy.”

“I… I expect that’s true…” Logan looked as though he still wanted to disagree, but couldn’t think how. He was too late. The others had taken him to be conceding defeat, and people were already returning home to gather their things. Logan’s wife hurried past him, dragging Jason with her, and Logan reluctantly followed. It was satisfying to watch him scurry away in defeat, though I wished the circumstances were different.

Soon the square was empty but for myself, Bryndine, and her soldiers. She stayed where she was, and I made no move to approach her; she simply looked at me for a long moment, as though searching for something. Uncomfortable with the scrutiny, I turned and strode towards my door to begin packing.

After five years of hiding, the time had come to leave Waymark behind and rejoin the world. Whether I wanted to or not.

CHAPTER FIVE

The controversy surrounding Bryndine Errynson began when she was seventeen years old. Like many members of the nobility, at sixteen she enrolled at the Academy. While most only undertook a single year of general study, Bryndine wished to stay on and earn her pin. This became an issue when she declared her chosen School: the School of Warfare, training ground for the finest military officers in the Kingsland.

The reaction was immediate and extreme. A woman becoming a soldier was seen as a violation of the Mother's way, and the Children incited the people into outrage over it. Bryndine was pulled out of the Academy at the order of King Syrid; Millum Wren, the Master of Warfare, was ejected from the Council for accepting her entry into his School.

However, Wren was later made High Commander of the First Company in Three Rivers, and there he continued to teach Bryndine. Seven years later, Bryndine Errynson had received the same training as any graduate of the School of Warfare, lacking only the pin to make it official.

— From Dennon Lark's *Life of Bryndine Errynson*

The sound was deafening. It exploded through the town, a crash of thunder that sounded so close it might have come from inside my own home. Leaving the drawers of my desk wide open and dropping an armful of writing supplies that I had been about to stow in my bag, I rushed to the door.

My hand froze on the handle. I could hear shouts and

screams outside, and the panicked whinnying of horses; my fingers trembled on the cold brass, refusing to do as they were told. I was suddenly aware of a thick lump of fear in my belly; it had been growing there for some time, I think, but I had been ignoring it, telling myself that we would be gone before an attack ever came.

I waited there with my hand on the door, listening, and after a short time, the cries outside died down. I heard muffled commands being given, but nothing like what I imagined a battle would sound like. I took a deep breath to steady myself and opened the door.

In the darkness outside, it was impossible not to notice the fire before anything else. The town was bathed in angry light and smoke billowed thick and grey around the roof of the Prince's Rest. The flames were spreading rapidly; a slight breeze had sprung up, and as I watched, the fire rode it across the roof of the Rest and leapt to the cottage that sat beside the inn. The horses still tied at the inn were thrashing about in panic as Bryndine's women tried to free them and lead them away, though it looked like most had already been rescued.

Bryndine and her soldiers were trying to maintain order: a number of them had formed a line from the well to the inn and were passing buckets of water along it to try to quench the flames; others sought to keep the terrified villagers inside their homes, packing to leave. There were more of them in the village than before—some of those who had been put on guard must have returned to help fight the fire.

"Leave the tavern," I heard Bryndine call, and I saw her huge form, outlined in smoke, amidst the line of soldiers at the well. As always, Sylla was at her side. "It's already lost. Form lines to those buildings, there and there." She pointed at the homes to either side of the tavern. "Douse the roofs, keep them wet. We need to stop it from spreading." They immediately set to work, following her commands with trained efficiency. Whatever I thought of the woman, she clearly had a firm command of her company.

Iayn Gerynson rushed by my door, and I grabbed his huge, hairy arm to stop him.

"What happened?" I demanded, fear causing my voice to

reach an embarrassingly high pitch.

"Lightning, Scriber. Bolt of lightning, right out of the sky. My ears are still ringin'."

"That's impossible." I turned my eyes upwards; the sky was completely clear, not a cloud in sight. "Lightning doesn't strike out of a cloudless sky."

"It's that damn woman, they said she was cursed!" Gerynson freed his arm from my grip easily and moved away, heading in the direction of his home. I knew he had spoken out of superstition and ignorance, but the terrible dread in my gut only intensified.

I stood just outside my door, watching as the Prince's Rest burned to the ground. Josia's small form was visible, rushing back and forth between the well and her home, desperately trying to save the inn even though the soldiers had given it up. I could hear her sobs from where I stood. I felt a twinge of pity for her—Josia's relentless cheerfulness had always bothered me, but of all the people in Waymark, she was probably the only one I didn't truly dislike. She didn't deserve this. I took a step towards her, though I don't know what I intended to do; as Bryndine had declared, the Rest was clearly a lost cause.

It was then that I heard it, a low whisper coming from behind. My hands clenched convulsively and I whirled on my heel, peering into the thin aisle of darkness between my small cottage and the next. But there was nothing there; nothing but long, wavering shadows cast by the flames that were now at my back. Yet the whisper persisted.

"Who's there?" I asked, my voice barely audible. There was no answer, but I thought I might have seen something moving in the darkness beyond the homes that lined the east side of the road. It was difficult to tell; the smoke from the fire made my eyes water, and the constant shifting of the shadows created the illusion of motion where there was none. And still the sound of whispering drifted past my ears

"*We are the Burnt*," the whispers said, one phrase among hundreds of others, whispered by hundreds of voices speaking at once. A wave of anger and pain flowed over me, and I stumbled back in fear. Something caught underneath my foot and I fell heavily to the ground, the impact knocking the breath from my lungs. I knew those whispers. It was impossible; it was nonsense; but I had dreamed of those voices.

There was something there, in the dark. I could see forms moving in the shadows now; I was certain of it. I tried to scramble backwards, but my body was frozen. Most of the guardswomen were fighting the fire, and there was no one to sound the alert—those figures in the darkness would fall upon Waymark without warning.

"They're coming," I tried to say, but it came out as a croak, unheard amid the commotion in the village, and the figures in the shadows were getting closer.

"They're *coming.*" Not loud enough, but better; a real voice issued from my mouth. The shadowy forms were nearly at the line of homes now; they would be upon the village in moments.

"*They're coming!*" I screamed. And that was loud enough. I wrenched my arm up, pointing into the dark. The ringing of some twenty weapons being drawn at once echoed in my ears.

"I see them!" a woman yelled; one of Bryndine's, a voice I did not recognize.

"With me! Protect the villagers!" I heard Bryndine command. "For the Promise!"

One of the dark forms lurched forward into a sprint, charging directly at me; the others followed closely behind, swarming into Waymark. As the first man entered the light, I almost thought I knew him—he looked like Josia's husband Hareld, and for a moment I hoped that these were not the rebels at all. But the man brandished a heavy axe in his hand, and he was closing on me swiftly.

I could not move. My mind screamed for my body to stand and run, but all I could do was stare in horror at the man who was moments from ending my life. I squeezed my eyes closed, waiting for the blow to land.

Metal crashed on metal, and my eyes snapped open again. Bryndine Errynson towered before me, the Burner's axe recoiling from her heavy round shield. She did not flinch, though her shield arm was badly wounded, and I could hardly believe she was not crying out in pain. She had said she might need to use the arm, though I had told her it would be foolish—I thanked the Mother and the Father that she had not listened.

She swung her sword in a vicious riposte that tore almost entirely through the man's neck. I flinched, expecting to be spattered with hot blood, but none came. Though his neck was yawned open grotesquely, the man barely bled at all as he slumped to the ground.

"Find cover, Scriber!" Bryndine barked over her shoulder, sprinting towards the oncoming attackers. They poured through the gaps between homes now, outnumbering Bryndine's women three to one or worse. Yet they made almost no sound; no battle cries, no grunts of pain or effort. I could still hear the whispers in my head, but their mouths did not move.

I did not seek cover. My body still refused all commands as I stared at the near-headless man at my feet. The lack of blood from his wound somehow made it worse; it was unnatural, against everything I had ever learned. I remembered where the whispers had come from in my dream: hundreds of men and women, naked and bearing awful wounds that did not bleed. Finally a slow, thick flow of dark red blood—nearly black—oozed from the gaping hole at the end of the man's neck. A warm, sticky pool began to spread, seeping under my hands and beneath the seat of my pants, and I almost cried with relief.

The man's head had fallen at an awkward angle, pulling against the thin flap of skin and muscle that held it to the body, and with a sudden motion, it flopped onto its side. Dead, empty eyes seemed to stare directly at me. There was no doubt now—it was the face of Hareld Kellen. A single thought raced through my mind: *that explains why he was late coming home.* With a hysterical giggle, I vomited the contents of my stomach onto the blood-soaked ground.

I sank into a terrified trance then, watching the fight unfold as though it were a performance acted out with marionettes. None if it felt real. The noises of battle seemed muffled, indistinct; I could see weapons clanging together and people screaming, but in my ears there was only a dull muddle of sound. All I could hear clearly were the whispers from my dream: "*All will burn… We will have vengeance…*"

The villagers fled into the homes on the other side of the

road while Bryndine and her twenty or so women held back the attackers. The women were badly outnumbered, but none of them had fallen, while the Burners had taken heavy losses already—to my untrained eye, it seemed the rebels fought clumsily and without coordination.

I saw a slender redheaded woman of Bryndine's company darting between foes, distracting one for a companion then lunging at another; a squat, stocky blond woman barrelling into a group of three men like a barbarian warrior and cleaving them down with her axe; Tenille's sword flashing in the firelight as she expertly disarmed her foe. Bryndine and Sylla fought side by side, and I was unsurprised to see that Sylla wielded her longsword with a terrifying ferocity, striking with blinding speed as she guarded her Captain's flank. I know little enough about combat, but it was clear to see that these women were extremely skilled.

Bryndine Errynson put the rest of them to shame. She wielded in one hand a sword that most could only have held with two, swinging it in heavy arcs that cleaved through armor and flesh and bone as easily as if she were chopping rotted wood. Her shield was a wonder to watch too, despite her wounded arm—the big steel disc moved with incredible precision and speed, deflecting blows that I scarcely even saw coming. She wasted no effort on useless motion, simply broke an opponent's attack on her shield, waited for an opening, and then cut her foe down with a single stroke. I had thought Sylla the more dangerous of the two, but where she often needed to land three or four decisive blows to fell her target, Bryndine rarely needed more than one.

Several men of Waymark waded into the fray, refusing to keep to their homes despite Bryndine shouting for them to find safety. Unarmored and armed only with makeshift weapons, they soon paid the price for their mistake. Iayn Gerynson chopped into a man's side with a heavy shovel, but as he was pulling it free, another of the rebels rammed a sword into his back. Iayn fell to his knees. He tried to stand, but the man he had struck—seemingly unhindered by the deep gouge in his side—caved in the big tanner's head with a spiked mace. Other men fell as well, but I recognized few of them through the smoke, and then the rest were retreating in terror while Bryndine and her women guarded their retreat.

I could only watch as it happened, as men I had known for years were cut down. The terror growing in my chest locked me in place, a terror more pure than anything I had ever known. The voices in my head grew louder, wilder. They were angry and in pain, and so I was too, and it only added to my fear. But at least I could claim one small grace: I was not the focus of their attention.

And then I felt that change.

It was like the slow turning of a great invisible eye; an unseen force gradually becoming aware of my presence. I had been caught eavesdropping, hearing something I was not meant to hear. The macabre chant focused on me, every word resounding as clearly as ringing crystal. "*Pain,*" the voices chanted. "*Fire. Death.*" I realized with dread what was coming.

"*BURN,*" the voices ordered. And I did.

CHAPTER SIX

The King's Army is one of two bodies created to uphold Erryn's Promise. While the Justices of the White Hall determine what it means to keep the Promise and whether or not a King has done so, the Army is the instrument by which it is actually kept. They have protected the Kingsland faithfully through seven recorded Barbarian Incursions, and more than one rebellion from within our own borders.

Each of the six baronies of the Kingsland has its own Army brigade, made up of five to ten companies of four hundred men, each led by a Captain. Each brigade has a primary company—the First in Three Rivers through to the Sixth at the Bridgefort—whose Captain is also Commander of the brigade. The Captain of the First Company serves as High Commander of the entire King's Army.

— From Dennon Lark's *Military History of the Kingsland*

The constant bumping of the wagon's wheels on the rough country road shook me awake. My back was pressed against the sharp corner of a wooden chest, and several bulging canvas bags surrounded me, giving me little room to move.

The first thing that came to my mind was panic. My hands leapt to check for the terrible burns that I was sure must cover most of my body—but there was no pain, no melted flesh glistening red on my arms or legs. I remembered the agony of burning vividly, but little after it; I could only imagine that I must have fainted. My head ached, and memories of whispered voices and fire flickered through my consciousness. I felt like I was going mad.

It was some time after midday judging by the sun shining full down upon me; I had to squint my eyes against the brightness. A low buzz of voices filled my ears, and for a moment I feared the whispers had returned, but as my eyes adjusted to the light I saw that the wagon was surrounded by hundreds of soldiers, marching in columns or mounted upon horses. They wore the tabards of the King's Army, with a numeral one sewn in gold beneath the King's burning tree—the First Company. Scattered among them were the villagers of Waymark, the women and children sitting in wagons or riding double with the soldiers while the men marched alongside.

From the look of the countryside I could tell that we were well away from Waymark, on the road heading east to Barleyfield. I was not sure exactly what had happened the night before, but by the fact that I was still alive, I guessed that the First Company had arrived to defeat the rebels.

I became conscious of several voices closer and louder than the rest, audible even over the rumbling of wagons and clip-clop of hooves. Bryndine's voice I identified almost immediately, and then Sylla's, speaking to a third woman whose voice I didn't know. I tried to stay silent and still, though the autumn chill in the air made it difficult not to shiver. They did not seem to notice that I had awoken, because their conversation continued unabated.

"It was strange, yes. I did not see him wounded." That was Bryndine's voice, in answer to something I had not heard.

"Strange? Bryn, he was shrieking like his head had caught fire," Sylla replied. It was not hard to deduce that I was their subject. I didn't like it, but it was understandable—why should they have faith in my sanity when I was beginning to doubt it myself?

"Might he have an illness?" a soft voice asked uncertainly. "My uncle used to have the shaking sickness. It would come on him when he got upset."

"That may be, Genna," Bryndine said. "I only hope he was not harmed in some way I did not see. My cousin may have need of him."

"Your cousin is an ass," Sylla muttered. "Why bring him a Scriber? At least in his condition he won't be able to report you to the King." I could not imagine what they were talking about, or what Bryndine might be reported for. But I knew that her cousin, Uran Ord, was the current High Commander of the First Company, promoted after the death of Millum Wren two years before. It sounded as though he had been wounded.

"Sylla…" The soft voiced woman—Genna—sounded concerned. "You shouldn't say such things."

"I will not wish misfortune on my cousin to save myself, Sylla," Bryndine said sternly. "We are soldiers in the King's Army. We have sworn to uphold Erryn's Promise. Such suggestions do not become us."

"Sorry, Bryn. I didn't mean…" Sylla's gruff contrition trailed off midway. She did not seem a woman accustomed to making apologies. "I wouldn't trust that Scriber to treat a bee sting, though."

"He treated my wound well enough."

"It's twice as swollen as it was!" Sylla protested.

"He warned me not to use it. I'm afraid I am not the most obedient patient."

"You just distrust anyone who is rude to the Captain, Sylla," Genna teased gently. "He did help us get the people out of Waymark."

"They would have come with us either way," Sylla grumbled.

"But perhaps not willingly, Sylla," said Bryndine. "As happy as you might have been to truss them up and carry the lot of them off in the wagon, I am glad we had Scriber Dennon's help."

I was not comfortable with Bryndine's praise. My memory of the previous night was not clear, but I recalled a hazy image of her shield repelling Hareld's axe—she had saved my life. I reminded myself that she had put it in danger to begin with by failing to warn the village when she first had the chance. I could not forgive her for that. A Scriber never forgets.

"Besides, Sylla, bringing the Scriber might help our case," said Genna. "The Army Scribers are mostly Warfare trained, even Tenille. They can perform field treatment at best. If the Captain produces the Scriber who saves the High Commander, it won't be ignored."

"If he even *is* any better than the rest." Sylla seemed disinclined to give me the benefit of the doubt. "He's just the local Scriber for a little nothing village. All we know about him is that he can stitch a wound and wrap a bandage. That's hardly more than field medicine."

"I have reason to believe he has had the appropriate training, Sylla. I will bring him to Uran as soon as we make camp." Bryndine's tone was decisive, and Sylla let the matter drop with a sullen grunt.

I wondered what Bryndine had meant about my training. It was true that I had excelled in many fields at the Academy despite my focus being History; I was an accomplished student in the Schools of Medicine, Arts, and Politics, and I had even done some study in the Sciences. But Bryndine had acted as though she didn't recognize my name when we first met, and if that was so, she had little reason to think more highly of my skills than Sylla did.

I was struck with the unpleasant feeling that she knew more about me than she had let on; perhaps she had spoken to Tenille. I would not be able to keep my history a secret when we arrived in Three Rivers in any case, but still, it irked me that Bryndine Errynson might have yet another reason to look down on me.

The women were done talking about anything that interested me, and I had questions that needed answering. I sat up in the back of the wagon, trying to act as though I had only just awoken.

As I crawled over the wagon's cargo towards them, the three women noticed me and ceased their chatter. Sylla and Bryndine turned towards me, and Genna—who I recognized as the stout blond-haired woman I had seen charging a group of rebels the night before—turned her eyes away, focusing on steering the horses with unnecessary intensity.

"Scriber Dennon," Bryndine greeted me. "Are you well?" She was too polite to directly ask me about my fit, but I heard the question lurking in her voice. I ignored it.

"I'm fine, Lady Bryndine." The mistake in rank was an accident, but the look on Sylla's face told me it had not gone unnoticed. I corrected myself before she could. "Sorry—Captain Bryndine. How did I get here? When I—" I paused, trying to think of a delicate way to avoid admitting I had fainted. "That is, the last I recall, the village was overrun by rebels."

Bryndine quickly filled in the gap between when I had lost consciousness and the moment I had awoken in the wagon. It went much as I had suspected. Her company had held back the rebels as well as they could, given their numbers, but were unable to clear the road in order to evacuate the villagers. Fortunately, the First Company had arrived before they were overrun, and their appearance had sent the Burners running. None had been apprehended—the rebels had vanished as suddenly as they had arrived.

"Do they actually call themselves that? The Burners?" I asked, remembering what the whispers had said: *We are the Burnt.*

"I don't know, Scriber. They might. It links them to King Erryn, and we believe that Erryn's Promise, or the King's supposed failure to uphold it, may be their motivation. But it could just be a name that spread because someone thought it clever. We know little about the rebels—none have been captured alive." Bryndine looked at me quizzically. "Why do you ask?"

"I thought… I thought I heard one of them use another name. The Burnt. Was I the only one?" I glanced between them hopefully. If someone else had heard the voices, then perhaps I was not losing my mind.

"You *heard* them?" Sylla peered at me suspiciously. "Scriber, nobody heard them. They never opened their mouths."

"I heard nothing, Scriber Dennon. Genna?" Bryndine turned to the third woman, who glanced shyly over her shoulder, avoiding my eyes.

"Nothing, Scriber. I'm sorry." Genna jerked her gaze back to the horses, as though embarrassed to disappoint me.

"If you are correct, Scriber, it may be the first thing we really know about these rebels. A small enough thing, but…"

Bryndine shrugged. "I will ask the others if they heard anything."

"It was nothing, I... I am sure I must have imagined it." The thought of her spreading word of my madness among her company was appalling to me. "I was not… in my right mind." Sylla snorted in amusement at that, but said nothing.

"It is strange, though," Bryndine mused. "They stay so silent, strike so suddenly and disappear so cleanly. It suggests discipline, but they fight clumsily, like none of them have ever held a sword. We should not have been able to hold off so many, not for as long as we did, and with so few casualties."

"How many were hurt?" I felt a twinge of guilt for failing to ask earlier.

"Six men from Waymark were killed, and one woman was apparently badly burned. The High Commander took a blow to the head, and five of his men died. Between the villagers and soldiers, we carry thirteen wounded in the wagons." She bowed her head. "One of my girls was badly hurt. She… will likely not survive the journey."

"I'm sorry," I said—but silently, I damned Bryndine to the Dragon. *If she had only warned me when she first came to Waymark, none of it would have happened!* I had hoped never to feel the weight of another life on my shoulders, but if this girl died, she died defending me. "Is there anything I can do for her?"

"Only the Father can help her now," Bryndine said. It was a mildly sacrilegious claim—the Father watched over warriors injured in battle, but the Children were fairly adamant that those warriors must be men. "She was stabbed through the stomach."

She was right: a gut wound was a slow, painful death sentence without expert medical treatment. The surgery was beyond me, even if it could be done on the road, lacking proper equipment. But it felt wrong to so easily accept the girl's fate. "With the proper facilities… the Academy…" I stammered lamely.

"We aren't at the Academy, Scriber." Sylla's eyes flashed dangerously. "You think we'd just let one of ours die if there was something we could do?"

"He didn't mean it like that, Sylla." Genna came to my

defense, laying a calming hand on her friend's shoulder—but still she avoided my gaze. This timid, gentle-voiced woman was completely different than the one I had seen charge three armed men without hesitation the night before.

"There may be someone else you can treat, Scriber," said Bryndine. I already knew what she was about to ask of me, but I could not let on that I had been eavesdropping. "The High Commander took a heavy blow to the head. He has been in and out of delirium since."

When they did not know I was listening, the women had mentioned that Uran Ord had some complaint against them, and that they hoped to use me to get back in his good graces. I wondered what was more important to Bryndine: her cousin's life, or his favor?

"A blow to the head?" I repeated, considering my options. If his complaint was a matter of fluids creating pressure in the skull, then a trephination might suffice, though I didn't relish the notion of boring a hole in the High Commander's skull. But if it was more than that, my skills would likely be insufficient. "There may be something I can do, but I was pinned in History, not Medicine. No doubt I can do more for him than an Army Scriber, but…" I shrugged my shoulders. I could not refuse to treat the King's nephew, but I did not want that responsibility. If Uran Ord died under my care, it would go very badly for me, especially considering the other marks on my record.

"Whatever you can do will be appreciated, Scriber Dennon," Bryndine said.

With little left to say, we lapsed into awkward silence. After a time, I crawled back to the rear of the wagon. I had no desire to speak to Bryndine further now that my questions had been answered, and I had noticed my chest sitting near where I had woken. I opened it and saw that someone had finished my packing; clothes, books, and writing supplies were all stowed neatly in the box.

I rummaged through and found my journal, a quill, and some ink. I had not yet recorded the previous night's events, and I could practically hear Illias' voice in my head, scolding me for putting it off. I had been unconscious, of course, but the

Scriber's instinct was ingrained too deeply in me to accept excuses. Though the shaking of the wagon made my hand rough and uneven, I began to write what I remembered of the attack.

* * *

The sun was low in the sky when the wagon came to a stop, and I was forced to put away my journal as dusk descended. By the time the long train of soldiers and villagers behind had gathered at the chosen site, it was full dark, and the First Company was busy erecting camp by lantern-light. Bryndine took the time to issue orders to her company before bringing me to see her cousin, and while she did that I stood stupidly in place, watching the soldiers set up camp with no inkling of what I might do to help.

The people of Waymark milled about among the men of the First Company, though scattered amid four hundred soldiers, fifty villagers were hard to pick out. Those I did see had nothing but smiles for me, and a few even greeted me with enthusiastic handshakes. I saw Penni making moon-eyes at the young soldiers, and was surprised when she rushed over to embrace me and kiss me on the cheek before running away giggling. I had thought the villagers would be resentful, considering I had called them all fools less than a day before; such warm treatment was wholly unexpected.

It was not until I spoke to Logan Underbridge that I understood. He shouted my name as he jogged towards me, his round cheeks still flushed red from the long march.

"Scriber Dennon! Glad to see you up, looked like you got hurt pretty bad." He clubbed me on the shoulder enthusiastically with a meaty hand. "I was a fool last night and I don't mind sayin' it—if you hadn't got us movin', and seen them Burners, we'd all be dead and burned, and that's a fact. Them Dragon-damned women would have seen us all killed!"

That was the answer, of course. The townsfolk were making a hero out of me so they didn't have to admit Bryndine had saved them. I did not mind them hating her; though they did not know it, she had chosen to leave the village in danger for a full day without warning. But the women she commanded deserved credit for what they had done. I wanted no part in this mass denial.

"I did nothing praiseworthy, Logan. I was unconscious for most of it. Those women saved you, not me."

"They didn't!" he insisted. "It wasn't them got us out, it was the First. The Bloody Bride and hers only made it that long on account of you seen the Burners comin'. They hardly knew what they were doin' with those weapons."

It was a laughable claim—I had seen Bryndine and her company fight. A girl was dying from her wounds as we spoke; wounds taken saving our lives. She might have been dead already. At that moment, I wanted nothing more than to punch Logan in his jowly red-cheeked face. But before I could, Bryndine intervened, begging Logan's pardon and escorting me away to see her cousin. It was for the best—I would only have hurt my hand, and looked a fool. I am not skilled at violence.

Uran Ord's tent had already been erected by that time, a massive canvas structure that dominated the camp around it. Tent is almost too small a word to describe it—it was closer to a personal pavilion, probably large enough to fit the entire population of Waymark, if not comfortably. From a spire on the top, the banner of the Ord family—twin towers, gold on dark grey—flew proudly above the smaller brown flag of the King's Army. I was not surprised by the ostentatious structure, impractical as it was. Uran Ord was the eldest son of Baron Uldon Ord of Highpass, and his family's taste for opulence was no secret.

A cleanly shaven brown-haired man of perhaps forty years stopped us as we approached the entryway to Ord's tent. He wore a Lieutenant's red cord on his shoulder.

"Lady Bryndine, the High Commander is being attended by our medics. No one is to enter." His expression was sour, and he pointedly avoided referring to Bryndine by rank.

"This man is a Scriber, Lieutenant Ralsten, and better trained than any in my cousin's ranks. Are you willing to take responsibility for the High Commander's death when this man might have saved him?"

I shifted uneasily—this was the second time Bryndine had

mentioned my training. She had to know who I was; of course she did. Even if Tenille hadn't told her of me, she had lived in Three Rivers most of her life, within walking distance of the Old Garden where the accident had happened. It had been foolish to hope that she did not know me. I resolved to confront her when I had finished with the High Commander, though the idea of broaching the subject myself went against every instinct I had.

Lieutenant Ralsten scowled at Bryndine, but pulled the entry flap open. "He may enter. You will return to your company and await the High Commander's judgement."

Whatever she had done to anger her cousin, it must have been serious. She saluted and left, making no attempt to defend herself. Curious, I watched her go, until Ralsten cleared his throat to regain my attention and ushered me into the large tent.

The light inside was dim, emanating from a few oil lanterns set around the Commander's cot, and the smell of sweat and vomit wafted through the air. Two Army Scribers hovered over the cot where Uran Ord lay, speaking in low, worried tones. They turned as I drew closer, and I gripped my collar, tilting my pin at them so it caught the light.

"Thank the Mother and the Father, they found someone," one of them—a tall bald man—whispered with relief. They stepped aside, allowing me a full view of the patient.

As soon as I saw him, I knew that there was little I could do.

His face was bruised and misshapen where he had been struck; the upper left side of his forehead dimpled inwards grotesquely beneath his thick black hair. Beside him was a bucket he had clearly been sick in more than once; the odor rising from it was foul. He was conscious, but his blue eyes were glassy and unfocused, and he seemed unaware of his surroundings. A spasm ran through him as I watched, his right arm and leg twitching violently for a moment before falling still.

"We need to drain the blood from the skull," the other Scriber, a heavyset man with dark hair, informed me. "But neither of us has the training." He gestured helplessly.

"You *needed* to do it half a day ago. From the look of him,

I'm surprised he is not already dead." Uran Ord would undoubtedly be an invalid for the rest of his life even if he survived; the pressure on his brain had likely already done irreversible damage. But one could not simply refuse to treat the High Commander of the King's Army.

I knelt beside the cot. "Go to Captain Bryndine's wagon and get the trephining drill from my chest. I'll also need a sharp knife, and make sure they're both sterilized by alcohol and fire." I closed my eyes, trying to think what else I might need. It had been a long time since I had even practiced the procedure. "Something to cut his hair with. Bandages too, this will be messy. And light, I will need more light."

The two men scrambled to obey, clearly glad to have passed on the responsibility for the High Commander's life. Warfare trained Scribers knew combat better than anything; these two had a medic's training, which qualified them for quick patch-up work in the field, likely even amputating limbs. But in the area of head and brain injuries, the Academy was only just beginning to make strides—few had the experience to confidently treat such ailments. I was no expert myself, having only practiced on false skulls at the Academy.

Even if I had been able to make the attempt earlier, it would likely not have been enough. From his apparent symptoms I suspected there was bleeding within the brain itself, not just the tissue surrounding it, and the severity of the wound suggested a serious skull fracture, which meant many small fragments would likely need removal. If either of those things was true, the surgery required was far beyond my abilities.

A young page came into the tent carrying two more oil lanterns, and I directed him in their placement around the cot. Shortly after that, the medics returned with the tools I had asked for. At my direction, they sat Ord up in bed and cut his hair as closely as they were able with a pair of barber's shears, cleaning the stray hairs away with a wet cloth and wrapping a bandage around his brow to catch the heavy blood flow that always came with a cut to the head. He remained docile throughout, staring ahead with clouded eyes, though several times he cried out to someone who was not there, and the spasms passing along the right side of his body were frequent and unpredictable.

"Do not let him move," I instructed as I gingerly set the knife against his bare scalp. Taking a shaky breath, I pushed the blade down, starting the incision.

Ord let out a tiny whimper as I sliced into his scalp. His blood flowing copiously out over my hands, staining the bandage above his eyes a deep crimson. But he did not struggle—he was too far gone. For all I knew he was reacting to some vision only he could see rather than the knife cutting into his head. Even a fully successful surgery would not return his mind to him, I suspected, but even so I forged ahead. It was the only thing I could do: he was the King's nephew. If he died while I was in the tent, the consequences would not be pleasant for me.

I peeled back the skin of his scalp along the incision, revealing the skull. The fracture where he had been struck was immediately obvious; the bone was cracked and depressed inwards, pressing in on the brain. Had I been more skilled, I would have attempted to lift the shards out of the depression, but I did not trust myself to do such delicate work. If I could make the trephination without complications, there was a chance it would relieve the pressure long enough to get Uran to the Academy for further surgery; anything beyond that was outside the limits of my ability.

Trembling hands forced me to stop, and my stomach heaved, but I mastered my nerves and took the trephining drill in my hand. There was resistance as I began to turn the drill, and I wasn't sure I had the strength to penetrate the bone, but then the teeth engaged and slowly began to bore through.

By the time I penetrated the skull and the layer of soft tissue beneath, my arm ached badly, and sweat beaded on my brow. Blood spurted around the drill bit, spattering my shirt and gushing over my hands, thicker and faster than I was ready for. Pressure was certainly being released; for a terrifying moment I thought that it would not stop. But as I held my breath, the flow slowed to a manageable level.

I had done it. My held breath burst from my lungs in a triumphant laugh. I shook my sore arm to loosen the tense muscles as I looked to the two Army Scribers with a satisfied smile.

"It's done," I told them. "He just may survive this."

When I looked back, the High Commander was no longer breathing.

"No." I put two fingers against his neck; there was no heartbeat. Desperately, I pounded a fist against his chest once, then again, but it did no good. In the brief moment I had looked away, Ord had slipped quietly into oblivion.

"No, no, no! It was done!" I lashed out with my foot and caught the bucket sitting near the cot. The foul smell within the tent grew fouler as vomit spilled across the ground.

"He is with the Father now." The bald medic put a hand on my shoulder. "You did all you could."

I wrenched myself away from him. "It doesn't matter." I rubbed my temple, forgetting that my fingertips were stained with the High Commander's blood. "They'll say I killed the King's nephew."

Their faces both went white at that—it hadn't occurred to them that we might be blamed for Ord's death.

"No, they can't… We didn't—" the heavier man stammered. "We only held him! It was you that did it!"

"Your concern is touching," I replied sarcastically. "But don't worry yourself. It will be me they blame. I make for an easy scapegoat."

"They needn't blame anyone." The voice came from behind the medics—from the High Commander's cot. Both of the other men turned towards the sound, blocking my view. My heart beat wildly in my chest as I shoved between them to look upon the cot where the dead man lay.

Uran Ord looked back at me, his blue eyes clear and alive.

CHAPTER SEVEN

The Brothers of the Sky and the Sisters of the Earth, collectively known as the Children, are the preachers of the Mother and the Father. Their traditions are taken from the Book of the Divide, one of the few texts to survive even through the Forgetting, presumably dating back to a time before the cataclysm destroyed ancient Elovia.

The Children maintain holy places known as Gardens in nearly every village, town, and city in the Kingsland. The main feature of a Garden is a grassy area of carefully tended vegetation where the Children give sermons, as plant life is the symbol of the Mother and Father's love. To quote from the Book of the Divide, "Though forever parted, their love lives in all things that grow in the Earth and are nourished by the Sky". Beyond that, however, the Gardens have little in common—they range from humble shacks on grassy fields to ornately designed structures surrounding verdant courtyards, like the historic Old Garden in Three Rivers.

— From Dennon Lark's *Religions of Cendonia*

"Forgive me if this seems strange, Scriber, but I could not let my men hear me asking these questions." Uran Ord sat on the edge of his cot, his head wrapped in white cotton bandages that masked the deep incision in his scalp. For a man who had been dead a quarter-hour before, he was surprisingly talkative. He had sent his medics away, and for the last quarter-hour or so, had questioned me thoroughly on subjects that he had no business not knowing the answers to.

"It's not unprecedented for a blow to the head to interfere with memory, High Commander," I said with an assurance I did not feel. "But I would *strongly* recommend that you go to the Academy for examination." I had been trying to convince him of this since he had awoken. It was not uncommon for a head wound to cause some memory loss, but it was *very* uncommon for a man to rise from the dead. I should have been relieved that he lived—it saved me from being blamed for his death. Instead, his unexplained resurrection made me more nervous.

There was a low hum in my skull that made my head ache. The stench and the dim light in the tent did not help, but it was more than that; it felt as though there was a presence in the air that I could not see. *I truly am going mad*, I thought glumly.

He gestured impatiently. "I assure you, I am fine. You did your job admirably; I won't forget it."

He kept insisting that my treatment had saved him, but it was not true. I had seen him dead, felt his lack of breath and pulse myself. How he had come back I did not know, but it was imperative that he be looked at by a Scriber pinned in Medicine. "High Commander, you must—"

"*Enough*. I am well, Scriber. Now answer my question."

"I have told you, Commander, I am not part of your company. I don't know the officer's names. There was a Lieutenant Ralsten watching outside your tent, that is all I can tell you." This was one of the issues Ord had questioned me on at length—he had no memory of any of his men, or even his own cousin. I had been able to tell him why they were here; about Bryndine, and Waymark; but I was unable to tell him the names of his men.

"Did he seem loyal to you? Would he help me in this quietly?"

"I haven't any idea, Commander. He appeared concerned about your well being, I suppose."

The noise in my head intensified and my headache grew worse as the conversation went on. I knew the sound, though I hadn't wanted to admit it to myself; whispered voices, many speaking as one. I almost wept. Ever since I had dreamed of them, I could not seem to escape those voices. Soon, I knew, they would call for me to burn, and I would have no choice but to do as they told. I needed to get out of that tent.

"Please, send him in for me." Ord dismissed me with a wave of his hand, but as I turned away, his voice stopped me. "And Scriber—do not tell my cousin of this conversation. I… would not worry her."

It was strange, I thought, that he would be so concerned for a cousin whose name he could not remember. But I was happy to agree; I had my own issues to speak with Bryndine about, and no desire to prolong that conversation. Eagerly, I ran for the exit, nearly sprinting out into the night.

The fresh air silenced the sound of voices, and I gasped it in gratefully, aware but uncaring that Lieutenant Ralsten was eyeing me suspiciously.

"What happened, Scriber? The others said that the Commander had come back to his senses, but that I should not enter. Why was I not called in immediately?"

"He will see you now, Lieutenant. He simply had some questions for me first."

"Is he recovered, then?"

I chose my words carefully. "He is… much improved. It may take time for him to be as he was."

"But he will recover with time? I warn you, Scriber, it's on your head if he doesn't."

"Of course it is. I should have thought of that when someone else shattered his skull," I said dryly.

Ralsten narrowed his eyes and was about to respond, but I cut him off.

"Lieutenant, for good or ill, his recovery had little to do with me. Go, he is waiting for you."

As I walked through the camp back towards the wagon that held my things, I was stopped several times by people from Waymark. Word of Uran's recovery had apparently already spread, and now they had one more thing to congratulate me for that was not my doing. I was not polite in setting them right on the subject, but most simply refused to hear my protests—though I did send Penni Harynson away weeping with a particularly rude rebuke.

The cloying, ignorant admiration of the villagers would

have been bad enough, but each time I was forced to stop and talk was also a moment longer standing there in my filthy, bloodstained clothes. I had not changed since the attack, and my clothing was stiff with dried blood and sweat. All I wanted was to put on a clean shirt and pants and wash my hands and face.

I was pulling a change of clothes from my chest in the back of the wagon when Josia Kellen approached me. I did not notice her immediately, until she spoke my name in a thin, broken voice.

"What is it, Josia?" I asked, annoyed at this latest interruption. "If you're here to talk about the Commander, I had nothing to do with his recovery. I'm busy."

"You saw her do it, didn't you?"

"Saw what, Josia? I don't—"

"You saw her kill my Hareld."

I was taken aback by the dangerous edge in her voice. She did not sound like the kindly, overly talkative woman I knew. "Josia, he was trying to kill me. Bryndine stopped him."

Josia cocked her head, as though listening to something far away, and for a moment, I thought I heard the faint sound of whispering—but no, it was nothing, just wind in the trees.

"He wouldn't!" she insisted. "She *murdered* him!"

She had lost her home and her husband in a single night; she deserved sympathy, more than any of the others did. But this was dangerous talk. Bryndine was the King's niece, and while her reputation led to a good deal of insults and mockery, Josia sounded as though she was on the verge of attacking with more than just words.

I climbed down from the wagon to speak with her. "Josia, I'm sorry. This must be… hard for you." I tried to make my voice comforting, but it sounded unconvincing even to me. "But Hareld… he was—"

"He *wasn't with them!*" she shrieked, wrenching herself from my grasp. She backed away several steps, staring at me with tears in her eyes. "I thought you would understand. You *saw* it."

Again, I thought I heard a quiet whisper in my ear—it sounded like "*Vengeance*". *It isn't real*, I told myself. *I'm imagining it.* But I saw Josia's eyes go wide as she turned away from me.

"Josia, wait!" But she didn't stop, and I couldn't follow—it felt too much like giving in to the voices I was hearing, admitting they were real.

I was certain that she couldn't have actually heard the whispers—there were no whispers to hear. Whatever was happening to me, it was only in my head; it had to be. But still, I resolved to warn Bryndine when I spoke with her, for Josia's sake. If she did try anything stupid, Bryndine could probably subdue her without harm.

When I had changed my clothing, I went to find Bryndine. She and her company had built up their own fire on the outskirts of the main camp, though I did not know if they were avoiding the other soldiers or if the other soldiers were avoiding them. Several women loitered around the fire talking; others were busy seeing to the horses, sharpening weapons, and doing various menial tasks. I still had not gotten a clear count of their numbers, but my earlier estimate of about twenty seemed accurate.

As I approached the fire, I recognized a few of the women around it. Sylla stared sullenly into the flames as she sharpened her longsword, and I wondered why she was not with Bryndine. Genna sat with two other women—a slim redheaded woman I recognized from the battle in Waymark, and a wildhaired blonde who was telling a story full of extremely foul language. The last woman I knew was Tenille, who stood with her back to the fire, speaking to two younger women who immediately moved to follow whatever order they had been given.

Tenille saw me coming before the others. "Dennon," she greeted me. "I'm glad to see you on your feet again." The women around the fire turned towards me, save for Genna, who focused her eyes on the ground in front of her.

"What happened to you anyway, Scriber?" asked the foulmouthed blond woman. "You were screamin' like a cut-rate whore, I thought one of the village girls was havin' a little fun watchin' the fight. Some folk, the danger gets them goin'." She grinned at me and I felt my cheeks redden.

Genna's face flushed redder still. "Orya!" she squeaked, horrified.

Orya just laughed, raising a hand to scratch at the wild tangles of hair atop her head. "Mother's teats, Genna, it's a joke. He don't mind." She looked to me for verification. "You know I don't mean nothin' by it, right Scriber?"

I did mind, in fact. I was in no mood to be mocked on this particular subject; not while the voices still haunted me at every turn. But I didn't know what to say. I was certain that any attempt to defend myself would only make me look more foolish.

"Missing the point as usual, Orya," the red-haired woman said, her blue eyes sparkling with amusement. "The Scriber was just calling for reinforcements. What brings the High Commander running faster than the sound of a cut-rate whore?"

Laughter broke out around the fire, and Orya guffawed louder than anyone. I found myself chuckling along with them—Uran Ord's taste for seedy brothels was one of the nobility's worst kept secrets. Only Sylla remained silent, grimly sharpening her blade. I wondered if she was even capable of laughter.

"That's hardly appropriate, Deanyn," Tenille scolded, trying and failing to keep the smile off her face. "The High Commander is wounded."

"Rumor is that the Scriber's already taken care of that," Deanyn said. "Besides, I'm not speaking ill of him. I'm just admiring his devotion to putting money in the hands of the less fortunate."

Another round of laughter. Apparently Bryndine's women were not fond of the High Commander. I wondered if Deanyn realized the favor she had done me; if so, it had been accomplished deftly, making Ord the butt of the joke in my place with a single comment. Whatever her intent, I was grateful.

"He'll be back to his charitable pursuits soon," I said. "But it wasn't my doing."

Deanyn shrugged. "The less you did for him, the more I like you, Scriber."

"Damn right!" Orya slapped her palm belligerently against the stone she sat on. "If there's any luck, the next whore he gives it to'll have the pox."

The other women were nodding, and some voiced their agreement. Even soft-voiced Genna looked angry—I could finally see in her the woman I had watched fight with such savagery the night before.

"That's enough." Tenille had tamed her expression, and now her face was stern. The insults died down immediately. "The Captain will be… pleased to hear that her cousin is well."

"Where is Captain Bryndine?" I asked. "I need to speak with her."

At that, Sylla finally spoke. "She doesn't want to be disturbed, Scriber."

"She will want to know about her cousin," Genna said.

"She said she wanted to be alone," Sylla growled. "She certainly won't want to see *him*. I'll tell her."

"Tell her what, Syl?" Deanyn asked. "The Scriber was there, he knows the man's condition. You're upset that she didn't let you come with her is all. You can't stand guard over her every moment of the day."

The argument seemed to get through to her—or else she simply realized she was outnumbered—and Sylla lapsed back into silence with an angry snort.

"You'll find her on the hill there." Tenille pointed into the darkness to the east of the camp, where a low rise was visible, silhouetted against the night sky. "She's with Janelyn." I did not know the name, but the sadness in her voice answered any questions I had.

"Janelyn is the girl who…" I trailed off, unable to come up with a tactful way to finish the question.

Tenille took my meaning and nodded. "She died a few hours ago. We built her a pyre on the hill, but the Captain wanted some time alone before we send her to the Father." She looked up at the crest of the small hill. "It has been long enough, I think. We'll go to her together." She raised her voice to catch the attention of the company. "On your feet, women. It's time."

* * *

I did not speak to Bryndine until after the ceremony was

done. Instead, I stayed and watched. It was sacrilege to burn a woman—the Children taught that women were to be buried, returned to the Mother in the Earth, while men were burned in order to free the spirit to rise to the Father. But I did not protest. Janelyn had died of battle wounds, and the Father was the patron of warriors. The girl had earned a warrior's rest.

It was a simple rite. Few words were said. Bryndine commended Janelyn's soul to the Father and set the pyre aflame, and the gathered women all saluted in unison, then stood a silent vigil as the body burned. Through the flames I could see the girl's face. She was young, barely twenty years old, and her hair was cut in a short, boyish style clearly modeled after her Captain's. I wondered why these women were so devoted to Bryndine. This girl, at least, had died because of her.

It was a long while before the body burned away, but eventually little was left of the pyre or the girl but smoke and ash. As the women began to slowly file back to camp, I pulled Tenille aside.

"Tenille, did you tell Bryndine about me?" I needed to know before I spoke to Bryndine myself.

She shook her head. "You know Dennon, not every Scriber hates you for the Old Garden. You couldn't have known that wall would collapse."

"Maybe not every Scriber. But most. They don't forget—it says so on the pin. Did you tell her?"

Tenille smiled slightly. "You have a point. No, I didn't tell her. I didn't have to. Did you really think the King's niece wouldn't have heard of you?"

"I had hoped." So Bryndine had known me when we first met. Another thing she'd hidden from me. "How do you work with that woman, Tenille? Do you know she was in Waymark the day before the attack and didn't say anything? She knew it was coming!" I gestured to the guttering remains of the pyre. "That girl would still be alive if she'd warned us!" I was speaking too loudly, I knew—several nearby women turned towards us curiously.

Tenille's smile faded, and her face went cold. Gripping me tightly by the arm, she dragged me away from the others. "You are twice the fool everyone thinks you are, do you know that?"

she hissed. "Those women will break your legs if they hear that talk about Bryndine, and I'll let them! You don't have the first idea what really happened."

"She told me she was scouting—"

"We *were* scouting. We are allowed to do little else. Ord told us the plan was to take the Burners by surprise before they attacked at all. We spread out across the area trying to find where they planned to strike. The Captain had to keep quiet because we didn't want them to catch word of the ambush.

"But the High Commander lied to us. His plan was always to let the Burners attack once we found their target—to get them all in one place. Then they could be surrounded and captured; they couldn't disappear again, like they always do. Ord didn't want us telling the villagers because he needed you there as *bait*." She spat the last word through gritted teeth. "When the Captain found out, she tried to reason with him, but he wouldn't listen—he wanted to be the man who caught the uncatchable Burners. So she disobeyed his orders, and brought us to warn you."

"She should have warned us to begin with," I insisted stubbornly. "I don't care what the plan was; she put us all at risk." Tenille's story might have lessened Bryndine's culpability in the attack on Waymark, but it did not entirely clean her hands.

"Dennon, Ord was furious. After the battle, while he was still lucid, he blamed her for letting the Burners escape again. He is going to tell the King. Bryndine has fought to be recognized as a soldier her whole life, and they're going to take it away. From her, from all of us. For saving you and the rest of those… ingrates." Tenille gestured towards the main camp, where the villagers of Waymark mingled with the First Company. "Think about that before you run your mouth off again."

Releasing my arm, she turned back towards the camp. "She still needs to know that Ord will live," she said over her shoulder as she walked away. "And you might consider thanking her."

I was left alone on the dark hill. The women had returned to camp by then, taking torches and lanterns with them, and the only light remaining came from the stars and the dying embers of Janelyn's pyre. In that dim light, I could see the huge, solitary shadow of Bryndine Errynson, still standing alone by the remains of the fire. I didn't know what I wanted to say to her now, not after what Tenille had told me, but despite that, I found myself approaching her.

"Scriber Dennon," she said without turning away from the ashes. "What news of my cousin?"

"He lives." I had promised Ord that I would not tell her of his memory loss, but Tenille's story had not left me sympathetic towards the High Commander. "But I am concerned about his mind. He could not remember why we were here, or who his officers were; not even your name."

"Do you think he will recover?"

"I don't know."

She nodded slowly. "He meant to have the King strip me of my rank, before he lost his senses. I suppose his men will remind him."

"Why did you not tell me what he had done? Why let me blame you?"

"He is the High Commander of the King's Army. The people must have faith in him if we hope to maintain Erryn's Promise."

"You could tell the King what he planned. Counter his complaint with your own."

"My uncle will not take my side against Uran, Scriber Dennon. I imagine he already knew of the plan."

"You still should have warned us, whatever your orders. It might have saved lives."

"Yes. I know." She never moved her eyes from the fire, or let so much as a hint of emotion color her voice.

I wanted to grab her and shake her, to provoke some kind of reaction. Instead, I changed the subject. "A woman from Waymark blames you for her husband's death," I told her. "Josia Kellen. She is not in her right mind. She may try something."

"The innkeeper? I thought she had been burned in the fire. Did you treat her?"

"No, I just spoke with her. She had no injuries I could

see." A shiver went through me—there was another kind of burning, one that left no mark.

"She was trying to put the fire out at the inn during the battle when she collapsed, screaming. Some of my women heard her say she had been burned."

I rubbed my temple with two fingers. "She… It must have been the stress. I fainted myself." Josia could not have suffered the same hallucination I did—it made no sense. But the fear did not leave me. She could not have heard the voices, but if she had, what did it mean? I didn't want to consider the possibility. "More importantly, if she does something foolish… be gentle with her. She lost more than most last night."

"I will not harm her, Scriber."

"There is one more thing." I steeled myself to ask the question I had been avoiding. "You know who I am. Why did you hide it?"

She did turn to look at me then. "I suspected. I knew the name Dennon Lark. But I saw no reason to bring it up. You clearly wished to avoid recognition."

"But why trust me to help you, or treat your cousin? You know my reputation."

"That you were responsible for the collapse at the Old Garden while searching for the Archives? A tragedy, certainly, but it has little bearing on your training. When they tell stories of you, most forget to mention that before the accident you were quite the prodigy among the Scribers."

Her level tone set me off my guard. With Bryndine, I could never tell where I stood—her face and voice betrayed nothing of what she felt. Most people, when they found out who I was, reacted with anger that I had dared to defile holy ground, or that I had led men to their death; they found something in the rumors to hate me for. I knew how to cope with that kind of scorn—by retreating. I had done so for five years. But this, I did not know how to take.

"I'm responsible for more than that," I said. "There was nothing there, just an empty chamber, another piece of the Underground. I defiled holy ground. I destroyed a priceless work of art that we have lost the means to recreate. I desecrated a piece of history. That is a violation of every oath a Scriber swears!" I had tried to hide my past for too long; I could not accept that it mattered so little to her. I wanted to explain to her the wrong I had done, to make her understand, to make her hate me. I was comfortable with being hated. "And I did it for a tall tale. A children's song! People died for nothing, and I'm responsible for it!"

"You couldn't have known what would happen." Her expression remained inscrutable. It was too much for me to take.

"*Don't do that!*" Five years worth of anger exploded out of my mouth. "Don't you *dare* say that, like it was nothing. Damn it to the Dragon, what does it take to make you care? What is *wrong* with you? Raise your voice, scowl, *something*; don't just stand there!"

"Would it make things any different? What's done is done."

"Is that what you tell yourself? Is that how you could watch that girl burn without even a frown?"

She did not frown then, either, but her voice was cold. "I do not have to explain myself to you, Scriber Dennon."

I almost struck her. She was well over a foot taller than me, almost twice as broad in the shoulders, and as strong in one finger as I was in both arms, no doubt. But I almost struck her. I was angrier than I had ever been—and worse, I barely understood why. The only thing that stopped me from attacking her was a low, quiet noise. A whisper.

"*All will burn.*"

The rage that always came with the whispers struck me in the chest like a hammer, but rather than making me go through with the attack, it stopped me. Was the anger I felt even my own? Was I about to attack the King's niece because of a voice in my head? *Mother below, I'm truly losing my mind*, I thought, fighting to control the fury being thrust upon me.

"Scriber, did you hear something?" Bryndine was instantly alert, peering into the darkness.

"You heard it?" I was pleased and terrified in equal parts. If she heard the whispers too, perhaps I was not mad—though if it was not madness, I did not know what else it could be. But then I realized she did not mean the voice. There was another sound, footsteps on the grass. I turned towards the noise, scanning the hillside with Bryndine.

There was a glint of light in the dark; starlight on metal. Staring in the direction it had come from, I saw a figure in the shadows, climbing the hill towards us.

"You shouldn't have killed my Hareld." Josia Kellen's voice crept up the slope, thin and sad. I could see her now; somehow she had laid hands on a sword, and she pointed it at Bryndine accusingly. "You shouldn't have killed him." It should have been ridiculous, that small motherly figure waving a sword at a woman twice her size. But the look on her face, the way the shadows hugged the creases and wrinkles in her skin—she could have been a creature from legend, a spirit in the dark.

Bryndine stepped in front of me. "Drop your sword," she commanded, though she had no weapon of her own; she had not brought her sword to the rite.

Josia lunged, thrusting the tip of the sword forward like a spear. Terror and instinct took hold of me, and I leapt backwards. But Bryndine didn't flinch. With speed that would have been surprising had I not already seen her fight in Waymark, she sidestepped the thrust and brought a hand down hard on Josia's forearm. With a cry of pain, Josia dropped the sword; Bryndine caught it before it hit the ground and levelled it at the other woman's throat.

"Don't hurt her!" I called, running to Bryndine's side. She did not lower the blade.

"I will not. But what are we to do with her? She is clearly not well."

I had no answer. "Josia, please, you have to tell her you won't do this again."

"They said I had to," Josia sobbed, dropping to her knees. "They said I had to get revenge. They'll burn me if I don't!"

I gaped at her open-mouthed. She had to be speaking of the same voices I heard. What else could she mean?

"Who told you that? The Burners?" Bryndine asked.

"No, no, I can't…" With sudden, appalling force, she hammered a fist into the side of her head. "They're here! Don't ask about them! They're going to—"

Faintly, as though from far away, I heard voices whispering: "*Burn.*"

Josia screamed. And kept screaming. She collapsed on the ground, writhing and rolling as though trying to smother invisible flames. I heard cries of alarm coming from soldiers in the camp as the shrieking rolled down the hillside.

"What is this, Scriber?" Bryndine lowered her sword, looking to me for some explanation.

I knew what it was. I had felt it myself, not long ago. But there was no way to explain it. Or more accurately, there was no way to explain it that did not end with me looking as mad as Josia.

"*It burns!*" Josia arched her back against the grassy hillside and, with a final heartwrenching wail, went still. I crouched by her side, hoping she had only fainted from the pain. But she was not breathing.

Bryndine knelt down beside me. "Scriber Dennon? Is she…"

"She's gone."

People were running up the hillside now, and soon we were surrounded by soldiers demanding to know what had happened. By the light of their torches I noticed something I had not before: about halfway down the slope, an ancient fireleaf grew amidst the scattered trees that speckled the hill. It was surrounded by fallen leaves.

As they took Josia's body away, Bryndine tried to explain what had transpired as best she could. But I stayed silent. I was preoccupied with one thought:

Josia had heard the same voices I did. And they had killed her.

CHAPTER EIGHT

The voices plague me through every waking hour, and even in my sleep I cannot escape them. I dreamed of the Burnt again last night. I fear I may be losing my mind.

— From the personal journals of Dennon Lark

The following days of the journey to Three Rivers were not pleasant for me. Word spread about Josia's death, and rumors naturally followed. The predominant story was that Josia had confronted Bryndine about the blasphemous funeral pyre, and Bryndine had killed her for it. As a result, Bryndine and her company were shunned and avoided—but that had been true before the incident, so little changed for them. Unfortunately, it was also common knowledge that I had been with the women when Janelyn was burned, and that I had witnessed Josia's final moments.

Overnight, my status among the villagers shifted from hero to pariah. Ordinarily, this would have been acceptable, even desirable—I had not wanted their praise or their company to begin with. Josia had been the only one of them I could tolerate. But after my argument with Bryndine, I did not feel terribly welcome among her company either, and the soldiers of the First had no use for me at all now that Uran Ord was well again.

I have always been a man who enjoys solitude, but there was little opportunity for me to study or write on the long march to Three Rivers. Without my books, or any significant interaction with the others, there was nothing to distract my mind from the questions that plagued me: Had Josia truly heard the same voices I did? And if so, would I share her fate?

With death and madness at the forefront of my thoughts, I began to notice the fireleaf trees scattered around the countryside. They were not uncommon by any means, and their bright flame-red foliage made them easy to spot, even amidst all the other trees whose leaves were tinted red by autumn's brush. Sometimes when we passed one growing close enough to the road, I thought I could hear the voices again, whispering their terrible words for my ears alone—but whether the sound was real or remembered, I could not say.

All of the fireleafs we passed were encircled by fallen leaves; it was clearly not a phenomenon restricted to the Waymark area. Exactly what that meant eluded me—I only knew that I had seen a burning fireleaf the first time I had dreamed of the Burnt, and that the dream had come soon after the leaves began to fall. Several nights, I woke screaming from that same dream, the pain of fire lingering on my skin.

On our fourth day of travel, the road took us through the fields of grain that surrounded Barleyfield for miles, and the possibility of leaving the procession when we reached the town occurred to me. Barleyfield was large enough to already have Scribers working there, so work might be scarce, but it would be better than returning to Three Rivers—and perhaps if I could resume my quiet, private life, the voices would cease.

As we drew closer to town, we passed great swaths of wheat and barley that had been burned and trampled into muddy brown ash. The few farmhouses that had not been completely destroyed appeared abandoned. Under normal circumstances, there is no barony but the Bridgefort with more arable land than Three Rivers, or more men working the fields. Yet the countryside we walked through was ravaged and deserted, and staying in Barleyfield was less appealing with each smouldering homestead I saw. If the Three Rivers Brigade could not keep the Burnt—I could not help but think of the rebels by that name, at least to myself—from putting field and farm to the torch even in the King's own lands, then the capital might be the only safe place remaining.

We arrived at Barleyfield itself several hours after dark on the fifth day after leaving Waymark. The Seventh Company was already billeted there to protect the town's rich farmlands against the Burnt, but the people were eager to make extra room for the First if it meant an increased Army presence for even a single night. Few citizens were forced to open their doors to the soldiers though; the once mildly thriving town was half-deserted. It was not hard to find empty homes to sleep in.

While the soldiers prepared to leave the next morning, I asked around about the diminished population. The threat of the rebels, it seemed, had already driven many to pack up their things and make for Three Rivers to claim protection under Erryn's Promise. Most of those who remained in Barleyfield only did so because the dangers on the road were too great to risk without military escort; they planned to leave with us. Some few stubborn locals were determined to keep their homes as long as the Seventh remained garrisoned there, and there was some talk of trying to harvest what they could from the fields before it was all burned. The harvest had been poor this year even before the attacks, and the realm needed to be fed, but still, few were willing to leave the safety of the walls.

I learned a great deal about the rebels from the people of Barleyfield. What little I had known of them came from Illias' letters, and I had not realized how truly ineffectual the Army's protection was proving against the Burnt. The attacks were near-impossible to predict, and even when the scouts managed to spot them in advance, none of the rebels were ever captured. As soon as the battle turned against them, the Burnt would simply melt away into the countryside, leaving only their dead behind.

Much of what I heard, though, was only rumors and speculation: that the rebels used forbidden Elovian lore to call down lightning and shake the earth; that they were really the vengeful Wyddin, come to destroy mankind once and for all; that they were savage barbarians from the Plains who had somehow sneaked by the Crossing. How they recruited was a mystery, but stories abounded of men and women disappearing after an attack, only to later reappear fighting alongside the Burnt.

Though I was uncomfortably aware that my own experiences with strange dreams and disembodied voices fit in nicely with many of those theories, I had to dismiss them as nonsense. A Scriber works with knowledge and evidence—I could not accept that there was some mysterious Wyddin sorcery at work. The most reasonable story claimed that the Burnt were simply radicals trying to prove that Erryn's Promise was not being upheld by King Syrid. If that *was* their goal, it was working; I heard no small amount of grumbling about the King's failure to put a stop to the raids.

But the most important thing I learned was that staying in Barleyfield was not a desirable option. When the First Company departed, leading nearly five times as many citizens as they had been when they arrived, I remained among them.

It was another twenty leagues—some six days of travel for a group of our size—from Barleyfield to the Saltroad, which gave me ample time to consider my options. As the days passed, I thought more and more of Illias' letters. I had never wanted to return to the Academy or to the capital, but I had little choice now. And given that I had no choice, it would be good to see Illias Bront again. All I had to do was turn north on the Saltroad towards Highpass while the rest of the procession journeyed south to Three Rivers.

When we made camp the last night before reaching the main road, I went to see Uran Ord. I hoped that he still felt some gratitude towards me, even though I had not actually been responsible for saving him; I needed an escort that only the High Commander could grant. The trip north to Highpass would be unacceptably dangerous alone.

I found no one outside his tent, but I heard voices within. Pulling open the flap, I peeked my head in. Bryndine, Uran, and Lieutenant Ralsten were inside, engaged in argument.

"She disobeyed direct orders and ruined the entire plan, High Commander!" Ralsten was saying insistently.

Bryndine stood silently at attention, seemingly unaffected by the accusation. Uran Ord, however, looked vaguely uncomfortable, and kept glancing sidelong at his cousin as he listened to his Lieutenant.

"And she will be punished, Ralsten. But I have the command of this train and the protection of the citizens to think about. I see no reason to worry about—" Ord paused, only for a sliver of an instant, but I could tell that he had nearly forgotten her name. "—Bryndine's punishment right this instant." Whether because he was embarrassed at his inability to remember her or angry because of her disobedience, Ord clearly did not want Bryndine there.

Not wanting to get involved, I made to leave, but the slight motion attracted Ord's attention.

"Scriber Dennon?" I froze, mortified that I had been spotted with my head poked halfway into his tent. "Please, come in." He motioned for me to approach, and I pushed the flap fully aside and entered, my face hot with embarrassment.

"I didn't intend to interrupt," I apologized.

"Nonsense. We were just finishing here. Cousin, you may go." He gestured for Ralsten to take Bryndine away.

"Uran—" Ralsten began to protest, but the High Commander fixed him with a sharp stare and he fell silent.

"I only wanted to let you know that I will be leaving for the Academy when we reach the Saltroad," I said. "I wondered if you might spare some men as an escort."

"I'm sure we can arrange something," Ord replied. As his gaze came to rest on me again, I felt suddenly lightheaded. A cold sweat broke out on my forehead. Something in this tent, something with Uran Ord, was terribly wrong. I had felt it before and hoped it was only in my mind, but this was the second time Ord's presence had affected me so. A familiar sound floated past my ears; a whisper that only I could hear.

"High Commander, no!" Ralsten was not quiet with his objection. "We'll need every man to protect these people from the Burners." He hadn't yet taken Bryndine away; I suspected he did not want to leave Ord alone with me.

"Please, forget that I asked. It was a foolish request." I turned to leave. I needed to get out before another fit struck, before the voices whispered for me to burn.

"I will escort him," Bryndine volunteered. "My women should be more than sufficient to see the Scriber to Highpass."

That stopped me mid-step. I turned to face her, stunned. Considering what I had said to her after Janelyn's service, I had assumed she wanted nothing more to do with me.

"A fine idea, cousin!" The High Commander seemed inordinately pleased with the suggestion. "We lose no men, and the Scriber is protected."

"Uran! She has to come back to Three Rivers. She must go before the King!" Ralsten sounded as though he couldn't believe what he was hearing.

"I will return to Three Rivers for my punishment when Scriber Dennon is safe," Bryndine promised. "You have my word."

"There you have it, Ralsten. You wouldn't doubt the word of an Errynson, would you?" Ord smiled thinly at his lieutenant. "The matter is settled." They proceeded to discuss the details, but the noise in my head was becoming too much to bear. With a muttered apology, I excused myself.

As soon as I was outside again, away from Uran Ord, the sound stopped. I could not imagine why Ord's presence affected me so powerfully. I had heard the same voices when I was near Josia, but just a few words, as though I was overhearing only part of what she was being told, and from a great distance. It was different in Ord's tent; it felt as though the whispers were emanating directly from him.

A dreadful thought occurred to me: what if the High Commander of the King's Army was somehow working with the Burnt? But that couldn't be—he had helped fight them back, and been badly wounded doing so. I rubbed at my temple. The constant fear of the voices was getting to me. Ord made me uncomfortable, but the idea that he might be a traitor was simply implausible. Whatever was happening, and however scared I might be, I would not let fear override reason.

"You have made yourself scarce these last days, Scriber," Bryndine commented as she exited the tent a few moments later. Ralsten followed close behind, scowling at us before stalking away angrily.

"If I had known you were going to miss me, I might have visited," I said dryly.

Bryndine didn't smile. "I simply wanted to extend my

gratitude, and I have not seen you."

"Gratitude? For what?"

"For attending Janelyn's ceremony. You did not have to do that. The women appreciated seeing her recognized by someone outside the company." I noticed that she did not say that *she* appreciated it; as always, she was a cipher. I could not begin to guess how she actually felt. Any illusions of understanding I might have had were proven false by the very fact that she was still willing to speak with me after our argument.

"Don't thank me for that. She was wounded defending us. The entire village should have been there."

"But they were not. You were."

I waved my hand irritably. "It was nothing worth mentioning. Is that why you volunteered to help me, or did you just hope to avoid punishment a while longer?"

"I volunteered because Ralsten would have convinced my cousin to deny you an escort. I would not have it said that the King's Army let a Scriber risk the roads alone in times like these. It would be a breach of Erryn's Promise."

"I don't think that Erryn meant for the Army to accompany every person who sets foot on the road. That seems an impractical promise to keep."

"Even so," she replied.

I decided not to press the issue—I had my escort, and I did not want to talk her out of it. "The High Commander seemed pleased to let you go. I assumed he would want to keep you near him until he can bring you to King Syrid."

"Perhaps he simply tires of my company." It sounded like a jest, but she didn't smile. "Truthfully, I think he is embarrassed that he cannot remember me. He has been avoiding me since his recovery, and was none too pleased when Ralsten insisted on bringing me to him."

"He is still not himself, then?" Unbidden, the suspicions I had buried earlier rose back to the surface.

"Far from it, Scriber. I don't mean to speak ill of him, but before he was wounded, my cousin would never have let me leave; not after disobeying him as I did."

We spoke briefly about preparations for the trip after that, then parted. I went to my chest and began to remove the items

I needed—the wagons would be going on to Three Rivers, and I could not carry the chest on horseback. I packed my journal, some clothing, and some extra quills and ink in a bag; most of my books I had to leave behind. I asked one of the soldiers to see that the chest was brought to the Scriber Registrar in Three Rivers, where I might retrieve it later, but I assumed I would not see it again.

As I made my preparations, my thoughts wandered. Something Bryndine had said earlier had planted a seed in my mind, and it had sprouted into a distinctly unpleasant question. Her cousin had been avoiding her, she had said. He was sending her away when he would never have done so before his injury. He had asked me not to tell her of his strange behavior, moments after his unlikely recovery.

What was Uran Ord so determined to hide from Bryndine?

* * *

We reached the Saltroad before noon the next day, and parted from the First Company and their legion of civilian followers. No one was sorry to see us go—they were quite pleased to be rid of the cursed Bloody Bride.

We ran into a problem almost immediately: Bryndine and her company had their own horses, but I did not, nor could the First Company spare one.

"He'll ride with me," insisted the red-haired woman who had saved me from embarrassment a few nights before. Deanyn was her name, I remembered. "I'm not carrying much. If he doubles up with most of you, we'll just have two people who need to find mounts and one horse with a broken back."

She was not far from the truth there; she was quite slender, and carried only a thin-bladed sword where most of the others were more heavily armed. The thought of trying to share Bryndine's horse was laughable—it was a massive beast, but even it would falter under that much weight.

So I rode with Deanyn, and found her to be pleasant company. She had a quick wit and an easy demeanor, and her presence acted as a bridge between me and the other women.

She pulled me into conversations that I would otherwise have avoided, and while I occasionally wished for some solitude, in general I found that the company made the time pass much easier.

Orya told interesting, frequently obscene tales and bawdy jests; Tenille shared stories and lessons from the Academy or spoke of her husband and children in Three Rivers; and no matter what the subject was, Deanyn had a wry observation that never failed to amuse. There was entertainment too: a stout, young woman named Nalla sang in a clear, beautiful voice; clever-fingered Varrie, who had spent her youth among travelling entertainers, played along on her lute. Everyone was more at ease away from the First Company—I heard more out of Genna than I ever had, and at one point, I was startled to see Sylla actually smiling, if only for a moment.

I was finally able to get an accurate count of the group—they were seventeen in total, counting Bryndine, and by the end of the first day Deanyn had introduced me to all of them. Debra was a woodcutter's daughter from Timberhold and had arms that might have been thicker than Bryndine's. Leste had grown up on the trading vessels that sailed between Ryndport and the Raen Empire; she had the black skin of the Raenish, and spoke their tongue fluently, but her Plainstongue was accented and slightly stilted in diction. Wynne was the youngest in the company, just short of her twentieth year—well read and intelligent, she had sought to be a Scriber, but could not find sponsorship or afford admission to the Academy.

There were many others: tall, gorgeous Kaelyn; the twins Elene and Selvi, who could both core an apple with their bows at a hundred yards, and who I could not reliably tell apart; silver haired Hylda, at least ten years older than the rest; disciplined Ivyla and terribly scarred Rylene. After a few days travelling with the women, I found myself growing comfortable enough to converse even without Deanyn's prompting. It was a rarity for me; I have never been a terribly social person.

Bryndine, however, kept a certain distance between herself and her company. She was more open with them than with me, certainly, but she was their Captain before she was their friend. Still, it was clear that the women loved and respected her greatly, and they followed her orders without question. I didn't understand the admiration—Bryndine's stone-faced poise annoyed me to no end. But it seemed wise to keep that to myself, as long as I was surrounded by armed soldiers who adored her.

The journey went by without incident. Apparently the rebel attacks were much less common in the Salt Mountain foothills, the raid on Waymark notwithstanding. Of course, the company of soldiers dressed in the uniforms of the King's Army may also have played a role in our safe progress.

Better still, the voices had been silenced; I had not heard so much as a whispered word since we turned north, and the Burnt no longer haunted my dreams. Fireleafs were scarce in the foothills as well, and though I saw a few of them far distant from the road, they failed to evoke the strange dread I had felt previously. After a few days, I could almost make myself believe that the whispers had been nothing more than the effects of stress and fatigue. Almost.

As we drew nearer, the Salt Mountains loomed larger and larger over the foothills. The Dragon-worshipping clansfolk who lived there claimed that the mountains were once waves, frozen by the Sea God in the midst of a terrible storm so that his people would have a land to call their own. Looking at the sharp peaks of dark grey-blue stone rising in the distance, I could almost believe the legend.

In the late afternoon of the third day, the twin towers that guarded the pass became visible, rising straight up out of the mountainside like the hilts of some giant's swords, driven into the stone long ago. Those towers were the symbol of Highpass; the sigil of the Ords, who had ruled there since before the Forgetting. After five years away, I was home.

CHAPTER NINE

The Scribers were founded in 687 AB by King Delwyn, known as the Scriber King. The Forgetting had been in effect for nearly two centuries when he came to power, and reading and writing were still illegal by the laws King Ullyd had set in place. Seeing how the Kingsland had floundered economically and politically over two hundred years of ignorance, Delwyn abolished those laws and put an end to the Forgetting at last.

He created the Scribers to ensure that such a thing would never happen again, and charged them with recovering as much as they could of what had been lost. To protect their autonomy, the Scribers' Academy was built not in the capital, but in Highpass. It was Delwyn's intention that if ever a new Forgetter came to power, the Scribers could go into hiding in the Salt Mountains with their books, so that the history of the Kingsland would never again be destroyed.

— From Dennon Lark's *The Scriber King*

Highpass looked like it had burst out of the mountainside all at once in an eruption of quarried stone. Buildings protruded wherever a decent surface could be found, their straight angles standing starkly against the ragged edges of the cliffs. Numerous small plateaus, connected to one another by switchback paths, each provided space for a handful of homes. Atop the flat cliffs to the west, the shops and the manors of the wealthy were built so close to one another that it looked as though the slightest nudge against one would send them all tipping off the precipice. And high up the road, the two guard towers stood like a pair of stone soldiers, watching the pass into Salt Mountain territory.

The Academy, in contrast, sat on a single broad table of stone carved from the mountain east of the city proper, with its own access from the Saltroad. When we reached the fork between the two, Bryndine bid Tenille to take the rest of the company along the west road into Highpass, to announce their presence to Baron Ord and request quarters. Bryndine herself would come with me along the eastern path, fulfilling her promise to escort me to the Academy.

"Shouldn't you go with them?" I asked hopefully. "Your uncle would probably prefer for you to call on him yourself." I didn't want to be alone with Bryndine; it was never comfortable.

"I said that I would see you to the Academy," Bryndine replied, as though it was the simplest thing in the world.

"I think I can find the way from here."

"If the Captain says we're going with you, we're going with you, Scriber," Sylla said indignantly. Of course she was going to join us; that was the one thing that could make conversation with Bryndine even more awkward. Now I would have to watch every word I said for fear that Sylla would assume an insult to her Captain and break a bone in retaliation.

"You're like to get knifed on the way up if you're alone," Orya informed me seriously. "A Scriber's a good mark, usually has some coin. Thieves're always watchin' the Academy road for folk travellin' alone. It's easier than workin' the city with the guards about. Probably more dangerous goin' that last bit by yourself than the whole road before it."

I raised an eyebrow. "You know a lot about it, do you?"

"Grew up hidin' in caves and climbin' the cliffs here. I mighta cut your throat myself before the Captain found me." The shocked look on my face made her laugh. "Don't worry, Scriber. I don't do that no more." She solemnly raised two fingers and made the sign of the Divide, turning it into a lewd gesture halfway through and grinning wickedly at me. "I swear it on the Father's cock."

"How pious of you," I said sarcastically.

She was right, though. Highpass had more than its share of cutpurses and thugs. The caves, cliffs, and chasms of the mountainside city offered hundreds of shadowy places for the criminal element to hide, and they took full advantage of it. The guardsmen and the Army tried to keep these hiding holes clear, but the thieves knew the secrets of the mountain better than anyone, and ambushes were common. That was how my father had been killed, and following in his footsteps had never much appealed to me.

"I suppose I'll need the escort," I admitted.

Bryndine and Sylla left their horses with the others to be stabled, and I clumsily hopped down from Deanyn's mount.

"Go easy on him, Syl," Deanyn said. "I need him back alive, he still owes me from the dice last night." She gave me a wink and a wave as the company rode away.

It was about a half-hour from the fork to the Academy campus, but the uncomfortable silence made it feel longer. Every time I considered speaking I looked at Sylla, glowering at me with her dark eyes, and thought better of it. I had my own reasons for keeping silent as well—I didn't know what kind of welcome I would receive upon our arrival. I had returned to the Academy only one other time since the catastrophe at the Old Garden, immediately afterwards. The reception had not been warm, needless to say. I had gone into hiding in Waymark shortly after. I tried to put such thoughts aside, however, as I looked up the east road and saw the Academy for the first time in five years.

Seven squat six-sided buildings rose from the broad man-made plateau, all of simple make, constructed of closely fitted blocks of polished marble. Six of these buildings sat at the corners of a sprawling hexagonal campus that was carpeted with lush green grass—an uncommon sight against the stony grey of the mountain. In the center of the campus, between the six Schools, stood the seventh and largest building: Delwyn's Hall, home of the Scribers' Council, and the greatest library of history and knowledge since the Archives. Despite everything, the sight of those buildings sent a thrill through me. I felt like a child again, gazing with wonder at the Academy from the

Highpass cliffs.

A high iron fence enclosed the campus, to keep those who were not pinned or enrolled from sneaking about—though I knew from experience that a child could fit between the bars in some places. Stone gatehouses stood around the fence at three points, to the west, north, and south, controlling entry from Highpass, the Salt Mountains, and the Saltroad respectively.

After a tiring half-hour climb up the road, we found ourselves standing before the southern gatehouse. I didn't recognize the Scriber who intercepted us at the gate, and by the bland look on his face, he did not recognize me either. I affected a confidence I did not feel as I unfastened my pin and handed it to him, hoping that he would not know my name. I wasn't eager for Bryndine and Sylla to see what my brethren generally thought of me.

Those hopes did not last long. As the gatekeeper examined the back of my pin, his bored expression twisted into an angry scowl.

"Lark? You've got some backbone, don't you?"

"Not particularly, no. May I pass?" I bit back the many less polite retorts that came to mind—they would only make things worse.

"You've stayed away this long, why not head back to whatever hole you were hiding in? Or have you come up with some more priceless relics to destroy looking for the Archives?" He spoke with a mocking sneer, and made no move to return my pin. "Or is it the Wyddin now? Some other fable?"

To my chagrin, Bryndine stepped forward to address the man. "If I am not mistaken, any Scriber with a valid pin is permitted entry to the Academy."

"This one gets in over my dead body," the gatekeeper replied, though even before he was finished speaking his eyes flickered to Bryndine's nearly eight foot tall form, and he swallowed nervously.

My embarrassment made it difficult to hold my tongue. "Sky and Earth, what do you think I'm going to do, tear down Delwyn's Hall?"

"Why not? You tore down the Old Garden; at least the Hall can be rebuilt."

"And of course I did it with malicious intent, and now I roam the baronies seeking out historical sites and ruining them. How fortunate for the Scribers that you were here to stop me!"

The gatekeeper's face flushed a furious crimson. "You aren't getting in! Good men died at the Old Garden!"

He was not wrong about that.

"By the Mother and the Father," Sylla muttered, stalking by me to grab the gatekeeper by the collar. She had kept silent until now, and her sudden movement took me by surprise—I had imagined she would enjoy watching me put in my place. She shoved the man up against the gatehouse wall with some force. "If the Captain *says* to let the Scriber in, you let the Dragon-damned Scriber in!" I almost laughed, despite my humiliation—she had said nearly the same thing to me a half-hour before. Her frustration at those who did not heed Bryndine was as consistent as it was intimidating.

"Let me go!" The gatekeeper struggled against Sylla's grip, but she had fingers like steel—I remembered the pain of her grasp myself. "*Intruders!* Intruders at the gates!" Another man came rushing out of the gatehouse, his sword drawn, and a group of observers began to gather on the other side of the gate. I rubbed at my temple, and tried to casually use the gesture to hide my face from the growing crowd. I had expected to be poorly received, but still, I had not been prepared for this.

"Sylla." Bryndine clasped the other woman's shoulder. "This is not helping."

Sylla shoved the man hard against the stone wall a second time, then reluctantly let him go. He dropped to his knees as she released him, and my pin fell from his hand, skipping across the dirt. I knelt and retrieved it, fastening it to my collar.

The other guardsman rushed forward to help his companion up, keeping his sword at the ready. "What is this, Yurrel?"

"That's Dennon Lark, Ibyn! He wants in the gate."

The students who had gathered beyond the portcullis reacted to the sound of my name with jeers and taunts, and the second guardsman's expression darkened.

"Dennon Lark… Haven't heard your name in years. Most of us hoped you'd have the good sense to stay away." His gaze flickered to the two women with me, and he paled slightly as he noticed the full Errynson arms on Bryndine's tabard. "But he's still a pinned Scriber, Yurrel. Open the gate."

Yurrel climbed to his feet and sullenly tromped into the gatehouse. A moment later, I heard the metallic clanking of chains, and the portcullis began to rise.

"Thank you, Scriber Ibyn." Bryndine inclined her head towards the man.

"I'm not doing you a favor. You'll find no warmer welcome inside than you did here. And not just because of Lark, either. There are some who still don't like the trick you tried to pull with the School of Warfare. But it won't be me who denies the King's own niece." He waved us onwards. "Go on, get your business done, and then leave us be."

Some of those waiting past the gatehouse had dispersed when it became clear that there would be no violence, but many stayed, and we entered the campus to the sound of angry shouts and hurled insults. Bryndine and Sylla flanked me to either side, keeping the crowd at bay, but even so we were shoved and jostled frequently as we hurried towards the School of History, where I hoped to find Illias.

"He mentioned that the Old Garden can't be rebuilt, and you said something similar a few nights ago. Have the Scribers made no progress with Elovian architecture?" Bryndine asked as we cut across the grassy campus. "I thought I had heard of advances in that field."

"The School of Sciences has nearly solved the problem of supporting domes and arches that size, yes. But the glasswork…" The stained glass images suspended above the Old Garden courtyard had been one of the greatest works of art left from before the Forgetting. They were irreplaceable. Even if the techniques were recovered, any attempt at repair would only result in a pale imitation; the tangible weight of history was not something that could be replicated. "The School of Arts has tried, but…"

There are some things I will never forgive myself for, and Bryndine had found one. It was not a subject I liked to dwell on. She seemed to sense my reticence, and we walked the rest of the way to the History building in silence.

Illias' private study was on the top level of the building,

and I led us straight there. It was easier once we were inside; those within were busy with classes or sequestered in silent study, and had not witnessed the scene at the gate. My presence went largely unnoticed as we climbed the stairways to the fourth floor.

When I knocked on his office door, a muffled grunt of invitation answered. He was in; that was a blessing. I had feared I might have to search the entire campus for him. I entered hastily, not wanting to risk being seen by anyone who knew me, and Bryndine followed. Sylla remained outside by the door—it was hardly necessary to stand guard in the middle of the Academy, but given our reception at the gates, I could understand the impulse.

"What is it? I've work to do." Illias had his head down, bent over a thick tome with age-yellowed pages, so that all I could see was the thinning grey hair atop his head. His quill hand was scribbling down words on a pile of clean, new paper, and he barely took the time to look at it as he copied. A smile I could not repress teased the corners of my mouth upwards. This was exactly how I remembered him. Morning, noon, and night, always bent over a book in study, or copying old works to ensure their survival.

His office had not changed either; it looked exactly as it had when I was ten, sitting at his desk and listening to his stories of times past, the stories that led me to a lifelong love of history. Dozens of oil lanterns hung from the ceiling and candles littered every flat surface. The many sources of flickering light cast hundreds of shadows that danced merrily along the walls. Illias hated a dark room; he hated not being able to read.

"Illias…" I didn't know what to say. It had been too long.

His head snapped up at the sound of my voice, and a warmth tingled through my veins at the sight of his familiar lined face, the grizzled grey beard that grew all the way down his neck, the piercing intelligence in his faded blue eyes. "Is that… Denn?" His mouth curved into a joyous smile, revealing crooked yellow teeth. It was not a handsome smile, but to me it was the most welcome thing in the world.

"Illias, I—" My words were choked off by a sudden tightness in my throat. There were tears in my eyes as the old man rose from his seat and rushed towards me, pulling me into a tight embrace.

"My boy." His voice was thick with emotion. "You don't know how often I've hoped it was you on the other side of that door." Then, more sharply: "It's been five Dragon-damned years." He released me and took a step back, cuffing me lightly on the side of the head. "What took you so long?"

"Well," I answered, still blinking back tears, "they held me up at the gate."

CHAPTER TEN

The Wyddin were said to possess great power over the Earth and Sky and all natural things, letting them control the weather and possess the bodies of animals and other such tricks. If the legends of Elovia are to be believed, the Sages harnessed this power. They used it to raise great palaces and temples from the Earth, to call down rain on their crops, and to decimate opposing armies by summoning lightning upon them and sundering the ground beneath their feet. In the end, though, the power was more than the Sages could control, and the Wyddin destroyed the kingdom utterly.

Clearly, much of this has been exaggerated and fictionalized over time. But I hope that by studying the old legends, I can come to understand some kernel of truth behind what really destroyed Old Elovia. It may make a good final project, to earn my pin.

— From the personal journals of Dennon Lark

From the moment Bryndine and I sat down at his desk, Illias struggled to contain himself. He was barely able to sit still while we reminisced. I knew the man well—he wanted to tell me something, and would be impossible to talk to until he did. I feared what it might be. I did not want to discuss any real Scriber business; Illias still wanted me to resume my work with him, and I was not ready for that. But after a quarter-hour of barely getting through to him, I realized it was pointless to avoid the issue.

"Out with it, old man. What are you hiding?"

Instead of responding to my question immediately, he pulled open a desk drawer and drew forth a thick sheaf of papers covered in musical notation and lyrics. Lifting them a few inches above the desk, he released them with a theatrical flourish so that they fell with a heavy thump. "Look at all of it, Denn! This is everything we've found since you left."

I didn't move, but Bryndine leaned forward to examine the papers. "Music? Is there some meaning here that I am missing, Master Illias?"

It must have seemed strange to her; an historian so giddy over a stack of songs. But I knew what they were, and all the enjoyment I had felt at seeing Illias again drained out of me in an instant.

"You've heard of Adello, of course?" Illias looked up at Bryndine with an eager expression that I knew well. He was a born teacher; there was little he loved more than finding gaps in knowledge and filling them in. But these were gaps I would just as soon he left unfilled.

"The bard?"

"Yes, of course you know him. Much of the famous songs and myths that are popular today are his work. And you know he lived during the Forgetting, I assume."

"Vaguely, yes. I had never given him much thought." Bryndine motioned for Illias to continue.

"When Dennon was a student here, he put a great deal of time into the idea that we could learn much about our past by looking into such things. Tales passed down orally, rather than the written words that were destroyed in the Forgetting. Many such songs and stories were put to the page by the early Scribers after the Forgetting, but Denn sought out and transcribed many bits and pieces of old folk songs himself as well. He began by looking into the legends of Old Elovia."

I tried to interrupt. "Illias, don't. None of this—"

He simply talked over me, ignoring my protests. "His work impressed the Council enough that he was granted full Academy backing for his research after he was pinned. He and I worked to develop a number of popular theories about ancient Elovian history. But it was quite by accident that our pursuit turned towards the Forgetting and the Archives. One of Adello's songs…" He turned to me with frustration in his eyes. "What was it called again, Denn?"

"*Curse of the Sages*," I answered with a sigh, shifting uncomfortably as I resigned myself to hearing the story of my failed career. One did not easily stop Illias when his didactic instincts took over.

"Yes, I always forget the name. In any case, it is commonly thought to be a tale of the Elovian cataclysm, and as such was included in our research. A Prince's love of reading leads him to dark Wyddin lore recorded by the Sages, and it destroys the kingdom. You may have heard it."

"It does sound familiar," Bryndine agreed. "There is some extra meaning to it?"

Illias nodded enthusiastically. "An entirely *different* meaning, in fact. Adello is mainly known for his songs of times long past—*Erryn the Burner* and *The Wyddin's Wrath* and so on, the sort of tales tavern minstrels like to play. *The Sages' Curse* seems to fit in perfectly at a glance.

"But Denn noticed something peculiar about it. It makes no specific mention of time or setting; it only speaks of how the Prince is corrupted by Elovian lore concerning the Wyddin. And much of the melody, as well as the description of the Prince, is similar to another piece—one that had never been attributed to Adello. *The Golden Prince*. A somewhat scandalous ballad, considering it is written from a male perspective, about the singer's adoration for the apparently handsome and virtuous Prince Fyrril."

"The Forgetter's son?"

"Ullyd's son, yes. I'm glad to see you haven't forgotten everything you learned here." Illias flashed his best teacher's smile, the one that had encouraged me so many times in my youth. I had almost forgotten that he would have taught Bryndine when she attended the Academy—he was not just telling a story, he was testing his student's memory. "We hadn't credited *The Golden Prince* to Adello—it is rather different from his usual work. Fyrril was a contemporary of his, not a legend, and the song is rather shamelessly flattering.

"But Dennon noticed the similarities, and took the two

songs to the School of Arts. They decided it was very likely Adello had written both, based on the style and arrangement, and the nearly identical terms describing the Prince." Illias peered intently at Bryndine's face, looking for signs of enlightenment. "Now, what do you suppose that showed us?"

She thought about it for a moment before answering. "It is Prince Fyrril in both songs, I suppose?"

"Yes!" Illias pounded a triumphant fist on his desk, shaking the candles perched on it and making the shadows in the room jump. "And if both are about Fyrril, *Curse of the Sages* must not be about the Elovian cataclysm. That was centuries before Fyrril's time. It *is* about the evils of Elovian knowledge, but during the Forgetting! Ullyd needed to spread fear to ensure the people supported his anti-literacy laws, and he must have commissioned Adello to help.

"Not only that, but Fyrril had previously been thought of as little more than a footnote in history. He was Ullyd's oldest son, but there is no record of his rule, not a single song or tale. But we now believe that he may have actually rebelled against his father, perhaps even tried to prevent the Forgetting—something that merited such a public condemnation. We would never have found any of it without Denn's fine work." He smiled proudly at me.

This was not something I wanted to be congratulated for. "If any of it is true. I am not considered a reliable source these days."

"It is an interesting study either way, Scriber Dennon," Bryndine said. "Is this what led you to search for the Archives? If Fyrril rebelled, he might have saved the books before they were burned."

I was mildly impressed that she had put it together so quickly. "That is what I thought at the time," I said. "But it was a fool's errand." The bitterness in my voice surprised me—the wounds of my past were closer to the surface here. "Hundreds have gone looking for the Archives on some wild theory, and it never ends well. They say Prince Willyn was seeking them when he disappeared—one of the few men to fail out of all six Schools at the Academy. That is the sort of company I am in. The last in a long line of idiots."

"One mistake doesn't invalidate all your work, my boy," Illias protested. "That's what this is, the continuation of your work." He tapped the stack of music on his desk. "I've had every Historian at the Academy scouring Delwyn's Hall for transcripts of old songs that cover similar themes. The School of Arts has identified hundreds of them as Adello's since you've been gone. He was apparently quite prolific in his work for Ullyd. There is a trove of knowledge about the Forgetting here."

"What can we learn from these?" I asked. "That reading is evil? That knowledge corrupts? These songs were written to scare people! They tell us nothing about what actually happened!"

"You thought differently once. This is what we *do*, Denn. We uncover the past as best we can."

"I was *wrong* when I thought there was something in those songs. Look what happened!" I swept my hand in a vaguely southward direction, towards Three Rivers. "I tore apart an irreplaceable piece of history. What will I do next time, burn down the Kingshome?"

"It was an accident, Denn. You can't let that—"

"Nine men *died*, Illias!"

The old man sank back in his chair with a weary sigh. "I gather you are not here to return to your research, then?"

"I'm sorry, Illias. I can't. I shouldn't have come." This was becoming crueller than I had intended. I had only wanted to see Illias again, but of course it had raised his hopes. He had never hidden the fact that he wanted me back at the Academy. "I just wanted to see you, that's all this was meant to be."

"And I am glad you came. If that is all this is, it will still be the best surprise I've had in years. But Denn… Stay here tonight, at least. Have a look at the songs."

"I can't stay here, Illias. If you'd seen what happened at the gate… I'll find an inn."

The old man gave me a look that nearly broke my heart. But staying at the Academy was out of the question. It had been a mistake to come to Highpass at all; it was not fair to Illias. I had to leave, and soon.

"My uncle will have a room for you, Scriber Dennon,"

Bryndine offered. "I must tell him about Uran's wound, and he will want to reward you for your efforts on my cousin's behalf."

Staying with Uldon Ord and Bryndine would barely be better than staying at the Academy. But I would never convince Bryndine to hide the story of her cousin's injury. I considered asking her to leave me out of it, since I had not actually done anything of use, but she was difficult to anticipate—she might tell him anyway, out of honor or propriety or the like. And I could not refuse a summons from the Baron of Highpass. It would be easiest to simply accept the invitation, as much as I wished not to.

"That would be best. It will make it easier for me to join you when you return to Three Rivers." I stood up from my seat. "We should go."

"Wait." Illias held up the stack of songs, his eyes begging me to accept them. "Just look at them." I couldn't bear to refuse. After everything Illias had done for me, he deserved at least this small concession.

"I will look them over. If I notice anything of interest before I leave Highpass, I'll tell you. But that's all I can promise."

Illias smiled, though there was not much hope in it. "I… wish you well, then, my boy." He turned to Bryndine and clasped her hand fondly. "M'Lady, it was good to see you again. You have my thanks for seeing Dennon here safely—it was kind of you. Millum Wren would have been proud."

"Thank you, Master Illias. I have always tried to uphold the Promise, as he taught me."

"He was a good man," Illias said. "I was sorry to hear of his passing. Replacing him with Uran Ord is a bit like replacing your sword with a dull dinner knife, if you don't mind my saying."

"My cousin is… not the man Millum Wren was." Bryndine's response was polite, with no direct confirmation of the insult to the High Commander, but the slight hesitation hinted that she and Illias were of the same mind. "Few are."

"Yes." Illias nodded sadly, and for the slightest moment I felt his eyes on me. "Few are."

CHAPTER ELEVEN

Started by King Ullyd the Forgetter approximately five hundred years after the Burning, the Forgetting is perhaps the single most defining event in the history of the Kingsland, excluding the Burning itself. Ullyd instated harsh laws against reading and writing, burned books, and killed scholars. This dark period lasted nearly two centuries, continued by his successors even after King Ullyd's death.

The greatest loss of all was the Royal Archives in Three Rivers. A repository of all surviving history and craft that had been collected since the founding of Elovia thousands of years before, the Archives were a symbol of the very thing that Ullyd feared so much. When he ordered them burned, the past of the entire continent burned with them.

— From Dennon Lark's essay, *Consequences of the Forgetting*

I had expected Uldon Ord's hospitality to be tiresome, but not quite so tiresome as it ended up being.

I saw the Baron and his wife only briefly when we arrived—Bryndine and I were brought to a large audience chamber where they waited, and she outlined the story of their son's injury and recovery, giving me far more credit than I deserved. The Baron thanked me for my aid, insisting that I attend a small dinner they were having later that evening. Though I very much did not want to, I lacked any way to politely refuse an invitation from the Baron of Highpass and the King's sister, and was forced to accept.

If I *could* have come up with any excuse, I would have done so eagerly. The Baroness obviously did not want me there. Hyrna Errynson was an imposing woman, more than six feet in height—several inches taller than her husband, who was not a small man. Her face was pinched into a perpetually sour expression, her golden blond hair pulled back into a severe bun, and when she peered down upon me, I knew what an insect must feel like in the moment before being squashed. It was clear that she knew who I was and disapproved of my attending the dinner, but she did not openly gainsay her husband's invitation. Despite her low opinion of me, though, she saved her most disapproving looks for Bryndine—the sight of her niece in Army browns did not please her.

The Baron himself was considerably less frightening, despite his size. He had the look of a man who had once been muscular, but lost most of it to fat—his broad shoulders and chest still held the impression of strength, despite his sagging flesh. Seemingly oblivious to his wife's disapproval, he made a grand showing of his gratitude, but the magnanimity felt insincere, a charade put on for the sake of appearances. He ordered his men to escort me to my quarters and supply me with whatever I needed to prepare for the evening, and I followed them out, glad to escape from the Baroness' judgmental gaze.

The rooms were very fine, all velvet and satin and gilded trim, but I did not spend much time enjoying them right away. Instead, I immediately had the servants draw me a hot bath. Scouring off the grime and blood of the trek from Waymark was uncomfortable but incredibly satisfying, like peeling off an old scab.

When I returned to the bedroom, my coarse, travel-stained clothing was gone, replaced with a dashing outfit of Highpass grey and gold. The fine Raen silk was lighter than breath against my skin, and it was easy to see why my own clothes had been deemed insufficient by comparison.

It was all very luxurious, but I had no illusions about the evening. Years earlier, when I was being lauded as the Academy's most promising young graduate, I had attended many such formal events. Despite all the elegant trappings, they were never anything but a dreadful bore, and the Ord's affairs were worse than any. The family claimed to be of purer Elovian stock than any bloodline left in the Kingsland, and tried to prove it by only hosting the most prim, proper gatherings imaginable.

Finally, the appointed hour arrived, and I was led to the dining chambers. I ended up seated at a remote corner of the table, far from the Baron and Baroness—my invitation was borne of propriety, not of any desire for my actual company. An elderly landowner sat at my right, in deep conversation with his neighbor about the dreary minutia of taxation, and to my left, an enormously obese noblewoman tried to catch the attention of the handsome young men seated at the other end of the table.

I caught bits and pieces from the others, mainly Uldon Ord boasting to the younger nobles of serving with King Eddyl during the seventh Barbarian Incursion thirty years before. I made a concentrated effort not to engage with anyone—the only thing less interesting than being ignored for the whole night would be actually speaking to the guests.

Hyrna Errynson's hand in the seating arrangements was obvious—in addition to hiding me far from the influential guests, she had surrounded her niece's seat in eligible nobles, all of them from old, wealthy families. Bryndine's chair was still empty; she had not yet arrived in the dining hall. The thought of her being wooed by any of the pompous young fools at the table was so ludicrous that I could not help but smile. Not one of them would stand taller than her shoulder, and she could probably best any three in a fight.

When Bryndine finally arrived, I nearly fell out of my chair in shock. She wore a ruffled dress of Errynson brown and crimson and a formal shawl that barely fit around her broad shoulders. Her short boyish hair was hidden under a fashionable lace cap, and matching lace gloves covered her large hands. The effect would have been transformative, but she wore it so uncomfortably that I could only see how poorly it fit her bulky frame; how little she belonged among these people.

She kept her back straight and her chin up as she moved to her seat, maintaining a grim dignity. When her aunt introduced her to the other guests, she acknowledged them tersely but politely, her mouth set in a thin, determined line. Even seated, she loomed like a giant over the men to either side of her. The fat cow beside me tittered into her hand at the sight and tried to disguise it as a cough; everyone heard, and despite Bryndine's effort to appear unaffected, I saw her cheeks flush.

"Geryn is a very impressive young man, Bryndine. He has been running his father's holdings for years, and stands to inherit them all." The Baroness gestured at the young man seated to Bryndine's right, and they exchanged awkward courtesies. "Geryn, surely your father has told you that a good wife is necessary to running a household?"

"Y-yes, m'Lady, he has." The quaver in his voice revealed his discomfort; he was a handsome lad, and I am sure he envisioned his future wife being much more comely than Bryndine Errynson. The rumors of how young Herryk Rafynson had died all those years ago could not have helped either—what young man wanted a bride that might kill him?

"Bryndine, what of you? You *must* find a husband soon. I fear my brother has been too distracted by his work to do his duty as a father." The woman's approach to courtship had all the subtlety of a drunken Ryndport sailor in a dockside brothel.

"I have been busy with the Army—"

"There will be no talk of that blasphemy at my table, Bryndine," her aunt interrupted sternly. "Elarryd has been remiss in letting it go on so long." She frowned at her niece with a distaste that bordered on overt disgust. "It is that woman's influence, no doubt. I fear you are paying the price for your father's… poor choices." She was speaking of Bryndine's mother; it was no secret that Hyrna Errynson had strongly opposed her brother's marriage.

Bryndine met her aunt's eyes with defiance, but to my surprise, her usual iron composure did not last. After a moment, she broke eye contact and hung her head.

"I'm sorry Aunt Hyrna. I didn't mean to offend."

I don't know what possessed me to speak. Pity, I suppose. "I have to admit," I said, "I was glad for Lady Bryndine's blasphemy when she saved my life." My tone was conversational, but even so, I was directly defying the Baroness. The chatter at the table died instantly, and I cursed my foolishness as all attention turned to me.

"Scriber Dennon, you forget yourself!" Uldon Ord barked, his chins quivering.

"My apologies Baron; Baroness." I cast about for a delicate way to extract myself from the situation. "I only meant that Lady Bryndine did a great service to the people of Waymark, not that it was an appropriate place for a woman. No doubt her success was due more to Erryn's blood than anything." I hoped that would save me from punishment—it would be hard to fault me for admiring the royal family.

"No doubt," Ord agreed after a brief silence. He seemed cautiously appeased, or at least willing to let the awkward matter drop. "But mind yourself in the future, Scriber. Now, let us talk of other things. As my wife says, this is not fitting discussion for the table."

The insipid conversation among the guests slowly resumed, but Hyrna Errynson remained quiet for a long while, staring at me with disapproval etched in her sour face. And Bryndine looked at me as well, with what might have been puzzlement; it was certainly not gratitude. Given our less than warm relationship, it had probably shocked her as much as it did me when I came to her defense.

Her reprieve came to an end before long—her aunt touched her on the arm to get her attention, and introduced the next of her potential suitors. Glad to have evaded both women's attention and come through my social gaffe essentially unscathed, I resolved to keep my mouth shut for the rest of the meal, and lapsed into quiet boredom.

* * *

Bryndine called upon me later in the evening, several hours after the dinner ended. I hadn't expected visitors, and was surprised when I heard the knock at the door; more so when I opened it and saw her. Sylla was with her, and appeared no more pleased to see me than usual, but she did not batter down the door or try to twist my arm off, so I counted myself lucky.

Bryndine looked much more at ease than she had at dinner. The ill-fitting dress had been exchanged for a simple shirt and trousers, and although it was still strange to see her out of her boiled leather and Army browns, she looked almost like herself again.

"Scriber Dennon." She inclined her head slightly in greeting. "May I come in?"

I shrugged. "If you please." I did not know what she wanted, but if I tried to send her away, Sylla would probably snap my neck. And besides, I was glad for the interruption. I had been staring at the stack of papers Illias had given me for an hour, trying to decide what to do with them, and getting nowhere.

Sylla moved to take up guard outside the door, but as Bryndine stepped inside, she gestured for the other woman to join her. "My uncle's guardsmen will suffice, I think, Sylla. If you are seen outside, everyone in the manor will know about my visiting the Scriber at this hour. And I've enough rumors to deal with already."

"Why *are* you visiting me at this hour?" I asked. "I'll assume you haven't simply been overcome with desire."

"Watch yourself, Scriber." Sylla stared knives at me, but I was used to that; I was becoming a decent judge of which comments would get me a glare and which would risk *actual* knives.

"I apologize. But the question still stands." I led them to the table where Illias' songs sat untouched, and gestured for them to sit before doing so myself. The rooms I had been given were well furnished—the table was as big around as the massive bed, inlaid with gold trim, and surrounded by velvet-upholstered chairs. I held it back, but the ludicrous situation made me want to laugh: I should really not have been allowed to entertain the King's niece in gilded chambers on velvet cushions.

"I came to let you know that we will be leaving for Three Rivers tomorrow, as early as possible," Bryndine informed me. As she seated herself, the delicate chair beneath her creaked ominously under her weight.

"So soon? Surely you want to spend more time with your aunt and uncle?" I raised an eyebrow meaningfully. We both knew why she wanted to leave, but I had a small hope that she might actually explain herself for once.

Unexpectedly, she dipped her head in acknowledgement of my unvoiced meaning. "My aunt does not care for my choices, and I have no wish to subject myself to her disapproval. But that is not the only reason to leave. You should not have spoken against her at dinner; she was against your presence to begin with, and that did nothing to endear you to her."

"I'd have said worse if I'd been there," Sylla grumbled. "It's the first time I've agreed with the Scriber." I glanced at her, surprised, but she only glared at me, then began to leaf absently through the papers on the table.

Bryndine's solemn expression hardened. "It is not your battle to fight, Sylla, nor Scriber Dennon's."

I had always thought that Bryndine's position in the Army was because of her family's influence, but it was becoming clear to me that her blood provided as many obstacles as benefits. It was hardly a boon for the Errynsons to have her flaunting the Mother's law all over the Kingsland. I wondered at the determination it must have taken to defy her family for so long. I could not have done it; I had fled the Academy at the first sign of disapproval. The thought made me feel small, and angry with Bryndine for making me feel that way.

"So the King's sister is displeased with me?" I asked. "Lovely, there go my hopes of ever being made a Baron."

"She does not want it to seem as though the Ords have forgotten your role in the accident at the Old Garden—it would not please the Children." Bryndine sounded almost contrite as she explained. "But my uncle thought it would look ungrateful to turn you away after saving Uran, and insisted on offering his hospitality. You would have been removed after your comment at the table, but it would not have been seemly to take back guest rights so abruptly. Tomorrow, they will ask you to leave quietly."

"Who can blame them? I would not want me as a guest either." I tried to be flippant, but it came out caustic. "The mad Scriber who tore down the Old Garden chasing fables—hardly fitting company for good, pious people."

"You always speak as if there was no reason behind your

actions, Scriber," said Bryndine. "It could not have been so frivolous—something must have led you there."

"Nothing sensible." I did not want to explain myself to her, but she had heard much of it from Illias already. *Better tell her now and have done, or I'll spend the entire trip back to Three Rivers fending off questions*, I reasoned. "You know most of it already."

"I know that you suspected Prince Fyrril might have saved the Archives, but why beneath the Old Garden?"

"Sky and Earth," Sylla groaned. "Are you two going to start talking Scriber talk?"

"Well, I don't want to bore you." Despite my decision moments before, I was willing to take the escape Sylla offered.

"Please, Scriber Dennon. I would like to know." Bryndine gave Sylla an apologetic look. "I'm sure it will not take long."

"I will be brief," I confirmed. "I'm sure you'll understand when I say this is not my favorite subject."

I paused briefly to gather my thoughts, and when I continued I spoke quickly, to be done with it as soon as possible. "It seemed strange to me that Adello had gone from singing a… almost a love ballad to Fyrril, to denouncing him as a traitor. Especially when he still described him in the same terms: golden-haired and handsome and so on. I convinced myself that he might have been in on Fyrril's rebellion—an agent within Ullyd's court. If Fyrril knew he was losing and that he could not rely on written records, he might have tried to conceal directions in a form that would survive through the Forgetting, so that those after him might find where he had hidden the Archives."

"Adello's songs." Bryndine nodded thoughtfully. "The bard would have been forced to support Ullyd to avoid execution, so the message would have to be obscure. Farfetched, but not impossible. But why the Garden?"

"It was a guess. Adello's work for Ullyd is very religious in nature." I tapped the pile of songs on the table, picking a random line from the one on top. "Look here: '*The Mother's condemning finger*', or here, '*the path to the Dragon's realm*'—pick any song and you'll find more of the same. The Old Garden is a religious site, and very near the site of the Royal Garden, where the Archives once stood. The two buildings would have been close enough for a passage to connect them through the Underground, to smuggle the books unseen.

"So Illias helped me convince the Council, and they convinced the King—we were granted permission to dig beneath the Old Garden. If we found no evidence that it lay over a part of the Underground, we would stop. But we did find a chamber."

"I believe I know the rest," Bryndine interrupted mercifully. I did not wish to speak of what happened next: the empty chamber, the east wall's collapse, the deaths that I had caused. "But your reasoning was sound, Scriber. I would not call what you did 'chasing fables'."

"It was sheer idiocy. Clues hidden in song? A child's fancy."

"He's right, Bryn—he's an idiot. These songs are all the same, it's all just stupid moralizing." Sylla had continued to flip through the songs as I told my story, but I was taken aback to learn that she had actually been reading them. Literacy was not common among the low-born, unless they had Academy training.

Bryndine noted my surprise. "I teach all my women to read and write, Scriber Dennon."

"Shocking, isn't it?" Scorn filled Sylla's dark eyes. "You're not the smartest one in the room just because you've got your pin, Scriber. I know enough to see that all this 'books are the path to damnation' babble isn't a secret message, which puts me a step above you."

I should have been insulted, but something else distracted me. "Say that again."

"You're an idiot," Sylla said.

"No, not that. Books are the path to damnation, you said."

"What of it? That's what these all say, more or less."

I picked up one of the sheets and looked at the lyrics written there. It was right in front of me—how had I missed it before? I grabbed another of the papers, and another; it was the same on all of them.

Bryndine cleared her throat, and I realized I had been silent for a long time. "What is it, Scriber Dennon?"

"I..." I did not want to admit it to myself. It was a child's fancy, as I had just said; it was completely absurd. I had already ruined my life going down this very road. But my mind was in motion after five years of relative inactivity, and I could not resist the momentum. "...I may have just found the way to the Archives."

CHAPTER TWELVE

Save for Master Illias, the Scriber's Council is an inefficient, idiotic, ignorant body, completely obsessed with politics and appearances over actually keeping their oaths. I suppose it is hardly a surprise—the Schools were originally intended to vote for a Master based on merit, but any vote on something so intangible is bound to become a contest of popularity. And when the Masters make decisions based on pleasing the nobles and trying to keep favor among their Schools, the Scribers as a whole suffer for it.

But even if it is for all the wrong reasons, I cannot blame the Council for distrusting me. I barely trust myself.

— From the personal journals of Dennon Lark

As Bryndine had warned, the Baron and Baroness quietly ejected me from their manor early the next morning. The servants woke me from a dream—a dream of men dying as stone and glass rained from above.

Shortly after sunrise, I found myself loitering in the street outside the stables as Bryndine's company packed and saddled their horses. I had my own mount for the trip to Three Rivers, at least—Bryndine had managed to get that much out of her aunt and uncle, a final reward for the service I had not actually performed for their son.

Bryndine insisted that I tell Illias of my theory before we left. I refused at first; the clarity I had experienced the night before felt weak in the light of day. But when she looked at me with her damnably blank face, it felt like she was judging me, and I relented. I could not let her see my weakness; I wouldn't give her the satisfaction.

At least she spared me the need to return to the Academy—she sent Ivyla to fetch Illias. And with every moment that passed waiting for him to arrive, I grew increasingly doubtful. It was the dream that had ruined my confidence. I could not stop thinking of the men who had died because of my last search for the Archives.

I had felt something the previous night that I had not in a long time: the ecstasy of intuition, of pulling together disparate threads of information into a cohesive idea. That joy had driven me to the Scribers in my youth, and it had blinded me to the folly of my actions then. Had it done the same last night? And then there was the fact that I had started hearing mysterious voices and having painful fits. How could I trust my conclusions when I feared I was going mad?

"Don't look so concerned, Dennon." Deanyn had taken to dropping my title, a familiarity that most of the other women eschewed. "The man is a friend of yours, is he not? At worst he disagrees with you—he isn't going to tar and feather you for a bad idea." There were few secrets in Bryndine's company—the women all knew of our late-night discussion already.

"It's not a bad idea, though!" Wynne brushed a lock of brown hair from her face, her green eyes wide with excitement. "It could be the greatest discovery since the Forgetting!" She had taken to my wild theory instantly. Despite a lack of formal schooling, her passion for knowledge was impressive—if she hadn't lacked money or sponsorship, she might have made a good Scriber.

"If there is anything to it at all." My stomach repeatedly tied itself into knots and then untied them again. It might actually be worse if Illias believed me—humiliating myself again would be bad enough without damaging his reputation as well.

"There may not be, but it is a sound enough theory to be worth investigating," said Bryndine, striding out of the stables with Sylla and Tenille at her side, all of them leading horses laden with supplies. "If you do not act on it, you will never know."

"It's more than that," said Tenille. "It is a Scriber's duty to pursue any opportunity to learn of the Kingsland's past." She had sworn the same oath; once she had learned of my epiphany, any chance of keeping it from the Scribers had disappeared.

I scowled. "Tell that to the Council. They'll have none of it, not coming from me, and not after the damage that has already been done at the Old Garden."

"Then they will be breaking their oath, not you," Tenille said. "You don't have to tell me of the Council's problems—I know better than anyone, except maybe Bryndine. But their obstinacy doesn't free us to ignore our vows."

"I'm going to tell Illias, aren't I?" I retorted peevishly. "I'll look like a fool, but I'll follow my oath; I don't need reminding."

"I don't know why you're all so concerned about this," Sylla said. "The Scriber is addled in the head. There's nothing hidden in those songs." Despite the enthusiasm of her comrades, she was persistent in questioning my sanity.

"You don't know that!" Wynne came instantly to my defense; it was almost touching how much the young woman wanted to believe me. "His ideas make sense, Sylla!"

"Anyway, Syl, didn't I hear it was your sage words that inspired him?" Deanyn asked with feigned innocence. "You shouldn't be so modest."

Sylla just grumbled under her breath, fiddling with her horse's bridle.

"Enough. Master Illias is coming." Bryndine held up a hand to silence the conversation. "Back to work, all of you—this is a matter for the Scribers." She led them back towards the horses, leaving me alone in the street.

Ivyla led Master Illias towards me, weaving through the light morning activity on the street. But they were not alone, and the sight of the bald, paunchy figure walking with the two of them tightened the knots in my stomach so badly that I feared they would never come loose.

Hantarin Redmond, Master of Politics, was essentially in charge of the Council. The Masters were all equal in rank, of course, according to custom—but that did not stop Master

Hantarin from controlling every decision they made. With favors, flattery, and the sycophantic support of Joryn Ivynson, the Warfare Master, he made sure every vote went his way. Of all the Council, he was the one least likely to believe my theory; agreeing to support me in my previous mistake had cost him and the Council a great deal of political favor.

Why he was with Illias I did not know, but I nearly bolted when I saw him. *Let Tenille tell them if she is so concerned about oaths*, I thought. But Illias was already disappointed in me, and I did not want to let him down again. Taking a deep breath to steady my nerves, I held my ground as they approached.

"Scriber Dennon." Redmond's voice was smooth and guileless to the ear. "How nice to see you again. I was with Illias when this young lady brought your message, and I must admit, I was curious what our most infamous graduate had come up with." His smile appeared genuine, but that was what made him so skilled at manipulation—he never seemed less than completely earnest.

"Master Hantarin insisted on coming," Ivyla explained. I felt badly for the young soldier. She clearly feared that she shouldn't have brought Master Hantarin back with her, but she was the disciplined, obedient sort; she could not have refused a Master Scriber's demand. Behind Ivyla's back, Illias shrugged apologetically, but I knew that he could not have stopped Redmond either. The Master of Politics was far too careful to let someone with my reputation leave before he learned why I had come. Especially after hearing that I had enjoyed the Baron's hospitality.

"It is an honor to have the attention of the Master of Politics." There was not a hint of sincerity in my voice. "Thank you for showing him here, Ivyla. You may go." Ivyla nodded and stepped away to join her comrades as they made ready for the journey to Three Rivers.

"Well, don't make us wait!" *Us*, Redmond said, though he knew full well that I had only asked for Illias. "What is it you had to tell us?"

I chose to direct my explanation at Illias, and tried to ignore Redmond as much as propriety allowed. "I looked at those songs you gave me."

Illias' eyes brightened immediately. "You found something?"

"Are you two still working on those old songs? How disappointing."

"Hush, Redmond." Illias gave the other Master a cross look. "Let him finish."

Unconcerned, Redmond gestured for me to proceed.

I swallowed nervously, but managed to force the words out. "It was something Sylla said—that books are the path to damnation. That is, the songs all say that the path to the Dragon's realm is paved with knowledge, reading, books and so forth. It occurred to me that it might not be a purely metaphorical path." I handed a sheet to Illias, upon which I had underlined several key phrases. "The books are damnation, so the path to damnation in these songs—"

"—Might be the path that leads us to the Archives," Illias finished. "That's inspired, Denn! We were so busy looking at what the songs might be telling us to do that we missed the obvious: the truth is in what they tell us *not* to do!"

Illias' enthusiasm was infectious, and I excitedly pointed to a line on the sheet I had given him. "Here, for instance, it speaks of the Mother trying to warn Prince Fyrril: '*With censuring hand she showed that knowledge is an evil road*'. Similar lines appear in most of these. It's always the Mother, never the Father, and she's always pointing or gesturing at something evil, warning people that it will lead them astray."

I could see the understanding dawn in Illias' eyes. "You're not suggesting…"

I let it out in a rush. "It could be a reference to the Old Garden—not as the place the books are buried, but as a signpost, pointing the way. The stained glass of the Mother and the Father reaching across the Divide towards one another. I think Adello is telling us to go in the direction her hand is reaching." I caught my mistake too late and corrected myself lamely. "*Was* reaching, rather."

Master Hantarin let out a sudden bark of laughter. "Surely you're joking, Scriber Dennon. You understand that the Council could never let you go anywhere near the Old Garden again?"

"Redmond—"

"No, Illias. I understand that you're fond of him, but Scriber Dennon has made the Scribers look quite foolish in the past." Redmond looked to me, his face a carefully composed mask of sympathy. "It's not personal, son, but we simply can't put any more resources into these fancies of yours." He sounded eminently reasonable, and any confidence I still felt eroded away. It had been insane to think the Council might listen to someone with my history. Scribers never forget—and Master Redmond was one of the most powerful Scribers in the Kingsland.

Illias' arms tensed and anger flashed in his eyes. He looked as though he was ready to attack his fellow Master.

Not wanting Illias to make trouble for himself on my account, I intervened hastily. "I understand, Master Hantarin. Thank you for hearing me." I gave a small bow, then laid a hand on Illias' shoulder. "I have nothing left to say but my goodbyes to Master Illias."

The Master of Politics gave a satisfied nod. "I am glad you can see reason; I feared you might not be so wise. I must return to the Academy, but I wish you a safe journey."

As soon as Redmond was out of sight, Illias let out a stream of profanity. "That pompous, Dragon-damned son of a whore! I hope the Father shoves a bolt of lightning right up his ass!"

A throaty chuckle came from behind me. "Some mouth you got, for a Scriber." Orya stepped up to clap Illias on the shoulder. "I like it. That other one seemed like a right prick."

"Not that we were eavesdropping, of course," Deanyn said as she and Wynne joined us.

I looked around for Bryndine, but she was not with them—apparently she had meant what she said about leaving the matter to the Scribers. Irrationally, that irritated me; she was the one who had pushed me into this. She could have at least cared enough to listen in.

"How could he ignore everything you said like that?" Wynne demanded, hands on her hips, the very image of indignation. "Aren't Scribers sworn to seek the truth?"

"That matters less every year." There was an edge to Illias' voice that I didn't recognize.

"It's for the best, Illias. There's no reason they *should* listen to me."

Illias gave me a long, level look. There was something behind his gaze, a determination that made me nervous. "You were talking about the stained glass at the Old Garden. The Mother points—" He made the same error I had, and paused to correct himself. The Mother at the Old Garden was little more than shattered glass now. "Pointed west. That is not a very specific signpost."

"Why does it matter?" I asked. "The Council won't let us do anything about it."

"But you have an idea. I know you well enough to know that, my boy."

"I thought…" I hesitated, but Illias just waited, staring at me with uncomfortable intensity until I continued. "It's always the Mother pointing—the goddess of the Earth. That could mean… perhaps a tunnel, under the ground. Fyrril and his people would have had to get the books out of Three Rivers unseen. We know they could have gone through the Underground from the Archives to the Garden, but after the east wall fell, we never had the chance to check the west."

"So we will dig beneath the west wall and see if they went that way." His tone was firm, decisive; this was not hypothetical. "With luck, we'll find something that will make the next step clear. If Adello really did hide this clue in his songs purposely, there must be others."

"Illias, you can't—"

"I *will*." He squared his shoulders and looked me straight in the eye. "Denn, I am an old man, and I am tired of arguing with the Council. I swore an oath, and I mean to make good on it before I die. No matter what Redmond and his dogs say."

"It's a waste of time, Illias. Redmond was right." My doubt was only worsened by Illias' belief in me. If he pinned his hopes on my insane speculation, I was sure he would be disappointed.

Wynne looked positively crestfallen. "Don't say that, Scriber Dennon!"

"Where're your balls, Scriber?" Orya actually sounded

puzzled—like retreat was a foreign concept to her. "Just go have a look around, if there's nothin' there, no harm done."

"I *won't* go back to the Old Garden."

"It was *one mistake*, Denn," Illias said, sympathy and exasperation battling each other in his voice. "What happened was not your fault, and if this theory proves true, it was barely even a mistake. You may be willing to give up because of that, but I am not."

"They won't even let me in," I protested, spreading my hands helplessly. "Korus would put a stop to it the moment he heard." Korus Creven was the Royal Scriber—and an old rival of mine from the Academy. He had the King's ear, and he would not sit idly while Syrid allowed me a chance to remove the stigma from my name.

"If you're never going to get in anyway, there's no reason to protest so much," Deanyn pointed out with a wry smile.

It was obvious that nothing I said would dissuade them, but I could not be part of it. "I can't stop you from coming with us, Illias, but you'll have to do this without me." I looked at my toes as I spoke, so that I would not have to see the judgement in their eyes.

"If I have to, I will, Denn." Waving a hand in the air to get her attention, Illias shouted, "Captain Bryndine!"

Bryndine walked briskly over from the stables. "Master Illias. What can I do for you?"

"I'm going with you to Three Rivers. How soon can you get me there?"

"Four days, perhaps, without killing the horses to do it. But it will be a hard pace."

Illias nodded with satisfaction. "The Council cannot convene with a member absent. They'll have to wait a week to make the claim that I've abandoned my duties, and the debate will take at least a few days after that before they can vote to remove me. Until then, I am the Master of History, and it is within my rights to pursue this."

"You'll lose your seat on the Council!" The prospect horrified me—he was going to risk his entire career because of my harebrained idea.

He set his jaw stubbornly. "Not if I find something first."

CHAPTER THIRTEEN

Three Rivers is the capital of the Kingsland, where the Errynson family has dwelled for centuries in the palace known as the Kingshome. When Erryn first sailed downriver from the Wasted Plains, he and his people made their camp at the junction of the Salt, Rynd, and Conqueror's Rivers and burned away the First Forest around the fork to claim the land as their own. That camp grew into Three Rivers—named, like the Kingsland itself, by the old barbarian sensibility of straightforward description.

The city as it stands is not the same city Erryn ruled from, however—there is evidence that at some point before the Forgetting, a fire razed much of Three Rivers to the ground. The most telling proof is the Underground, a series of basements and cellars showing signs of the fire that were apparently built over and forgotten in the reconstruction. The criminal element uses most of this network of tunnels and buried rooms for illicit activity, but still more remains sealed away.

— From Dennon Lark's *Cities of the Kingsland*

We made the journey from Highpass to Three Rivers at a pace that left me little time to dwell on the consequences of Illias' decision, though I did find myself worrying about his physical well-being. Covering seventy leagues in four days was no easy ride for me, and I was half Illias' age. But for the most part, the saddle sores and deep muscle pain that plagued me for much of the distance diverted my attention from anything else.

There was one thing that cut through the pain, however—perhaps because it carried the threat of an even worse agony. As we left the foothills, the voices returned. They were faint and infrequent, never so focused as they had been the night Waymark was attacked, and the dreams of burning did not return, but it was enough to make me wary again after having been free of them for several days. Whenever I found myself riding beside a fireleaf, I slapped my mount into a faster gallop and put the orange-red leaves behind me as quickly as I could. I was certain that the Burnt would come upon us at any moment, and the slightest glimpse of movement in the hills sent my heart racing faster than my horse. But no attack came.

It was early afternoon on our sixth day of riding when Three Rivers came into view. As we rode south down the Saltroad, the entirety of the Kingsland's greatest city spread out over the hills and valleys before us, a vast wrinkled blanket of stone and straw and timber thrown haphazardly over the countryside, cut into thirds by the rivers that gave the city its name. East of the Saltroad, the Salt River journeyed with us towards the heart of Three Rivers, where it would join with the Conqueror's River from the eastern plains and form the Rynd, stretching off into the west towards Ryndport and the sea.

Three Rivers had never shown much evidence that intelligent planning went into its layout. Save for the Kingscourt to the east, where the historic buildings and noble estates sat along carefully laid cobblestone streets, the city was a mashed together disaster of styles, from thatched-roof cottages to stately marble manors and anything in between. A maze of interrupted roads and circuitous pathways dissected the southern Commoncourt and the western Tradecourt, and numerous arbitrarily placed bridges spanned the three rivers that separated the districts. Navigation through those streets was near impossible for anyone but long-time residents, and even they sometimes struggled with it.

But the city I looked upon now was nearly twice as large and a hundred times as disorganized as the one I had last seen five years before.

A crude wooden palisade had been constructed some

distance from the walls, and within its perimeter milled what must have been tens of thousands of refugees. Even the new boundaries could not contain their number—tents and crude shelters spilled outside the palisades in all directions. As we drew up to the edge of this overflow, the stench of human waste and unwashed flesh made my stomach heave violently.

Bryndine noticed my discomfort and reined her horse over to mine. "The smell is hard to take, but we will be within the true walls shortly. Try not to breathe through your nose." She surveyed the makeshift shanties with a critical eye. "There are more here than when I left—the Burners force more people from their homes every day."

Instead of answering, I held my breath against the smell as best I could, and motioned her onwards impatiently. I felt for the plight of the refugees; it was the same as my own. But the stink made it difficult to maintain sympathy, and I wished to be through it as soon as possible.

Soldiers of the Nineteenth Company patrolled up and down the Saltroad within the palisades, keeping the refugees from blocking the roadway and generally maintaining order. As we rode by, I noticed more than a few of them scowling at Bryndine; but when she looked, they only saluted. No matter what they thought of her, she was still an Errynson.

At the gates, a Lieutenant of the Nineteenth halted our progress and approached Bryndine. "Captain Bryndine, King Syrid wishes to see you immediately."

"I am at the King's command, Lieutenant." Bryndine turned to me and Illias and dipped her head politely. "It appears this is where we part, Scribers."

The Lieutenant cleared his throat. "Actually, Captain, the Scribers are to come as well."

"Of course we are," Illias said, chuckling cynically. "I imagine Redmond sent a bird the moment he learned I was gone. He knows how to play this game; he'll have divested the Council of any responsibility for my actions."

The man had said *Scribers*, plural, it occurred to me. "I'm not a part of this, Lieutenant. There's no reason to take me to the King."

"I'm sorry, but my orders are to see you all to the

Kingshome. If you aren't needed, it will be cleared up there." The man gestured to a nearby soldier, who brought forth a horse and helped him mount it. "Please come with me—we should not keep the King waiting."

I balked at the notion. "This is a waste of time! I'm not—"

Bryndine leaned over and gave my mount a slap on the flank, startling it into motion. "When the King summons, we can only obey, Scriber Dennon." She kicked her own mount forward and her company followed her through the gates and into the capital. I went along grudgingly. Bryndine was right: I would never convince an Army man to disobey the King's orders. They would almost certainly send me away when we reached the Kingshome, but until then, I had no choice but to follow.

We were escorted south through the crowded markets of the Tradecourt, where the noise of peddlers shouting their deals and customers haggling over wares echoed in the narrow streets and made conversation between our group all but impossible. Eventually the Lieutenant cut east, leading us over the Salt River by one of the larger bridges, reserved for Army use and patrolled by men of the Twenty-Fifth. As we crossed into the Kingscourt, the change was palpable—the noise of the Tradecourt was like a physical weight pressing in from all sides, and the quiet streets of the noble district offered nearly instant relief.

Unlike the rest of Three Rivers, the Kingscourt was a calm, lovely place—the guardsmen who patrolled the area at all hours of the day were well-paid to keep it so. The cobbled streets were shaded with carefully groomed elms, and though it was early autumn, few leaves lay on the ground—there were people here whose sole job was to keep the streets clear of such things.

We rode through beautifully tended gardens and squares built around marble fountains and exquisite statuary, and at one point the road cut through a small park with a large fireleaf at its center. I squeezed my eyes closed and tried not to draw attention to myself as a low whisper floated through my head; I did not want to let on that a seemingly harmless tree could disarm me so, especially not here among the homes of the most influential people in the Kingsland.

As we drew closer to the Kingshome, the buildings became more and more opulent, yet less and less impressive by comparison to the palace. The wide street was home to many grand sights—the partially collapsed Old Garden with its massive domed entryway that still baffled the School of Science; the newer Royal Garden, built where the Archives once stood; the huge manor of the Lord Chancellor; the great marble stairway before the White Hall, guarded by several white-cloaked Justices—but none of them were so awe-inspiring as the ancestral home of the Errynsons.

The Kingshome was a marvel of Old Elovian architecture, techniques lost since the Forgetting: arches and pillars so delicate the stone might have been spun on a loom; vaulted rooftops of impossible inclines; steeples tall enough to pierce the Divide. It shone in the late afternoon sun, smooth white marble and glittering gold, and from every spire flew the banner of the burning tree, ablaze in brilliant crimson.

The Lieutenant brought us as far as the courtyard just within the gates of the palace, where he and Bryndine's company were asked to wait. A guardsman in Errynson livery escorted Bryndine, Illias, and me further into the palace. I tried to explain that the King would have no use for me, but my complaints were not heeded; as Bryndine had said, I had no choice but to obey.

We were not taken to the throne room—the King sat on Erryn's Chair to receive important guests of high status, not two Scribers and his niece. Instead the guard led us to a large, airy council chamber where King Syrid waited.

The moment we entered, the whispers began, swarming through my head like a hundred angry wasps.

Uran Ord was there—he had to be. Though he stood beside the King of the entire realm, my eyes went first to him, not Syrid. Ord's head was still tightly bandaged, the cloth wrapping pulled tight over the dent where his skull had been crushed inwards. How he could still function with such a wound was beyond my understanding. I tried not to make eye contact with him, but no matter where I looked the invisible swarm of voices buzzed in my head, calling my gaze back to the High

Commander. Rubbing my temple with two fingers, I fought desperately to keep my composure, focusing my attention on the King as best I could.

Syrid Errynson sat at the back of the room on a high-backed chair of gold and velvet. To his left there was an empty chair of similar opulence, a chair that had presumably sat empty since the death of Queen Anya; to his right sat his brother Elarryd, the Lord Chancellor of the Kingsland.

Their father, the much beloved King Eddyl, was remembered as a ruler of great cleverness and wisdom, and as a warrior of great strength. His two sons, at a glance, appeared to have divided those traits amongst themselves. Syrid was drawn and gaunt, slouched under the weight of the crown that sat atop his bald head, but there was an intelligent look to his face and his keen eyes were always in motion. Elarryd was almost the King's exact opposite, broad-shouldered and deep-chested, with long golden hair like some hero out of legend.

I had heard stories, and seen firsthand the size of their sister Hyrna, but it surprised me just how tall both men were. Neither was as large as Bryndine, but their height—near seven feet—was impressive. It is said that the blood of ancient barbarian heroes and Elovian kings give members of the royal family their legendary stature, and looking at them, I believed it.

Finally, I noticed the fourth man, standing on the opposite side of the King from Ord. A handsome man, brown-haired with arrogant eyes—I knew his face well. Korus Creven, the Royal Scriber, gave a mocking bow as our eyes met, and I understood immediately that this meeting would not go well for me.

"Your Majesty." Bryndine knelt before her uncle, and Illias and I followed suit.

"Rise." Syrid had a look of annoyance on his face as we stood, but I saw the Lord Chancellor smile warmly at his daughter.

"I bring Master Scriber Illias Bront and Scriber Dennon Lark, your Majesty." Bryndine stepped to the side and took a rigid military stance, letting the King's gaze fall upon me and Illias. He did not look pleased.

"Master Illias. I have word from the Scribers' Council that

you are here against their wishes," the King said with a frown.

Illias looked the King directly in the eye. "That is true, your Majesty. But I am the Master of History still, and it is my prerogative to follow whatever path I deem necessary to uncover the Kingsland's past, until such time as the Council removes me." It was true—the Masters of the Council were officially allowed to pursue their goals without the King's interference. Still, I worried that Illias was only hurting his chances by addressing Syrid so brazenly. Though the law said he needed no royal approval, in reality he would never be allowed to set foot in the Old Garden without permission.

"I understand that they may do just that by next week's end."

"And I will continue my work until they do," Illias replied.

King Syrid raised a questioning eyebrow. "What work is that, Master Illias? Master Hantarin's message was scant on details."

"I have reason to believe that there is more to be found at the Old Garden," Illias said. "There may be a tunnel beneath the entry dome on the west side, through which books from the Archives may have been smuggled."

"Your Majesty, if I may speak," Korus interjected smoothly. The King gave him a slight nod, and he continued, "It would be unwise to allow any Scriber access to the Old Garden—there would be public outcry, and the Children would be most displeased. But it is doubly inadvisable to do so when Scriber Dennon is involved, given his history."

"I have nothing to do with this!" Distracted by the whispers flitting past my ears, and overly eager to counter Korus, I nearly failed to properly address the King. As he turned his eyes on me, I hastily tried to cover the lapse. "—your Majesty. I have no wish to enter the Old Garden. Do not deny Illias on my account."

Korus could barely contain his glee. "But it was your theory that prompted this, was it not?" This must have seemed an ideal chance for him to take some measure of vengeance. I had outdone him in nearly everything when we were at the Academy, so much so that when it became clear I would always be Illias' favorite, Korus had changed his focus to the School of

Politics. Though he had become Hantarin Redmond's most prized student, and was now one of the most influential Scribers in the Kingsland, he had never forgiven me.

I hesitated, but I couldn't bring myself to lie in front of the King. "…Yes."

Without breaking her stance or so much as shifting her eyes towards Korus, Bryndine said, "I have heard Scriber Dennon's reasoning, and I believe it to be sound, your Majesty."

Uran Ord took a step forward, and I almost thought he would lunge at Bryndine, but he stopped himself. "I must object, Majesty. I have told you of my cousin's lapse in judgement—how can we trust her in this?" When he spoke, the whispers grew more frantic—agitated for reasons I couldn't understand. I rubbed my temple vigorously and concentrated on ignoring them.

Elarryd Errynson had been silent until now, watching the proceedings thoughtfully, but now he came to Bryndine's defense. "My daughter is many things, but she is no fool, Syrid. This may be a pursuit worth some amount of public disapproval. Can we risk allowing the Archives to remain lost because of past mistakes?"

Korus' responded with such conviction that I was sure the argument was lost. "There is no evidence that the Archives were saved at all, Lord Elarryd. This is a misguided fancy, nothing more."

The Lord Chancellor was not dissuaded. "Let us hear the Scribers out, and then we will know whether or not it is worth pursuing. It can do no harm, Syrid."

The King nodded tersely, motioning for Illias to proceed. With unusual brevity, Illias summarized my theory, handing over several sheets of musical lyrics to support the claims.

"There seems to be some substance to this, Syrid." Elarryd studied the papers with an interest that surprised me. Though he was Lord Chancellor of the realm and had a reputation for wisdom and intelligence, his warrior's build and bearing made it difficult for me to see him as a man of knowledge.

The King looked at his brother with doubt in his eyes. "You would have me searching for old books while the Burners tear my kingdom down around me?"

"Those old books have much to teach us. You know that as well as I, we both spent time at the Academy." Elarryd's tone was calm, convincing; the practiced voice of a man who had spent years guiding his brother's decisions. "Warfare and weapon-smithing, medicines and surgical techniques we have lost—things that might aid in this fight, and even if not, certainly in those after it. And it will hardly tax our resources. I am sure Master Illias can manage the matter, with your blessing."

Syrid pinched the bridge of his nose. "Damn it to the Dragon, Elarryd. It is not a good time for this. We have the Burners to deal with yet, and no matter how many of the bastards we kill, they never seem to run out. The realm starves with the poor harvests of late, and I have thousands of refugees begging for food that I cannot provide, claiming I have not fulfilled the Promise. I do not want the Children inciting them to riot over this. Besides that, it will earn the Council's ire."

Elarryd smiled wryly at his brother. "That is usually the way of it. Nothing ever happens when it would be most convenient."

There was frustration in the King's eyes. "You could not have waited until the rebels were dealt with, Master Illias?"

"If I gave the Council time, they would have stopped me, Majesty."

Korus could not restrain himself any longer. "Your Majesty! You cannot move against the Council on this." The barely contained joy had left him, replaced with tense indignation. It must have been torture for him to watch the argument turn in my favor—or what he saw as my favor, though I was not fighting for it. "This is not the time to risk losing the support of the Children, the Scribers, and your people. If you support another of Lark's theories—"

Elarryd cut him off before he could go further. "Then let us remove Scriber Dennon from the matter. His name will not be mentioned, and he will not enter the Old Garden. Give Master Illias access until such time as the Council removes him—he has perhaps a week before that happens, ample time to look into the matter. If he finds anything, the Council will have to admit their mistake. If he does not, all you need do is abide by their decision to dismiss him at that time, and they cannot say you have ignored their wishes."

Syrid drummed his fingers on his chair as he mulled the suggestion over. "The Children will still be a problem."

"That is not insurmountable," said Lord Elarryd. "Without Scriber Dennon's involvement, they have less reason to oppose the intrusion. If a tunnel is found, the Scribers will not be long under the Old Garden's walls; if it is not, they will be gone by week's end."

"So be it." The King thumped his fist decisively against the arm of his chair. "You have one week, Master Illias—make good use of it. Scriber Dennon, you are not to set foot within the Garden." Though I had not wanted to take part to begin with, something twisted in my gut at the King's declaration—some small piece of hope I had buried long ago finally laying down to die. It was not a pleasant feeling.

"This is unacceptable!" Uran Ord's bellow was far louder and angrier than was proper in the presence of the King. There was no reason for him to care so much about this; the matter barely affected him, and he was not known for his piety. But for reasons I could not begin to guess, he was furious, and the voices surrounding him shared that fury. "*All knowledge burns*," they hissed, and each word sent a new wave of pain throbbing through my head.

Syrid looked at his nephew with irritation. "If my High Commander finds it so difficult to accept his King's decision, perhaps I need a new one."

"Your Majesty, surely you can't mean to let these Scribers defile—"

"Enough, Uran!"

The High Commander shut his mouth sullenly, but his eyes were filled with rage, and though only I could hear them, the enraged voices did not cease.

The King waved a hand towards me and Illias. "Korus, help Master Illias with the arrangements. The guards will see Scriber Dennon out. We are done here, and I have a family matter to discuss with my niece."

He could only mean the matter of Bryndine's disobedience to the High Commander. I had nearly forgotten that she stood to be punished for trying to save the people of Waymark. It was an injustice, but there was little I could do about it, even if I had been allowed to speak for her—I could not have gotten more than a few words out past the terrible noise in my head.

I tried to catch Bryndine's eye as the guards led me from the room, to give her some indication of my support. But she only continued to stand at attention before the King, her face a solemn, impenetrable mask.

* * *

"What was the King's mood?" Tenille asked, pacing a matted path into the grass in the front courtyard of the Kingshome.

"Not pleasant. But he agreed to let Illias into the Garden, so…" I shrugged. "I can't say how he will deal with Bryndine." It was a weak answer, but I was too distracted to give better—Uran Ord monopolized my thoughts. There had been a powerful anger in him, and in the voices I had heard; it might constitute a danger to the King. I felt I should tell someone, but how could I explain it without sounding mad? And to whom?

Rubbing my temple, I surveyed the courtyard around me. It was large and open, with entrances to the different wings of the palace in all directions. The main doors, huge panels of varnished oak, sat at the end of a wide path lined with tall marble pillars. Guardsmen were posted at all doors, and there were a number of them gathered to one side of the area, standing around a patch of earth where the grass had been worn away over the years by many armored feet. Two men were sparring in the middle of the small crowd, while the others shouted their encouragement.

The sight of the guardsmen tempered my fears somewhat. The King was well-protected, and from threats more real than voices in my head. I took comfort in dismissing the voices as some flight of fancy, but there was a deeper fear beneath it—the fear that I was only lying to myself. Though I tried not to, I couldn't help but think of Josia Kellen, lying dead on a dark hill.

But there was nothing I could do either way. Even if I tried to warn the King or his guards, no one would listen.

Sylla spat on the grass at my feet, bringing me back to the conversation. "We all know what Syrid will do," she said. "He's been waiting for the excuse."

"The King could have disbanded us at any time." There was no optimism in Genna's quiet voice. "He might not now."

"If Bryn hadn't refused to let it drop, he'd never have let her wear Army colors to begin with," Sylla retorted. "If she's in the Army, at least she's under his control. But that's not going to be enough now that she's disobeying orders. We're done."

"We're not." Deanyn leaned serenely against a marble pillar and spoke with a seeming lack of concern. "Whatever happens, I have no plans to go anywhere. We may not wear the same uniform after today, but you lot won't get rid of me that easily." An easy smile lifted the corners of her mouth. "I say we go out tonight and get good and drunk. If things go one way, it's a celebration; the other way, we'll drown our sorrows."

Unsurprisingly, Orya was the first to voice her support. "Now *that's* an idea. All the cryin' in the world won't help more than a good drink. And if it's good news, first round's on me."

Tenille stopped her pacing long enough to frown at the two women. "This is not something to be taken lightly, you two. Be serious."

"I take drinking very seriously," Deanyn replied, affecting a solemn expression.

Tenille snorted—a mix of amusement and annoyance. "You don't have to convince me of that." She paused, and her frown relaxed into a slight smile. "To be honest, I could use a drink."

A chorus of agreement followed Tenille's admission.

"Tonight then," Orya said. "The Doused Tree. And Father bugger any of you who try to get out of it!" She looked meaningfully towards Genna—the quiet woman's cheeks went red at the obscenity, but she indicated her acceptance with a nod.

"What delightful companions you've found since last we spoke, Lark." I turned to see Korus standing behind me, eyeing Orya distastefully. "So ladylike." He must have foisted Illias off on a subordinate as soon as he was able, just to catch me before I left.

"I'll show you ladylike." Orya was completely unruffled, and followed up the statement with an obscene gesture.

Korus pointedly ignored her. "Why did you come back, Lark? Was it not enough to destroy a priceless piece of art? When this new idiocy of yours goes wrong, it will embarrass the King at a time when he needs the people's support most."

"I already told you, Korus, I didn't want any part of this. I tried to tell Illias not to come."

"Not hard enough, it seems." A shallow, cruel smile played across his lips. "At the very least you are being kept out of it—I shudder to think what the Children might do if you were allowed back into the Old Garden."

"They're not letting you in, Scriber Dennon?" Wynne frowned. "It was your idea."

"No, I… I told you, I don't want to be part of it, Wynne." Despite what I said, disappointment still lingered. The short time I had spent studying Adello's songs in Highpass had stoked a long dead fire inside me; quenching it again was no easy thing. "Korus is right, it would only cause problems."

"Mother in the Earth, Lark. You've somehow found someone with little enough sense to *believe* in you." Korus sneered at Wynne. "You do know who this man is, don't you girl? You would be hard pressed to find a Scriber less qualified for the work."

"Don't be so hasty, Korus. There's always you." Tenille stepped forward, putting herself between me and the Royal Scriber. "Leave off. Dennon hasn't done anything wrong." She had no more reason to love Korus than I did; he had been part of a very vocal opposition to her unusual training at the Academy.

He tried to maintain his bravado, but backed away a step at Tenille's advance. "Tenille. Lady Bryndine does like to surround herself in false Scribers, doesn't she? That's hardly a surprise, I suppose—she prefers false soldiers as well."

There was sibilant sound from behind, metal scraping on leather, and I turned to see Deanyn casually holding her drawn sword in hand. "Don't mind me, Scriber Korus. Just playing with my false sword." She tested the edge of the blade against her thumb. "But wait, that's quite sharp, isn't it? That can't be right. We could hurt someone with these."

Korus went slightly pale at the implication. "I am the Royal Scriber! I won't be threatened by the likes of you!"

"What about the likes of me?" Orya cracked her knuckles, her wide eyes and wild hair giving her a distinctly unstable air. "Like you said, I'm no lady. I wouldn't know if it's good manners or not to hit the Royal Scriber."

Orya and Deanyn's show of defiance prompted the support of the other women. Wynne, who I had never thought of as threatening before, glared at Korus with an ire that I hoped never to see turned in my direction. Genna's timidity evaporated as she clenched her hands into fists. Dark-skinned Leste placed her hand on the hilt of her saber; Debra needed no weapon but her heavily muscled arms to look threatening.

Even those I barely knew came to my defense—I had said no more than two words to Rylene during our travels, but the scowl on her scarred face was chilling as she stepped forward. Only Sylla remained still, but as she glanced between Korus and me, I got the impression that it was only because she couldn't decide which of us she wanted to hit more.

Korus, finally realizing that these were not women to be trifled with, looked absolutely terrified. He half-turned to leave, then glanced back over his shoulder, opening and closing his mouth as though he couldn't decide whether to stand his ground, call the guards, or simply bolt. It was priceless.

"That's enough," Tenille interceded. "Korus is right, we'd be punished for harming him."

Masking his relief with arrogance, Korus gave a curt nod. "Yes, quite sever—"

Tenille continued, interrupting the threat. "Of course, a smart man like him must realize that whether or not we were punished, he would still be hurt. A smart man might leave Scriber Dennon alone and go."

Korus opened his mouth to respond, but Tenille just tipped her head towards Orya and raised an eyebrow. He took another look at the wild-eyed blond woman, clamped his mouth shut, and stomped away in a petulant huff. Snorts of muffled laughter followed him; the women enjoyed his ignoble retreat as much as I did.

But in his absence, I found myself uncomfortable. I hadn't expected these women to come to my defense so readily, and I didn't know what to say to them. Embarrassed and awkward, I muttered an unintelligible thanks, avoiding eye-contact, and hurried towards the main gate to leave.

"Dennon, wait."

I looked over my shoulder to see Deanyn striding after me.

"What is it?" My voice came out more snappish than I'd intended, but she didn't seem to mind.

"Come out with us tonight."

I was taken aback by the offer. "What? Why?"

"You seem like you could use a drink. Banned from the Old Garden and all."

"I didn't want to be part of that," I insisted, though it rang false in my own ears.

She shrugged. "Come anyway."

"I—Perhaps. I will think about it."

Not one to push, Deanyn just gave a simple nod. Her easy manner made it difficult to maintain my embarrassment.

Mustering my courage, I asked her, "Why did you all… do that? Defend me."

She shrugged. "Why wouldn't we? We've been travelling together for weeks. You're not bad company on the road. You might be a bit of an ass sometimes, but who isn't?" She grinned to show she was joking. "And you've helped the Captain out a few times; I can count on one hand the people who are willing to do that. I like you. Most of the others feel the same way. Wynne in particular, though your pin might have more to do with that than your personality."

"Most of the others barely know me," I objected. "And I *know* that Sylla loathes me."

"Sylla is a different story." She looked like she might explain, but instead she just smiled teasingly and said, "In any event, it needn't be entirely about you. Korus insulted us too."

Once again, I didn't know how to respond. Not to the mild accusation of narcissism—which, I was fairly certain, had been said in jest—and certainly not to the admission of affection. I opened my mouth to speak, but no words came to mind.

Mercifully, she did not wait for me to say more. "You really should come out with us. You have few enough friends that I've seen; I could be one, if only to show you how it's done."

I gave her a weak smile. I couldn't refuse the offer now; she had been kinder to me than I deserved. "I will be there, but I may come late. I have to see the Scriber Registrar here first. Obviously I cannot work out of Waymark any longer, and the Academy will want to know where to collect my dues." That, at least, gave me an excuse not to spend the entire evening in some run-down tavern.

Just then, the great oaken doors of the Kingshome creaked open, and Deanyn whirled to look. Over her shoulder, I could see Bryndine's tall form silhouetted in the massive doorway. The women turned towards their Captain as she approached, waiting for news, dreading what it might be.

But I did not have to wait for Bryndine to speak to know the King's decision; I needed only to look at her. On her face—usually so carefully composed—she wore an expression of absolute despair.

CHAPTER FOURTEEN

They say that Bryndine Errynson recruited her company from all corners of the Kingsland, saving many of them from dungeons and stockades, and sometimes even the gallows. I can believe it, though not for the reasons that most do. The truth is, in most baronies, they'd probably clap a woman in irons just for daring to go against the conventions laid out in the Book of the Divide. And the women Bryndine leads do no small amount of that.

Sky and Earth, people can be so stupid.

— From the personal journals of Dennon Lark

It was near sunset when I finally arrived at the Doused Tree; after leaving the Scriber Registrar, it took me more than an hour to find the place among the mess of roads in the Commoncourt. It looked much like any other dilapidated building in the Commoncourt, but I knew it by the sign outside: a flagon of ale upended over a flaming tree. There was no doubt it was the tavern Orya had named.

The tavern was lively that night. Even from the street, I could hear the sounds of drunken revelry within. No surprise, that—by its poor lighting and general state of disrepair, I assumed it to be the sort of low-price, low-standard place that would make great profit from the refugees coming into the city. Even the poorest and most wretched of those living in the tents beyond the walls would part with their coin for a stiff drink; it let them forget their dire situation, if only for a night. I was not overly eager to spend the evening in such a place, but I felt obliged to at least make a brief appearance.

At least I was arriving late. It would be easier to excuse myself given the hour.

Bryndine's women had already claimed three tables and were well into their cups when I entered. The other patrons gave them a wide berth, watching them with sideways glances full of suspicion, but the women didn't seem to care. The entire company was there as far as I could tell, and their attitudes were surprisingly buoyant, given that they had been officially discharged from the Army hours before. The drinking may have had something to do with that—the tables were littered with empty flagons.

Orya and Debra were engaged in a one-sided arm wrestling match at one table. At another, Tenille and Wynne were deep in discussion over Theryn's *Philosophy of Duty* with a skinny dark-haired man I vaguely recognized. Nearby, Kaelyn flirted with several smitten young men, while Varrie entertained the others with coin tricks and prestidigitation. A surprising number of women had husbands or lovers with them: Hylda held hands with a short, balding man, and Rylene's escort seemed not to mind the scars on her face at all. Even Sylla had come, though she did not look to be enjoying herself—she sat wedged into the corner of the common room, talking little and drinking heavily. Bryndine, however, was notably absent.

"Dennon!" Deanyn spotted me and waved me over to her table. "I kept a seat for you."

I picked my way through the room towards her, unpleasantly conscious of the many eyes that fixed upon me at the revelation that I was with the Bloody Bride's company. Trying to avoid any more attention, I kept my head down until I reached the table. Deanyn was seated with Genna, Wynne, Tenille, and the man I couldn't quite name—he wore a Scriber's pin, which was likely how I knew him. Tenille's husband, I assumed. I took a seat between Deanyn and Genna, and the latter visibly flinched as my arm brushed hers. Clearly embarrassed by her reaction, she took a deep drink and did not look up at me.

"Scriber Dennon," Wynne greeted me excitedly. "You've read Theryn, haven't you?"

Deanyn laughed. "No introductions, then?"

"Oh!" Wynne looked abashed. "I'm sorry. I was just…" She trailed off, blushing, and gestured for Tenille to present the familiar-looking man.

"Dennon, this is my husband Vance." Tenille leaned warmly against the man, who wrapped an arm around her as he extended his free hand for me to shake.

"A pleasure." I returned the handshake. "I think we might have met before…?"

"We've seen each other around the Academy. I was pinned in Medicine, but I studied History as well." Vance looked slightly uncomfortable, but I decided not to take it personally. He must have known who I was, being married to Tenille, and few Scribers who knew me would go so far as to shake my hand at all.

"So…" I shifted uncomfortably in my seat, trying and failing to think of some interesting subject of conversation. "Is Bryndine going to be joining us?"

"She is with her father, but she said that she would be along later," Tenille answered.

"I may miss her then. I can't stay long." Unable to think of a proper excuse, I kept my reasons vague. "I have… things to do in the morning."

Arching an eyebrow, Deanyn gave me a knowing smile. "We wouldn't want to keep you from anything important. But at least have one drink—I'll even pay for it."

"That seems fair," I acquiesced. "Red wine…" I looked around the dingy room with some scepticism. "If they have anything besides ale."

They did, though it was no fine Raenish red, or even a decent Bridgefort vintage—it tasted like the grapes had been stomped on a stable floor. Still, after a few sips, I found myself relaxing somewhat.

"Scriber Dennon, I was going to ask you about your views on Theryn." There was an eager glint in Wynne's eyes as she brought the conversation back around to the philosopher.

"By the Mother and the Father, more of this?" Rolling her eyes, Deanyn stood, grinning to take the edge out of her next words: "I'm going to join the interesting people." She moved over to the next table, where Orya and Leste were in the middle of a dangerous-looking drinking game involving knives.

Philosophy seemed a harmless enough topic to pass the time while I finished my single glass. I leaned forward, resting my elbows on the table as I spoke. "The thing to understand about Theryn is that he was writing shortly after the Forgetting ended, so much of his talk about complete obedience to the King can be read as satirical..."

* * *

An hour and innumerable drinks later, I had explained my views on various philosophers to anyone who would listen; joined Nalla in a rousing rendition of Adello's *The Burning King*; and lost arm wrestling matches to Orya, Leste, and finally even Genna, who had drunk enough to actually make eye contact with me during the contest. It felt good to dull my senses, to let the wine wash away the constant fear of disembodied voices. To drown the euphoria of discovery I had only just reawakened, and the unexpected grief at having to let that feeling go once more.

But as the night wore on, the mood among the women grew increasingly morose, and my own disposition fared no better. Spirited drinking games gave way to dejected discussion about their unjust punishment. Bryndine had not yet arrived, and I felt badly for the women waiting for her—I suspected that the Captain they loved so dearly was not coming at all.

Eventually, I found myself in the sort of solemn, confessional conversation that only comes when one mixes depression with heavy drinking. Once again I sat with Tenille, Vance, and Genna; Deanyn had returned as well. Wynne had left to join some of the others in making insulting toasts to the King and the High Commander, and Orya had taken her seat. It seemed backwards, the well-read young woman throwing out curse-riddled salutations while the usually foul-mouthed Orya discussed her hopes and disappointments, but alcohol and unpleasant news make people act strangely—my still being there at all was proof enough of that.

"Maybe it's for the best," I suggested to Tenille, forcing my tongue to enunciate the words through the slurring effect of the wine. "You have children."

Tenille frowned. "Most soldiers do, but no one cares when they're men. I want to *protect* my children." She spoke quite clearly—she and Vance had imbibed sparingly, at least by comparison.

"Better her than me." Vance gave his wife an affectionate squeeze. "I wouldn't last a day. We're proud of Tenille. It should be people as well trained as her out there, man or woman."

"Only thin' 'at matters is, we don' got cocks." Orya's normally rough speech was even harder to understand when she was drunk, and she was further gone than anyone at the table. She took a deep pull from her mug, then slammed it down. "Ne'r mind us bein' better'n any Dragon-damned man in th'Army!" Her voice carried loudly through the common room and garnered foul looks from the other patrons, but many of the women around her showed their agreement with shouts and raised glasses.

"Why do it then?" I asked. "I'd have quit long—" I paused to belch, covering it with my hand. "—ago. Gets you nothing but scorn."

"Well, we *don't* do it." Deanyn attempted glibness, but it sounded like sorrow. "Not anymore."

Tenille tried a more serious answer, but I could tell her heart wasn't in it. "We fight to serve—"

"Bryndine." Genna's voice was soft, but somehow the sound of it silenced the others. "We do it because of Bryndine."

"Not anymore," Deanyn repeated quietly.

Genna looked at me with only faint hesitation—although she, like Tenille, had held back from drinking too much, the ale had made her bolder than usual. "Scriber Dennon, you know how people speak of her. She protects us from scorn by taking it upon herself. We're here because—" Halfway through the sentence she realized she had become the center of attention and halted abruptly, then flushed red and finished in a nervous rush, "—because she brought us here."

Orya nodded emphatically. "I'd've lost a hand or worse, stealin' in Highpass." She illustrated the point with a pantomimed chopping motion towards her wrist. "But the Cap'n stopped it. Army wage was more'n I'd make in a year, 'fore she foun' me."

"I had the Warfare training, but no opportunity to use it before Millum Wren introduced us," Tenille agreed. "And she inspired many of the girls to seek her out themselves. Wynne wanted a chance to serve the Kingsland when she couldn't get into the Academy. And Janelyn—Father rest her—begged to join us the moment she came of age."

"Didn't go well for Janelyn. Sometimes it's better… not to get what you dream of." I drained the last of my wine and peered glumly through the empty glass. Dozens of bubbles and imperfections warped my view of the women sitting across the table; Genna and Orya melted down like used candles.

"Don't you dare diminish her death!" Tenille's anger surprised me, and my fingers fumbled, letting the glass fall to the table. "You've read the Book of the Divide, Dennon. Women who wish to do more with our lives than tend to a husband have few paths to choose from. Bryndine gave us one. Janelyn knew the risks, and chose willingly—as any soldier does."

I raised my hands in surrender. "No disrespect. Janelyn helped save my life. You won't hear me saying she wasn't fit for the Army. But why choose to fight for people who hate you for it?"

"Some of us wouldn't have been allowed any choice at all without Bryndine," whispered Genna. "Fathers can force their daughters into marriage. To men who..." Her voice broke, and she looked down at her hands.

"Erryn's Promise says that all citizens are free and equal, but daughters and wives are treated as property more often than not," Tenille said with no small amount of bitterness. "Mother forbid we try to make the kingdom safer for our families. Bryndine seeks to correct that where she can. Not many have the courage to challenge the King's niece when she cites the Promise. The Army will be poorer for her loss."

Deanyn laughed, but there was no joy in it. "That's an

understatement. She was the best officer they had." Raising her mug and her voice, she shouted, "To the Captain!"

"Th'Cap'n!" Orya slurred with feeling, liquid sloshing out as her cup flew upwards.

In short order, all three tables were raising a loud toast to Bryndine. I joined in half-heartedly. For all that they claimed Bryndine had done for them, I could not help but feel she should have been there for them at that moment. The same thought seemed to occur to many of the women as they saluted their absent Captain; a pensive silence fell over them after they lowered their drinks.

"Sky'n'Earth, that's too far!" A belligerent voice cut through the muttered conversation in the common room, and I looked to see a square-jawed bald man rising unsteadily to his feet from a nearby table. "You lot bein' 'ere is bad enough, but now yer toastin' the dragon-Damned Bloody Bride, bringin' the Mother's wrath down on th' rest of us? We're good, Gods-fearin'—"

Sylla was upon him before he finished speaking, driving her fist into his stomach. She had been silent the entire night, not moving from her spot in the corner; I had nearly forgotten she was there. But as soon as she heard him insult Bryndine, she flung herself at the man with a swiftness that I could barely believe, particularly from a woman who had been drinking so heavily for so long.

As the man doubled over, she grabbed him by the hair, slamming his head down into her raised knee. Blood streamed from his broken nose, and he slumped to his knees cursing, but Sylla was not done with him. A final, savage blow to the temple sent him sprawling to the floor unconscious. The room was silent; no one could quite believe the ruthless efficiency of the beating they had just witnessed.

"Who else has something to say about the Captain?" Sylla demanded.

"You shouldn'ta done that, bitch." A large man with a protruding gut stood from his seat at the bar, advancing towards Sylla. Her dark eyes flashed dangerously in response.

He made it no more than two steps before a blur of blond hair and sinewy limbs crashed into him. I could hear Orya laughing, of all things, as she carried the big man to the ground.

Chairs clattered against the hardwood floor as nearly everyone in the tavern rose, and then, complete chaos. Leste dodged a fist and countered by cracking her mug into the head of the man who had thrown the punch. Selvi or Elene—I still could not tell the twins apart—pinned a man's arms while the other sister battered him with her fists. Three men surrounded Ivyla, and her vicious defense proved that she was not entirely the honorable and unimaginative soldier I had thought. She evened the odds by lashing a foot into the largest man's groin and striking another in the face with a solid backhand, but the third caught her jaw with a roundhouse punch that sent her reeling.

A moment later, I could no longer tell one woman from the next in the tumult of bodies grappling through the tavern. Orya's reckless laughter floated over everything, giving the mayhem an air of dream-like madness.

I tried to make my way towards the door to escape, but my wine-weakened legs faltered and I staggered sideways into a hefty man with a thick beard and furious eyes. His elbow snapped back into the side of my face, and I cried out as my cheek split open.

Falling to the floor, I scrambled on my hands and knees towards the nearest table. Vance was cowering beneath it already, and he greeted me with a helpless shrug. A drunken chuckle escaped my lips; we looked absurd, two scared, skinny men trembling behind the furniture while women brawled violently all around us.

The fight came to an end as suddenly as it began. With a bellow, the tavern-keeper gained everyone's attention, threatening to call the guard. When it became clear that might not be sufficient, he added a lifelong ban for anyone who threw another punch. The latter proved much more effective.

When the violence had ceased, he turned to Tenille. "I want you lot out, and don't come back. The wife warned me not to let you drink to begin with. I called her foolish. If their coin's good, what's the harm, I said. Well, I'm the fool now, I reckon."

"Sky'n'bloody Earth, it's him started th' ruttin' thing."

Orya pointed at the man Sylla had left senseless on the floor, wheezing through the ruin of his bloody nose. It did not make a convincing case for their innocence.

"We'll go," said Tenille, helping her husband to his feet as she spoke. When she bent down below the edge of the table, I saw that a nasty bruise was already forming around her eye. "Come on, women. Staying won't do us any good."

Some of the women muttered quietly, glaring at the other patrons, but they followed Tenille out the door. I clambered out from beneath the table and hurried after them.

It was late evening by then, nearly midnight, and most of the women said their goodbyes and began to stumble home. Tenille and Vance bid me farewell and took their leave, Vance fussing over his wife's bruised eye. As I watched them go, I realized that I had nowhere to stay myself. I had thought to take lodging at the Doused Tree, but that was out of the question now.

Deanyn and I were among the few still lingering outside the tavern, and she flashed me an ironic smile. "Well, are you glad you joined us?"

"Overjoyed." I raised a hand to the gash on my cheek, and my fingertips came back bloody. "You came out better than most," I commented, looking her over. Besides two very light scratches on her forehead from what might have been fingernails, Deanyn appeared untouched.

"Doesn't feel that way." Gingerly, she laid a hand against the right side of her torso. "One of them hit me with a stool."

"Could have a broken rib." Without thinking, I reached out a hand to probe the injury.

She flinched as I made contact, but didn't pull away. "I feel like you're skipping over an important piece of this courtship, Scriber."

In my inebriated state, it had not occurred to me that I was essentially groping her without permission. "N—nonsense," I stammered. "This is purely medical."

She chuckled, and the motion made her wince. "Of course it is. Is anything broken?"

"Not that I can tell."

"Impressive medical expertise, that," she teased. "But if I

am not mortally wounded, I should go. Do you have a place to stay?"

I shook my head. "I was going to rent a room here, but that seems unlikely now."

"If you can't find a better place, I have a room at the River's Song in the Tradecourt."

I nearly choked with shock. "I… that is generous, but…"

"Calm down, Dennon. I'm not trying to seduce you." She smirked at my artless reaction. "I only meant that there may be rooms available there. The cheaper inns are mostly full. People don't want to stay outside the walls if they can avoid it."

"Oh." Despite my embarrassment, I was relieved. I was fond of Deanyn, but it had been a long while since I had been with a woman, and longer still since I had made anything like a friend. I would only have ruined things, given the opportunity.

As she turned to leave, a question came to my mind. "The others all had some reason for following Bryndine. Why do you?"

She shrugged. "Why not?" With a mischievous grin, she strode away down the dark street.

I thought about following her to the River's Song. I did need a place to stay, though the Tradecourt inns were expensive—how Deanyn could afford one on an Army wage was something of a mystery. But when I moved to follow her, the combination of the blow to my head and the effects of the wine left me lightheaded, and I ended up leaning on the tavern wall to support myself. I eased myself down into a sitting position with my back against the wall, waiting for the world around me to stop its drunken swaying.

It was then that I realized I was not alone. Sylla sat against the wall a few feet from me, holding her head in her hands.

I was scared to speak—she didn't like me at the best of times, and I had just watched her beat a man into unconsciousness in mere moments. So I sat in silence, holding my breath, hoping she would not notice.

Eventually, she raised her head and looked at me. "Go away, Scriber." Her expression was not one I had seen her wear before. She was annoyed by my presence—that was not new—but beneath it there was a grief that made her less imposing than usual. It may have been the wine, but I found myself feeling sorry for her.

"Do you have somewhere to go, Sylla? A husband..." I realized how unlikely that was even as I said it. "...or family, friends?"

"Would that make you happy, Scriber?" She laughed bitterly. "If I told you a tale about protecting my family, like Tenille? Or would you prefer something sad like Genna, nearly made to marry the man who raped her so her family wouldn't be shamed? You could pat my head and pretend to understand. Maybe we'd become friends."

"I didn't mean—"

"I *killed* my husband, Scriber. Not such a sympathetic story, is it? They'd have hung me for it, but Bryndine claimed I had the right to defend my life under Erryn's Promise. The truth is, he was a drunk and he beat me, but I wasn't afraid for my life—I did it because I hated him. I wanted him dead."

I stared at her uselessly, completely speechless, but she did not need any response. As far as I could tell, she was speaking just to say the words aloud.

"So no, I have nobody. Nobody but Bryndine ever cared. I can't just call this ill luck and go back to my life." Her voice was thick with emotion, but I couldn't say whether it was sorrow or fury. "Bryndine was my life."

I don't know if she expected me to recoil in horror, to call her a murderer, or simply to leave her alone. But it was those last four words that struck me more than the story that came before them. "You could still stay with her, couldn't you?"

She looked at me with disgust. "And be a burden on her? She'll *have* guards. Her father will marry her to a wealthy Baron or landholder, with more men than he knows what to do with. She would take me with her, but she would do it for my sake, not because she needs me. I couldn't—" She must have seen the sympathy in my eyes, because she stopped abruptly, and her face twisted with fury. "Why should you care, Scriber? I don't want your pity." She pushed herself to her feet. "I don't want anything from you."

She stalked away into the darkness, and I watched her go silently. Anything I said would only have made things worse.

The only person who might have reassured her was not there, had not bothered to come.

Sylla might have deserved her misery; she had killed a man, though he hardly sounded like a great loss to the world. Perhaps I should even have been concerned for my own safety, having just learned that a woman who disliked me was capable of murder. But all I could think was that Bryndine should have been there to talk to her.

As Sylla moved out of my sight, I made a decision. Not a wise decision, but one largely facilitated by my dark mood and inebriation.

I was going to go see Bryndine, and I was going to ask her why she had deserted her company.

CHAPTER FIFTEEN

It is possible that I have treated Bryndine somewhat unfairly.

— From the personal journals of Dennon Lark

The Kingscourt is heavily patrolled at night, but I had just enough wits about me to get over the bridge and past the guardsmen. It helped that I was wearing the elegant silk clothing given to me in Highpass, and in the darkness the stains of food and drink were not immediately obvious. But it was my pin that ensured unhindered passage. Even at that time of night, the guards were hesitant to stop me when I flashed the golden inkwell at them and claimed important business with the Lord Chancellor. Luck played a large part as well; if any of them had decided to come near enough to smell the wine on my breath, they would never have let me by.

It was not until I reached the Lord Chancellor's manor that I realized I would never be allowed in so late. There were men at the gate, and Elarryd's household guard would certainly know that their master had not summoned me.

Somewhat bafflingly, in retrospect, it struck me as a good idea to climb the wall around the manor. I crept around the side of the estate where no street lanterns could betray my presence and tried to scrabble up the tightly fitted stonework. My fingers found no purchase; the gaps were too small, the stones too smooth, the wall too tall to simply grab the lip and pull myself over.

I thought I could see a larger gap in the stones above my head, and jumped to try and reach it, but it was too high. With the sort of logic that only a drunk man can fathom, I decided that I needed a running start, and backed away to the other side of the street. Hurling myself forward as fast as I could, I leapt with my arms outstretched, reaching for the handhold I thought I saw—but there was no gap, only a stray shadow. My hands crashed painfully into solid stone, and I toppled backwards to the ground, crying out as I landed hard on my back.

The Lord Chancellor's guards were upon me before I regained my feet, hoisting me roughly and dragging me around to the front gate of the manor. When they threw me up against the wall, the light of the nearby lanterns glinted off my pin.

"A Scriber?" The first guard was understandably puzzled. "What are you doing here?"

"He's drunk, I smelled it when we were moving him," the other said. "And look at that cheek—he's been in a fight already tonight."

"What's a drunk Scriber want here?" The first man prodded me in the ribs.

Confidence seemed a better idea than apology. "I need to see Bryndine. She knows me, tell her Dennon needs to speak with her."

"At this hour? I don't think so."

"I need to talk to her!" I insisted belligerently.

"Scriber, you ain't getting in. Might be we should have you arrested for trying to break into the Lord Chancellor's manor, but you're pinned, and I don't want it on my head if you have real business here. Come back in the morning."

I could see that I wasn't going to get anywhere with the guards, but I was determined to see Bryndine, and drunk enough that my next action felt less idiotic than it actually was.

"*Bryndine!*" I bellowed, twisting my head towards the manor house. "Bryndine, it's Dennon!"

"Shut your mouth!" One of the guardsmen cuffed me across my swollen cheek and I squealed in pain.

"What is going on out here?" Elarryd Errynson's deep

voice sounded from beyond the gates.

"Trespasser, your Lordship. Caught him trying to climb the wall." The guard sounded almost sheepish. "Beg pardon, Lord Elarryd. We shouldn't have let him wake you.

"Let me see him."

The two guardsmen hauled me through the gate; on the other side, the Lord Chancellor of the Kingsland stood waiting outside his front door. He wore silken nightclothes and an annoyed expression, his blond hair mussed from sleep.

"Scriber Dennon. I thought I heard your name. Father in the Sky, are you mad? Is this about being banned from the Garden?"

"I need to speak with your daughter, your Lordship." Despite my drunkenness, I could tell that I was treading on dangerous ground. "I—I'm sorry for waking you."

"You need to speak with my daughter?" Elarryd was incredulous. "It is past midnight!" He leaned slightly closer, and his face darkened even further. "Are you drunk? Sky and Earth, this is… Do you know what could have happened to you? I am the Lord Chancellor of the realm! You could have been killed for skulking around my home, and it would have been thought just!"

"Father, it is fine. I will speak with him." I had not noticed Bryndine until she spoke; she was hidden in the shadows behind the doorway. Unlike her father, she did not look to have been sleeping—she was still dressed and tidy.

"Absolutely not, Bryndine. Such behaviour cannot be rewarded. And I would not have him wake your mother."

She stepped outside and laid a hand on her father's shoulder. "Please, Father, return to bed. This is my concern."

Elarryd took a deep, frustrated breath, then nodded. "Fine. I will trust you to handle him." He turned to the guards with what I hoped was grim humor. "But if he starts bellowing again, by all means, kill him."

Bryndine and I replied simultaneously, her voice far less nervous than mine:

"Thank you, Father."

"Thank you, your Lordship."

"And Scriber Dennon, remember this: I would be very

displeased if you said anything to upset my daughter." The Lord Chancellor looked me meaningfully in the eye, then turned and strode back into the house.

"Come, Scriber. We will speak inside," Bryndine said, and I followed her through the front door.

She led me into a large study off the main foyer, with a fire still burning in the hearth despite the hour. The decoration was surprisingly humble. I had expected gold and velvet, but the Lord Chancellor's manor was plainly adorned, with few valuables on display.

Bryndine seated herself in a chair before the fire, and motioned for me to take the seat beside her.

"You have been drinking." She swept her eyes over me as if she could gauge my sobriety at a glance. "Are you sober enough to speak sensibly?"

"I am a Scriber," I said, offended despite the fact that I had not made a sensible decision in hours. "I always speak sensibly."

She accepted my word with a nod. "You are here to ask why I did not join the women at the tavern, I assume?"

I should have heeded her father's warning, but I was in no condition to be wise. "They worship you! You should have been there, to… reassure them, give them some sort of hope!"

"And if there is no hope to give?"

"Father above, are you completely heartless? They were devastated!"

"Is that what bothers you, Scriber Dennon? My composure? My… heartlessness? You have said as much before."

"It bothers me that you can desert those women when they need you most!"

She looked into the fire silently for a time before speaking again. "Do you know why I chose to serve in the Army, Scriber?"

"No. I don't." A few weeks before I might have attributed it to her high birth, the whim of a spoiled noble. But not anymore.

"My parents were only allowed to marry because Father made it an issue of Erryn's Promise. My mother is not of high birth, as I'm sure you know." She looked at me as if expecting a snide remark, but I said nothing, so she went on. "They often told me that as long as the King's Army stands in defense of the Promise, every citizen is free to live a life of their choosing. I grew up idolizing the Army for that.

"But the Promise is not always perfectly followed. My uncle would not allow me to wear the uniform, not even at Millum Wren's request. I could imagine doing nothing else, so I went where the Army was called and gave my aid whether it was asked for or not. You must have heard some version of that story as well." A hint of bitterness crept into her voice. "The Bloody Bride loves killing men so much that she joins whatever battle she can find, or the like.

"It caused a great deal of public outcry, particularly when I started gathering other women to join me. In time, my father convinced the King that he could better control us if we *were* part of the Army. We were given only safe assignments, far from the public eye, but still I counted it a victory, for myself and for the Promise. Every day since, I have had to fight to hold on to that victory."

"What does this have to do with anything?" I demanded. My wine-addled mind had no patience for stories—I had come to berate her, not to be lectured.

"Only this: my position was hard-earned, and always precarious. The men would have been glad to claim that I was too soft to be a soldier, too womanly, too emotional. Any excuse would have been enough for my uncle to remove me. I have spent years practicing to hide my feelings from sight. I am not heartless; I have only done what I had to do." She hung her head. "Though now it seems it was all for naught."

"That changes nothing," I said. "If you care, why did you not come tonight?"

"Why is it so important to you, Scriber?"

"Because you are supposed to be braver than this!" I had not meant to say that; I had barely realized I felt it. "I was perfectly happy to hide in Waymark, you know. And then you came along, with all your talk of duty. You took all the bile thrown at you by the people and the Army and your family and you just kept going. You made me feel like a coward, and I *hated* you for it!"

Rising from my chair, I began to pace angrily before the fire. "Do you know why I told Illias about my idiotic theory, or gave that little speech in Waymark?" I glared at her, daring her to answer, but she just stared inscrutably back. "I didn't want to look weak in front of you! And then tonight you did what I would have. You ran away. So now I have to wonder, what was the Dragon-damned point of any of it?"

"You do not understand." I was surprised by the despair in her voice. "How could I face them? They have lost everything because of me. Everything they fought for. What could I possibly say to them?"

"Anything at all would have been better than staying away."

Her eyes narrowed; her jaw clenched. I could almost see the last of her self control evaporating. "And what of me?" she asked. "Am I not entitled to be upset? I have lost everything as well, everything I spent my life gaining!" She pounded a fist against the arm of her chair, and the wood splintered beneath her knuckles. "Sky and Earth, why must you always bait me, Scriber?"

It was the reaction I had hoped for since meeting her in Waymark, but seeing her iron mask shatter at last did not bring the satisfaction I had expected. "It was never my choice to stay with you! Why even agree to speak with me, if I anger you so? Why carry me in your wagon, or bring me to Highpass? You could have rid yourself of me at any time!"

"Would that I had," she snapped. "You have never been anything but rude and arrogant." She was silent briefly, and then her face softened and she slumped back in her chair. "But in a way, that is what drew me to you. You *are* rude, but no more or less so to me because of my blood or my sex. There is a certain honesty to it. And I suppose you are only being honest now. Perhaps I deserve your anger."

I stared at her for a moment, trying to control myself, and then I could not hold back anymore. I began to laugh—not some mild chuckle, but a mirthful torrent from deep in my belly that doubled me over and sent me collapsing back into my seat.

"What is so amusing, Scriber? If you are too drunk to control yourself, you may leave." There was still anger in her voice, and I knew I should be careful, but I was helpless in the throes of my amusement.

"It's… just so perfect!" I gasped for breath. "I dislike you for being brave, and you… you keep me near because I am rude?"

Her lips rose into a slight smile, then a larger one, and then she was laughing with me, and I realized I had never heard her do so before. The sound was as clear and vibrant as a Garden bell; not at all what I expected. It was a long while before we composed ourselves.

When she had collected herself once more, Bryndine said, "We are both fools, it seems, but neither of us need be cowards."

Finally mastering my laughter, I straightened in my seat and looked at her with apprehension. "What do you mean?"

"I will speak to the women. You are right; I owe them that much. And you will go to Master Illias, to see how you can help."

"I can't help," I protested. "I'm forbidden from the Old Garden."

"That does not mean that there is nothing for you to do. At the very least, you should be nearby in case he finds something—it was your theory, and you may be needed."

"I don't want any part of it."

"You forget that I was with you when the idea came to you." Bryndine's tone was firm; a Captain's voice, brooking no argument. "I saw your face. You will not convince me that it doesn't matter to you."

"It does," I admitted. It was not something I would have said aloud if I had been sober. "I've wanted little else since I was a boy. If there is something there to find, it could be the greatest discovery since the Forgetting. But I… I still dream of the men who died the last time."

"You always will, Scriber. Just as I will always remember Janelyn. That is the way of these things. Come with me tomorrow." Again, she said it like an order, not a request.

Somehow, I found myself nodding. "I… would like to help Illias. If I can. Without going into the Garden." It felt like a weight had lifted off my chest, and I laughed with relief. "Sky and Earth, I would love it. I am beyond tired of teaching children and tending scrapes."

Bryndine smiled. "Good. Now, it is late, and you are not entirely sober—you should not be wandering the streets." She stood and extended her hand, helping me to my feet. "Come, I will show you to the guest quarters. We have much to do in the morning."

CHAPTER SIXTEEN

Without Bryndine Errynson, the dig beneath the Old Garden would have ended before it began. She and her company were instrumental in one of the greatest discoveries since the Forgetting.

— From Dennon Lark's *Life of Bryndine Errynson*

The sun was too bright, the autumn air too chill, and my head ached like Uran Ord's must have after the rebel's mace stove in his skull. That last, though, was almost a relief, coming as the normal result of too much wine rather than the chanting of unseen voices. I had not slept well either, waking repeatedly throughout the night from terrible dreams of destruction and death at the Old Garden. As Bryndine and I approached the partial ruin of the Kingsland's oldest house of worship, I wondered what I had been thinking when I agreed to come.

I wondered again why I was there when I saw the two figures standing with Illias and Korus outside the domed entrance of the Old Garden: the Eldest Brother and Sister, he in a sky-blue robe and she in an earthy brown. I could guess their rank by their hair—I did not know how they walked without tripping over it. The Children never cut their hair after taking their vows, something about growing as the plants sacred to the Mother and Father do. It made it easy to identify those of seniority and high esteem. Their hair always grew well past their waists.

I knew their faces, too, as we drew nearer. Brother Cyril, the Eldest Brother of the Sky, was a short, skinny man with a gaunt face and wispy grey hair that reached to his ankles. Stout, jowly Sister Olynna, Eldest of the Sisters of the Earth, had longer hair still, the end of her brown braid brushing lightly against the ground. The leadership of the Children had not changed, apparently, since they censured me for my role in the Old Garden's destruction five years ago.

Illias' incensed gesticulation made clear that whatever conversation he and the Eldest were having, it was not friendly. "The King has given his permission," he insisted as we came within earshot.

"And we are allowing you entry, Master Illias, but the King cannot control the will of the people." Brother Cyril spoke as though he had just woken from sleep, but it was not due to the early hour; he had sounded much the same five years ago. The old man always sounded tired—the effort of supporting his head under all that hair, I suspected.

"The will of the people?" Illias snorted contemptuously. "Better to call it the will of the Children—dishonesty is a sin, is it not? This is your doing. You've put the fear of the Dragon in them with your preaching!"

"You question the truth of our words?" Sister Olynna made the sign of the Divide in the air before her. "May the Mother and the Father help you, Master Illias, if you cannot trust their chosen servants." She shook her head in a show of saddened disapproval. This was the true leader of the Children, not the tired old man beside her—Olynna was shrewd, calculating, and an exquisite performer when she needed to be. She had been especially convincing the day she and Brother Cyril had publically condemned my soul to the Dragon.

"It is somewhat strange that Master Illias cannot find a single man willing to help him dig," Korus said, affecting concern, though the smirk on his face made his true feelings obvious. It was then that he noticed Bryndine and me approaching, and that smirk grew into a malevolent grin. "Lady Bryndine, an honor as always. And Scriber Dennon! What luck. You are an expert on the Old Garden, perhaps you can advise us."

As the eyes of the Eldest fell upon me, I realized that my arrival could not have come at a worse time. I had expected Illias to already have digging underway, but clearly the Children were resisting the attempt, and my presence was just another thing they could protest.

"This is an outrage!" exclaimed Sister Olynna. "You dare to bring this man here? Has King Syrid no respect for the sanctity of this place?"

The loudness of her voice sent needles of pain through my head, but I tried not to show outward sign of my discomfort. It could not help for them to know I was suffering the consequences of a night of indulgence.

I tried to repair the damage as best I could. "The King did not send me," I said. "I am only in Three Rivers because my home was attacked by the Burners. I heard that Illias was here, and only thought to visit him. I meant no harm."

Korus' smile disappeared; he had clearly hoped for something more incendiary. But he could not contradict me, not when the King had commanded that my involvement be kept silent.

Bryndine caught on immediately. "The Scriber asked me to escort him. The city can be confusing to those who do not live here. It is my fault, Eldest. I should have known better than to bring him here."

Brother Cyril gave her a sour look from beneath drooping eyelids. "Your judgement is hardly something to be relied upon, Lady Bryndine."

Bryndine bowed humbly, and when she bent forward over the tiny Eldest Brother, her huge form cast him entirely into shadow. I found myself fighting back a chuckle.

"You have my deepest apologies, Eldest," she said. "With your permission, we will take our leave."

Olynna waved her away. "Of course. Take this man away. His presence offends us."

It was difficult to keep my temper under control around the woman, even knowing that Illias' career was at risk. "Likewise," I muttered, and though my voice was low, I was certain she heard me. She narrowed her eyes, but said nothing.

Apparently it was beneath her dignity to trade insults with a heathen like myself.

"Wait a moment, Denn," Illias said. "If I might have a moment to talk to an old student, Eldest?"

"Are you sure, Master Illias? Dennon Lark is… a poor choice of companion, especially for a man of your station." Olynna eyed me with contempt as she spoke, and I imagined how satisfying it would be to yank on that ridiculous braid.

Illias gave the Eldest Sister an indignant look as well, but managed to hold his ire in check. "It will be brief."

Sister Olynna nodded curtly, and Illias pulled Bryndine and me a safe distance away.

He kept his voice low. "What are you doing here, my boy? I thought you wanted no part of this."

Bryndine took responsibility before I could answer. "It was my suggestion, Master Illias. We hoped to see if Scriber Dennon could be of use without breaking the King's ban. If we have caused you trouble, I apologize."

Illias shook his head. "Don't worry over that—you could not have worsened the situation. The Children have spread the word that no one is to give me any aid, and no Scribers will help for fear of earning the Council's ire. I am at a loss, truly. I cannot proceed without workers, and I haven't much time." He gave me a small, sad smile. "I am glad to hear that you want to help, Denn, but I fear we have already lost this battle."

Accepting defeat would have been an easy escape, but I could not quite bring myself to do it, not with Bryndine watching, not after everything we had both said the night before. And besides that, an inspiration had come to me, chasing the lingering haze of last night's wine from my mind. I wanted to see where it led.

"They claim that they will honor the King's wishes, though?" I asked. "It is only a lack of workers that stops you?"

Illias nodded, looking at me curiously.

"Then if you *can* find help, they will have to let you dig, or else directly disobey the King."

"Yes, but where—"

"It so happens that Bryndine's women are in need of employment."

Understanding lit Illias' face, and then excitement. "By the Divide, Denn, I have missed you these five years! That is perfect!" He turned to Bryndine hopefully. "What about it? Will you help?"

"Nothing would please me more, Master Illias. But I am hardly in favor with the Children—they will likely object."

"They have no strong grounds to do so," I said. "You are no longer with the Army. And you are of the King's blood." I was convincing myself as much as her—saying the words aloud, I could almost believe them. "It puts them in a difficult position. They would have to not only object to the King's decree, but deny his niece as a blasphemer, which would show tremendous disrespect to the Errynsons. They may not want to throw down that gauntlet."

"I thought you were pinned in History, not Politics, Scriber Dennon." Bryndine smiled very slightly at me—more than I was used to, from her. "It is worth trying."

"Master Illias!" Sister Olynna called out impatiently. "Are you quite done?"

Illias turned to her with a smile. "Done, Eldest Sister? No, I rather think I am just beginning."

* * *

The plan worked perfectly. Though they did not like it, the Eldest had little choice but to let Illias proceed with the dig—they were unwilling to openly offend the royal family when simply waiting a week would rid them of Illias just as surely.

The women embraced the work with enthusiasm. It gave them reason to stay together—as well as payment for their services, as Illias still commanded the coffers of the School of History—for at least another week. By the next day, the excavation was well under way.

I could not enter the Old Garden myself, of course, but the Lord Chancellor's manor was only a short distance away. Despite the embarrassing circumstances by which I had first come there, I was allowed to stay. In fact, when Bryndine told them of my role in keeping her company together, her parents welcomed me quite warmly. Unlike most of Bryndine's relatives

I had met, Elarryd and Branwyn Errynson were nothing but supportive of their daughter's desire to serve the Kingsland.

Wynne acted as a messenger, keeping me apprised of their progress. At first she had little to report, but her passion for the work was evident even when she could tell me nothing but that they had removed more rubble from the Underground chamber beneath the Garden. The girl really should have been a Scriber. I found myself wishing I could share in her enthusiasm. But whenever I saw her I felt only stomach-twisting dread—every time, I was certain that she had come to tell me of some awful disaster.

With little to do but wait for Wynne's visits, I spent my first free day reacquainting myself with the twisting streets of Three Rivers. It was a different town than it had been when I left five years before. Always crowded, it was doubly so now with the constantly arriving refugees, yet the lively, animated quality that had once possessed the Kingsland's capital was gone. People still haggled with merchants, but they did it desperately, with the implication that a lower price might mean survival for another day. Many begged for food, though there was little to be found; with the crops in Three Rivers and the Bridgefort failing, people horded what they had. Children no longer played in the streets—they stayed to their homes, or their tents in the filthy sprawl beyond the walls. What bound the city now was not a sense of community, but a sense of fear.

Everyone I spoke to had a different tale or rumor about the Burnt: that they could command the weather, make crops wilt and decay, even control minds. But for the most part, people would not speak at all. Even my Scriber's pin was not enough to quell their distrust. With so many joining the Burnt, any stranger was treated as a threat. Thinking back to that night in Waymark, when Hareld Kellen had charged at me with an axe, I could hardly blame the frightened citizens for their reluctance to trust a new face.

After that day, I kept to the Lord Chancellor's manor. I was already hated by most anyone who knew my name, and wandering the streets with the mood in the city being what it was felt like tempting fate.

On the fourth day of digging, Wynne arrived at the manor,

breathless with excitement, to tell me that they had cleared enough debris to begin searching for the theoretical passage under the west wall. She assured me that safety was their first concern, but still I sent her back to Illias with a warning to proceed cautiously.

That night I lay awake in bed, consumed with the fear that morning would bring terrible news. When I did finally fall into sleep, it was a sleep plagued by nightmares of men dying under falling glass and stone.

The next morning, when the servants woke me shortly after sunrise to tell me Wynne had arrived, I knew beyond doubt that the worst had happened. With growing terror, I dressed myself and descended the stairs to meet her, my heart beating so wildly that I feared it might shatter my chest.

And then I saw her face, and I realized why she had come—the reason that I had tried so hard not to consider, had scarcely even thought possible.

Her expression was one of absolute elation. "We found it, Scriber Dennon," she said. "You were right!"

CHAPTER SEVENTEEN

The story goes that when the Mother and the Father wanted children, they first created the Dragon, the Sea God, collector of damned souls. He was too powerful and tempestuous, and he denied their love. Then they created the Wyddin, but the tree spirits were subservient to their core, and sought only to please their makers. The final, favorite children of the gods were humans, who were mortal and thus reliant on divine guidance, but also possessed dreams and desires of their own.

But humans could not live in the primordial realm where Earth and Sky were one, so the Mother and the Father created the Divide, separating the realms—and themselves—forever. Should they ever cross the Divide to be together, it will collapse and the Sky and Earth will rejoin, destroying mankind. For our survival, they sacrificed a love beyond mortal ken.

The vast majority of Kingslanders believe that story. Needless to say, ruining the oldest and holiest of Gardens has somewhat harmed my reputation.

— From the personal journals of Dennon Lark

"The King can go swim with the Dragon for all I care, Denn. You are coming with us," Illias insisted.

For the second time that week, I stood outside the huge dome of the Old Garden's entrance. Acting on Illias' command, Wynne had practically dragged me from the manor towards the Garden, explaining the situation as we walked: they had uncovered the westward passage just before dawn after working throughout the night, and by sunrise, had cleared the old tunnel enough to pass through. At that point, Illias had decided that they would go no further unless I was there—despite the fact that I was forbidden by royal decree to enter the building.

"Illias, we've discussed this! Even if I was willing to disobey the King, I wouldn't go in there." I could barely even look at the building without seeing the faces of the men who had died there. Bryndine had talked me into helping from a distance if I could, but I was not ready to do more than that—entering the Old Garden was out of the question.

"You only need to enter the Garden to reach the tunnel," Bryndine said. "You will be within the walls for mere moments. I think we can justify that to my uncle." She was becoming as bad as Illias. Neither of them would give me any peace.

Wynne shifted impatiently, eager to get underway. "Just think what we might find down there! You have to come, Scriber Dennon."

"Just go," I said. "I'll be waiting to help interpret anything you find. You don't need me."

"But I *want* you there," Illias replied. "This is your discovery, Denn." He threw his hands up in frustration. "Damn it to the Dragon, you need to find a way beyond all this self pity!"

I rubbed at my temple. "I said I would help, and I will. Why is that not enough?"

Illias had never looked so annoyed with me. With a level of anger usually reserved for his fellow Council members, he said, "Because I didn't teach you to sit and wait while others do your work for you!"

My own anger flared in response. "And what a disappointment I must be! You'll never let it go, will you? You are not my teacher anymore, Illias! You're just an old man trying to use me to prove you haven't wasted your life, and I *can't!*"

He struck me across the face. Hard. The force of the blow reopened the gash on my bruised cheek, and I cried out in pain.

"Wasted my life?" Illias' face twisted with a rage I had never before seen in him. "*Never* say that to me again, boy! I do not need you, or anyone, to prove the worth of my life!"

I stared at him open-mouthed. This was the gentle, kindly

man who had raised me, and yet I barely recognized him now. I wanted to apologize, but in the face of such fury, I could not find the words.

"If none of my students ever amounted to anything, I would still not count it a waste. But you, Denn—you are worse than that by far. I almost wish that you *were* a failure. It would be easier to take than this… cowardice! You could accomplish great things, if you were not so paralyzed by the thought of making a single mistake!"

I had never felt so small in all my life. It was bad enough to be torn down by the one man whose opinion I valued above all, but to have it witnessed by others was worse still. Bryndine's expression betrayed nothing, but the disappointment on Wynne's face was unbearable.

And Illias was not done. "I am not the one wasting my life, Dennon. You are. And it breaks my heart." His anger was fading, but the sorrow that replaced it was no easier to take. "You *will* come with us, or I swear by the Divide, I am done with you." He half-turned away, as though he couldn't bear to look at me.

I couldn't speak; I wanted to cry. *It wasn't supposed to be this way. I was going to help.*

Bryndine stepped towards me and grasped my arm. "Master Illias, do you mind…"

Illias gave a brusque wave of his hand, and Bryndine led me a short distance away.

"We spoke of this, Scriber." Bryndine's grey eyes looked like steel as she fixed me with a stern gaze. "You need to come with us."

"I can't."

"You can," she said, "but you are afraid to."

I jerked my arm from her grasp. "Yes. I admit it, I'm afraid. I'm a coward. You were right from the beginning." It always came back to this. No one made me feel inadequate quite as well as Bryndine.

"Fear doesn't make you a coward, Scriber. But you may want to consider what this fear will cost." She looked pointedly back at Illias.

I am done with you, he had said. Illias was the only family I had. I could not lose him. And I would only be in the Old Garden for a moment. Much as I didn't want to admit it after all the fuss I had made, Bryndine was right.

Still, I was not quite willing to *admit* that she was right, at least not to her face. Instead, I shouldered past her and strode towards Illias. The old man turned to face me as I approached, but I kept my head down—it was too difficult to meet his eyes just then. My voice lodged in my throat, but I forced myself to speak. "Illias, I'm sorry," I whispered, staring at my feet. "I'll come."

It was not Illias who answered.

"I think not, Scriber Dennon." Sister Olynna's voice. Startled, I turned to see her approaching, led by a young Sister whose hair barely reached past her ears.

"How fortunate that Sister Gretyl came to me in time," Olynna continued. "I only thought to look at this tunnel of yours, but now I see that the Mother brought me here for another reason."

Illias rounded on her, his ire finding a new target. "I can have the women collapse what is left of this place with a word. Is it worth that much to you to stop Dennon from passing through?"

He was bluffing; Illias would never deliberately destroy an historical site. Sister Olynna had to suspect as much, but still the threat left her speechless for a moment—the Eldest were not accustomed to dissent.

"You… you are not serious, Master Illias. You have sworn oaths against doing such a thing, and the punishment would be—"

"The punishment would be too late. The Garden would still be gone." He spoke with such intensity that I almost believed it, despite everything I knew about the man.

Olynna turned to Bryndine. "You would not allow your women to do this."

I found myself holding my breath as I waited for Bryndine's response. She could undermine Illias with a word, and she might—lies and threats were not her way. The side she chose would very likely decide the issue, and I realized with some surprise that I was not sure which resolution I would prefer.

"It is not for me to allow or disallow, Eldest," said Bryndine. "I am no longer their Captain."

"It is your choice, Olynna." Illias gestured to the dome behind him. "Let Denn through and we will follow the passage away from here and leave the Garden in peace. It costs you nothing."

The Eldest Sister looked us over with a cold eye. "Fine, then. Bring him with you. But I will not be silent about this, Illias. The people will know of your sacrilege. The King will know."

"If we find what we are looking for, nothing you say will matter," Illias replied. "And if we do not, you would always have condemned us."

Olynna glared at him with a hatred so fierce that it had to be impious. But she said nothing more, only turned and stormed away with Sister Gretyl hurrying behind. I was torn between disappointment and gratitude as I watched her go. For better or for worse, there was nothing standing between me and the Old Garden now.

Illias smiled gratefully at Bryndine. "Thank you for the support, Captain." His eyes fell on me, and it looked as though he might say something, but instead he turned towards the Garden. "Come—we have work to do."

Stepping into the Old Garden for the first time in five years, I could not help but feel I was dreaming. And my dreams of the Old Garden never ended well.

The entry dome was just as I remembered it—enormous, empty, and echoing. Each footstep against the polished marble floor reverberated endlessly. A mosaic of religious imagery spanned the curve of the dome above. It was not perfectly preserved—tiles were missing here and there, and in some places large swaths of stone were bare—but what remained was impressive. The scenes told the story of creation: the Mother and the Father before the Divide, the Dragon and the Wyddin, the birth of mankind.

To the north and south stood large oaken doors leading into the halls that encircled the courtyard, halls filled with offices and dormitories for the Children who had once lived and worked in the Old Garden. Those doors were roped off—the structure had not been in active use for decades, not since Syrid's grandfather King Eryk had declared it a historical site sixty years before. The Eldest of the Children dwelled in the nearby Royal Garden now, built over the ruins of the Archives by King Eryk's command.

Opposite from the entrance, on the east side of the dome, were the double doors that led into the courtyard—the Garden itself, where the Eldest had once preached to Kings and Queens. I had led nine men to their deaths beyond those doors, and it was all I could do not to turn and flee as I approached them now.

When Bryndine pushed the heavy oaken doors open, I could see into the courtyard, and I balked. It looked as though it had been untended for years. The grass grew long and thick, and weeds sought to strangle what few flowers remained. Hedges that had once been carefully groomed and sculpted were now bushy and unkempt. But it was what lay beyond all that wild growth that stopped me: the place where the grass ended and the pit began. The place where the east wall had crumbled and collapsed, where a priceless artwork had been destroyed, where men had died. Stepping through that door would be stepping into my nightmares.

But Illias was watching, so I gathered all the courage I had, and followed him through.

I could not help but look upwards as I passed the doors. Suspended in the open air overhead was the great glass image of the Father, wrought in bright blues and soft whites and brilliant yellows, the sky and the clouds and the sun all at once. His face was a study in tragedy, somehow showing every moment of thousands of years spent separated from his love, and he reached forth one hand longingly towards... nothingness. Where the Mother should have been, yearning towards him across the Divide, there was only empty space, lending new meaning to the Father's anguished expression.

For a thousand years and more, the Mother and the Father had resisted rain and snow and wind and the natural downward pull of the earth. But they had not been able to survive me. The Mother was gone, and the Father was ready to follow his love into death. The impossibly delicate frame that held the glass figure up was failing. Whatever work of engineering had held them both in the air for so long had needed both halves to support itself, and while the School of Arts had tried to bolster the Father with thick iron bars and chains, it did little good. The glasswork god sagged more every year, dropping panes of colored glass from his slowly warping frame.

With my eyes focused upwards, I nearly blundered into the great hole that was the east side of the courtyard. Wynne grabbed my arm and pulled me back from the edge, looking at me with concern.

"Careful, Scriber Dennon. It's steep," she said.

I nodded but did not reply, forcing myself to look down.

A makeshift scaffolding of wooden stairs had been erected since I was last there, descending down into the Underground chamber some twenty feet below. Much of the rubble that had once filled the chamber had been cleared away by Bryndine and her company. Instinctively, I looked for the bodies that I saw every night in my dreams. I half expected to see broken corpses pulling themselves from the debris, but Bryndine's women had been thorough; not a stone remained to mark where the men had died.

In my mind, though, I saw them still. A Scriber never forgets.

The women waited for us below. Debra and Leste hauled away a heavy rock, and Orya steadied a support beam while Rylene helped wedge it into place. Deanyn saw me looking and smiled. Only Illias and I remained above; Wynne and Bryndine were already descending the stairs.

"Denn…" Illias spoke softly, laying a hand on my shoulder. "I know this is not easy for you. What I said—"

"I deserved it." My voice sounded strange in my ears, flat and empty.

"Let's not linger here," Illias said. "It will be easier for you once we have moved on." But he did not descend; he waited with me until I was ready. Despite what had happened outside, I loved him for that.

I did not want to go down into the darkness. I could not see the west end of the Underground chamber; it continued on under my feet, back towards the Old Garden's dome. Continued on beyond where the sun could reach, beneath the earth and the huge stones of the Garden, beneath hundreds of tons of heavy, crushing weight.

But it also led to what might be the greatest discovery made in five hundred years. And I could be a part of it. For just a moment, I let myself feel excitement instead of fear. It did not last long, but it was enough.

"I'm ready," I said, and I stepped onto the stairs.

CHAPTER EIGHTEEN

Prince Fyrril Errynson, the eldest son of Ullyd the Forgetter, was thought for centuries to be of little historical significance. Little information on his life survived the Forgetting. A single song by the minstrel Adello gave rise to rumors of an illicit relationship between the two, and according to the Salt Mountain clansfolk he spent time there in his youth, meeting with the Barrock to renegotiate their mining treaty with the Kingsland. No record of him as King exists, and as such, it was concluded that he must have died before taking the throne.

It is only recently that the truth has been discovered: Prince Fyrril may be among the most important figures in the Kingsland's history.

— From Dennon Lark's *The Forgetting Remembered*

Several hours later, sweating in the stuffy, stale air and the heat of the lanterns, I regretted coming at all. It was a miserable experience from the very beginning.

Only six of us had entered the tunnel, for safety's sake—it had seemed unwise to bring a group of twenty into an untested passage that had been sealed for centuries. Illias and I were among the six, of course, and with us came Wynne, who had begged to be included; Bryndine and Debra for their muscle, in case we encountered any obstacles; and Sylla, because she flatly refused to stay while Bryndine went. Despite being the only pinned Scriber in Bryndine's company, Tenille had opted to stay behind, rightly pointing out that if the worst happened, she might need to lead the women in a rescue effort.

It made for a quiet group. Though I did not blame him for his anger earlier, I still felt awkward with Illias, and Bryndine and Wynne had witnessed me at my most pathetic. I could barely look any of them in the eye. Sylla despised me, and I was too nervous to speak with her—now that I was sober, the story of how she had killed her husband filled me with more fear than pity. And as for Debra, I did not know her well, and she was a terse woman, not given to lengthy conversation.

In that silence, I could clearly hear every other sound in the passage. I jumped at each creak and rumble, terrified that the tunnel would fall. Trapped underground with only dim lantern light to see by and waiting for a disaster I was sure would come, every moment felt like a scene from my worst nightmares. And there were other sounds too, more than just natural ones. Every so often, soft voices would drift through my mind, whispering terrible words. It felt much like when I passed a fireleaf on the road, but there were no fireleaf trees there under the ground. Perhaps we were passing beneath them. In any event, my nerves were raw and frayed after the first quarter-hour of exploration, and it got no better from there.

Progress was slow. At several points, we were forced to stop and clear the passage where the ceiling had collapsed inward. Bryndine and Debra did most of the work—the tunnel was not wide enough for more than three people to stand abreast, and Bryndine and Debra together were worth at least three people of a more conventional size. The blockage was always fairly minor, and never took more than a half-hour to clear, but it did not inspire much confidence in the tunnel's integrity. I was particularly terrified when we passed beneath the Salt River; when I heard the roar of water rushing overhead, I was sure that the ceiling was falling.

After some four hours of walking, we came to another chamber. It was little more than a large basement with fire-blackened walls, like most of the Underground, but in one corner was a set of stone stairs leading up to a trapdoor in the ceiling. The way continued on west from there, but it was badly blocked—the west wall of the room and the passage beyond had partially crumbled, and it looked to be worse than the small cave-ins we had already encountered.

Illias brought us to a halt. "We must be very near the city walls now," he said. "We should try that door, it may bring us above ground. I would like to get my bearings, and if we need more hands to dig out the passage, it would be better to bring them in this way."

I agreed with enthusiasm, though more because I was desperate to see daylight again than anything else.

Debra climbed the stairs and pushed on the wooden trap-door, but it did not move. She tried pulling, and got no better result. "The bastard's stuck," she grunted as she yanked downwards on the metal ring that served as a handle.

Working together, she and Bryndine were eventually able to wrench the wooden door open, showering themselves with dust and debris. It led up into a small shaft with a wooden ladder inside, perhaps ten feet in height.

The ladder was not sturdy, but it held together surprisingly well for its age—it supported Debra's weight, though she nearly fell when one rung broke under her feet, and I thanked the Mother and the Father that Bryndine had not risked attempting the climb first. Another wooden door sat at the top of the shaft, but this one was partially rotted, and Debra easily tore it away. Beyond it there was nothing but tightly packed earth.

It appeared to be a dead end, but Debra took her pick-axe from her belt and scraped at the obstruction, causing another shower of dirt to rain down the shaft. At the sight of the falling earth, my heart almost stopped. "What are you doing?" I shouted up at her. "You'll bring the roof down on us."

"There's not more'n a foot of earth above, Scriber," Debra called back down. "I'm already through."

I peeked up after her; she was right. A dim light was visible at the top of the shaft.

As it turned out, we had dug our way into the earthen wine cellar of a merchant on the edge of the Tradecourt. He took quite a start when we walked out of his basement, but he became very cooperative when Illias and I showed him our pins and told him we were working with the King's niece, though Bryndine was forced to remain below until we could find a ladder that would hold her.

When we exited the house, we found ourselves mere yards from the city wall. Illias had been right in his estimate. "We need to clear the passage," he said, his voice rising with excitement. "If it goes beyond the wall, it as good as proves that the books were smuggled out of Three Rivers."

"But to where?" I asked. I had been mulling the question over throughout the day, and still had no answer. "Ryndport is the obvious choice—it is the Prince's seat, and it lies to the west. But it has been searched a dozen times. There isn't any practical place the Archives could be hidden there."

"We can only hope we find something that tells us, my boy," Illias replied. "Perhaps Fyrril left some sign, something that relates to Adello's songs. We've come this far on your theory—there must be something to it. For now, we need to bring the rest of the women to help clear the tunnel." It felt good to have his confidence again, though I did not entirely share it.

Wynne volunteered to fetch Tenille and the others, and they arrived back within the hour with the necessary tools and a new ladder. I can't imagine the owner of the house was pleased when twenty of us invaded his basement, but he hid it well.

The collapse was quite bad, and Illias was meticulous in ensuring that the tunnel was properly supported as the women hauled the debris away, so the work went slowly. We still had not broken through by the time daylight dwindled into dusk.

When evening fell, Illias halted the digging. The women had worked through the previous night, and he was unwilling to deny them their rest again. But I could see the worry in his eyes as we parted; he had only a few days left before the Council voted to remove him.

It was not until mid-afternoon the following day that the last of the blockage was finally removed, and we were able to continue. But as it turned out, we did not have far to go.

Perhaps a hundred yards beyond the cave-in, the tunnel came to an end in another chamber. It had the look of a smuggler's lair, a dirt cave dug out by hand. The back of the cavern sloped upwards into a wall of loose dirt. It was not hard to guess that there had been a passage there once, used for bringing illicit goods in and out of Three Rivers, but it had long since caved in on itself.

But it was not the nature of the chamber that interested me; it was what the chamber contained.

Five simple wooden chests sat in the earthen room, sealed at the seams with a coating of ancient yellowed wax. Atop the center chest lay a sealed silver scroll case, glinting in the lantern light. It was engraved with the sigil of the burning tree.

"Is that…?" I could hardly believe my eyes.

"The royal sigil," Illias breathed reverently. We both knew what it meant—someone of the royal family had left these chests. Someone like Prince Fyrril.

I picked up the silver cylinder and began working at the wax seal as delicately as I could. It had been there for centuries, and I did not want to risk damaging the contents.

Meanwhile, Debra and Bryndine levered a chest open with their picks, and the musty smell of old paper wafted out. Inside were stacks and stacks of books, each stamped with the symbol of an unfurled scroll.

"What is that?" Sylla asked, pointing to the marking.

"The Archival seal," Illias answered. "These books come from the Archives. I have only ever seen three other books with that seal."

"So the Scriber was right." She sounded disappointed.

Bryndine ran a finger over the spines of several books and read the titles off one by one. "*One Hundred Recipes*, *the Goose and the Gelding*, *a Woodworker's Guide*. This one says *Eldeis ce Ina*, I believe. The script is Elovian, I do not know all the letters."

"It means… something like 'Law of Coin'," I said, glancing at the book her finger rested on. "Taxation laws, perhaps." I was interested in that one, though it sounded dry—the Scribers had very little knowledge of Elovian laws.

"You speak Elovian, Scriber Dennon?" Wynne asked with a look of awe.

I shook my head. "Not truly. No one does. We have a book of Elovian nursery rhymes at the Academy—one of the three books left from the Archives. I taught myself what I could from it, but the vocabulary and grammar are limited. Most of the language is lost."

"These books will change that." Illias grabbed me in an enthusiastic embrace. "We've done it, Denn!"

I returned the embrace half-heartedly. There was something nagging at my thoughts, something that was not quite right. *These books… the titles Bryndine read… surely the Archives had more to offer than this?*

"This can't be the entire Archives, though," Sylla said, echoing my doubts. "There's not even a hundred books here."

"It might be all they could save," suggested Wynne.

"Why bring them beyond the walls and leave them, though?" I wondered aloud. "And those titles did not sound like the greatest knowledge history has to offer. This is a great find, no doubt, but…" I hesitated. The further I went with this pursuit, the harder it was to escape it. I was not certain I wanted to commit to another idea.

But it was impossible to resist; this was the work that I had loved since I was a boy. "There must be more," I said. "These chests must be what they were forced to leave behind—they would have taken the more important ones elsewhere." As I spoke, I flaked the last bit of wax from the silver scroll tube, and tipped it so that the rolled parchment within fell into my hand. With great care, I began to unroll it, though I needn't have worried—the case had been sealed well, and the paper remained surprisingly supple.

It was a page torn from a journal, written in a clear, strong hand. I looked at the date—early autumn, in the five hundredth year after the Burning. Five hundred years ago almost to the day. As I read on, a cold fist of fear closed around my heart.

Father is no longer himself. Adello suspects sorcery—he says he can hear the whispers of it in the air, and it drives him to distraction. The rebels have been known to use such Wyddin tricks. It is only since Father was wounded in battle with them that he has changed.

At first I hoped he was simply frustrated at the rebels' unpredictability; the way they attack out of nowhere and disappear just as suddenly. But he has become a stranger to me. He speaks like a madman, preaching against the evils of the written word, threatening to burn the Archives. And his fear spreads to the people. All this when he should be concentrating on stopping the rebel attacks. Instead, he lets them happen, and does nothing.

But only Adello believes me—even my brother will not listen. Oryn adores Father too much to see any flaw in him.

I need the Archives. If the knowledge to undo this spell exists, it will be there. I cannot let them be burned. My men have found a way under the city walls. We cannot save every book, but I intend to smuggle the most valuable of them to my manor in Ryndport.

Adello begs me to reconsider. He fears that opposing the King will be my death. My own fear is that if I do not, the rebels will burn the kingdom to the ground.

And then, scrawled in a hastier script below:

I am Prince Fyrril Errynson, and with this act I have openly rebelled against the King. Whoever reads this, if my men and I have failed, I beg of you—go to Ryndport. Find the books and finish what I started. I will leave what trail I can. And whatever they say of us, know that our motives were pure. We sought only to keep the Kingsland from destruction.

"What does it say?" Wynne tried to peek over my shoulder.

"Is it a message from Fyrril?" asked Illias.

"It's a page from his journal," I replied. "Dated 500 AB—the early years of the Forgetting." I handed the page to Illias.

He looked it over briefly. "The father he mentions is Ullyd, of course. And this brother, Oryn, interests me—I have always wondered who sat the throne after Ullyd, if not Fyrril. The rebels, though… we have no record of them, if they were not part of Fyrril's own rebellion."

"But they sound familiar, don't they?" My gut twisted with dread. Dread, and terrible certainty. "Mysterious rebels, unpredictable attacks, rumors of sorcery?" Silently, I added *strange voices* and *sudden madness* to the list, thinking of Uran Ord, of Josia and Hareld Kellen—and of myself.

"If not for the year, it could be describing the Burners." Bryndine frowned. "What are you suggesting, Scriber Dennon?"

It was so obvious, and yet so completely impossible. "Everything that is happening right now," I said, "has happened before."

CHAPTER NINETEEN

Is there something more to these voices, or are they only in my head? I need to know. I need to find Fyrril's research.

— From the personal journals of Dennon Lark

"Do you mean to say that the Burners have existed for five hundred years, Scriber?" King Syrid arched an eyebrow. "Nonsense. What have they been doing until now?"

Bryndine had insisted that we tell the King of what we had found immediately—Fyrril's message made our previously academic pursuit very relevant to the security of the kingdom. So it fell to me to explain myself to a King who still saw me as the man who had torn down the Old Garden, and a Royal Scriber who was all too happy to discredit anything that came out of my mouth. It was not a task I relished.

"I do not think that it is the same group, your Majesty," I said, trying to keep the impatience from my voice. "But the similarities must be more than coincidence. These rebels may have found some record of the ones Fyrril mentions. We know so little of their motives; perhaps that is because they have some information we lack. Some secret that allows them to move so quickly and strike so suddenly."

"Surely you do not believe these claims of sorcery, Lark?" Korus asked with a sneer.

"No," I answered, though it was not wholly true. If the voices I heard were some Wyddin magick that the Burnt had uncovered, it would explain a great deal that I desperately needed explained. "They clearly have some secret we do not understand, some trick these other rebels had first. We must see where this leads—it may be vital to stopping them. And besides that, it is our duty as Scribers. I believe you swore the same oath I did, Korus."

"Scriber Dennon is right," said Elarryd. "If it was only the books, the trip to Ryndport could wait until the danger has passed, but if there is a chance of learning more about the Burners, we must take it."

To my surprise, Korus nodded his head. "Their findings are… not insubstantial," he said grudgingly. "It is worth pursuing. But I would not leave it in Scriber Dennon's hands, Majesty."

At that, Illias stepped forward. "With due respect, your Majesty, that is not your decision. Korus forgets that the Scribers are not under the King's command. I am the Master of History, and I have charged Dennon with following Fyrril's trail while I see the books back to the Academy."

Illias had informed me earlier of his intention to return to the Academy. He had already sent a bird to Highpass to deliver the news and save his seat on the Council—there was at least a day left before the vote could be taken to remove him. When I asked him why he would abandon the search after putting so much effort into it, he had given a number of reasons: that his "old bones" were not ready for another hard ride; that the wagon back to Highpass would be much more comfortable; that someone needed to ensure the books were properly cared for. I suspected, though, that his chief motivation was to force me to take charge.

"I don't care in the slightest who leads this nonsense, Master Illias," Syrid said. "I do not share your confidence—five hundred year old books have nothing to teach us of the rebels. But if my councillors wish it, you have my blessing. I cannot spare an escort for you, however. We need every man to defend against the Burners."

"We need no soldiers, your Majesty." Illias gestured

towards Bryndine. “Your niece and her company have agreed to join Dennon.”

Syrid frowned. “Bryndine is no longer with the Army. She should not be acting as some… mercenary. It reflects poorly on the Errynson name.”

“Don’t be foolish, Syrid.” Elarryd spoke to his brother in a way few others would dare. “The Scriber needs some kind of escort. No one is going to notice, and if they do, we will say Bryn is going along to visit Prince Alyn.”

“It has been some time since I have seen my cousin, Majesty.” Bryndine’s face remained expressionless, but her voice had a hint of amusement in it.

“Fine, fine. It doesn’t matter.” The King threw up his hands. “Let us be done with this. I have more important things to consider.”

Bryndine and Illias turned to leave, but I stood my ground. I would get no better opportunity than this.

“One last thing, your Majesty. I have concerns about the High Commander.” I could no longer justify staying silent, not after reading Fyrril’s note. If there was even a chance that Ord had been somehow possessed or ensorcelled by the Burners, as ludicrous as it seemed, I had to say something.

The King gave a wry snort. “You are not the only one. What are these concerns, Scriber?”

His response was not entirely unexpected; I had hoped for something like it, given the annoyance he had shown his nephew during my last audience. “I fear he has returned to service too soon after his injury, your Majesty. If it is not too much of an intrusion, may I ask if you have noticed any strange behavior from him of late?”

“He has not been entirely himself,” Elarryd said.

“He has been acting like a fool, you mean,” the King growled. “The last useful plan he had was weeks ago, and your daughter ruined it.”

Bryndine bowed her head at the accusation, and I was tempted to defend her. Uran Ord’s “good idea” had been to use Waymark as bait for the Burners. But angering the King would not help me make my point.

“I fear that he is not fully recovered, your Majesty,” I said as sincerely as I was able. "A head wound is more than just a physical danger; there can be mental effects as well. Bed rest may be the best thing for him."

"Majesty, Uldon Ord will be furious if you remove his son," Korus warned. "As will your sister. They will take it as an insult." There was an actual political concern there, but I felt sure that his intention was more to contradict me than to advise the King.

"Am I to suffer an incompetent High Commander because I fear my sister?" Syrid drummed his fingers on the arm of his chair and looked at me thoughtfully. "I will take your advice under consideration, Scriber Dennon. Is that all?"

It was the best result I could have hoped for. With luck, the King would send Ord back to Highpass, and even if not, at least he had reason to keep his nephew from making any important decisions. It was in Syrid's hands now; there was nothing more I could say.

"It is, your Majesty." I bowed before the King, then followed the guards from the room.

* * *

"You will do fine without me, Denn," Illias said, patting my shoulder. "It was your ideas that took us this far, not mine."

The courtyard of Lord Elarryd's manor bustled with activity. Bryndine and her women busied themselves strapping supplies to the horses, making ready for the journey to Ryndport. Though they were no longer entitled to wear the tabards of the King's Army, it was strangely comforting to see the company back in their rough travelling clothes and boiled leather armor. A number of Scribers worked alongside them, hauling the heavy chests retrieved from the Underground into the wagon that waited in the street.

Word had come from the Academy the day before, commending Illias for his work—it made me smile, imagining the distaste on Master Hantarin's face as he put his name to that letter. With the Council's approval, every Scriber in Three Rivers was suddenly eager to lend a hand in getting the books to Highpass. Even Korus had come, if only for appearances.

He stood on his own, watching the work with a sour face and making no move to help.

"You don't need to keep saying that, Illias." I grinned at the old man. "I am not trying to get out of it this time." In truth, I was eager to get underway, though not because of any newfound confidence in my abilities—if there was something in Ryndport that might explain the voices I had been hearing, I needed to find it.

"I wish you would bring help, though. Bryndine and her women are capable, to be sure, but a few pinned Scribers…"

I shook my head. "I have Tenille, if I need her. Anyone else would only be trouble. I am still not popular, and I'll not spend the trip trying to keep a group of resentful Scribers under control." It was only half true. I was more worried that I might be seen having a fit, or reacting to invisible whispers. Until I could say for certain that it was not madness, I would not let another Scriber see me like that.

"If you insist, my boy. It is in your hands now."

"Illias… about the other day, at the Old Garden…" I did not want to raise the subject, but it might be the last time I saw him for weeks.

He raised a hand to stop me. "Don't apologize, Denn. I went too far."

"Even so, I'm sorry if I have ever… disappointed you."

"I am proud of you, my boy. Never doubt it." He gave my shoulder a comforting squeeze. "I just wish *you* would take some pride in your accomplishments from time to time."

"I'll be proud when my accomplishments outdo my failures," I said.

Illias rolled his eyes. "What other Scriber has discovered so much in recent memory? But be stubborn about it if you wish, my boy. I am just happy to see you working again."

Before I could reply, Branwyn Errynson approached us with an offering of hot tea. "I hope I'm not interrupting, Scribers. I thought you might like a drink."

Branwyn was a slight woman with light brown hair, blue eyes, and delicate features. It was hard to imagine that she had given birth to a giant like Bryndine; clearly her daughter had inherited more from Lord Elarryd's side.

"Thank you, Lady Branwyn." It was a bit strange to have the Lord Chancellor's wife waiting on us; she could just as easily have sent a servant. But I accepted a cup and took a sip, and Illias did the same.

"I wanted to speak with you before you left, Scriber Dennon," Branwyn said. "To thank you again for helping Bryndine. I was worried for her—she has never wanted anything but to serve in the Army."

"She was doing Illias a service by assisting him," I replied, uncomfortable with her gratitude. "I had little to do with it."

"It was your suggestion, Scriber," she insisted. "Bryndine told us what happened. She is never happy without a purpose to serve, and you gave her one when she needed it. I know she is grateful to you as well, though she might not show it freely."

It was pointless to argue; I didn't want the attention, but clearly I was helpless to stop it. "I am glad I could help, then."

"My husband wants you to know that if ever you require a favor from him, you need only to ask. He would have seen you off himself if he were not in council with the King."

"The Lord Chancellor is most generous," said Illias. "That is not an offer many men hear in their lives."

"I—I thank you, my Lady," I stammered. "And Lord Elarryd."

"You are most welcome, Scriber Dennon." Branwyn smiled at my obvious discomfort. "And don't look so nervous. You have nothing to fear here." With that, she left to speak with her daughter, who was overseeing the last of the preparations.

By the time we finished our tea, the horses were packed and ready. I said my final goodbyes to Illias while the women bid farewell to their own loved ones. Bryndine bent down to give her diminutive mother a peck on the cheek; Tenille embraced her two young boys and kissed her husband. Hylda's daughter clung tearfully to the silver-haired woman—the girl was quite pregnant, and did not want her mother to go.

When the goodbyes were done, we mounted our horses and followed Bryndine from the courtyard. But as we filed from the gates of the manor, I heard a clatter of hooves. Not from our company, but from the north, towards the Kingshome, and approaching rapidly. And with the hooves, there was a low whisper—the word "*Pain*" hissed in my head.

"Stop!" It was Uran Ord, galloping down the street to meet us. He was dressed for battle, his bandaged head covered by an open-faced helm, and his sword was drawn. As he neared, the voices grew louder.

Some two dozen men of the First Company followed him, and it took only moments for them to surround the gates of the Lord Chancellor's manor, blocking us in. I recognized a few of them from the journey out of Waymark; Lieutenant Ralsten was notably absent. While those within the courtyard rushed out to see the source of the commotion, I tried to sidle my mount back through the gates, away from the armed soldiers of the First Company.

"What is the meaning of this, Ord?" Illias demanded.

"I'll not let her leave! She hasn't the right!" Ord was a hurricane of fury and noise; at this distance the voices whirling around him were deafening. But it was not only him. It felt as though his men were part of it now, or some of them at least, and their presence amplified the cacophony. I wanted to block my ears, but I knew it would do no good.

Korus stepped through the gate, his hands raised in a calming gesture. "This is not seemly, High Commander. The King has already given his approval."

Ord levelled his sword at Korus. "And where were you then, Scriber? You allowed this to happen! They cannot be permitted to pursue this nonsense!" He jabbed his blade at the air to emphasize his point. I barely heard him; I could only hear the hundred voices behind his words, screaming, "*It must burn!*"

"What could I have said?" Korus was defensive now; he had never taken criticism well. "I don't like it, but they *found* something."

Bryndine nudged her horse forward. "Let us pass, cousin," she said. Her voice was hard as stone.

Ord replied with an enraged roar, kicking his mount into motion and cleaving his sword down at his cousin's unprotected head.

Bryndine's horse danced backwards and the blade whistled through empty air. Her hand flew to the hilt of her sword, and in a single, smooth motion, she pulled the heavy blade from its sheath.

Within an instant, every blade within thirty yards was bared. Bryndine's women hesitated, waited for orders; the men of the First gave no such pause. "*Death*," I heard the voices wail, and then the First Company attacked.

The ring of steel tolled through the air as the women were forced to defend themselves. Sylla spurred her mount forward to deflect a strike at her Captain's exposed back, and other men and women crossed blades in the periphery of my vision. But I could not tear my eyes from Bryndine and Uran Ord.

Ord charged forward again with a snarl, launching a deadly blow at Bryndine's neck; she struck it aside with an effortless sweep of her sword. But she did not strike back. Instead, she held her position and shouted, "Stop this, Uran!"

Without hesitation, Ord pressed the attack. Their blades met once, then again, each clash sending the High Commander reeling back from the strength of Bryndine's parry. With a frustrated grunt, he sliced sideways at her chest with all his might, but she leaned back just slightly, letting the blade pass by and sending him lurching sideways in his saddle. Bryndine advanced, smashing her sword down on his like a blacksmith hammering an anvil. The force ripped the weapon from Ord's hand and sent it crashing to the ground.

Ord thrust his hand out to the man beside him. "Your sword!" The soldier instantly reversed his blade, offering it to the High Commander hilt first.

"Surrender!" Bryndine commanded, looking at her cousin with disbelief. "This is madness!"

But I could hear the voices urging Ord on, screaming for blood and vengeance, and I knew he would not stop until she was dead.

Or he *would* not have stopped, except that at that moment, Korus yelled, "You're doing exactly what they want you to, Ord!"

To my surprise, that caught the High Commander's attention. He looked up at Korus, the anger on his face giving way to confusion. And when the High Commander hesitated, his men instantly pulled back. It did little to thin the tension; the women watched them like hawks, keeping their swords at the ready.

Korus rushed to explain. "Lark told the King that you're unfit to serve because of that head wound. You couldn't have chosen a better way to prove him right. If you have any interest in keeping your position, you need to stop this immediately."

Ord lowered his hand. The soldier beside him withdrew his sword, returning it to its sheath; the other men did the same. The voices descended into a low chant. For a moment, I dared hope that we might leave without bloodshed.

Then Ord laughed, and the sound of it sent ice through my veins. It was not the laughter of a sane man. "Fine then." He turned his eyes back to Bryndine. "Go. It doesn't matter. There is nothing you can do."

He took up his reins and led his horse away, his men following in silence.

"You were right, Lark," Korus grumbled, obviously unhappy to admit it. "I will tell the King. Ord needs to be dealt with."

Bryndine looked at the retreating column of men thoughtfully. "Something is certainly not right with him," she said. "He has never been unskilled with a sword. I should not have defeated him so easily."

Illias raised an eyebrow. "I think his actions are of more concern than his skill right now. It is lucky that you raised your concerns when you did, Denn."

I did not answer; I was barely listening. Ord's last words repeated endlessly in my mind as I watched him disappear down the street. Not the last words he had spoken to Bryndine—though those were chilling enough—but the ones that only I could hear:

"*All will burn.*"

CHAPTER TWENTY

I have never believed the legends of the Wyddin. Tree spirits who can possess the bodies of animals, jealous children of the Mother and the Father seeking vengeance against mankind. The source of magick. It always sounded like nonsense to me. There was no magick in Elovia, I was sure of that. The Sages could not harness the power of something that does not exist.

I may have been wrong.

— From the personal journals of Dennon Lark

For the first three days of the long ride down the Searoad towards Ryndport, I could not stop thinking of the whispered threat Uran Ord had left in his wake. Korus had promised that he would see the High Commander stripped of his rank, and I had no reason to disbelieve it, but still I worried. "There is nothing you can do," Ord had said to Bryndine. What had he meant by that?

Three days out of Three Rivers, I found out.

I heard the voices before we saw the men. For days, I had been hearing whispers whenever we passed one of the many fireleafs that grew in the hilly interior of the Three Rivers barony, and so I barely noticed the noise until Selvi and Elene galloped up alongside Bryndine to make their report. The twins were the fastest riders and the keenest eyes in the company, and

Bryndine often sent them afield to scout. One of the two—Selvi, I believe—said, "Men coming from behind, Captain. About thirty of them, looks like they're with the Army." Though they did not seem concerned, both women had their shortbows out and ready.

I looked back over my shoulder, squinting against the light—it was still early in the day, and the sun was bright in the eastern sky. Sure enough, I could see them: a group of riders, barely more than dots on the road now, but quickly gaining.

It was then that I realized the voices were growing louder.

Bryndine brought the company to a halt with a raised hand. "We will see what they want. They may have a message for us."

"*Fire*," the voices chanted. "*Vengeance. Death.*" They came not just from the approaching men, but from all directions, a murder of crows screeching inside my head. It was worse than Ord's interrupted assault at the manor; this was more like that night in Waymark, the night the voices had made me burn.

"*It must not be found*," they wailed. "*All will burn.*"

They were coming to kill us. I knew it instantly and without doubt. They wanted Fyrril's books to remain hidden, or to be destroyed, though I did not know why. Uran Ord had tried to stop us more than once, and had failed; now it had come to this.

"Don't stop," I begged Bryndine. "We need to get away from them."

She gave me a questioning look. "What do you mean, Scriber Dennon? The Army is no enemy of ours."

"*Please!* If you have ever trusted me at all, trust me now. Those men mean us harm!" The wailing in my head was too much to bear; I clapped my hands over my ears. I could barely keep from screaming. "It is not only them! They're all around us, they're coming, I can hear them!"

"What do you hear, Scriber?" Bryndine looked at me doubtfully as I gripped my head and peered frantically back at the soldiers.

They had cut the distance between us in half, and now I could see the brown of their uniforms. They rode in complete silence, yet the fury of the voices tore through me. They knew me now; I felt that unseen eye turning towards me once more, as it had in Waymark. *They only find me when I'm frightened,* some part of me realized, a strangely detached thought in the midst of my terror. But it did not help; if anything, it made me more afraid.

"*BURN.*"

I did scream then, as the flames devoured my skin.

"*Ride!*" I yelled at Bryndine, consumed by rage and pain. And for some reason, this time she listened.

I bent over in agony and felt myself toppling from my saddle, but Bryndine reached out and grabbed me by the collar. With impossible strength, she lifted me onto her horse one-handed. Clutching me to her chest, she grabbed the reins of my mount with her free hand.

"You heard him! We ride!" she shouted, spurring her mount forward and leading mine alongside.

I shook in Bryndine's grip, but she held me tightly, not letting me fall. Fire that only I could see ran over my limbs, melting the flesh from my bones, burning the hair from my head. But somehow, I fought through it enough to open my eyes.

As the company galloped away from the approaching men, the voices hissed in anger. We had discovered their ambush, but they were not yet thwarted. "*Kill,*" they said, and hundreds of men and women poured over the hills on either side of the road, sprinting towards us. If we had stopped and waited at the sight of the Army uniforms, we would have been crushed in that furious pincer. But we were nearly by them now. We were going to escape.

And then the earth began to shake.

The horses faltered on the quaking ground, but they were trained for combat, and their riders were skilled. The women mastered the frightened animals and rode on. But our pace slowed, and the rebels closed in from behind.

"*Burn. Burn. BURN.*" the voices cried, and lightning struck just behind us with an ear-splitting crash. This was the sorcery Fyrril had warned of; lightning and earthquakes, the Wyddin magicks I had so long dismissed as superstition.

I watched through agony and fire as Genna's horse reared

at the sound of thunder, throwing her from its back. The stocky woman rolled and came to her feet in a smooth motion, axe in hand; her mount was already gone, galloping into the hills. Several of the women made to stop, to go back for her despite the fact that it would destroy our small lead. But when Genna looked over her shoulder at us, there was a fury in her eyes I had seen only a few times before, and I knew what she meant to do.

"Go!" she shouted. And then she charged directly at the oncoming horde.

She closed the short distance in an instant, swinging her axe in a deadly arc. With a single sweep, she cut two of them down; she felled another with a vicious backhanded strike. As she cleaved through a half dozen rebels, I almost believed that she could stop them, that she could single-handedly hold back the entire horde. But the sheer number of them was too much. A moment later, the swarm pulled her down, and she disappeared from sight.

We did not stop; there was nothing we could do for her now.

Genna's doomed assault had delayed the Burnt just slightly, and I felt a moment of hope as I watched them fall behind. When I turned my eyes forward, that hope evaporated. Ahead of us, more rebels rushed from the hills, hundreds more, blocking the road completely. There was nowhere to go.

I heard a terrible shriek as my left eye burst from the heat of the flames; a moment later I realized it was my own voice. Clinging desperately to my senses through the pain, I craned my head around, looking for some way out, some respite from almost certain death. Two hundred yards north of the road, there was a fireleaf tree, its branches nearly bare save for a handful of red leaves. It was the last thing I saw. My other eye split open like an overripe fruit, spilling its innards down my cheek, and my vision went black.

But in that darkness, I saw an image from my dreams. "The fireleaf," I gasped to Bryndine. "Tell them you'll burn—"

Flame poured into my mouth, burning away my voice. I felt the soft flesh of my throat sear, heard the crackle as it blackened and split. I could not even scream as I lost consciousness.

* * *

When I awoke, the Burnt were gone.

Like the last time, there was no evidence of burning anywhere on my body. I felt no pain, and the eyes that had failed me could now see perfectly well. I glanced around to get my bearings.

The company clustered around the fireleaf tree I had seen before fainting. Dusk was falling, but most of the women held torches, and a small campfire burned a few feet from where I lay, casting a flickering orange light around the foot of the tree.

Wynne sat beside me, and when she saw that my eyes were open, she called out, "He's awake, Captain."

I groaned and sat up. "What happened?" I asked.

"I don't know, Scriber Dennon." Wynne's features creased with concern. "Are you all right?"

"Not particularly." Her eyes widened, and I clarified quickly, "But I'm not injured."

As Wynne fussed over me, Bryndine approached with Tenille and Sylla at her side, Deanyn following closely behind.

Deanyn gave me a small smile. "Well, you're alive. That's something."

"Genna," I said, remembering the woman's brave charge. "Is she…"

Bryndine bowed her head. "She is gone. We went back for her once the Burners left, but we found nothing, not even the men she killed. The rebels cover their tracks well."

"I'm sorry." I lowered my eyes. I had liked Genna, despite her shyness around me; she was a gentle soul. "But… why did they leave?"

"I hoped you could tell us, Scriber," replied Bryndine. "We did as you told—we threatened to burn this tree, and the Burners retreated. How did you know they would do that? *Why* would they do that?"

I hesitated to answer. They had seen the lightning and felt the ground shake, but would they believe me? Whatever I told them, it would not sound sane.

Wynne filled the silence with a guess of her own. "Could it be religious? Trees are holy to the Mother and Father."

Tenille shook her head. "The Book of the Divide says the plants were put here for us to use; they're holy, but not protected. But the rebels may be some sort of fanatics, I suppose."

"It's nothing like that." I climbed to my feet, leaning against the trunk of the tree for support. "Or rather, I wouldn't know if it was." I did not want to continue; they would think me mad. But I knew now that I was not. The danger was real, and I could not hide the truth from them any longer. "I… I hear voices. Voices no one else seems to hear. They call themselves the Burnt, not the Burners. I—"

"This is insanity." Sylla's voice cut through my stammered explanation. "The man is out of his mind."

"He's just had some sort of fit," Wynne said, crossing her arms and glaring at Sylla. "He's disoriented, that's all."

"And yet, he knew they were coming, and he knew how to escape them." Bryndine looked at me with searching eyes. "And we all saw the lightning, and felt the tremors. Fyrril's message said something about the whispers of sorcery. Scriber, are you suggesting…" She paused, clearly struggling with the idea. "Some sort of magick? Some Wyddin trick?"

"I cannot explain it any other way." I spread my hands. "I have heard the voices ever since Waymark. I don't know what it is, or how they do it. But surely you've noticed the strangeness about the rebels. They can't be caught. They appear without warning all over the Kingsland. They called lightning down on us, you all saw it; lightning struck in Waymark as well, out of a clear sky."

"There is some truth to that, Captain," said Tenille, though she did not seem comfortable admitting it. "I noticed strange things as well. In Waymark, they never spoke out loud, and some of them kept fighting when I was convinced I'd killed them. They barely even bled. I… thought it was just the heat of battle, or my imagination, but…"

Sylla crossed her arms. "I saw them bleed plenty."

"Not while they still fought," Tenille said with growing conviction. "Only after they died."

"But why did you not speak of this before, Scriber?"

Bryndine still did not look convinced, and she was not the only one—even Wynne, usually my greatest supporter, looked sceptical.

I narrowed my eyes in annoyance. "Would you have believed me? Look at their faces." I gestured at the other women. "They barely believe me now, after everything we just saw. I only just believe it myself, and only because I can't think of an alternative."

Bryndine nodded slowly. "You are right, I suppose. But what do the rebels want? Have you heard anything of importance in these whispers?"

I could only shake my head. "I know nothing about their motives. But they attacked because they do not want us to recover Fyrril's research, I am certain of that. I hope that if we find those books, it might explain some of this. I need to understand why I am hearing these voices, why they can make me have these… fits."

"What of the fireleaf?" Bryndine asked. "What significance does it have to them?"

"I honestly don't know. I had a dream, in Waymark. The Burnt surrounded a burning fireleaf tree, and they… did not seem pleased."

Bryndine raised an eyebrow. "A slim thing to hazard our lives on."

"Positively fat, I'd say, compared to the alternatives we had," Deanyn remarked.

Bryndine nodded without speaking, turning her eyes up towards the flame-colored foliage of the tree that towered over us.

After a moment, Wynne asked, "What about the rest of Fyrril's note, the spell on his father? Can they really control minds?"

"I can think of nothing else that would lead men of the King's Army to ride us down," I said.

"My cousin." There was no doubt in Bryndine's voice. "That is why he has been acting strangely, why he was so eager to be rid of me after Waymark. I might have recognized something was wrong, and told my father. You suspected this when you warned the King about him, didn't you Scriber?"

"Yes," I admitted. "And they likely made Josia Kellen attack you for the same reason—so that you could not expose Ord." I braced myself for her anger—she would not be pleased that I had hidden my suspicions about the High Commander.

But she only said, "You did well, then. Your warning and Uran's display when we left the city will surely see to his removal." There was a distant look in her eye; she was already thinking about what this new information meant, about our next step.

"*If* we are to believe this," Sylla said, "what do we do about it? I know how to fight against a sword, not… whatever this is."

Determination flashed in Bryndine's eyes. "We go on. If these Burnt seek to stop us, then they must fear what Fyrril knew. I do not understand how any of this can be, but our path is clear. We cannot waste this chance. We will send word of what we know to the King when we reach Ryndport."

"Shouldn't we turn back?" I asked. "They will come after us again as soon as we move. We're only safe as long as we have a fireleaf to threaten, we can't possibly make it to Ryndport."

She smiled slightly. "They cannot attack if they cannot find us. We will not go by the road."

CHAPTER TWENTY-ONE

The ride to Ryndport has thus far been the most harrowing experience of my life. I do not know if my sanity will survive the trip.

— From the personal journals of Dennon Lark

The next day, Bryndine led us north off the Searoad and into the hills. Perhaps ten leagues from the road, we cut back west towards Ryndport. We rode in the shallow valleys between hills, staying out of sight, sending Selvi and Elene out periodically to scout our surroundings from atop whatever rise was nearby. The twins often saw the Burnt searching for us; small bands roaming the countryside in the distance, or sometimes dangerously near. Even divided to cover the area, each group outnumbered us badly.

Small villages dotted the hillsides, but we saw none that were not burned or abandoned, a testament to the danger of the rebels who sought us. Any settlement too small to defend itself had been laid waste weeks before. We avoided even the ruins; it was tempting to take shelter in an abandoned building for a night, but too obvious. They would be looking for us there. There were fireleafs in the hills too, but we kept our distance from those as well. Bryndine suspected that the threat of burning would not work so well a second time, and if the Burnt thought we might try it again, they would be searching near the trees.

I could hear the whispers at all times. They sought me relentlessly, and they were never far off. It was a terrible sensation, being stalked by a hunter I could hear but not see. The voices had only ever noticed me in the past when I was terribly afraid, as I had been the day before, or the first night I heard them in Waymark, so I tried to distract myself from my fear by talking to the others. I shared jokes with Deanyn and spoke of history and philosophy with Wynne; sang with Nalla and let Varrie try to teach me to juggle; and whenever idleness threatened, I studied Adello's songs, looking for clues to the location of Fyrril's books. But through it all, I was always conscious of the whispers. I could not banish the creeping tide of unease; I could only try to keep from drowning in it.

In my dreams, I had no such defense.

The first night after we left the Searoad, when Deanyn shook me awake from a nightmare of fire and pain, I knew that the Burnt had found me, and that they were coming. It was sometime before midnight; no one had slept for more than a few hours. I had no choice but to wake them. We had to leave before the Burnt arrived.

"You are sure it was more than a normal dream?" Bryndine asked when I had explained myself.

"They know where we are. We need to go."

She sighed, but acquiesced. "You would know better than I, Scriber. We will move on."

From that night forth, the women took shifts watching over me at night and waking me every hour. If my dreams were of the Burnt, the company was roused and we rode on. And I dreamed of the Burnt more often than I did not.

After two days, I could barely stay awake in my saddle—and we were still at least ten days from Ryndport. The more tired I became, the more difficult it was to distract myself from my fears, and though I could not be sure, I strongly suspected that succumbing to terror would give away our position.

Several times, we were nearly caught. Selvi or Elene would rush down from a hilltop to report that the Burnt were approaching, and we would force the horses to run for all they were worth, though our mounts were no better rested than we were. We always put the rebels behind us; the Burnt were mostly on foot, and those with horses were not skilled riders. They could not match our speed as long as we kept moving.

Ten days after we left Three Rivers, we fell prey to the second ambush.

We had crossed the border into the Ryndport barony earlier that day, by my estimate, and it felt like a victory, like we had finally outrun the rebels. It made us complacent. I woke from a long, terrible dream of the Burnt to find Hylda asleep; it had been her turn to wake me. I did not know how long I had slept, but it was more than an hour, and already I could feel the voices screaming in my head, terribly near.

"Wake up! They're here!" In a state of near-panic, I roused the others, praying to the Mother and the Father that it was not too late.

They were light sleepers, Bryndine's women, trained to be on their feet at the first sound of danger, but still they were too slow. By the time the entire company was awake and mounted, the Burnt were nearly upon us. They marched between the nearby hills in two groups, each of at least two dozen rebels, flanking us from the north and south.

"Stay together, and do not stop for anything," Bryndine ordered. "Ride!"

We rode. Pushing the horses as hard as we could, we put some distance between us and the rebels, just enough that I dared to think we might escape.

But the Burnt were cleverer than I had thought. The hills to either side grew steeper as we rode; too steep for the horses to climb. They had driven us into a ravine. And then I saw the rest of them, some thirty strong, blocking the path forward while our pursuers rushed in from behind. It was the same trick they used on the road, but this time there was no way out, no fireleaf to threaten, just sheer bluffs on both sides.

"*All will burn*," the voices screeched, echoing the words they had spoken the day we left Three Rivers, the rage-filled warcry I had heard so many times.

"Do not stop!" Bryndine repeated her order. "Our only chance is to break through. Ride them down!" She kicked her horse forward and drew her sword.

For once, I was too distracted to be properly terrified. I am no great horseman; it took all my concentration to stay in my saddle as we surged forward. I kept to the middle of the group, counting on the women to protect me.

The company met the Burnt in a screeching crash of metal and hooves. The noise was terrible, and yet our foes were silent—only I could hear their voices screaming in rage.

The ground began to shake, and lightning struck no more than a foot away from me. My nostrils filled with the stink of burnt flesh and horsehair, and I watched Hylda's mount slump to the ground, as dead as the woman on its back. Hylda's daughter had been pregnant, I remembered. The baby would never know its grandmother.

I had no time to dwell on her death. Angry voices shrieked in my head, and the Burnt closed in from all sides.

The rebels could not match the women in skill—they relied entirely on their overwhelming numbers and their magick. But on foot against trained, mounted soldiers, those numbers were not enough, and their sorcery was as dangerous to them as to us in such close quarters. The furious charge of Bryndine's company scattered their front line like leaves in a storm. Debra trampled one down and beheaded another; Kaelyn followed in her wake, disembowelling a third man with casual grace. Tenille's sword rose and fell with steady precision, a counterpoint to the savage fury of Sylla's strikes. And at their head rode Bryndine Errynson on her huge warhorse, dwarfing all those around her—a colossus among ants. Every stroke of her giant blade ended in death.

But despite taking terrible injuries, many of the Burnt kept their feet, kept fighting; their wounds did not bleed. Just like in my dreams, just like Hareld Kellen. The grass beneath us was stained with red, but it did not come from the Burnt who still stood. Their blood spilled only after they finally fell, the consequence of some magick I could not understand.

Varrie cried out behind me and I looked back just in time to see her horse fall—a crack split the earth beneath them, catching the animal's hoof. The Burnt swarmed over the girl. She had just enough time to impale a man on her sword, and then I watched her die, her skull split by a rebel axe. Her body tumbled into the growing rift in the ground.

I urged my horse forward, trying to coax some last reserve of speed to outrun the chasm opening behind me. Deanyn and Orya rode hard to either side, guarding me against attack as we fled. With bone-crunching force, Orya kicked a lunging rebel full in the face, and Deanyn knocked a spear aside with her sword and sliced the attacker's throat with a single motion.

A hand grabbed my leg. Instinct made me kick downwards, but the grip was too tight; the hand did not come free. I looked down and saw one of the Burnt clinging to me, dragging against the ground as he tried to pull me from my mount. His face was blank—no malice, not even a hint of concern for his own safety. Terror pounded in my chest as I looked into those empty eyes.

My horse slowed at the extra weight, and I clutched tightly to her neck as my saddle slipped sideways beneath me. My concentration broke, and the fear surged beyond my control. The voices wailed like damned souls in my mind, and I knew that at any moment I would hear that undeniable command—"*BURN*".

Instead, I heard Orya shout, "Watch your leg, Scriber!"

A flash of metal, and the man fell away. Only his hand remained, still clutching at me for an instant before its fingers relaxed and it dropped to the ground.

My eyes followed Orya's sword upwards, and she laughed her wild, half-mad laugh at the fear on my face. "No time to wet yourself. Keep ridin'!" She pointed ahead.

The path was laid bare before us. Bryndine and the others had cleared the way.

Laughing with relief, I galloped out of the ravine and onto a low plain. The Burnt still followed, and the voices still pounded in my skull, making my head ache, but they would never catch us on foot, not across open ground. Whatever sorcery they had was failing, weakened by the bloody swath Bryndine and her women had trampled through their ranks. As we broadened the distance between us and them, the lightning ceased, and the ground went still. In moments, the rebels were mere specks dwindling on the horizon.

That was the last time the Burnt came so close, and

though the cost was high, it was not as high as it might have been. We lost only three: Hylda and Varrie I had seen fall, and Nalla died later that night of her wounds. Leste had been stabbed in the thigh and Ivyla took a deep cut to her side, but neither required much more than cleaning and stitching; others had minor injuries, nothing of great concern.

There was no time to mourn the dead. They, like Genna, would have to wait until we reached safety to be remembered as they deserved.

It was another week before we reached Ryndport, a week of painful dreams, little sleep, and constant, searching voices. The Burnt did not catch us again, but the fear was always there; we could never rest easily. The only way to avoid another attack was to keep moving.

But as we approached the sea, the voices grew fainter. There were few fireleafs near the coast, and just like in the foothills of the Salt Mountains, that seemed to mean fewer of the Burnt. For the last two days, I did not dream at all of the burning fireleaf, or the naked men and women who did not bleed. Someone still woke me every hour, but I was always able to return to sleep.

Shortly before sunset on the last day, when we crested a hill and saw the sea spread out before us, glittering blue-green until it met the sky, I nearly wept. After more than two weeks of terror and torture, with our horses nearly dying beneath us, we had arrived in Ryndport.

CHAPTER TWENTY-TWO

Founded by Prince Rynd the Explorer, Ryndport is the Kingsland's main port of trade with the Southern Isles and the Raen Empire. The shipping merchants who live there are the wealthiest citizens in the Kingsland. In Rynd's honor, it is customary for the King's eldest son to oversee Ryndport in place of a Baron, from the time he comes of age until he ascends to the throne.

It is also the Kingsland's most diverse city—the realm is peopled by citizens of many cultures, from Salt Mountainers to the dark-skinned men and women of Raen and the Isles, but Ryndport is the main point of access for most foreigners, and the city where most remain after arriving. Like the rest of the Kingsland, the main population of the city is descended from the barbarians who followed King Erryn, but in Ryndport, one in three people hail from other lands, or have ancestors who did.

— From Dennon Lark's *Cities of the Kingsland*

We entered Ryndport ragged, tired, and bloody, a sorry sight amid the rich markets of the coastal city. Bryndine wasted no time ordering the guardsmen to escort us to her cousin, and we were led through crowded streets towards the Prince's estate.

Unlike Three Rivers, there was no chaos to Ryndport's design—it was not the largest city in the Kingsland, but it was by far the wealthiest, and the merchants who lived there put a great deal of coin into its beautification. Each home was larger and more ornate than the one before it, and the broad, straight roads were paved with polished white stone and lined with exotic plants brought by ship from the Southern Isles. There was a poorer element, I knew, the sailors and workers necessary to keep such a town running, but they were as well hidden as the money of their wealthy employers allowed.

The Prince's manor sat atop a hill on the southern side of the city, looking down over the markets. Despite its elevated position, it was not nearly the grandest home in Ryndport—Erryn's Promise meant that the shipping merchants who did most of the trading also kept most of the coin. But it was grand all the same, a three-floored building of sand-colored stone on well-kept grassy grounds, shaded by the strange broad-leafed trees of the Southern Isles.

Prince Alyn came rushing out to meet us as we rode through the gates. A huge, broad-shouldered man of more than seven feet, he was the largest of the Errynsons I had yet seen—save for Bryndine, who still stood a half-foot taller. Shaggy blond hair framed his face, and beneath his bright blue eyes he wore a wide smile.

"Bryn!" he bellowed, practically pulling his cousin from her horse and crushing her in an enthusiastic embrace.

"Hello, Alyn," Bryndine said with weary amusement.

"I swear by the Divide, woman, you're taller every time I see you." Releasing her, the Prince stepped back and looked her over with concern. "But you look awful. What happened? We expected you days ago."

"The rebels forced us to take a… different route." Bryndine outlined the terrible ordeal, including the voices, the strange sorcery, and my suspicions about Uran Ord.

Alyn's large frame tensed as she spoke, and when she was done, he asked, "Are they still pursuing you? Do I need to prepare for an assault?"

Bryndine paused to consider before answering. "They have not yet risked attacking such a well defended city. But it would be wise to station more guards and alert the Ryndport Brigade."

"I will. And I'm sorry, Bryn. I can't imagine what you've

been through." The Prince squeezed his cousin's shoulder. "If I'd only known, I would have sent men after you."

"There is nothing you could have done," Bryndine said. "We were not on the road; your men would not have found us."

"Still, I can't help but think I should have done something when you were late arriving. It must have been horrible. But…" He paused, a slight hint of disbelief marring the concern on his face. "Magick, Bryn? You've had a hard journey, I know, but you must see how foolish that sounds. Magick is for children's tales about the Wyddin. There must be some other explanation. Sorcery is hardly necessary to make our cousin act like an idiot."

"We saw what we saw, Alyn," Bryndine replied. "And I trust Scriber Dennon about the rest." I was absurdly grateful for that; the fear that I was simply insane had never left me, even after everything we had seen. "But you need not believe everything," she continued, "so long as you believe that we need to find those books."

The Prince nodded his head in affirmation. "Of course. You'll have any help I can give you. You know that. I had a bird from the Academy several days ago requesting my aid."

That caught my attention. "The Academy? Did they mention… is Illias safe?"

"He arrived there more than a week ago, with the books you found."

I had feared for Illias ever since we were attacked, though it had been eclipsed by the other concerns of the journey. The books from Three Rivers were of little importance to the Burnt, but I had not been certain that *they* knew that. It was good to know that he had not been waylaid.

"So, what do you need from me?" Alyn asked. "Anything in my power is yours."

"We have had a difficult journey," Bryndine replied. "You and I can speak more later, but now I must send a bird to Three Rivers, to warn the King about Uran and the Burnt. After that, we will need a place to rest."

"Ah. About that…" Embarrassment painted the Prince's features. "Sending the message is easy enough, but I've called all my companies to active duty, so the barracks are crowded. The rebels are scarce near the coast, but the inland villages need my protection."

Bryndine understood immediately. "You've no room for us."

"You will stay with me, of course, but your women…"

"We can stay with my father," Deanyn volunteered. "He has more than enough space."

I caught her eye and raised an eyebrow; she had never mentioned her family to me. She saw me looking, and raised her shoulders in an unapologetic shrug.

"Then I only have one other request," said Bryndine. I could hear the sorrow in her voice, though it did not show on her face. "I would have a service for those we lost, if there is a Garden that will have us."

The Prince, as it happened, had a private Garden on his estate, and after Bryndine composed her message to King Syrid, we were escorted there. It was almost a miniature replica of the Old Garden—a large anteroom provided entry, set into a wall that separated the Garden from the rest of the grounds. Despite their clear disapproval of Bryndine's company, the Children there performed their duties with solemn dignity. The Brother and Sister performing the rite commended the women to the Mother, of course, as was proper, but I know I was not alone in asking the Father to accept their souls instead—the first time I had prayed sincerely in years.

When the service was done, the Children left us alone in the Garden. As when Janelyn had died, the women stood vigil silently in the light of the setting sun, and I stood with them.

I do not know what the others were thinking in that silence, but my own thoughts were wracked with guilt. *Genna, Hylda, Varrie and Nalla*—I etched their names in my mind beside Janelyn's, and those of the nine men who had died at the old Garden. They would still be alive in Three Rivers if I had not needed an escort. Now they were just four more names on the list of people I had led to their deaths.

* * *

It was well into evening by the time we were ready to leave

the Garden. As the company filed out, Bryndine tapped me on the shoulder and gestured for me to hold back.

She motioned the others onward. "Tenille, you have command for the moment. Go prepare your horses—make sure they are fit to ride. The journey was hard on them. I must speak with the Scriber."

Tenille led the women away towards the stables, leaving Bryndine and I alone in the Garden's antechamber. In the darkness of the evening, the room had an eerie feel to it. Stone reliefs of the Mother and the Father watched us from the walls, their features cast into shadow by the dim yellow light of the lanterns.

"I have something I need to ask you, Scriber. I have waited until now because we had other more pressing concerns, but I need to know."

"What is it?" I asked impatiently. I did not want to talk; after two weeks of riding with almost no rest, I just wanted to collapse into bed and sleep for a week.

"The woman from your village who died. Josia. Whatever it was that happened to her after she attacked me, it looked very much like what happened to you on the road."

"It was… similar. What of it?" I knew what she was asking, but I did not want to think about it.

"Will these voices drive you mad as they did her? Can I trust you? And… will they kill you, in the end?"

All questions I had asked myself thousands of times. "I don't know," I answered. "But they haven't yet. I am still sane, as far as I know, and very much alive."

She stared at me intently, judging the truth of my words. "Josia said that she attacked me to stop the voices from burning her. It has not occurred to you to seek relief the same way?"

"Of course," I said with blatant sarcasm. "It worked so well for her."

She appeared to accept that. "A fair point."

"Is that all, then?"

"Not yet. I would have you tell me what you know of the Wyddin. My cousin's reaction today was not far from my own—it seems absurd. The Wyddin are creatures of legend."

I sighed with exaggerated irritation, rubbing at my temple.

"And then I can sleep?"

"Yes."

"Fine, but I know little more than anyone—it's all myth." I leaned against the wall as I explained; the effort of standing was becoming exhausting. "The Book of the Divide tells us that the Wyddin were created before mankind, the second of the Mother and the Father's attempts to make satisfactory children. People say they hate humans for replacing them in the Gods' affections, but the Book says little about that.

"Supposedly they have some power over Earth and Sky. There are stories of them possessing animals when they need to, but otherwise they have no physical form of their own—they live as spirits inhabiting the plants and trees. If the Burnt really have uncovered some sort of Wyddin related magicks, that may be why the fireleafs are important to them, I suppose."

"Little that I have not already heard." She sounded disappointed. "The stories of men using Wyddin sorcery come from Elovia, yes?"

"The Elovian Sages were said to be masters of such things," I confirmed. "Legend says they could control the Wyddin and channel their power for the aid of the kingdom. But they eventually lost control, and the Wyddin destroyed Elovia in vengeance. I always assumed that was a fable. That some natural disaster destroyed the kingdom and they blamed the Wyddin afterwards."

"But perhaps it was true," Bryndine mused. "It would explain much of what we saw, though I can hardly believe it. And if the Wyddin are real, what other legends might be true?"

"None, necessarily." My Scriber's instincts came to the fore, trying to put logic to the impossible. "Even the Wyddin may not be real. We only know that these powers exist, not their source. Perhaps they are simply some science we have lost, turned into sorcery by time and faulty memory. I hope that the books Fyrril saved from the Archives have more to say about it."

"If not, we have paid a high cost for them," she said, her eyes darting briefly back to the Garden, where her women had been given their last rites. "Now that we are here, have you any idea where to begin looking?"

I shook my head. "Not yet. I may need help with that. I have looked at the songs, but if Fyrril has marked his trail with an existing landmark, like he did with the Old Garden… I am not familiar with the locations of such things in Ryndport."

"Deanyn and Leste hail from here. They can aid you with that."

"I will ask them. Tomorrow." I emphasized the last word pointedly.

Bryndine did not miss my implication. "I apologize, Scriber Dennon. I have kept you too long." She waved a hand towards the door. "Go, join the others. Deanyn will take you to her father's estate."

I turned to leave, but she made no move to follow. "Are you staying?" I asked.

"For a while longer." She kept her face blank, but I was beginning to understand Bryndine Errynson. She would stay in the Garden alone long after I left. She was not yet done saying goodbye.

CHAPTER TWENTY-THREE

Rynd Errynson is one of the few figures from before the Forgetting whose life is still well chronicled. Often called the Explorer, Prince Rynd founded the city of Ryndport when he was still a young man. He forged west beyond the borders of the Kingsland where the First Forest still grew until he and his men found the coast, and like his ancestor before him, he burned back the trees to create a new settlement.

He led expeditions across the Dragon's Sea, and became the first man of the Kingsland to set foot in the Southern Isles and the Raen Empire to the far west. Monuments and statues in Ryndport proclaim his many achievements, and the kingdoms he opened trade with still remember his name. Though he ruled as King for many years, he is nearly always remembered as Prince Rynd, for his accomplishments before taking the throne.

— From Dennon Lark's *Rynd the Explorer*

"You are Deanyn *Syvanson?* You might have said something!"

I gaped at Deanyn with absolute bewilderment. The Syvansons were far and away the wealthiest family in the Kingsland. Randyn Syvanson owned most of the shipping fleet that did trade with the Raen Empire; his fortune was beyond reckoning. And Deanyn had just told me that she was his daughter.

Deanyn laughed. “If I’d said something, I’d have missed the look on your face. I stand by my choice.”

“Knocked me on my ass when I found out too, Scriber,” Orya said, slapping me on the back. “Girl drinks like a sailor, fights like a street rat, and I’ve heard her say a thing or two, made even me blush. Wouldn’t think she comes from money.”

“But… But… Why?” I stammered. “Why trudge around with the Army when you have…” I gestured towards the estate that loomed before us. “All this?”

Calling the Syvanson’s home an estate was like calling Three Rivers a village. Prince Alyn had an estate; the Syvansons had almost a town of their own. In addition to the absolutely enormous main house—with six floors and four separate wings, it dwarfed every other structure in Ryndport—there were ten other buildings on the sprawling property. I could not imagine the purpose of even half of them.

“As I’ve said before: Why not?” Deanyn shrugged.

“I thought you were being amusing!”

“I was,” she replied. “That doesn’t mean it wasn’t true. Do you know how boring it is sitting in a manor all day, going to some formal affair every night where all they talk about is trade agreements and shipping routes? I prefer excitement, and following Bryndine was as good a way as any to find it.”

“Surely your parents don’t approve. Will they even let us stay?”

“They… care very little about what I do.” Some emotion flashed across Deanyn’s face, but it was gone before I could identify it. “Embarrassment is not really an issue when you have as much money as my father does. I wouldn’t have brought us here if I thought they would turn us away.”

“As amusing as it is to watch Dennon’s eyes bulge,” Tenille broke in, “could you two continue this inside? I’m nearly asleep on my feet, and I doubt I’m the only one.”

Chastened, I held my tongue as Deanyn cantered her mount towards the gates. Two men stood guard. She addressed them by name. “Harrick, Bryndon. Open the gates, will you? I bring illustrious guests to meet my parents.” She gestured towards the company, all of us filthy and haggard from our long journey.

"Right away, Mistress Deanyn," one of them—Harrick—answered, lifting an iron key from around his neck and fitting it into the gate.

"Who shall we say is coming?" Bryndon peered uncertainly at our less-than-impressive group. "Your father will want to know."

"I'll tell him myself. We wouldn't want you two to leave your posts." Deanyn looked over her shoulder and motioned for us to follow. "Come on, then."

She led us through the gate and across the vast grounds towards the main house. Another pair of guards waited at the door. When Deanyn dismounted and approached, they recognized her and sent for her mother, who arrived shortly thereafter with a retinue of servants following behind.

"Deanyn. We didn't expect you." Deanna Syvanson did not sound particularly surprised or pleased to see her daughter; she was simply stating a fact.

"And yet here I am." Deanyn embraced her mother somewhat stiffly. "We need a place to stay. My friends and I have had a difficult trip."

"Of course. I will have rooms made up." She glanced past her daughter at the rest of us, her mouth pursing with mild distaste. "And baths." With a wordless flick of her hand, she directed several men to see to our horses, then beckoned us through the door.

Despite our tattered state, she had little interest in what had happened to us, or to Deanyn, though she was polite in her apathy. After arranging for servants to show us to our rooms and tend our needs, she excused herself, leaving Deanyn with a cold peck on the cheek.

"Tell my husband that our daughter is here," she ordered one of the servants as she left the room.

A few moments later, Deanyn's father appeared at the top of the stairs. He greeted his daughter with a slight nod. "Deanyn," he said. "It is good to have you home. The estate is at your disposal." Then, he disappeared back the way he had come. I could hardly believe the disinterest he and his wife showed in their daughter's well-being.

Deanyn saw the confusion on my face. "It's not as strange

as it seems," she said, answering the question I hadn't asked. "When you can have anything you want, nothing has much value."

I had no response to that, but I felt I should do something—in an awkward attempt at comfort, I hesitantly laid a hand on her shoulder. Surprise crossed her face for a moment, before it was replaced by a small, appreciative smile.

We stood in silence for a moment, and then she said, "You look exhausted, Dennon. Go, sleep. I'll see you in the morning."

She gave me a gentle shove towards one of the waiting servants, and I let the woman lead me away to my room.

* * *

I slept late the next day, but not as late as I would have liked. Perhaps an hour before noon, there was a knock at my door.

The sound pulled me from my sleep—the first dreamless night I had been blessed with in weeks. As I regained my senses, I found myself lying face down on a soft feather bed, a line of spittle dribbling from the corner of my mouth onto the goose-down pillow that cushioned my head. I had barely noticed the bedding the night before, as tired as I was, but now it seemed far too comfortable to leave.

"What is it?" I yelled in the general direction of the door.

A man's voice answered, "The Lady Bryndine Errynson to see you, sir."

Grumbling, I rolled from the bed and dressed myself. There was little point in delaying; Bryndine would not leave me be, not while there was work to be done. After a moment of debate, I retrieved Adello's songs from my bag. She would want me to determine where we should search; it was likely why she had summoned me. I was just as eager to find the books as she was, but even so my body was reluctant to cooperate—it took all my self control not to crawl back into bed. My respect for Bryndine had grown over the last few weeks, but I cursed her and her Dragon-damned sense of duty for not letting me sleep another hour.

When I was ready, the man who had woken me led me downstairs to a dining chamber where Bryndine sat with several other women, enjoying a breakfast of bacon and eggs, buttered bread, and a brightly colored drink that I assumed to be orange-fruit juice from the Southern Isles. Deanyn and Leste were there, presumably to act as our guides to Ryndport; Tenille, Wynne, and Sylla filled the other chairs. They talked among themselves in subdued voices, and no one smiled—it was difficult to enjoy even the lavishness of the Syvanson's hospitality while mourning lost friends.

"Scriber Dennon." Bryndine gestured to a seat beside her. "Join us. I took the liberty of gathering those I thought might be of use to you—we will discuss our plans while we eat."

I placed the stack of songs on the table and sampled a strip of bacon as I seated myself. "I would work better with a few hours more sleep," I said as I chewed.

"We cannot afford to dally," Bryndine replied. "Alyn's watchmen reported sightings of the Burnt early this morning. Few men, and never there long enough to apprehend, but we know they can congregate quickly. I fear our presence is drawing them here, and I do not want to put the city at risk longer than necessary."

I nearly choked mid-swallow. "If they are waiting for us outside the walls, how will we leave? They'll attack the moment we exit the gate."

If Bryndine shared my fear, she did not show it. "That is a concern for after we have found the books. But the less time we give them to gather themselves, the better."

Composing myself as best I could, I replied, "Let's not delay, then."

Taking the top few sheets from the pile of music, I handed them to Bryndine, who looked them over and passed them along.

"I have been looking at the songs," I said, "and there are some phrases that stand out. Here, *The Sage's Curse* says '*To the Dragon he was bound; his sins left him on hollow ground*'. The idea of 'hollow ground' beneath the damned is common in these songs, threatening to give way and drop them into the Dragon's realm. It could refer to a cavern of some sort, a hiding place."

"There are many caves in the sea cliffs," Leste said in her slight Raenish accent. "But these all flood with the tides."

I acknowledged her with a nod. "I had already thought of that. They wouldn't serve to hide the books. But the key may be the Prince himself, standing upon hollow ground—perhaps the books are hidden beneath a statue or some other image."

"There are no statues of Prince Fyrril," Tenille objected.

Wynne looked down at the sheet of music, pursing her lips. "It doesn't have to be Fyrril, does it? Even if it is about him, the song never mentions the Prince by name. That could be on purpose."

"A good point. It could mean any image of any Prince," I agreed.

"That makes things harder," Deanyn said. "If you counted all the statues of Rynd in the city, they might outnumber the citizens."

"It should be on the edge of the 'Dragon's realm'—the sea." I looked at Leste and Deanyn as I spoke. "Does anything come to mind?"

"There are at least a dozen statues by the seaside." Deanyn frowned, absently pushing her food around with her fork. "I don't know."

"The largest one, I am thinking of," said Leste. "On the cliff north from the docks. It is the first thing seen, sailing into the bay."

"On the cliffs—over top of the caves. That would put it on hollow ground." I realized I was grinning, caught up in the pleasure of solving a mystery. "We need to look at that statue."

Bryndine stood from her chair. "Then we should go right away. Tenille, send Ivyla to notify my cousin." She strode purposefully from the room and the other women followed. Grabbing a heel of bread and a handful of bacon from the table, I hurried after them.

We set out immediately. Leste was an efficient guide, and she knew the streets of Ryndport well; less than a half-hour later we stood before a huge statue of Prince Rynd on the cliffs overlooking the bay. Shortly after we arrived, Prince Alyn joined us, leading several men up the cliffside path.

"I doubt you'll find much, Scriber," Prince Alyn said as he

dismounted, gesturing towards the statue. "The old boy's been there forever, but he's nothing special. But whatever you need, my men are yours."

The statue was carved from dark granite and stood some forty feet tall, though five feet of that was the base—a solid block of heavy stone perched precariously close to the edge of the precipice. I stayed several steps back; the sheer weight of the thing looked as though it could collapse the well-eroded sea cliff beneath it at any moment, and it was a long fall to the sharp rocks below.

"What do you make of it, Scriber Dennon?" Wynne asked, peering dubiously at the stone Prince.

I pulled my gaze back from the cliff's edge to study the statue. It was little more than a roughly sculpted chunk of stone. The Prince's face and clothing were only scantly detailed, intended to suggest a form from afar to sailors entering the bay, not to be viewed up close. He faced away from us, gazing out into the empty harbor—there was little for Rynd to watch over at this time of year, when autumn storms interfered with shipping routes and kept most ships docked for the season.

"Not the most inspiring work, is it?" I observed. "I hoped it might indicate a direction like the glasswork at the Old Garden, but unless Fyrril hid his books at sea…"

"There's a plaque on the side," said Tenille, leaning in to read the words engraved upon the sheet of bronze set into the statue's base. "*Rynd the Explorer. Founder of Ryndport, discoverer of the lands beyond the sea. Let our ambitions sail beyond the shores of the familiar, towards the lands of the impossible.*" She frowned. "A fine sentiment, but not much use to us."

"You're sure the books couldn't be in the caves? There are plenty down there." Deanyn bent over the edge of the cliff, looking down at the cave-riddled rock below. Just watching her made my stomach clench and my head spin.

Swallowing my nausea, I replied, "They are too damp even when they aren't flooded. If the books were stored there, they would be long since decayed."

"Well, maybe Prince Fyrril wasn't the sharpest fellow," Deanyn said. "There aren't many other hiding places around here."

I shook my head. "The caves have been searched thoroughly more than once," I said. "The Scribers have spent centuries looking for relics of the past. Whatever we are looking for, it won't be so obvious."

Bryndine tapped a knuckle against the large stone base of the statue. "The ground he stands on is supposed to be hollow—perhaps there is something hidden in the base?"

"It's solid stone, though." Wynne circled the huge granite block, looking for a point of access. "How would we get in? Do we break it?"

The thought of wrecking another monument that had stood for so long made me cringe. "Check the plaque," I suggested, hoping Fyrril had left us an alternative to breaking our way in.

Wynne pulled a knife from her belt and rapped the pommel against the bronze plate. To my great relief, a low ring answered—there was definitely a hollow of some kind beneath the metal. Excitement shot through me, and I rushed forward to join the women by the cliff's edge, my fears briefly forgotten.

"It will come off." Leste drew a knife of her own and set it against the edge of the metal square.

I grabbed her by the wrist. "Wait. You'll only damage your knife, and scrape the statue. We'll need tools."

"It won't be a problem, Scriber," Alyn said. "I will send for a mason."

It was a half hour before the Prince's men returned with the craftsman in tow. In the end, his method was not much gentler than Leste's: he pried the metal back with his chisel, pulling the metal posts from the plaster that anchored them. But he assured me the plaque could be easily reattached with no serious damage.

Another quarter hour passed waiting for the man to finish, but finally he pulled the plaque free of the stone, revealing an opening of perhaps half a foot across. Impatience and enthusiasm getting the better of me, I lunged past the others to get a closer look.

The hole was empty.

"Well," said Deanyn, "that's disappointing."

CHAPTER TWENTY-FOUR

In the Book of the Divide, the Dragon is the God of the Sea, the first child of the Mother and the Father. He is unpredictable, like the sea itself, and a collector of discarded things—such as the souls of the damned. Those souls he takes are doomed to sink forever beneath the waves, tortured by horrible beasts created by the Dragon on a mercurial whim and then forgotten.

The clans of the Salt Mountains take a different view. During the autumn and winter, they come down from the heights to the coastal cliffs and survive off the sea. As such, they have come to revere the Dragon as the first among the Gods, claiming he created all others. He is said to have frozen the waves in a storm, creating the Salt Mountains as a home for his people.

That two countries developing so near to one another could produce such different beliefs from the same basic tale shows how greatly the environment and location of a civilization can shape its religion.

— From Dennon Lark's *Religions of Cendonia*

"We cannot go back! We haven't found anything!"

My protests did little to diminish Bryndine's resolve. "What can we hope to find?" she asked. "There is no trail left to follow. We must return to Three Rivers and tell the King what we have learned of the Burnt."

We had spent the rest of the day examining statues by the

docks, but it was half-hearted. It was clear to everyone that the empty recess beneath the statue on the cliffs should have held some clue. Whatever had been hidden there had been removed at some point over the last five centuries; there was nothing left for us to find. Depressed and defeated, we had returned to the Syvanson manor as evening fell to dine with the rest of the women and discuss our options.

The meal was lavish—too many courses to name, but the main dish was a delectable spiced fish served with fine Raenish wine, and afterwards, more sweets and pastries than all of us put together could finish in a lifetime. Propriety demanded such a showing, as Prince Alyn had chosen to dine with us. Deanyn's parents had little choice but to deliver a feast fit for royalty. The Syvansons joined us at the table as well, though they were as unimpressed as ever by our discussion.

"You have already sent a bird to the King," I said to Bryndine through a mouthful of fruit-filled tart. "There must be some clue left for us. Whatever was beneath that statue could still be somewhere in the city." I would not so easily desert the search—and not only for fear of the Burnt waiting for us outside the walls. I was determined to know the truth about the voices, and Fyrril's research was my best chance.

"My father is not like to believe claims of Wyddin and sorcery even if you delivered them in person, Scriber Dennon," Alyn said. "Bryn's message will probably be dismissed outright, I'm afraid."

"*Anything* we say will be dismissed outright unless we bring some sort of proof," I insisted. "We must keep looking."

"Where should we look, Scriber?" Sylla jabbed her fork in my direction and I flinched, almost expecting her to throw it. "Admit it: you were wrong, there was nothing there. That's the end of it. You've wasted enough of the Captain's time."

The woman terrified me, but I was sick of her taunts. "You realize that the moment we are done with this search, you'll be disbanded again? The Scribers are only paying you to help me." I aimed to wound, and I knew that staying with Bryndine was important to Sylla—I remembered as much from my hazy memory of that night outside the Doused Tree.

"Better that than dying for a madman. Don't pretend

you're our savior, Scriber. Women are dead because of you." She glared at me with murder in her dark eyes—and she was no stranger to murder. I remembered that too, and wished I had held my tongue.

"Enough." Bryndine's stern voice interrupted our quarrel. "Scriber Dennon, if you have some idea of how to salvage the search, let me hear it. Otherwise, we have no choice but to return."

"Just let me think for a moment," I said, pushing two fingers against my temple. "I haven't had time to think."

"He has no answer," Sylla said, sneering in my direction. "He's only trying to delay the decision."

"Shut up, Sylla!" Wynne's chair clattered backwards as she stood and slapped her hands down on the table. "Why can't you just give him a moment?"

Wynne's anger was the spark; exhaustion, grief, and disappointment were the tinder. The table erupted in a blaze of dissenting opinions and recrimination.

"This was a mistake," said Rylene. "We're useless here—we should be in Three Rivers." Her declaration elicited several nods of support.

Orya's lips curled up in disgust. "So we could sit cowerin' in city walls? We ain't with the Army no more, you think they'd let us fight? Scribers offered us coin and work, not takin' it would've been the mistake."

"But no one would have died," Selvi said in a small voice. She exchanged concerned glances with Elene. I could not blame the girl for speaking out—she was only thinking of her sister's safety.

Deanyn looked at the twins with a raised eyebrow. "Do you mean to tell me that our work is dangerous? If only I'd known, I might have taken up needlework."

It went on like that for some time. Some women wanted to return to Three Rivers; others simply wanted to stay together as long as they could. A small few—mostly Wynne and Tenille—argued for the importance of finding Fyrril's books, regardless of the risk.

But from some at the table, there was only silence. Bryndine watched the argument unfold with an unreadable expression. Prince Alyn fidgeted uncomfortably in his chair. Randyn and Deanna Syvanson looked as though they might fall asleep at any moment. And I stayed silent as well, trying to think of something, anything, that would justify continuing the search. Something that would prove I had not led those women to death for nothing. Something that would keep them from marching right back into the Burnt's grasp.

Ironically enough, it was Sylla who gave me the answer, for a second time.

"We can't keep listening to the Scriber," she said. "The Burnt are closing in. We'll be trapped here if we stay much longer."

Trapped here. Trapped as Fyrril would have been trapped, his father's armies approaching from all sides.

All sides save one.

My eyes met Bryndine's. "I know where to go," I said, but it was drowned out by the women's voices, shouting over top of one another.

It didn't matter; Bryndine understood. She rose, nearly eight feet in height, impossible to ignore. The women fell silent instantly.

"I believe Scriber Dennon has something to say." Bryndine looked at me expectantly.

"I know where the books are," I said. "Or at least where to look next."

"I trust you won't leave us in suspense." Bryndine raised an eyebrow ever so slightly.

"The mountains. He took them to the Salt Mountains."

No one spoke. Deanyn's father coughed quietly.

"How can you be sure?" Bryndine asked. "We found nothing."

"He had no other choice." I swept a hand east, towards the city gates. "Think of it—there would have been armies at his gates. He had rebelled against the throne. He had to get the books out, or they would be found and burned when the city fell. The King's Army would have cut off all routes of escape by land. The only way out was by sea."

"How do you know he moved them at all?" Sylla demanded. "Even if he wanted to, he may not have had the chance if he was under siege. Maybe they were burned centuries ago."

I shook my head. "Rynd's statue fits the clues too well, and there was clearly something hidden in that hole. A message like what we found in Three Rivers would have fit perfectly. He must have had time to move the books somewhere, and place something beneath the statue to lead the way."

"He could have sailed anywhere," said Tenille. "Why not Raen, or the Isles?"

"Because the journal entry we found in Three Rivers was written in autumn," I replied, my excitement swelling as I put the pieces together. "I saw the port earlier today; not a single sail was unfurled. No one is crossing the sea, not during the storm season. And Fyrril's rebellion began at the same time of year. The only option would have been to sail up the coast to the mountains. He was known there—there are records of him negotiating the mining treaty with the Barrock. He must have relied on their aid."

Comprehension lit Tenille's eyes. "Impossible lands," she breathed. "Even that was a message." There was awe in her voice—the Scriber in her overpowering the soldier, for a moment.

Deanyn cocked her head. "What are you talking about?"

"The inscription on the statue spoke of the lands of the impossible," Tenille explained. "The clansfolk say the mountains were made from waves frozen in a storm. What could be more impossible?"

A realization came to me then, as clear and perfect as a diamond. "Waves made solid by their God. The Dragon. The Dragon's realm in Adello's songs was never the sea—he has been leading us to the Salt Mountains all along."

"I don't doubt that you are right, Scriber," said Bryndine. "But even knowing that, we are no better off than we were. The mountains stretch from the coast to the Crossing. Where would we even begin?"

Wynne had been listening raptly, but now she spoke. "Prince Willyn," she said.

Confusion was writ on every face as they turned towards her, and her thrilled grin turned to doubt. But I had an inkling of what she meant. It was clever; she was thinking like a Scriber.

"Go on, Wynne," I prompted.

"I just thought… Someone had to take whatever was hidden in the statue, yes?" She looked at me for approval.

When I nodded, her expression brightened, and she continued with enthusiasm. "Prince Willyn was the heir to the throne, he governed Ryndport. He had access to the statue. Maybe he found some message from Fyrril. He's supposed to have gone into the Salt Mountains looking for the Archives—why would he have done that if something hadn't put the idea in his head?"

Though I had little to do with her deduction, I felt a certain pride. *Is this how Illias feels when a student does well?* I wondered. Suddenly the old man's devotion to teaching made a great deal more sense.

"A good thought," I said, smiling at the girl. "That narrows our search. The clansfolk can show us to the area where Willyn was last seen—their Storytellers have long memories."

Wynne beamed at the praise. *She should be earning her pin at the Academy*, I thought for the hundredth time. It was among the Academy's greatest flaws that so many like Wynne were denied because they lacked money and influence; I would never have gained entry myself if had not been lucky enough to meet Illias. *I could speak for her*. Illias would surely sponsor her at my recommendation.

"Lovely," said Randyn Syvanson, though his tone suggested a complete lack of interest. "You seem to have this well in hand. Shall we retire for the night?" That he and his wife found our company tiresome was obvious, but custom demanded that they not leave the table before the Prince.

Deanyn rolled her eyes. "Are we boring you, Father? I know it must be difficult, we are only discussing the safety of the Kingsland."

The Prince was quick to step in. "I apologize, Randyn. It is rude of us to speak of our affairs at such length at your table, but these are important matters. I believe we are nearly finished, if you'll permit us."

With a small sigh, Deanyn's father leaned back in his chair. "Of course, Prince Alyn."

Alyn turned to Bryndine. "I think you should go, Bryn. Better you leave by ship than rush into the Burners' ambush. The only issue is finding you passage—most ships are docked for the season, and the sailors will not be anxious to give up their shore leave to chance the Dragon's Teeth. Erryn's Promise forbids me from commanding them to aid you."

"We can provide a ship," Deanyn said, glancing sidelong at her father. "For the good of the kingdom. I am sure my father is eager to give any aid he can."

Our host shrugged and inclined his head slightly. "Of course. For the good of the Kingsland." He truly did not seem to care; Randyn Syvanson could buy a thousand new ships and have more wealth left than most. "But I cannot guarantee a crew."

"This is not a problem," Leste said. "I know many sailors."

Bryndine hid her uncertainty well, but the slight wrinkling around her eyes gave it away. "A journey into the Salt Mountains will take time, and the King must be told what the rebels are capable of," she said. "He must be warned about Uran and the possibility of others like him. As you say, Alyn, a bird will not suffice."

"We have no time to waste," I protested. "It is already midway through autumn. The mountains will be nearly impassable within a month."

"I will go to Three Rivers for you," the Prince declared. "I wish to see the state of things there for myself, and speak with my father. I will leave the Third in charge of defense here and bring the Ninth Company with me—better I risk the trip with four hundred soldiers than you with only a dozen."

Bryndine's mouth straightened into a thin, firm line. "I cannot let you face danger in my place."

"A full company of Army men will be more than equal to their untrained rabble, Bryn," Alyn said. "And it is you they are pursuing—if you are not with us, they may not risk attacking at all."

"What will you tell the King?" Bryndine asked. "He must know what we saw, and you do not believe our story."

Alyn laughed. "Always so dutiful. The Army would be

lucky to have more soldiers like you, and less like Uran." He feigned a wounded expression. "But I am hurt that you think I could deny my favorite cousin. Your story is hard to believe, but I trust your eyes and your mind. I will tell the King exactly what you told me."

Bryndine offered her cousin a rare, grateful smile, but it lasted only a moment before it was replaced by the solemn determination I recognized well. There was no doubt in her next words.

"Then we sail for the Salt Mountains."

CHAPTER TWENTY-FIVE

The people of the Salt Mountains have no true leader. They are divided into many nomadic clans, each with a chief of its own.

However, they appoint one man as their Barrock, a military and diplomatic figure in charge of relations with the Kingsland. The position dates back to before the Forgetting, when—according to the clansfolk—a King Elwyn, who they jokingly name "Salteater", tried to invade their lands, and a man named Barrock united the clans to repel the King's Army. Barrock then negotiated a treaty under which the Kingsland could mine the mountains, but had to pay for the privilege.

The clans also respect the guidance of the Storytellers, religious figures who are said to remember the entire history of their people. As they have no written language, the Storytellers pass their knowledge down orally, and must have near perfect memories. Due to the wisdom gleaned from these stories, they are trusted advisors to the clan chiefs.

— From Dennon Lark's *History of the Salt Mountain Clans*

Finding the clansfolk was not difficult. Midway into autumn, they were already gathered along the sea cliffs, and their camps were visible from the deck of the ship as we sailed up the coast. Navigating the rocky waters along the cliffs—called the Dragon's Teeth by the sailors—was a greater problem, but with Leste's aid we had been able to recruit an experienced and able crew. They sailed the Teeth swiftly, and within four days, found us a safe berth at one of the small docks the Mountainers used to launch their fishing boats.

As we unloaded our supplies and led our mounts from the ship, a group of clansmen approached us down the narrow cliffside path, all five of them dressed in thick white snowcat furs against the chill of the mountains. Huddled inside the too-large greatcoat Prince Alyn had provided—and despite the layers of heavy clothing I wore beneath it—I envied them their apparent warmth. In fact, I envied the women as well, seemingly impervious to the cold under their cloaks and leathers and woollen underpadding. Only I had to wrap my arms around myself to keep from shivering.

"Kingslanders," one of the approaching clansmen—a tall heavyset man with a beard—hailed us in a stern tone. "Why are you here? Our tribute for the mines came on the last half-moon."

Bryndine saluted the men as they drew near. "We seek the guidance of your Storytellers."

The man's eyes narrowed with distrust. "The Storytellers serve the clans and the Dragon, not the Kingsland. You will come with us to the Barrock. Kingslanders are his concern."

Bryndine nodded respectfully. "It would be my honor to speak with the Barrock. Tenille, see that the horses are made ready. Scriber Dennon, come with me."

Without instruction, Sylla fell into step beside us, and Bryndine accepted her presence without rebuke. The clansmen led us up the path they had come by, and then along the cliffs heading north. As we walked, I took note of the camps we passed through—I had never before set foot in the mountains beyond Highpass, and though I had read about them, it was an altogether different thing to see firsthand how the clansfolk lived.

They built no permanent structures; we passed mostly hide tents and covered caves. Few of the clansfolk let our presence distract them from the business of untangling fishing nets, gutting their daily catch, or simply sharing stories around the cooking pits. They went about these tasks with an eclectic collection of goods: steel tools forged in the Kingsland alongside stone ones of their own make; Raenish fabrics sewn to rough animal hides; fine glass jars mixed in among rough clay pots. The mining treaty with the Kingsland provided them with many things they could not produce themselves, and they let nothing go to waste.

The Barrock's tent was no larger or more impressive than any of the others, and nothing marked it as different, so I was surprised when the clansmen came to a halt. Their leader motioned for Bryndine to follow him inside.

"Scriber Dennon, join me," she said. "I may need you to help explain what we seek." She looked to the large bearded man for permission. "If that is acceptable."

The man gave a slight nod and lifted the hide flap that covered the entrance of the tent.

Sylla moved to join us, but one of the clansmen barred her way with an outstretched spear. Sylla tensed, and her hand twitched towards her sword.

"No more," the leader said to Bryndine. "Only you and the skinny man."

"I am in no danger, Sylla," Bryndine said. "Please, wait for us here."

For a moment I thought Sylla might disobey, but she reluctantly let her hand fall and stepped back. I could feel her angry glare behind me as I followed Bryndine into the Barrock's tent.

The Barrock sat cross-legged on a pile of furs at the back of the tent, sharpening a Kingsland-forged longsword. He looked much like the rest of the clansmen—a wiry man with dark hair and a short beard, dressed in plain hide breeches and a woollen shirt, bearing no regalia or badge of office. He was seated, but I could tell that he was no larger than myself. It did nothing to diminish his presence—he had a keen, slightly intimidating air about him, that of a man in full command of himself and his surroundings. He showed no surprise at our entrance, simply swept his dark eyes over us appraisingly and nodded in greeting.

"You are Elarryd Errynson's daughter," he stated, looking at Bryndine. "I see it in your face. I have met with your father many times. A wise man."

Though her height already forced her to bend down in the

low-roofed tent, Bryndine bowed slightly further. "You honor my family, Connig Barrock. My name is Bryndine, and this is Scriber Dennon Lark. We come seeking your aid."

The Barrock furrowed his brow. "My people do not take kindly to Kingslanders asking favors. Tell me what you need, and I will tell you if it is possible."

"We require a guide to the place where Prince Willyn was last seen alive," said Bryndine.

The Barrock slid his whetstone along the edge of his blade, a pensive expression on his face. "I can see no harm in that," he said after a moment. "The Storytellers will know. The Dragon has blessed them with all memories of our people. But it is rare for them to share their stories with outsiders, and I cannot make them help you. I can only ask. Sit, we will wait." He gestured to the fur-lined ground, then turned to the bearded man who had brought us to him. "Edred, fetch Teller Revik."

It was not long before the Storyteller entered the tent. He was old, grey-haired and slightly stooped beneath his rough spun robes, his deeply lined face twisted into a disapproving scowl. It was immediately evident that he was not pleased to see us.

"You disappoint me, Connig," he said in a hoarse, quavering voice. "The Storytellers are not at the beck and call of Kingslanders."

"Their request is small enough," the Barrock replied calmly. "And she is Elarryd Errynson's daughter. He has treated fairly with us. Hear them out, Teller Revik. If you wish to refuse them afterwards, I will not argue."

Revik made a disgusted noise in his throat, but nodded. Without speaking, he lowered himself into a seated position on the floor of the tent and looked expectantly at Bryndine.

"We mean no disrespect, Teller Revik. We only need a guide to show us to where Prince Willyn was last seen." Bryndine's tone was impeccably polite, even reverent towards the old man.

"It is remembered that we showed Kingslanders to that place, many years ago," Revik said. "They found no sign of the Prince. Why should we bring you back there now?"

"We believe that Willyn was seeking something hidden in

the mountains by Prince Fyrril," I explained. "A collection of books from the Archives. It would help us greatly to know where he was looking."

The Storyteller frowned. "Prince Fyrril was a friend to our people. He helped us to repair the treaty your selfish rulers scorned for so long, helped us to earn more than scraps from the Kingsland's table. This is remembered. We will not betray his secrets."

I was becoming annoyed with the old man's attitude. "Fyrril wanted those books to be found," I insisted, taking the scroll case we had found in Three Rivers from the pocket of my coat. "He left a trail that has led us this far. Here, read this." I took the journal page from the silver case and offered it to Revik.

"I do not know your letters, Kingslander," the old man said disdainfully. "We have no need of them here."

"I will read it to you." I unrolled the paper, and read the words aloud—with particular emphasis on the end, where Fyrril begged for someone to seek the books out in Ryndport.

When I was done, the Barrock held out his hand. "Let me see," he said. When I handed him the page, he looked it over, then nodded at Teller Revik. "The Scriber read truly, and I do not believe it to be a forgery, Storyteller."

"It does not speak of the Salt Mountains," Revik said doubtfully.

"No," replied Bryndine, "but our path has led us here. You must see that Fyrril wanted his work to be recovered. We believe that the threats he writes of have returned."

Revik stroked his chin, then heaved a deep sigh. "Very well. Fyrril was a brother to our people. I will respect his wishes." The stubborn set to his jaw relaxed slightly. "You are right, he did come to us with something precious to hide. It is remembered."

My eyes widened. "You have known this all along, and said nothing?" It was not truly surprising—the Academy had been unaware of Fyrril's importance until recently, and the clansmen offered nothing freely to the Kingsland. But I could not help thinking how different my life might have been if Fyrril's secrets had been revealed before I had ever thought to search the Old Garden.

Revik glared at me. "We do not share our knowledge without reason," he said. "But even if we did, it is not remembered what Fyrril hid, or why. He did not say, and we did not ask. We allowed him and his men to go alone into the mountains."

"Then you do not know where the books are?" Bryndine asked.

"No," the Storyteller answered. "I can tell you where your Prince Willyn was last seen. That is all."

Bryndine nodded respectfully. "Thank you, Teller Revik. That is all we ask."

"Then listen, Kingslanders, and I will tell you this story as it was told to me," Revik began in his tremulous voice. "As it has been remembered from the moment it happened and will be remembered until the Dragon's seas swallow the world once more."

CHAPTER TWENTY-SIX

I often wish that I had not brought these women with me. Too many have given their lives already. But when I stop to think about it, it is clear that without them, I would be dead ten times over, and certainly no closer to finding Fyrril's books.

If there is any justice in the world, Bryndine's company will be recognized for their service when we return.

— From the personal journals of Dennon Lark

Five days later, watching the clansmen ride away on their surefooted mules, I had to wonder if we were making a mistake.

There was nothing remarkable about the place where Willyn had last been seen. A flat stretch of ground beside a mountain stream, it was a fine place to make camp for a night or two, and nothing more. Apparently, Willyn and his men had been doing just that when the Stonewater Clan had come upon them.

The story Revik had told us after his unnecessarily ceremonial introduction was short and simple: Willyn had told the clansmen that he intended to forge north from this campsite, leaving the established trails; they warned him that to do so was unwise, that the northern slopes were prone to rockslides and prowled by hungry snowcats. The Prince had not heeded their advice.

Nor did we. The clansmen who had guided us there made it very clear that they would go no further if we meant to follow Willyn's trail, not with winter fast approaching. If we were still in the mountains when the snows came, death would be almost a certainty. But we had no choice. The Lost Prince was our last hope to find Fyrril's books.

Over the next few days, Willyn's campsite became a base for our search. Bryndine divided us into two groups to better cover the area—she, Sylla, Rylene, Deanyn, Leste, and Ivyla ranged to the northwest, while Tenille led Debra, Kaelyn, Orya, Wynne, and myself through the northeastern wilderness. The mounts could manage the mountain trails, but the terrain off the beaten path was too rough for them, so we were forced to walk. Each morning, we set out to search while Selvi and Elene stayed behind to watch the tents and tend the horses. Each night, we regrouped at the camp with nothing to show for our efforts.

There were no trails where we searched, only cliffs and ledges, ravines and barren valleys. From afar, the Salt Mountains looked like waves made solid, but this close, they only looked like what they were: cold, desolate rocks. None of us knew exactly what we were looking for—some sign of Willyn's passage, some cave or crevasse where Fyrril might have hidden the books from the Archives. We spent most of our days seeking safe passage through the treacherous terrain, finding nothing of particular note.

After a week of meandering through the mountains with no results, I began to despair. We knew too little to search with any accuracy, and there was no time left to wander blindly with the icy Salt Mountain winter threatening to arrive any day. In fact, on the morning of our seventh day of searching, snow had begun to fall lightly on the higher slopes. That same afternoon, hiking up a thin ridge at the edge of a long canyon, we found our path blocked by fallen rocks—the remnant of some past rockslide. I threw my hands up in disgust at the sight. We could not afford the time it would take to clear the way.

"We may as well see how much we can clear before nightfall," Tenille said with a sigh. "Debra, Kaelyn, with me. We'll work in shifts—the path isn't wide enough for more than three of us."

"What does it matter?" I asked, holding a hand out to catch a light dusting of snowflakes. "We have at most a week before the snowfall stops our search entirely, and it will take most of that time to move those rocks."

"We have come this far, and at your insistence, if I recall," said Tenille, tapping at the golden pin on her collar. "You and I are sworn to see this through. We cannot give up now."

"No, I suppose not," I admitted. "I'm sorry, it just seems so—"

"I know," Tenille interrupted. "But we have to try."

They set to work, and Wynne, Orya and I settled in to wait on the rocky ridge a short distance down from the blockage. To Orya's great displeasure and boredom, I spent the time teaching Wynne what I knew of Elovian letters and sentence structure—I had been giving her lessons at night in the camp, and she was a quick student.

About a half-hour passed before Debra jogged down and called for us to take our turn. Grumbling, I stowed my papers and ink back in my pack and pushed myself to my feet.

And then the mountain began to fall.

The noise came first, a great rumble and crack from above. The others looked upwards in shock and confusion, but I knew that sound instantly. For just a moment, I was back beneath the Old Garden, watching as the ceiling fell.

But it was only for a moment, and then I threw myself into motion, grabbing Wynne and Orya and pulling them with me. "It's a rockslide!" I yelled. "Down the ridge, quickly!"

A torrent of pebbles and dirt pelted against me as I sprinted down the narrow ledge with Wynne beside me and Orya—cursing loudly and furiously—at my back. Loud crashes shook the ground beneath my feet as stones tumbled down the mountainside. Sparing a quick glance over my shoulder, I saw Debra running not far back, Tenille and Kaelyn following close behind.

Kaelyn's foot slipped in the powdery snow that dusted the ground and she stumbled, falling back a step. Just a step, but it was enough. A dark shadow spread over the pretty young soldier as the rocks rushed towards her. I heard myself scream her name, saw her hurl herself forward—but it was too late. A huge boulder slammed into her, smashing her off the ridge.

I put my head down and pushed my aching legs to their limit, narrowing my focus to only the ground at my feet. A single misstep could have killed me, just as surely as it had Kaelyn. My lungs burned and my heart beat loudly in my ears—so loudly that I barely noticed when the rumbling stopped.

"Scriber Dennon!" Wynne shouted from behind. "It's over."

I slowed, looked back, finally took note of the silence. Ironically, the violence of the rockslide had left the path almost entirely clear. The rubble that had blocked the way had been carried down into the ravine with the rest of the falling rocks.

"Sky and Earth, I thought that was the end," I panted, bracing my hands against my knees. "Is anyone hurt?" I swept my eyes over the others in concern.

That was when I noticed Tenille was gone.

"Where is Tenille? Did she fall?" I searched the ridge again with my eyes, but there was no sign of her; no place her body might be hidden.

"Thought she was behind me." Guilt contorted Debra's face. "She was there when Kaelyn… I thought she was behind me."

"I see her!" Orya shouted.

I turned to see Orya crouched over the edge of the ravine, and my heart fell into my stomach. Joining her at the cliff's edge, I gathered my courage and peeked downwards. The ravine was more than a hundred feet deep, and the height made my vision spin. Falling to my knees, I gripped the earth with white-knuckled fingers, just barely mastering myself enough to keep my eyes open.

At the bottom of the ravine, a slim trickle of water ran through a riverbed filled with debris from the slide and a hundred slides before it. Directly below, a vast slope of fallen rocks piled against the cliff. There was no sign of poor Kaelyn, undoubtedly buried somewhere in the rubble, and I did not see Tenille at first either, until Orya pointed to a small ledge perhaps a third of the way down the cliff to my left.

Tenille lay upon the ledge, and even from this distance I

could see the awkward angle of her leg, the bone jutting from beneath the skin. The light snow had all but stopped, but a slight powder coated her motionless form. It was impossible to tell if she was alive or dead—there was no obviously fatal wound, but the fall might easily have killed her, and I could not see if she was breathing.

"Bugger me," Orya swore. "She looks bad. Think she's alive, Scriber?"

"I can't say from here," I said. "She would look considerably worse if the larger rocks had struck her, I think. If it was only the fall… it is not so far that survival is out of the question. I don't know."

Wynne leaned over my shoulder to see. "We need to get her," she said anxiously. "If she's alive, you can help her, can't you?"

"I don't know!" Getting to my feet, I stepped away from the edge of the cliff and began to pace, rubbing my temple with two fingers. "I don't know. I need to examine her."

Please let her be alive, I begged whatever god might be listening. *Kaelyn is already gone. Let just one more death on my conscience be enough.*

"I can pull her up," said Debra. "Need to get a rope around her though."

"How in the depths are we supposed to do that?" I demanded, gesturing angrily at the sheer cliff walls.

Orya stood and shrugged off her pack, pulling out a length of rope. "Told you before, Scriber, I grew up climbin' the cliffs in Highpass. Gettin' to her won't be a problem." Uncoiling the rope, she tied the end around her waist and yanked at the knot a few times to test it. With a satisfied nod, she tossed the other end of the long cord to Debra.

"Should I lower you down?" the big woman asked uncertainly.

Orya knelt again, peering down into the ravine with no sign of fear in her wild blue eyes. "Faster doin' it my way," she said.

Then, without warning, she swung her legs over the cliff's edge and dropped out of sight.

"Mother below!" I gasped, scrambling to the edge of the

ridge. Behind me, I was vaguely conscious of a panicked Debra pulling back on the rope to arrest Orya's fall.

I expected to see Orya dangling at the end of the rope far below, or crumpled against some ledge or outcropping. I did not. She clung to the cliffside several feet beneath the edge, searching for a foothold. As I watched, she began to descend, her hands and feet somehow finding purchase where I could have sworn there was none.

"Are you insane?" I shouted at her.

"Might be," she replied with a grin, and flung herself sideways through the air.

My lungs stopped working; my stomach threatened to leap out of my throat. Forgetting for a moment the rope cinched tight about her waist, I was quite certain she would plummet to her death on the rocks below. Instead, she reached out and grasped some invisible handhold, lurching to a stop and laughing with exhilaration.

I could only shake my head in amazement as she scampered nimbly down the cliff in heart-stopping leaps and drops. In no time at all, she was lowering herself onto the small outcropping that held Tenille.

"Is she all right?" Wynne called down.

Orya leaned down over Tenille for a moment, then answered, "She's breathin'. Hurt bad though."

"Can you wake her?" I asked. I did not want Tenille bouncing against the cliff when we pulled her up—better if she could help control her own ascent somewhat.

It took several attempts, but eventually Orya's prodding and slapping and yelling roused her.

"Tenille," I shouted. "Can you tell me where your injuries are?"

"B-broken ribs." Her voice was strained, and I could hear the wince in it; she had to yell to be heard from this distance, and with broken ribs that was no easy thing. "My right arm and leg."

I nodded to myself. With one leg and arm, she could at least hold herself upright and keep from scraping against the cliffside too badly, though the pain would be substantial. "We're going to pull you up. Orya, we'll send the rope back down for you."

"I'll get myself back up, you just see to her," Orya yelled back. She untied the rope from her waist and looped it under Tenille's buttocks, forming a makeshift seat.

When the harness was secure, Debra began to heave, cords of muscle bulging along her thick arms. Slowly, Tenille rose, gripping the rope with her left hand and extending her good leg to push herself back from the cliff. She said something to Orya as she started to ascend, but I could not hear what it was.

When we pulled her onto the ridge a short while later, Tenille's face was pale and drawn, and sweat beaded on her forehead. As we laid her on her back, she looked me in the eye and whispered in a strained voice, "Something is shining in the rocks." Then her eyes rolled back and she fell unconscious again.

I did not let myself dwell on her strange words. Kneeling at her side, I examined her as thoroughly as I was able. She was breathing regularly—her broken ribs had not punctured the lungs—but there were bruises all along her right side. Below her knee a jagged shard of bone penetrated the skin; her right arm was broken as well, but less badly. The pain must have been incredible—I could not imagine how she stayed conscious even as long as it took for us to pull her up.

"Hold her," I directed Wynne and Debra, gesturing to Tenille's thigh.

With the two women anchoring her in place, I pulled on her injured leg until the bone drew back beneath the skin, setting the break as best I could. After bandaging the wounded flesh, I did the same with her arm. There was little I could do about her broken ribs, and we would have to find something to splint the broken limbs—but barring some internal injury I could not treat, she would live.

"She is going to survive, I think," I told the others, relief coloring my voice.

"What did she mean about something shining?" Wynne asked. "She must have seen something below."

"A trick of the light, perhaps," I said. "Quartz or mica in the stones. Or…" A sudden, unlikely hope surged through me then, and I scuttled back to the cliff to look for myself.

Orya was already halfway down to the debris strewn riverbed, to my surprise.

"What are you doing?" I shouted, scanning the ravine floor for whatever it was Tenille had seen.

"Tenille saw somethin' while you were liftin' her," Orya answered. "Thought I'd have a look."

"Where is it?" I could make nothing out amid the stones.

Orya leaned precariously back from the cliff and pointed to a spot near the bottom of the pile of rubble. "Looks like metal."

I saw it then, a bright reflective glint between stones that shone for just a moment as the sun hit it through the clouds. Closing my eyes, I said a silent prayer to the Mother and the Father. *If something good comes of this disaster*, I promised, *I will be devout for the rest of my days.*

When I looked again, Orya was nearly at the bottom of the ravine. She dropped the last several feet and strode to the base of the stone pile, crouching down where I had seen the metallic gleam.

When she grasped the first stone to move it aside, she paused.

"This ain't no stone." She held the smooth yellow-white object up for me to see. Even from so far away, I recognized the vague shape of a human skull. "There's a mess of bones here."

Morbid as it was, my first reaction was elation. "Orya, you need to find that metal. I must know what it is."

Wynne sensed my excitement. "You think this is what we've been looking for, don't you?"

I nodded slowly, almost scared to admit it for fear of angering some capricious luck spirit. "Those bones could have been hidden here for a very long time," I said. "Buried in a rockslide, concealed for years until the pile was disturbed enough to reveal them. The Scribers would have found no sign of them when they searched."

At that moment, Orya's voice rang out from below. "Mother's teats, I can't believe it. Look at this, Scriber."

In her extended hand, she held a long, thin metal object.

Despite the distance, I could tell what it was instantly: a tarnished silver scroll case.

We had found the Lost Prince.

CHAPTER TWENTY-SEVEN

Prince Willyn was not a smart man. He badly wanted to be a Scriber, but none of the six Schools would give him his pin. Even for the King's son, no Master could justify rewarding such poor performance on exams, or such general ignorance.

And yet, it appears that he came closer to finding the Archives than anyone else for some three hundred years. This is, to say the least, somewhat embarrassing for the Scribers.

— From the personal journals of Dennon Lark

Willyn's scroll case held another page from Prince Fyrril's journal, dated a month after the one we had found in Three Rivers.

Adello sends word from Three Rivers, though he risks discovery in doing so. The voices are stronger than ever, he says—the sorcery has claimed many of the nobles, most of the officers in the Army. He begs to return to my side. I sent him a final message today, telling him of my plans; telling him that he must remain there, that if he and his songs do not survive, all our efforts are wasted.

We cannot hold here. Father and Oryn have brought the entire Army to Ryndport, leaving the rest of the Kingsland at the mercy of the rebels. And these walls were not made to hold back a siege. The storms have halted shipping, and our supplies dwindle. The city will fall within the week if we continue to fight. I have ordered a surrender at dawn tomorrow, and instructed the people not to resist when Father takes the city. I hope that will be enough to spare their lives when he realizes I am gone.

My men and I sail for the Salt Mountains tonight under cover of darkness. I am on the verge of understanding this sorcery, I think—the words of the Sages must hold the secret, though I fear whatever truths I may find come far too late. I know where I can hide the books when I am done. There is a small cave, in a valley that I discovered years ago while hunting with the Whiteclaw Clan.

I hope that whoever finds them can do more than I have.

On the reverse side, the entirety of the page was given to a hand-drawn map of the Salt Mountains. There was no uncertainty here, no hidden meaning or clues to be sought in song. The map showed the way to the last undiscovered remnants of the Archives.

Bryndine ran her finger along the route Fyrril had marked five hundred years before. "If we travel north along the ridge where you found the Prince and then east when the ravine ends, this valley should be no more than two days away."

It had taken us hours to carry Tenille back to the camp through the difficult terrain of the mountains. When evening fell and we had not yet returned, Bryndine and the others had come looking for us; with their help, we had arrived back at camp shortly before midnight. After a moment of silence for Kaelyn, most of the company had retired for the night. Those of us still awake—Bryndine and I, Wynne and Deanyn, and of course Sylla—sat by the fire, examining the page that had led Prince Willyn to his death.

"Prince Willyn was barely a day from the place when the landslide took him," I said, hardly able to believe it. "Of all the people to come so close…"

"Why did he not just tell the Scribers?" Wynne asked. "I thought he wanted his pin, wouldn't this have helped?"

I shook my head. "He wanted his pin once, but he left the Academy on… poor terms. He was angry with the Scribers. Perhaps he wanted to embarrass them by finding what they couldn't."

"That is… sad." Wynne's eyes were full of pity for the long dead Prince. "If the Scribers had given him just a bit of respect, these books might have been found two hundred years ago."

"If he had earned more respect, they might have given it to him," I countered, feeling an impulsive need to defend the Scribers of Willyn's time despite my poor relations with so many of their current number. "Willyn did not deserve a pin, by all accounts."

"Almost hard to believe, for a man who thought it a good idea to run off into the mountains without telling anyone," Deanyn said, absently tossing a twig into the fire. I grinned at her across the flames, and the corner of her mouth twitched upwards, ruining her deadpan expression.

Wynne did not smile. "I suppose," she said. "It still seems sad." It occurred to me that she might have related to the Prince's plight—she had wanted to be a Scriber herself, and had been disappointed.

"We cannot change what happened to him," Bryndine said seriously. "But we must act quickly if we wish to succeed where Prince Willyn failed. The snows have already begun. We will set out tomorrow. A small group, I think—no more than four, including you and I, Scriber."

"Are you sure you don't want more than three people to look after Dennon?" Deanyn asked. "He's trouble, that one. Gets in barfights, argues with the clergy."

Bryndine ignored the joke. "The fewer of us there are, the faster we can move, and with less risk of disturbing the mountain and causing another slide."

Breaking her long, glowering silence, Sylla said, "I'm coming with you."

Deanyn laughed. "Ah, that solves the problem then. She'll just kill him within the first hour."

Sylla only narrowed her eyes at Deanyn and kept silent. My stomach clenched tightly. I smiled and forced a chuckle to cover my fear, but knowing what I did about Sylla, Deanyn's jest felt more like prophecy.

"We should bring Orya too," I suggested. "She climbs like a spider. We may need her."

Bryndine nodded. "That is it, then. You and I, Sylla and Orya. We'll leave at first light. Deanyn, you have the first watch. Rylene will relieve you in two hours." She handed Fyrril's page back to me and stood. "Get some rest, Scriber," she said as she headed for her tent. "You will need it." Wynne and Sylla followed her to the sleeping tents, leaving Deanyn and I alone by the fire.

I was about to retire myself when I glanced down at the map Fyrril had drawn, and noticed something that made me snort with amusement.

"Is something funny?" Deanyn asked.

"More ironic than funny." I held up the map. "Waymark is directly south of us. No more than a week's travel from here, if I'm reading this correctly. I spent years telling the villagers Willyn never passed through there." Perhaps I should have been embarrassed by my mistake, but somehow it seemed fitting.

Deanyn grinned. "You, wrong about something? By the Divide, how can this be?"

"Your faith in me is overwhelming," I said, laughing. "It's too much for me. I'm going to sleep."

Rolling the map up and placing it back in its tarnished case, I pushed myself to my feet. Bryndine was right; it had been a difficult day, and I needed a good night's rest. I did not want to be tired and irritable in the morning—making Sylla angry was an easy way to get myself killed.

Deanyn, apparently, could sense my unease. "Don't worry too much about Sylla," she said. "I was only joking before. She's a fierce guard dog, but a tame one. She'll bark, but she won't bite unless the Captain lets her."

"I know," I said, though I was not half as certain as Deanyn sounded. Sylla had accused me several times of risking their lives for nothing—if we did not find the books, if they had been moved or destroyed in the last five hundred years, how would she react? By putting a sword through me, I suspected. It would be understandable, really. If it came to that, I might fall on her sword myself.

Deanyn could not hear my doubts, though, so she only nodded and said, "Good. Sleep well then."

As I ducked into my small tent, I heard her voice again.

"Dennon?"

I turned to face her. "What is it?"

There was real concern in her eyes. "Promise me you'll keep yourself alive. I'd consider it a personal favor."

Somewhat touched, I gave her a tired smile. "I will," I said. "Believe me, no one wants that more than I do."

She nodded. "I will hold you to it." She waved me into the tent, and when I crawled under my scratchy woollen blanket, I fell asleep almost instantly.

* * *

Travelling alongside Sylla, with so few companions to distract attention, was difficult to bear. Everything I did seemed to raise her ire; I could not so much as take a step without her snapping at me for making too much noise.

"Unless you want to bring every snowcat on the slopes down on us, you had better step quieter, Scriber," she would say, though no one had seen so much as a paw-print for the entire week we had been searching the mountains.

Though I had promised myself I would not antagonize the woman, I found it difficult to take her abuse silently. But when I offered a retort, it always met the same response—she simply laid her hand on the hilt of her sword, and I bit back any further insults and retreated.

Orya, at least, was better company. Not even Sylla's dour presence was able to repress her buoyant and frequently obscene spirit, so I did not lack for conversation. Bryndine, surprisingly, was also a good travelling companion—our relationship was approaching something like friendship, or at least mutual respect. During most of our earlier travels, she had talked more with the women than with me, but that day, she reminded me that she had spent time at the Academy by engaging in discussion on an impressive variety of scholarly subjects.

There were some slight snowfalls throughout the day, never lasting long, but enough to leave a thin white coat on the ground, and to make me nervous. Though we were moving at a decent pace, and could in theory reach Fyrril's cave and rejoin the others in as few as three more days, a single heavy snow could make the return trip near impossible.

By nightfall, we had reached the end of the ravine where the slide had happened. The ravine disappeared gradually, sloping upward until the steep cliffs relaxed into a gentle bowl, and eventually into two relatively level banks of bare stone surrounding the shallow stream all the way up to its source in the mountainside to the north. The weak flow of water did not come close to filling the entire riverbed—though it undoubtedly would in the spring, after the snowmelt—but it was clear and clean, and more than enough to fill our waterskins. We made our camp there that night.

We ate a short meal around the fire, then pitched our small canvas tents to keep the snow out while we slept. When the time came to determine the order of the watch, I offered to take a shift myself. With the full company, it was never necessary, but given that there were only four of us, it seemed selfish not to do my part.

Sylla laughed darkly at my temerity. "I don't think so, Scriber. I'd like to live through the night. What would you do if something came? A history lesson won't fend off a snowcat."

I scowled at her. "I would wake the rest of you if I saw something," I said. "I just thought you three might like a bit more sleep. Can you ever forgive such a terrible mistake?"

Sylla leaned forward with menace in her eyes, and again my fear overpowered my indignation. At some point during the night, she would be keeping watch alone while I slept; I would be at her mercy. I cast my eyes back towards the fire and shut my mouth.

"There is no need to be rude, Sylla," Bryndine said. "Scriber Dennon, your offer is appreciated, but we have trained for situations like this. Better you get a full night's sleep."

In the end, they determined that Bryndine would take first watch, then Sylla, then Orya. Orya and I took to our bedrolls; Sylla claimed that she did not yet feel like sleeping and remained by the fire with Bryndine.

Moments after she laid down, Orya's loud snoring rumbled in my ears. I envied her the ease with which she found her rest. Even without the noise of her snores I would not have been able to sleep. Instead I lay awake, imagining our small party trapped in the mountains by a sudden snowfall, slowly succumbing to the cold.

A short time later, I heard Bryndine say to Sylla, "He is quite terrified of you, you know." I suppose she thought I had fallen asleep, because she was quite clearly talking about me.

Sylla snorted. "Good. Someone needs to be able to shut him up."

"It is more than that, Sylla."

"I don't like him," said Sylla. "We never needed him before. Now all we do is follow him. All *you* do is follow him."

"The Kingsland faces a threat we know almost nothing about. If Scriber Dennon can lead us to answers, I will follow him wherever I need to. He is trying to help. Do not forget that he helped keep the company together after my uncle dismissed us."

"How could I forget?" The bitterness in Sylla's voice was palpable. "It seems everyone loves him for it but me. It's false hope, Bryn. As soon as he is done with us, we'll be disbanded again, and worse off than before. How many of us will be dead or injured by then? I… I don't want to see you hurt, especially not because of him."

"You told him about Gered." I had heard Bryndine use that tone before; she was telling, not asking. "That is why he is so afraid; you told him that you killed your husband. Why?"

"I was drunk."

"You wanted him to think you a murderer."

"Why shouldn't he?" Sylla asked gruffly. "It isn't as though I'm innocent."

"No. But you did not do it lightly or without reason. You would not harm someone who did not earn it."

There was a long pause before Sylla replied, and when she did, it sounded as though she was struggling to speak. "I know you think that. I know. You always think that I… that people are better than they are." She took a deep breath. "But if scaring the Scriber is what it takes to keep him from putting you in needless danger, then I will scare him. And if I need to, I *will* harm him. I would kill him if I had to, to keep you safe."

A chill went through me at those words. I could tell by her voice how truly she meant them, perhaps more than anything I had ever heard her say.

"I do not think I have anything to fear with you here," Bryndine said, and there was deep affection in her words. "But I chose this, Sylla. You should not worry so much about me."

"Somebody needs to. You spend too much time worrying about everyone else."

Bryndine laughed at that. "Then I suppose I should thank you for taking on that burden."

"You never have to thank me for anything," Sylla said. Then, a moment later, in the closest thing to good humor I had ever heard from her, "But if you want to, I don't mind."

Their conversation turned to lighter fare after that, and eventually I blocked out the noise. But I did not fall asleep for hours, kept awake by the images playing out in my head. I could still see us, snowed into the mountains, freezing to death. But it was never the cold that killed me. No, the way I saw it, Bryndine died first, her skin grey and frozen. My death came after, delivered on the edge of Sylla's sword.

* * *

I dreamed of the Burnt surrounding their burning fireleaf, but it was strange, different. I was not among them, but far away, atop a distant hill. I could see the tree burning against the night sky, and the figures circling it, silhouetted in flame, but the voices were quiet, with little power behind them. When those distant whispers commanded me to burn, no flames engulfed me. There was no pain, just fear—deep, gut-wrenching fear.

I woke with a shout and sat up without thinking, my head colliding with the low ceiling of the small tent. Disoriented as I was, I panicked, and soon I had pulled the tent pegs from the ground and thoroughly tangled myself in canvas.

"What're you shoutin' about, Scriber?" Orya asked, not bothering to hide her amusement. "Seems to me you hit first. The tent was just defendin' itself."

The sound of her voice calmed me somewhat, helped me remember where I was. If Orya was on watch, it must have been early morning, sometime around dawn. With all the dignity I could muster, I freed myself from the remains of my tent and looked around.

The ground was blanketed in snow and flakes filled the air, shockingly white in the grey pre-dawn glow. *We knew the snows were coming*, I told myself. *It was only a matter of time*. But I had dreamt of the Burnt—they must have known where we were, and I could not escape the feeling that they were striking out at us. If they could call down lightning, why not snow?

"How long has it been snowing like this?" I asked.

"Started not a half-hour ago," Orya replied. "Thought I'd give it a bit, see if it stuck before wakin' you all, seein' as the snows so far ain't lasted long."

I looked up at the dark grey sky for a long time, then said, "I don't think it's going to stop. Help me wake the others."

It did not take long to rouse Bryndine and Sylla, and when everyone was awake, I told them about my dream, and about my suspicion that the Burnt might know our location.

"We have to return to the camp," I said, though a part of me hated myself for admitting defeat. I wanted desperately to find Fyrril's books, and every Scriber's instinct I had screamed that I had to keep looking, but self-preservation won out. "We can still escape the mountains before the trails are blocked."

Bryndine tapped her fingers against her leg, her brow furrowed with thought. "You are not certain that the Burnt caused this snow, though?"

"No, but—"

"If they did, we can assume it will not end; it will grow worse if anything. If that is so, we are already too late, and there is little purpose to retreating. If it is not their doing, then the snow may still relent long enough for us to find what we came for—we are less than a day from the spot Fyrril marked. We must keep going."

Sylla could not have looked more appalled. "Bryn, it's not safe. We need to go back. The Scriber is right for once."

"You want to let a bit of snow scare us off?" Orya asked incredulously. "Why'd we come at all if we're just turnin' tail now?"

"I'm worried about more than just catching a chill," I said. As though taking my words as a challenge, a sharp gust of wind blew a torrent of stinging snow at me, and I hunched inside my greatcoat, pulling it tighter around me. "If we stay, we'll die."

Bryndine turned her gaze on me, and I was startled to see a glint of anger in those grey steel eyes. "And if we turn back, is our fate any better, Scriber Dennon? We have seen what the Burnt can do. Can you watch them tear down the Kingsland knowing you might have been able to stop them? My women have shed blood for this, died so we could get this far. Their deaths mean nothing if we turn back now. If you can live with that, I will not force you to stay, but I cannot. I will go on."

I should have known that Bryndine Errynson would not give up, would not betray the Promise she held so dear. A part of me *had* known, even as I was asking her to turn back. So her reaction came as no great surprise.

No, what surprised me was that I found myself unwilling to abandon her. I like to believe that it was courage, or honor; I did not want anyone's death to be in vain. But I have never been brave. It may have been little more than fear of trying to find my way back alone. Whatever the reason, though, I knew that I would go where she led.

"If you intend to keep going, I will come with you," I said, though I was quite certain the journey would end in my death, either by the cold or by Sylla's sword. "But when we freeze to death, remember that I warned you." I did not admit it aloud, but in truth I was relieved; I yearned to continue the search, but I could never have mustered the courage if Bryndine had not taken the decision upon herself.

Bryndine nodded stiffly. "I will not forget." She allowed a slight smile to raise her lips. "And if we live, I will remember that you came in spite of it."

The snow did not relent; as we travelled east along Fyrril's route, the weather grew worse. Soon the wind and snow had painted the entire world white—not just the ground, but the air itself. I could see only a few yards in any direction, and I had to squint against the chill bite of the wind to do even that. The women would have been invisible to me except that the dark brown of their leather armor stood out against the whiteness in the air. If we had been forced to climb, I think we would all have died; even Orya could not have scaled any kind of incline in those winds, blinded by snow, fingers frozen and clumsy. But the path did not lead us higher into the peaks, and there were no cliffs to scale. Though I was all but blind, I could tell we were descending, and I could only hope it meant that Fyrril's hidden valley was near.

As we trudged through the ever deepening snowdrifts, I thought I heard voices whispering. I could not be certain—they were impossibly faint, and the howl of the wind as it blew through the rocks made discerning any other noise difficult. Even so, it put my nerves on edge, and I could not rid myself of the feeling that the Burnt were watching us.

We walked for what felt like an eternity; in reality it was closer to five or six hours. The snow was up to my knees in some places, and my legs ached with the effort of each step. I was ready to collapse when we finally entered the small valley.

At first, we did not realize that we had reached our destination—we simply trudged onwards until we met the east slope of the valley, unable to see the sharp upward incline until we were already upon it. When Bryndine noticed the ground climbing beneath our feet, she called for us to halt.

"This must be the place," she shouted over the sound of the wind. "The cave should be here somewhere."

"If we can even find it under all this snow," I yelled back, but excitement was building in my chest. The greatest collection of lost knowledge and history left in the world might have been right beside me even as I spoke, and despite the very real chance that we would die looking for it, I could not suppress the thrill I felt.

Then, from the corner of my eye, I saw a flash of movement. I barely had time to react; I could see little through the snow but a slight shadow, a ghost of a form leaping at Bryndine's back.

Somehow, Sylla already had her sword drawn, was already moving. "Bryn!" she shouted, throwing herself between her Captain and the pale form as it pounced.

A flash of red spattered across the snow; Sylla was knocked from her feet. I heard her grunt in pain, saw her sword rise and fall as she grappled with her attacker, and then a heavy gust of snow hid her from sight.

Orya's sword was bared now too, and she started towards

the place where Sylla had fallen. "Sky and ruttin' Earth, what was—" Another white shape struck her in the chest, cutting off her words and pulling her down.

Sylla had struggled to her feet and was circling warily, holding her sword out in front of her. I could just barely make out the shape of the thing that had attacked her—it was pure white, almost invisible through the blizzard, prowling atop the snow on four legs.

I was not sure of what I saw, but I yelled my best guess as warning. "Snowcats!"

Bryndine, I saw, had armed herself and strapped on her shield. A white shadow lunged at her and she yanked the big metal disk into its path, only partially deflecting the attack. Claws tore along her right forearm. She stumbled backwards, blood dripping onto the snow at her feet, and swung her sword. The blade cut nothing but snow.

Terror gripped me and I dropped to my stomach, trying to hide myself. Snow worked its way under my coat, cold and damp against my skin; I barely noticed, just burrowed deeper, trying to stay beneath the animals' notice.

This was not right. I had read about snowcats; they were solitary hunters, not pack animals. I could not tell how many there were, but it had to be at least three or four, and even two would have been unnatural. And then I heard the voices, realized with stomach-churning dread that they really had been there all day, whispering behind the wind, and now they were saying, "*BURN*."

I felt… something. Not the pain I expected. It was as though my skin wanted to burn, but could not quite catch. Instead of agony, a strange clarity washed over me. When I raised my head, I could see every snowflake in the air individually, and the shape of the wind that carried them. I felt half-mad, and yet the world made more sense than it ever had before.

The white shapes of the snowcats should have been impossible to follow, camouflaged in white, never still for more than a moment. I saw every movement they made. Five cats crept silently through the blizzard, striking swiftly and darting away, driving the women apart. Separating them for the kill.

The women were blinded by the blizzard, their movements restricted by the knee-high snow drifts. They could not fight what they could not see, and if they could not fight, they would die.

Without knowing why, I rose to my knees, turned my eyes upwards. Cold flakes of snow landed on my bare face. "Please," I whispered, and the word felt powerful on my tongue, sounded foreign in my ears, like I was speaking to the Sky in a language I did not know.

The snow ceased.

I did not know how or why, and the clarity I had felt faded almost instantly, but I was sure of one thing: I had asked the snow to stop, and it had stopped.

And whatever I had done, it had been noticed.

Five pairs of dark predatory eyes fixed upon me as the snowcats turned. I felt the Burnt behind those eyes. They knew what I had done, could sense it the same way they sensed my fear, or found me in my dreams. There was a faint whisper—"*Death*"—and then the cats were in motion, racing towards me with single-minded ferocity, my companions completely forgotten.

Her vision no longer obscured, Bryndine severed a snowcat's spine the moment it turned its back. Sylla chopped halfway through another's neck, and Orya threw herself onto the back of a third, savagely stabbing her sword down through its ear and into its skull. The animals did not bleed as they fell.

The last two snowcats closed the distance towards me almost faster than I could see. One came from my right, breaking away from Bryndine; the other approached from directly ahead, Sylla and Orya slogging futilely behind it. The women could not match the beasts' speed, not with more than a foot of snow on the ground; the snowcats were born for this, running atop the drifts so lightly that they barely left tracks.

They converged on me from both sides, but the one in front of me leapt first, claws outstretched. Ten yards away, Bryndine put her whole body into a mighty swing of her sword, though she appeared to be striking at nothing. A flash of grey in the air, a glint of metal, and the leaping snowcat jerked sideways, crashing to the ground with six feet of steel buried in its ribs. I stared for a moment, unable to make sense of what I had just seen.

"Get down, Scriber!" Bryndine shouted as she surged forward through the snow.

Startled into motion, I threw myself flat against the ground, barely ducking beneath the last snowcat as it pounced. Sharp claws raked at my back, tearing my greatcoat and the clothing beneath, but finding no purchase in my flesh. The beast passed overhead, failing to disembowel me by a margin no thicker than my underclothes.

It landed behind me and to my left, the momentum of its jump carrying it a short distance away. When I looked back, it was already skidding to a halt in the snow, reversing direction. My feet slipped on the packed snow beneath me as I tried to stand, and I fell on my stomach, forcing the breath from my lungs. The cat would be on me in an instant, I knew. I did not want to die with my back turned. I rolled over just in time to see the sleek white animal descending. It was so close that I could smell the rotting meat on its breath. Sharp claws raked the air inches from my face.

They never reached me.

Bryndine slammed into the snowcat in midair, holding her shield before her like a battering ram. The force of the blow carried the beast to the side, its claws missing me by inches. Bryndine fell heavily on her hands and knees beside me; the cat landed on its feet, close enough to take my head off with one swipe.

The cat slashed at my throat, quick as instinct. Bryndine was quicker. Still kneeling, she swept her left arm across her body in a backhanded arc, driving the edge of her shield into the snowcat's head. The metal disk sheared through flesh and scraped bone, but drew no blood. Somehow, the cat kept its feet, clawed at me again, and then Bryndine's shield punched through its skull with a dull crunch. It slumped to the ground and moved no more.

Bryndine pushed herself to her feet. Her sword still jutted from the side of one of the beasts' corpses a few feet away, and she strode over and drew the blade free. A dark trickle of blood finally flowed from the wound it left, and she wiped her blade clean in the snow before sheathing it. I had been confused before, but now I understood that she must have *thrown* the sword—a sword that I could barely lift with two hands—hard enough and accurately enough to kill the cat from ten yards away. I stared at her for a moment with my mouth agape, trying to imagine the kind of strength and control that would have taken.

"Are you injured, Scriber?" Bryndine reached down to help me up.

I took her hand and stood, still trying to understand what had happened. "I'm… fine," I said. It was not entirely true—I had no wounds, but the moment of unexplained clarity I had experienced during the fight worried at my thoughts. *What is happening to me?*

"Dragon-damned cats came out of nowhere," Orya said as she and Sylla drew near. "What got them so angry?" She was limping, I noticed, and one of the cats had left four deep parallel gouges in her cheek that would almost certainly scar.

"It was the Burnt." I ran my eyes over my companions as I spoke, searching for signs of serious injury. Sylla clutched at her side where one of the beasts had parted her armor and underpadding to reach the flesh beneath; Bryndine had escaped the worst of it, though her right arm was wounded and bleeding.

Bryndine nodded, apparently unsurprised. "I thought as much. They bled too little, and snowcats do not hunt in packs as a rule." She looked at me for a moment in silent appraisal, then said, "It was fortunate for us that the snow stopped when it did. You hear the… the sorcery at times, Scriber. Was that…" She let the words hang without finishing her thought, but it was clear that she suspected my involvement in ending the snowfall.

I shook my head sharply, unwilling to confess until I knew exactly what I had done. "I don't know what happened. I… I'll understand more when I read those books. We need to find the cave."

"No we don't," said Sylla.

I swivelled to face her, ready to defend the need to keep searching despite the snowcat attack. After whatever it was that I had just experienced, I needed answers more than ever. But

Sylla's face showed none of the defiance I was expecting.

She pointed back the way she had come, and I saw it. Half-buried in the high snowdrifts piled against the valley's east slope, no more than twenty yards from where we stood, was the mouth of a cave. Fyrril's cave.

"We don't need to look for it," Sylla said again. "It's right there."

CHAPTER TWENTY-EIGHT

If not for the bravery of Prince Fyrril and the men who followed him, the entire history of the Kingsland would have been lost with the Forgetting. Much of that history survives today only because of Fyrril's rebellion, and because of the songs of a minstrel who was fiercely loyal to his Prince. Fyrril died to give some measure of hope to the Kingslanders who, nearly five centuries after his death, would face the same threat he had; he died without knowing if his sacrifice would ever be remembered. That it was not for so long is one of the greatest tragedies of the Forgetting.

— From Dennon Lark's *The Forgetting Remembered*

Beyond the mouth of the cavern, the passage turned sharply to the left and sloped uphill. The change in direction prevented the snow from travelling very far past the entrance, and the cold of the mountains kept the air crisp and dry. I could almost believe that the last tomes of the Archives might have survived there for nearly five centuries.

Bryndine and Sylla walked with me, Sylla moving gingerly due to the wound in her side. I had bound the women's injuries as best I could before doing anything else, and none of them had been terribly serious. The gouge in Orya's thigh could have severed any number of arteries, but had missed them all; despite the limp it gave her, she had insisted that she hardly felt the pain and volunteered to stand watch outside while we explored the cave.

The light grew dim as we went further in, but we had come prepared. Bryndine detached a handheld oil lantern from her pack and used it to light the way. It was not long before that light revealed something that nearly made me scream with rage.

At the end of the passage, our way was blocked.

An enormous stone prevented further progress, completely obstructing our path. Peeking through the slivers of space around it, I could see that the passage opened into a larger cavern just beyond, but the light of the lantern did not penetrate far enough to see what lay within.

My shoulders slumped. After coming all this way, it would be a cruel joke for our search to end here, but I did not see how we could get by. There were too few of us to move such a large boulder. Fyrril must have had it put in place to keep animals and the like from entering and damaging the books, but he would have had men with him to help. We did not have time to go back for the others and return before the winter began in earnest.

"Well," I said, unable to keep the bitterness from my voice, "I suppose this is as far as we go."

Bryndine regarded the boulder as though assessing an opponent. "I think not," she said, setting her lantern on the ground. "We will try to move it."

She was a big woman, and strong, but I was certain that she was overestimating her abilities. She had to be. The boulder must have weighed thousands of pounds—it nearly filled the passage, more than eight feet in height and six across. But there was an undeniable command in Bryndine's voice, and when she set her shoulder against the rock, Sylla and I moved to join her without hesitation.

I had seen Bryndine Errynson do amazing things. I had seen her swing her blade hard enough to cleave a man in two, seen her take blows that would have knocked me off my feet. Outside the cave, I had seen her kill a snowcat by throwing a sword that should have been impossible to throw as far and as well as she had. I had seen her fight—and win—while outnumbered ten to one.

This was the most incredible thing I had ever seen her do.

Though Sylla and I pushed beside her, we were less than useless; to say we helped at all would diminish what Bryndine did then. She heaved against the giant rock, the muscles in her arms and neck bulging and cording with the strain. And the rock moved.

At first I thought I had imagined the motion, but then I felt it again. The slightest movement, no more than an inch, but this time I heard the sound as the boulder scraped the stone floor of the cave. I was barely pushing, my feet scrabbling against the ground, unable to find leverage. Yet the heavy stone continued to inch forward.

Sweat beaded on Bryndine's brow despite the cold; her face was flushed and red, her square jaw clenched. She braced her foot solidly against the floor and put all of her weight, all of her preposterous strength, into another surge of effort. The boulder slid forward another half-foot, then a whole foot. Sylla and I fell back, unable to keep any kind of useful pressure on the stone.

Bryndine gave a final, titanic shove, and the boulder flew forward, rasping loudly along the rock wall. Then, slowly and ponderously, the giant stone toppled, falling into the cavern that lay beyond.

The crash of falling stone echoed painfully in my ears, and in the back of my head there was a vague concern that the rock might have damaged the books when it fell, but at that moment, I could do nothing but stare in awe at Bryndine. *The blood of barbarian heroes and Elovian kings*. I had never believed in the old saying about the Errynsons, but it occurred to me then that where Bryndine was concerned, it might have been more than just legend and gossip. I thought that Sylla might mock me for staring so openly, but when I looked at her, she was watching Bryndine, and her eyes held nothing but pure admiration.

Bryndine swayed on her feet, leaning against the side of the passage to steady herself, and Sylla immediately leapt to her side.

"Are you all right, Bryn?" she asked, her brow furrowed with worry.

Bryndine waved away the concern, though she was panting for breath and looked ready to collapse. "I will be fine in a moment. Scriber Dennon, take the lantern. Find the books."

Nodding, I took the handheld lantern and started into the cavern, clambering over the rock that had barred our way. I could already see a glimmer of metal by the lantern's light, and I hurried towards it. What I found took my breath away.

The cave went back some twenty feet, and against the far wall sat ten chests like the ones we had found in Three Rivers, all sealed and seemingly intact despite the long years they had waited there. Ten chests—twice as many as our last find, and if Fyrril was to be believed, full of the most important books the Archives had contained. Atop one of the center chests sat a flat rectangular box crafted of silver, with a burning tree embossed into its surface.

"They're here," I said, my voice breaking. "The Archives are here." There was something damp on my face, and I realized I was crying. This was everything I had worked for my entire life, and despite many, many bumps along the way, I had arrived at last. Those who had died had not died for nothing. The lost history of the Kingsland waited in those chests.

With something approaching religious reverence, I opened the silver box. A leather-bound journal lay within—Fyrril's journal, the source of the pages we had found in our search. A small piece of parchment lay on top of the journal, scrawled with a message in a hand I now knew well.

Whoever has discovered this place, I hope that it is not too late for you to make use of these books. This journal holds my story, all I have done and learned. In the chest beneath are all of the books I found relevant to my research. The others contain the most important works I could save from the Archives.

My men and I will do all we can to preserve the Kingsland, though it will almost certainly end in torture and execution. I have done little right, I fear, and the kingdom suffers for my failures. But perhaps if this information is used well, our deaths will have been worth something.

The despair in the short note was heart-breaking. Fyrril had given everything to defy his father and preserve these works through the Forgetting. He had deserved better than a rebel's death.

Bryndine laid a hand on my shoulder, startling me; she and

Sylla had approached from behind as I read the note. Embarrassed, I hastily wiped the moisture from my cheeks.

"We cannot afford to stay long, Scriber Dennon," Bryndine said. "It will be hard enough getting back with the snow as deep as it is already. We must try to outpace the next blizzard. Most of these books will have to remain here until the Scribers can return."

"I know." I tapped the lid of the chest in front of me. "We need to bring as many books as we can carry from this chest."

"We will take all we can. You can read them on the road."

Though I wanted to read everything in the cave immediately and a hundred times over, I shook my head. "Better that I read them somewhere safe, sheltered. They are old, and I don't want to risk damaging them." This was another thing driven into me at the Academy until it was instinct—a book was a precious thing, not to be read on horseback or around a campfire, not to be exposed to the wind and rain and grime of the outdoors. And these books were more precious than any I had ever handled.

Bryndine raised an eyebrow. "There may be vital information in Fyrril's journal. It is a long journey back to Three Rivers, if you mean to wait."

I smiled, thinking of my conversation with Deanyn a few nights before. "Actually, I know a closer place."

* * *

We arrived in Waymark a little over a week later.

Slogging through deep snow, our packs laden with heavy tomes, it had taken us four days to return to camp. After that it was a safe and uneventful journey south out of the mountains, despite a few light snows before we descended into the foothills. Tenille's injuries did not slow us a great deal—with her limbs splinted and her ribs wrapped, she had insisted that she could ride, ignoring my objections. To her credit, she kept pace with the rest of the group and gave no complaint, though every bump must have been excruciating for her.

It was torturous to hold myself back from opening the

books until we arrived in Waymark, but I was a Scriber, and Illias had taught me well. A week of waiting was nothing compared to centuries of history, and every text had to be handled with care until they could be preserved and recopied at the Academy.

We entered the village just before noon. It was deserted, as expected, and the fire at the Prince's Rest had claimed every building on the east side of the road. I had no particular fondness for the place—it had always been a hiding spot, not a home—but it was upsetting to see it so reduced, nothing left but ash and empty houses.

The fireleaf in the center of town still stood, untouched by the fire; the ground around it was an unbroken carpet of flame-red. Not a single leaf remained in the boughs of the tree, and for once, I was able to approach a fireleaf and hear no hissing voices calling for vengeance. It was not a comfort—I understood too little about the nature of the Burnt and their relationship with the fireleafs for the change to be anything but foreboding.

My little cottage with its roughly made Scriber's shingle was unburned, as I had hoped, and everything I had not been able to carry with me when I left was still there: quills and ink and parchment, a lantern and dozens of candles, and most importantly, my solid oak reading desk.

The women unloaded saddlebags full of ancient texts, stacking them carefully beside the desk. Between Bryndine, Sylla, Orya, and myself we had managed to carry much of the contents of that single chest from the cave: sixteen books, all of them written in Old Elovian. With my limited knowledge of the language, I could tell that they were all works concerning the Sages and the Wyddin, but delving deeper would be difficult.

When the books had been unpacked, Bryndine came to inform me of the plan. "We can spare the rest of the day here, Scriber Dennon, and we will stay the night. Tenille needs the rest; the ride was hard on her. We leave in the morning. Will that suffice?"

"I would prefer more time," I said. "Deciphering Old Elovian is not an easy thing."

"I understand, but we need to report anything you find to

the King as soon as possible. You will have more time when we arrive."

I spread my hands. "I will do what I can then. See that I'm not disturbed. And tell Wynne I may call for her later—I've been teaching her something of Elovian, and I may need an assistant for the translation."

She nodded and left quietly, closing the door behind her.

Opening Fyrril's journal for the first time after a week of waiting—after a lifetime of waiting, really—was among the most thrilling experiences of my life. It held the same wonder as reading my first words, as having Illias attach the pin to my collar at my graduation. It was the realization of a dream I had held since I was a boy. The true events of the Forgetting had been lost for five hundred years, and this was perhaps the only accounting of them left in the world. I would be the first man in centuries to know what had truly happened.

Some of the story was familiar, mirroring events I had lived through in the last few months: the beginning of the rebel attacks, assaults on small villages with no warning and no trace left behind; the panic of the people; the vain attempts of the Army to put a stop to it. But most of it was new, tales of figures whose lives had been all but forgotten.

Fyrril wrote of his father, a kind man and a good king who he loved dearly, whose apparent descent into madness broke his son's heart—a very different Ullyd from the reviled man history remembered. He wrote of his younger brother Oryn, so desperate for his father's approval that he supported the Forgetting and was named heir in Fyrril's place. And he wrote of his closest friend, Adello, whose loyalty never faltered, who dared to remain in the King's court, acting as a spy and informer after the Prince rebelled. The bard must have suffered greatly—if he had heard the voices that surrounded the ensorcelled as clearly as I did, every day in the capital would have been torture.

The journal outlined Fyrril's ill-fated rebellion from beginning to end. After Ullyd was wounded in battle with the rebels, he changed, becoming fearful of the written word. He gathered the support of the Children in his crusade against Elovian knowledge, blaming it for the rebel attacks. The people followed their King in this, burning books and murdering scholars. Finally, Fyrril felt he had no other choice; he rescued as much of the Archives as he could, and turned against the King.

Fyrril began his rebellion with the strongly held hope that he could still save his father and the Kingsland from the rebels' sorcery, but as his men died and his city was besieged, as more and more people turned against him, the Prince fell into despair. He blamed every loss and every death on his own inadequacy, his failure to find some cure for his father. As I read, I was struck by a desire to somehow speak with this man across the years that separated us, to tell him that it was not his fault, that he had done more than anyone could have asked.

Two pages were missing, the ones we had found, left as marks along his path. The entries surrounding those more clearly outlined the Prince's plan. Knowing he could not win, he had decided to at least preserve some record of the truth, so that others might eventually learn what had really happened, and perhaps fight back against his father. He sent a last message to Adello, telling of his destination in the Salt Mountains, where he planned to hide the books. He implored the minstrel to work clues into his songs for those who might someday follow Fyrril's trail. And then, with three hundred of his most loyal men, he abandoned Ryndport and left for the mountains, though the guilt of doing so nearly broke him.

Finally, I came to the last pages of the journal, the record of his last days in the Salt Mountains:

I have been a fool.

So many months wasted searching tomes for information on sorcery. It was never sorcery that gripped my father. It was not the work of men wielding some forgotten power. It was the Wyddin themselves. The voices Adello hears are theirs, crying for vengeance. How many times have I read those pages and missed what was right in front of me?

It is too late now for me to take this knowledge to the capital, to turn this battle back in my favor. I have lost. Too many have been possessed by the tree spirits already. But there is one final path open to me.

The fireleaf trees are their weakness. That is what they have been trying to hide; the Elovians knew, so their words had to be destroyed. When the trees burn, the Wyddin burn with them.

I have three hundred men left with me, perhaps two hundred more scattered among the baronies. When the books have been safely hidden, I will leave this journal for whoever may find it, and we will return to the Kingsland to burn every fireleaf we can. The Army will hunt us; the Wyddin will find us. We will be taken, and tortured, and killed. But we may destroy enough of the trees to free the kingdom. I do not expect to survive, but so many have died for me already. Why should I live when they do not?

May the Mother and the Father forgive me for failing my people so completely.

I turned the page, but there was no more; it was the last entry.

The Wyddin.

It was an impossible thought, and a terrifying one, but I immediately believed it. Really, it was only a small step from what we had already concluded. The failing crops, the earth tremors and lightning, all of it could be explained by the power of the Wyddin over Sky and Earth. They had sent the snowcats after us, and the Wyddin were said to be able to possess and command animals. I had assumed all of these tricks were sorcery, the sort the Sages might have used, but if it could be sorcery, why not the *source* of sorcery?

Fyrril's journal did not answer all of my questions, though. Why would the Wyddin attack us? Certainly tales existed of their jealousy towards mankind, but why here, why now? And no stories told of the Wyddin possessing humans, or driving them mad. No stories explained what was happening to me. The answers, if there were any, had to lie in the books Fyrril had left behind.

When I opened the door to summon her, I found Wynne already waiting outside. I ushered her inside and summarized what I had read, handing her Fyrril's journal so she could read the final entry herself.

When she was done, she looked up at me with wide, sad eyes. "What do you think happened to them, Scriber Dennon?"

I could not say for certain, but I made an educated guess. "The Forgetting lasted for almost two hundred years after Fyrril wrote this, which means Prince Oryn inherited the throne from Ullyd. As much as I wish I could say otherwise, Fyrril and his men must have been captured, executed as traitors." It was the only thing that made sense, considering that nearly all record of the poor, brave Prince and his doomed rebellion had been wiped from history.

"But no one has heard from the Wyddin for five hundred years. They're supposed to just be legends. The Prince must have burned enough trees to stop them."

"Yes. But he likely died to do it." The thought made me want to weep. The heroism of the Prince and his men should have been the stuff of legend; instead they had been killed and forgotten. "I mean to find everything I can about the Wyddin so that we can stop them again—hopefully without dying ourselves. I need your help."

Wynne nodded, her green eyes sparkling like emeralds at the idea of reading such valuable books. I imagined that my own eyes had looked much the same to Illias the first time he had let me open one of the old tomes from Delwyn's Hall. It was that more than anything that prompted my next question.

"Wynne, you wanted to be a Scriber at one time, didn't you?"

She blinked. "I… of course, but I couldn't afford… They didn't let me in."

"I could speak to Illias. He would sponsor you if I asked."

"You would do that?" Her eyes showed disbelief, but the corners of her mouth were already twitching upwards into a euphoric smile.

"Why not? You'd make a better Scriber than—"

Before I could even finish the sentence, she rushed forward and grabbed me in a tight embrace. "Thank you, Scriber Dennon!"

Instantly embarrassed, I pried myself from her grasp. "Well, don't get too excited," I said gruffly. "I'll have to see what kind of work you do tonight."

"I won't disappoint you," she said. There were actually tears in her eyes, which only made me more uncomfortable.

"Get to work, then," I said, shoving a book into her hands and gesturing to my work table. "Look for any words or phrases that might be relevant and bookmark the pages. I'll look through when I am done with this one."

We did not sleep that night. By lantern light, and by candlelight when the lantern ran dry, we scoured the books for information, making whatever sense of them we could. As the hours passed, I filled sheet after sheet of paper with scribbled notes and thoughts, littering my desk with hastily written translations of arcane Elovian passages. Though Wynne knew even less of the language than I did, her help was invaluable; she had an eye for important passages, and never forgot what page a certain phrase lay on, or whether we had seen a certain combination of words in another book.

I understood very little of what we found. In one tome, there was a reference to some sort of Wyddin elders granting the Sages power by teaching them to, roughly, "open their spirits" to something interchangeably referred to as the *Wyd*—a word I was not familiar with—and the "world-voice". This world-voice may have been related to the voices I heard, the ones that had killed Josia, but the book mentioned no danger in it, which was very much at odds with everything I had experienced. I had hoped for more information, something that might explain how I had stopped the snow outside Fyrril's cave, but the rest was simply too complex to translate.

Comparing and cross-referencing a number of the remaining tomes, we were able to decipher certain basic facts about the Wyddin. They were born of trees that the books called *threlea*—"birthtrees" by my best translation—and were tied to these trees. Each leaf was a spirit, and when they were mature the Wyddin often left their trees, causing the leaves to fall and then bud anew when the Wyddin returned. These had to be the fireleaf trees, though the writings made no mention of color, and I was left to wonder what it meant that the fireleafs in the First Forest grew green instead of red.

The books also told of their ability to possess other forms, but exactly *which* forms was not entirely clear. Only animals were mentioned specifically. One text claimed that the Wyddin did not gain the instincts or memories of the animals they possessed. If that same rule applied to human possession, it explained why they fought so awkwardly, and why Uran Ord had forgotten his cousin and his men. It also suggested that Josia had *not* been possessed—she had clearly remembered everything. No, she must have been like me, plagued by pain and voices until they drove her mad. I could not say which fate horrified me more.

Further on, though, the text indicated that the Wyddin could only take the bodies of the *revaen*, which roughly translated to something like "not awake" or "lacking awareness". I did not truly understand the term, but there was no mention of the Wyddin entering anything other than animals and plants, so I took it to mean that they could not possess thinking creatures. The Burnt, though, could clearly take human bodies. If they and the Wyddin were one and the same, they must have found a way to overcome that obstacle.

It was Wynne who found the phrase that truly convinced me this was the case.

"Scriber Dennon, look at this," she said, holding a huge, yellowed tome open for me.

"What is it?"

"We've noticed the Burnt don't seem to bleed properly, yes? Isn't this the word for blood?" She pointed to a paragraph midway down the page.

I perused the words carefully; it was a passage concerning animals possessed by the Wyddin. And there, right where Wynne pointed, was a short sentence that made me tremble as I read it.

Ae rael nima, it said—"They do not bleed".

By morning we had found few useful answers, but I had many more questions, two of which dominated my mind above all others. Firstly, if the Wyddin had so much power, why did they not simply crush us? They could have possessed the King himself instead of his nephew, as they had with Ullyd five hundred years before; they could have simply swallowed Three Rivers into the ground. Secondly, why was there no mention in any of the books about the Wyddin being dangerous in any way? Everything I read indicated that the Elovians had lived in harmony with the forest spirits, which contradicted every tale I had ever heard of the kingdom's fall.

We had very little to show for the night's work when Bryndine finally knocked on the door to tell us it was time to leave. As Wynne and I followed her outside, each of us carrying an armful of old texts, she asked, "Did you find anything, Scriber? Is there any way to stop them?"

How could I tell her we had found so little of use when so many women had given their lives to find these books? My mouth opened foolishly, but I was too ashamed to form any words.

Then, before I could think what to say, a whispered voice crept through my thoughts and drew my eyes to the fireleaf in the village square. The women bustled about its broad trunk, packing their gear and saddling their horses. Above their heads, branches that had been bare the night before bore a handful of leaves that looked like flame. I knew what that meant now: some of the Wyddin had returned to the tree in the night.

Looking at the newly budded leaves, I remembered that I *had* discovered something, perhaps the most important thing. The Burnt had done it to me more than enough times; it was a favor I would be glad to return. I turned back to Bryndine with fire in my eyes and an answer on my tongue.

"We burn them," I said. "We burn them all."

CHAPTER TWENTY-NINE

We made every effort to find Fyrril's books and return quickly. We braved the trip to Ryndport despite the danger and risked the Salt Mountains on the verge of winter; we made the journey back without delay, despite having more than a dozen ancient texts to examine.

We made every effort to report our findings to King Syrid in time.

We were too late.

— From the personal journals of Dennon Lark

I heard little from the Wyddin in the days after we left Waymark—the fireleafs we passed were bare and silent. The Burnt were not in their trees; they were marshalling their forces elsewhere. As we drew near to Three Rivers, though, the voices returned in force, whirling around the city like the first winds of a storm.

But I did not need to hear the voices to know that the city was suffering. As we rode down the Saltroad towards the capital for the second time in as many months, the sight that greeted us was a dismal one. The sprawl of tents and refugees that had once extended well beyond the makeshift palisades had shrunk by more than half. What was left of the camp was crowded into the wedge of land between the Salt and Rynd Rivers; the rest of the land around the capital was completely deserted. The palisades themselves were barely standing, scorched black in places and completely toppled in others. A few Army tents were visible beyond what was left of the wooden walls, brown canvas structures topped by the banner of the burning tree, but given how bad things looked, there were far fewer of those tents than there should have been.

A small group of Army men met us as we rode through the crumbled palisades, eight soldiers and a man wearing the red cord of a Lieutenant on his shoulder. All were on foot; there were no horses anywhere that I could see. The Lieutenant, I realized after a moment, was Ralsten of the First Company. I could barely recognize him—his eyes were sunk into tired, dark pits and he wore a tangled brown beard that hadn't been trimmed for weeks. The gold-stitched numerals that would have identified him as a man of the First had been torn away from beneath the burning tree on his breast; looking at the others, I saw that they had all done the same.

Ralsten eyed us with suspicion and lowered his head slightly in place of a bow. "Lady Bryndine."

Bryndine saluted the man. "Lieutenant Ralsten. What has happened here? Is the First in charge of the defense?"

Ralsten laughed sourly. "No companies out here, Lady. Just us." He spoke without the arrogance or military formality of the man I remembered; he sounded more exhausted than anything else.

Bryndine raised an eyebrow, but did not ask what he meant. "We need to see the King immediately."

"Don't we all," said Ralsten. "Little chance of it though. The gates are barred. You won't be getting in."

"What do you mean? This is urgent."

"I mean the gates are barred, Lady Bryndine. Come with me, I'll explain."

After a moment's hesitation, Bryndine nodded. Ralsten and his men had no horses, so we dismounted and followed them on foot, leading our mounts—save for Tenille, whose injuries made walking impractical.

Ralsten and his men led us by the hastily constructed living areas of thousands of sick, starving, filthy people. Everywhere I looked I saw emaciated children, and sunken-eyed mothers trying to feed their families with what looked like no more than water and weeds. Wounded men carrying makeshift weapons watched us warily as we passed. Of Army men, I saw few—there was perhaps one soldier for every hundred people.

"The first attack came almost three weeks ago now," Ralsten said as we walked. "It was the first time the Burners attacked such a large target, and we weren't prepared. There weren't enough men. The people were being slaughtered. The King ordered us to leave them out here and bar the gates, said it was for the greater good, the safety of the people inside the walls.

"Some of us couldn't accept the order. We left before the gates shut. There weren't enough of us to protect all the riverbanks, so we gathered as many as we could here and managed to mount a defense. But the rebels have been attacking every few days since, whittling us down. We have maybe seventy-five men left, and that number falls with every attack."

That Ralsten was among those who had chosen to defy the King surprised me; he had struck me before as the stubborn, duty-bound sort. I suppose, though, that I had not been wrong—I had merely misjudged where he thought his duty lay. But that was nothing beside the greater shock of his story: Three Rivers under siege, the King abandoning thousands to death.

"My uncle would not have done that," Bryndine said. "It is a complete violation of Erryn's Promise."

"He did, Lady Bryndine. He's different, they're all different. The nobles, the officers, the High Commander. Ever since Uran took that wound, he's been acting strange. When the King started taking council with him and pushed Lord Elarryd aside, everything went wrong."

Concern wrinkled Bryndine's brow. "Is my father safe?"

Ralsten nodded. "As safe as he can be under the circumstances. He and your mother are in hiding somewhere inside the walls. He's been sending what help he can, smuggling supplies and soldiers out through the Underground."

"And Prince Alyn?" Bryndine asked.

"He arrived just before the gates closed, and I haven't seen him since. The men from inside say he's deep in the King's councils, him and Uran."

Bryndine's shoulders fell. We both knew what that meant: the King and his heir had been taken by the Wyddin. We were too late.

"Have you sent word to the other baronies?" Bryndine asked, though she must have known what the answer would be.

Ralsten shook his head. "Lady Bryndine, I don't know if the other baronies are still standing. And if they are, the carrier pigeons are all inside the walls, sending whatever messages the King wants sent."

We walked in silent despair for a time, until Ralsten came to a halt near a large brown Army tent. "Our infirmary, such as it is," he said. "Your friend looks like she needs it." He gestured towards Tenille.

"I'm fine," Tenille argued as Bryndine helped her from her horse, but Bryndine ignored her protests. I questioned the Scriber within as Bryndine laid Tenille into a cot, and was satisfied—the man was pinned in Medicine, not Warfare. He was working with substandard supplies and in poor conditions, but he could do more for Tenille than I had.

"You did not walk with us all this way for Tenille's sake," Bryndine said to Ralsten after we left the tent.

"No," the Lieutenant admitted. "I had to talk to you. To make sure you hadn't changed like the rest."

"And?"

"You seem right enough," he said. "I haven't much choice but to trust you anyway. The truth is, there are too few of us to protect these people. Every time the Burners attack, hundreds go missing. The next time we see them, they're fighting against us, and we're more outnumbered than before."

"What can we do to help, Lieutenant?" Bryndine asked.

"Let my men see to your mounts first. We had to slaughter most of our horses for food—we're going hungry, but there's horse feed to spare." He nodded at the soldiers escorting us and they stepped forward to take our reins, leading the horses away.

When they were gone, he said, "Didn't want them here for this—best the men don't hear it if you bring bad news. I know you went looking for information on the Burners. Did you find anything of use?" The desperation in his eyes and the eagerness in his tone made clear just how badly he and his men needed the help.

Bryndine outlined what Wynne and I had found, and Ralsten listened attentively. I expected him to scoff, but when she was done, he only nodded.

"So the King is one of them." If Ralsten was surprised, it did not show.

"Yes," said Bryndine. There was little more she could say.

Ralsten spoke with resignation, as if voicing a conclusion he had come to days ago. "Then we have already lost. Even if we start burning the fireleafs, the King will send the Army out behind us. We'll be trapped between them and the rebels."

"Wait until the next attack comes," Bryndine said. "If we burn the trees now, it will only warn the Burnt. We might hurt or kill some of them, but as you say, they will stop us. If we wait, they will not expect it. It will not work well more than once, but it may shock them into retreat, or at least make them more vulnerable."

Ralsten was obviously taken aback; he had never much respected Bryndine as a soldier. "Not a bad plan," he said. "Not bad at all. Next time the bastards show their faces, we'll burn them off. At least we'll go down fighting." A savage grin stretched across his gaunt, bearded face.

I realized my hands were trembling, and I asked, "A last stand, then? Is that what it comes to?"

Orya's grin stretched the claw scars the snowcats had left in her cheek and made her look almost feral. "If that's what you're thinkin', Bryn, I'm with you."

"W—we all are," said Wynne.

Deanyn forced a smile. "Living was getting tiresome anyway."

It was plain on the face of every woman in Bryndine's company—they would follow her in this, and die with her if she asked them to. Only Sylla, at Bryndine's side as always, wore a different look: one of dismay. Not because she was afraid to die—I doubt Sylla ever gave much thought to her own well being—but because Bryndine might. I was humbled and ashamed by the bravery of these women. For my own part, I wanted to hide somewhere until it was over.

But Bryndine had another plan in mind. "No," she said. "It has not come to that, not yet."

"What, then?" I asked, glad for any option that might not end in our deaths.

"I am surprised you haven't thought of it, Scriber Dennon. We go to the Academy. The Scribers are sworn to the Kingsland, not the King. They will have to lend us their aid when they see the books. If the Council supports us, Scribers all over the Kingsland will do as they say. Hundreds of Warfare-pinned Scribers from every barony will desert the Army—enough to burn a great many fireleaf trees."

Relief washed over me, and I had to laugh. "It's a sorry excuse for a Scriber who forgets the entire Academy. Of course we go to them."

Bryndine turned back to Ralsten. "Lieutenant Ralsten, can you hold here for a few more weeks?"

"I don't know, La—Captain Bryndine. But by the Divide, we'll try."

Bryndine nodded. "We'll leave immediately, then. There's no time to waste."

"There is one more thing you need to see before you go," said Ralsten.

He led us deeper into the camp, to a flat patch of dirt where a small group—a mix of men in Army browns, commoners in piecemeal armor, and even a Justice in his white cloak—were sparring and running drills. As we approached, I saw a woman in boiled leather armor watching the current match. Her back was turned and I could not see her face, but she was short and stocky, with shoulder length blond hair.

"She said she's one of yours," Ralsten said. "Stumbled in a few weeks ago."

Bryndine voiced the hope we all shared. "Genna?"

The woman turned, and I knew that round, gentle face instantly. And yet, the joy I wanted to feel eluded me. It was too much to believe. I had seen her fall to the Burnt—would they have let her escape without making her one of them? I tried to focus on the whispers, but the air was thick with the voices of the Burnt, and if one of those voices came from Genna, I could not tell it from all the others.

The women must have shared my suspicions, because none of us moved. The company seemed to be collectively holding its breath, waiting to see what their lost member did.

"Bryndine?" Genna's face broke into a wide smile, and she started towards us. A warmth settled over my heart. *She knows us.*

"Genna, how… How are you here?" Bryndine asked.

"They left me. After they pulled me down, they left me there. They were too busy chasing the rest of you to see if I was dead. I don't know how long I was unconscious, but when I woke, they were gone. I couldn't find you, so I came back here."

I could feel the women relaxing around me, the excitement starting to build. Bryndine's mouth rose into the largest smile I had ever seen from her, and she started forward to embrace Genna.

Then, just for the slightest instant, Genna's gaze flickered in my direction, and her eyes met mine. She did not so much as flinch. Right then, I knew this was not shy, damaged Genna. This was something else.

But she knew us, I told myself, trying to deny what I knew to be true. It wasn't convincing. *Of course she knew us. Uran Ord knows us. The Burnt know us, and their voices are everywhere. It isn't her.*

She was a yard from Bryndine now, and one hand was at her side, reaching for something in her belt. I thought I saw a dull glint of light on metal, but no one else seemed to notice.

Words deserted me, and I did the only thing I could think to do.

Sprinting forward, I threw myself at the thing that looked like Genna. She was squat and sure-footed; hitting her was like colliding with a wall of stone. But the attack caught her off guard, and somehow I took her to the ground with me.

I tried to hold her down, but she was on top of me in moments, pinning my arms with her knees. She might have lacked Genna's training, but not her strength. In one hand, she held a small dagger, the dagger she had been about to use on Bryndine, and a hysterical thought floated through my head: *I was right about that, at least. I'm not just making a fool of myself.*

The dagger swept down.

Steel flashed, and then the hand holding the dagger was gone; Genna's arm ended in a raw red stump. The wound did not bleed. I jerked my head to the side as the severed hand fell to the ground, the blade it clasped barely missing my face. Over Genna's shoulder, I could see Bryndine standing with her sword bared, staring down at us in confusion and horror.

The wound did not slow Genna down for even an instant. She clawed at my throat with the hand that remained to her, and her fingers were just closing around my windpipe when Bryndine pulled her away, pinning her arms behind her back.

Genna struggled, but Bryndine's grip was too strong for her to escape. "You will all burn!" she shrieked. Then, abruptly, her body went still, sagging in Bryndine's arms.

"Genna!" Bryndine shook the other woman, trying to rouse her, and looked at me in panic. "I did nothing, she just… Scriber, help her!" She laid Genna's limp body on the ground, and I scrambled to her side.

Genna was motionless, her eyes wide and unblinking. She was not breathing. I felt for a heartbeat, but found nothing. I looked up at Bryndine and shook my head.

Bryndine's shoulders slumped. "She was… one of them?" Only moments before, she had been overjoyed by the reunion; now, sorrow made her voice break.

Though Genna's fingers no longer clutched my neck, I could not seem to properly find my breath. When I spoke, it came out hoarse and angry. "What do you think? She nearly killed you. And me." I immediately felt remorse for the sharp retort—Bryndine was not the true target of my ire.

"She's been with them all this time?" Ralsten asked incredulously. "Why in the depths didn't she act until now?"

"Because," I said, "she was waiting for us. The Burnt knew we would let her get close." *They let us believe she was alive, and then took it away.* I wanted to scream.

I forced myself to look again at the body, though the sight made my stomach roil. Blood was just now beginning to flow from her severed wrist, slow and dark. But not *only* from her wrist. A dark stain grew under her left arm, where her leather armor parted to reveal the padding beneath. When I touched it, my fingers came back red and sticky.

The revaen, *the book said.* All other thoughts fled from my mind. *They can only possess those lacking… lacking what?*

I grabbed the dagger she had dropped. *Forgive me for this, Genna,* I pleaded silently as I sliced through the straps on her armor and the padding beneath.

"What are you doing?" Bryndine demanded. "Leave her!"

"Wait. Look."

I peeled Genna's tabard and armored jerkin aside, revealing her bare torso. Just beneath her left arm, a long gash split her chest, cutting up towards the heart. No one could have survived a wound like that.

Bryndine frowned. "That is not where I cut her. How…"

The books had said that the Wyddin could take plants and animals, things without true self-awareness or identity, but not humans. *But if Genna was killed weeks ago…* "The *revaen*," I said. "Not just without awareness—without mind, or soul. The Wyddin can possess the dead."

Even as I said it, the full, terrifying implication of that truth dawned on me. "This is how they always disappear so cleanly, why they are never captured. They appear to die, leave their hosts, and nothing remains but corpses. The Wyddin themselves are already in some other group of dead villagers halfway across the Kingsland."

As she always did, Bryndine struggled to hide her emotions, but her anger was writ in the set of her jaw, the white-knuckled fists at her sides. "She was one of mine. The Burnt will answer for this." She was silent a moment, then, "They are already dead? All of them? The King?"

"I think so, yes."

Her voice was as cold as a Salt Mountain winter. "Then we need not show them any mercy."

I could barely hear her—the terrible voices all around Three Rivers swallowed her words. It was only then that I noticed how loud they had become; they had been rising since Genna attacked. "*We will have vengeance*," they screamed. "*All will burn.*"

I fought to control my panic. If I gave in to fear, I knew that I would burn. "She told them we're here." My voice sounded unnaturally calm in my ears. "They're coming."

Bryndine didn't hesitate; she started giving orders before I finished speaking. "Selvi, Elene, get your horses and ride north into the hills. Stay out of sight and make for the nearest two fireleafs. When the attack comes, burn them. If you can find oil, prepare flaming arrows—the fires will give away your position, and the further away you are the better." She pointed to each woman in turn, and each saluted upon receipt of her assignment. "Debra and Rylene, ride with Selvi; Ivyla and Leste with Elene. You may have to fight your way closer if the arrows do not work. Deanyn and Wynne, stay with Scriber Dennon, keep him safe. Orya and Sylla, with me."

The women set about their tasks immediately, and Bryndine turned back to Ralsten. "Lieutenant, gather your men. We need to organize a defense around the palisades."

If Ralsten objected to her taking command, he hid it well. Whistling for attention, he interrupted the training soldiers and called them over, sending runners to gather the rest. Other men gathered around as well, men who wore no uniforms and carried only improvised weapons—shovels and sickles, rough clubs and wood-chopping axes.

Ralsten directed two men to remove Genna's body. "She will be laid to rest with the dead after the battle," he said. Bryndine nodded, watching in silence as her friend was carried away.

Ralsten's men accepted our story as easily as the Lieutenant had. They had been fighting the Burnt for weeks, and it came as no surprise to them that their foes were something other than human. However, the idea that the rebels were not living creatures at all was accepted with less grace—an uneasy murmur rippled through the gathered men.

It was Sylla who voiced the question that must have been on everyone's mind: "If they're already dead, how are we supposed to fight them?"

"They do not fall easily," Bryndine said, "but we have killed them before. Scriber, is there anything in Fyrril's books that might help?"

I could only shake my head. "Nothing, but as you say, you've killed them before. It's possible that doing enough damage to the body drives them out, or perhaps certain types of injury—destroying the head or severing the spine seems to have worked in the past. The bodies may be as useless to them as they would be to us with such wounds."

Motioning Bryndine closer, I lowered my voice—what I had to say next was not something I wanted the entire camp to hear. "The truth is, we can't be certain wounding them does anything at all. It may be that they are only trying to hide their true nature by leaving a host when it appears mortally wounded. Now that we have the books, they must assume we know what they are, which would make the charade unnecessary. They may be… difficult to stop."

"Pray that is not true, Scriber," Bryndine said. "We have no choice but to fight them as though it is not."

Then, raising her voice for all to hear, she addressed the gathered soldiers, the frightened men and women of the camp. "Do not give in to fear! You have held these rebels back this long—knowing what they are can only be an advantage. They *can* be beaten. Strike for the head, the neck, the spine; they *will* fall. Do not give in to fear, and we will not fail!" Holding her sword high, she cried, "For the Promise!"

"*For the Promise!*" The men raised their weapons and echoed her cry, even those who did not wear the burning tree, and I found myself shouting with them. I could see it in their eyes, some spark of hope reigniting after long weeks holding against an implacable foe. Bryndine had given them the words they needed, and for once, I think, they saw her as something more than the King's strange, oft-maligned niece. For perhaps the first time, they saw her for what she was: a born leader. She strode towards the palisades, and they followed her almost eagerly. Soon, Deanyn, Wynne, and I stood alone beside the empty training ground.

"We should be with them," Wynne said, staring after her Captain.

Deanyn clapped the younger girl on the shoulder. "Trust me, Wynne, they don't envy us this task. Dennon's sure to do something foolish." She winked at me, and I made myself smile back.

It was not long before the sounds of battle began.

At the first cry, the first clash of metal ringing from beyond the palisades, Deanyn drew her long, thin sword from its sheath. Wynne had already strapped a light buckler onto her arm, and now she followed Deanyn's lead, pulling free her shortsword. In moments, the noise from beyond the walls grew to rival the shrieking of the Burnt in my head. I took several deep breaths, trying to keep in check the terror writhing in my gut.

"Let's get you some place safe," Deanyn said, gripping me by the arm.

It was a suggestion I was all too happy to accept, and I would have followed her, except that at that moment, I heard something. Through the wailing voices in my head and over the cacophony of battle, someone was screaming, "*It burns.*"

I had heard those words before. "Wait," I said, looking for the source of the scream. There, some forty yards from us, a woman had collapsed by her tent just inside the palisades. Without stopping to think, I ran towards her.

I heard Wynne yelling after me. "Scriber Dennon!"

I didn't stop, but I was peripherally aware of both women following behind me. When I reached the fallen woman, there was a girl of no more than ten kneeling beside her, her eyes wide with fear.

"I was joking when I said you'd do something foolish," Deanyn said as she and Wynne reached the tent. "You didn't need to prove me right."

I paid her no mind. The woman on the ground was convulsing wildly, and I dropped to one knee beside her.

"What happened?" I asked the child, though I already knew.

"She… she just fell. Help her, please!"

The woman screamed again, but this time she formed no words, just an incomprehensible howl.

"I don't know how," I whispered. The Burnt were doing this, just as they had to Josia, and to me so many times.

Just then, a brilliant light erupted on the walls not ten feet away, and a roar of thunder split the air. The young girl screamed.

As the after-image of lightning faded, I saw the burning

stakes of the nearby palisades collapse inwards. Rebels streamed through the opening. Women and children screamed and tried to flee, but the Burnt cut them down without mercy. Lightning flashed again, and a nearby tent exploded in flaming debris. The flames spread along the dried yellow grass to the tents nearby like a swarm of burning locusts, devouring everything in its path.

"Run!" I pushed the child towards the infirmary tent, away from the rebels and the raging fire. "We'll do what we can for your mother." The girl hesitated a moment, looked back at her mother, sobbed, and ran.

The first of the Burnt drew near, swinging his sword in a heavy downward arc; Deanyn caught his blade on hers just above her head. With a savage kick to the stomach, she sent the man stumbling back. "We need to get away from here ourselves, right now," she shouted.

The woman on the ground let out a desperate wail and then ceased moving altogether. I did not have to check to know that she was dead, like Josia. *Why not me?* I wondered. *Why am I still alive?*

"Scriber Dennon! Get up, you have to go!" Wynne's cry brought me back to my senses, and I surged to my feet.

Wynne and Deanyn fought side by side in an elaborate dance of blades, fending off five rebels now with many more closing in. A dead-eyed woman struck at Wynne's side and the young soldier caught the blow on her buckler, then ducked under a second man's slash so that it struck one of Deanyn's opponents in the shoulder. The stray attack sent the man off balance, opened his guard, and Deanyn's blade neatly severed his neck.

"Run, Dennon!" Deanyn yelled. "We'll keep them back!"

I should have fled, but I couldn't leave them to die for me. *The others should have set the trees burning by now.* The realization caused panic to rise up my throat; I barely kept myself from vomiting. *We're going to die here.*

Deanyn and Wynne shouted again for me to run as more men and women charged towards us, but I could not. I was no longer in control of my body; fear had turned my limbs to stone. I felt the Burnt turn their attention towards me, and braced myself for the pain.

Then, through the breached wall, I saw a burst of orange spark to life atop a nearby hill. Flames.

The fireleafs were burning.

"They did it!" Wynne pulled her sword from a man's back and pointed it at the distant fire.

I had no time to appreciate the victory. The voices of the Burnt changed pitch, became wails of agony that tore at my mind, and I screamed as their pain set my body ablaze.

The rebels surrounding us faltered, staggered; many fell to their knees. One collapsed limply to the ground, then another—either their fireleaf was the one burning, or the same pain that consumed my body had shocked them from their hosts. I did not know which, and I did not care.

The refugees did not let the opportunity go to waste. Some ran, easily escaping now that the Burnt were distracted. Others who had been fleeing turned to attack their weakened pursuers with rocks, sticks, cooking tools—whatever was at hand. Wynne and Deanyn went to their aid, their blades making short work of the rebels who were still able to fight back.

The Burnt who could still retreat fell back towards the opening in the palisades. Those that could not physically escape deserted their bodies, too mad with pain to be subtle about it—they dropped by the dozen, littering the camp with discarded corpses.

And still I burned. It was not like the flames the Burnt had forced upon me in the past; that, I now understood, had been only remembered agony, a memory of the suffering they had once known. This was what had *caused* those memories. The Burnt did not force me to share their torment—they were too distracted to do anything of the sort—but I felt it all the same. I was lost in an inferno of pain, the pain of thousands of spirits burning together, reflected and magnified through the strange connection that they shared. The connection that I somehow shared with them.

The pain, though, was not nearly the worst of it; worse, far worse, were the emotions that came with the fire, the anguish and terror and loss. Clawing at my temples, I fell to the ground, assaulted by memories of things I had never seen. Pain. Men in brown carrying burning brands. Fear and pain. A forest of green turned red by flames. Sorrow and fear and pain. A huge figure, a giant silhouetted in fire. *Hate.*

For a moment I thought that last image was Bryndine—I had never seen anyone else so large, so broad of shoulder, so heavily muscled. But no, the golden hair was too long, and there was a more masculine shape to the massive body. And then I saw the firelight glint off the iron crown on the figure's head.

Erryn. This was no recent memory; I was seeing the Burning, a thousand years in the past.

I heard a loud wooden creaking as the city gates opened behind us, but it was far away, unreal. My entire existence was the agony of burning, the pain of a thousand minds joined with my own. I might have felt hands lifting me, voices shouting in protest, but that was all a dream. The only reality was fire, and soon it burned me away into nothing, and the world went dark.

CHAPTER THIRTY

Erryn's Promise has often been imperfectly kept. Though the King is meant to serve the people, the people rarely have the courage to stand against a King who does not. The Justices of the White Hall are sworn to remove a King who has been judged a Promise-breaker, but in practice that is often a difficult task, as the Justices are adjudicators and gaolers more than true soldiers.

Worse still than simple Promise-breakers are the Kings who have defied the Promise while convincing the people that they were upholding it, such as Ullyd the Forgetter. A King who claims to act in the best interest of his subjects can do nearly anything in the name of Erryn's Promise, if the people are foolish enough to allow it—and too often, they are. When a King has the people's support, however misguided that support is, it is nearly impossible for the Justices to intercede. In the worst cases, the Justices are fooled themselves.

In this way, the Promise has been the Kingsland's greatest weakness at times, just as it has been our greatest strength at others.

— From Dennon Lark's *The Promise of a Kingdom*

"Wake up."

A sudden impact and a sharp pain in my side shocked me into consciousness. I did not know where I was, but the moment I woke, even before I opened my eyes, I became aware of invisible voices all around me. *I must still be in Three Rivers, at least*, I surmised. The whispers of the Burnt suffused every inch of the capital and the surrounding land.

As my vision focused, I saw that I was lying on the floor in a white room. A man in King's Army browns stood over me, poised to kick again. I groaned and held up a hand to show him I was awake, but it didn't stop him; his foot lashed out and caught me in the ribs, knocking the wind out of me.

"On your feet, traitor," the man said.

Standing was a painful proposition, but I did my best, hoping to avoid another blow. Disobeying every instinct my aching body had, I rose to my knees and then to my feet, nearly falling over again when a rush of dizziness stole my balance away. The soldier caught me by the arm before I toppled.

It took me a moment to determine my location. The room was entirely empty, and the white walls were featureless and austere save for a single barred window, too small and too high for me to see through. It was only when I saw the steel bars that blocked the entrance in place of a door that I knew where I was. The White Cells—the dungeons beneath the White Hall.

The soldier dragged me from my cell into the hallway, where several other uniformed men waited. Bryndine was with them, and they were taking no chances with her—she was bound in irons and her scabbard hung empty on her back. Six men surrounded her and held her chains, all clearly chosen for size and strength, though none came within a foot of Bryndine's height. The single man gripping my unbound arm was almost humorous in contrast, though the situation was anything but.

Bryndine nodded at me in greeting, as she might have if we encountered one another on the street instead of in a prison surrounded by guards. "Scriber Dennon. You are well?"

I inclined my head slightly, scared to speak aloud in front of the guards. Apparently my fear was justified, because the largest of the soldiers did not approve of Bryndine's question. "Shut up, bitch," he said, and drove a meaty fist into her stomach. She did not flinch. The man winced and surreptitiously rubbed his knuckles; I held back a spiteful grin.

"Good," said Bryndine. "We have been—"

"I told you to shut up!" The man drew his sword and

struck her hard in the side with the pommel.

Once again, Bryndine absorbed the blow. Her jaw clenched, but otherwise she showed no sign of discomfort. She turned her gaze on the man, cold and calm, and said, "I will speak when I wish. My uncle has summoned us"—she placed a slight but meaningful emphasis on her relation to the King—"and I do not think he wants me or the Scriber beaten to the point that we cannot answer his questions. But by all means, strike me again. The choice is yours."

The big soldier glared up at her. "Don't think the King'll save you. He hangs them that work for the rebels, you'll be no different." But he sheathed his weapon, all the same. "Let's go. He's waiting."

The soldiers led us out of the dungeon and through the White Hall. The stark white corridors were empty save for the soldiers guarding the White Cells—the white-cloaked Justices who presided over the courts and warded the cells were nowhere to be seen. Their vow to keep the King's power in check, I suspected, had not been popular with Syrid of late.

As we walked down the great white stairway that led from the White Hall to the street just outside the Kingshome, Bryndine explained what had happened while I was unconscious. After the Burnt fled, the city gates had opened and the First Company had emerged, surrounding the camp and demanding that Bryndine and all who travelled with her be given into their custody at once. Ralsten and his men had tried to fight back, but they had been vastly outnumbered. Unwilling to let them spend their lives uselessly, Bryndine had laid down her arms and surrendered herself.

"I am not certain who else they took," Bryndine said. "They kept us separated. The women I sent to burn the fireleafs had not yet returned; they may have eluded capture." Her hands were bound, so she tipped her head towards the men surrounding her. "Most of these men, I think, are… in control of themselves. They did not fight like the Burnt. But they think us traitors. Uran and my uncle have convinced the city of our guilt, though I do not know what crime we are meant to have committed."

The soldiers did not try to silence her again, though much

of what she said drew angry stares, and they handled us roughly in place of actually striking us. Even when it became clear that they would not hurt me for speaking, though, I said nothing. There seemed little point in discussion. We were prisoners of the King, and the King was of the Burnt. We would be dead by day's end.

We were taken through the gates of the Kingshome, but not to the small receiving chamber I had seen on my last two visits to the palace. No, the soldiers led us directly through the main doors and down the tall, arched hallway that led to the throne room. The King had summoned us to stand before Erryn's Chair. There was only one reason I could think of for that. *He means to pass sentence on us.*

The throne room was massive, over a hundred feet long and at least half that in width, with a high vaulted ceiling supported by slender marble columns. Sunlight streamed in from the dozens of windows that lined the walls, so that the room was always bright during the daylight hours. When the King passed judgements or made proclamations to his people, he did so from Erryn's Chair, and the throne room was built to allow hundreds of citizens to witness such events. It was filled near to bursting now. Citizens of Three Rivers crowded into every inch of free space, clamouring for a view of Bryndine and myself. Guardsmen in King's Army tabards lined the brown velvet carpet that led to Erryn's Chair, keeping the throng from blocking our path forward.

The people screamed at us as we passed by. "*Traitors,*" they cried, and "*Blasphemers!*" They shouted obscenities at Bryndine, calling her the Bloody Bride, accusing her of terrible, entirely imagined crimes. They threw curses at me as well, though less often—mostly I was beneath their attention, despite the fact that some of my crimes were real. I may have desecrated holy ground, but I was not as exciting a target as the King's niece. Some spat, but the guards kept them far enough away that it rarely reached us, and when it did it only spattered against boots and trouser legs.

At the far end of the hall, King Syrid sat upon Erryn's Chair, watching with a blank face as we approached. The throne of the First King was enormous and beautiful—carved, legend said, from the trunk of the first fireleaf Erryn had burned, orange-yellow wood shot through with veins of red and spots of charred black, varnished to a perfect shine. The back and the arms of the chair curved and twisted with the grain of the wood, curling into points like tendrils of fire. Above the King's head, the burning tree of the Errynsons was carved into the wood in exquisite detail, each leaf and lick of flame sharply defined.

The King's councillors stood to the right of the throne. Uran Ord was closest to Syrid, his head still bandaged and misshapen. Prince Alyn was next in line, and then Korus. The Eldest Brother and Sister were at the King's left side, and Sister Olynna shot me a satisfied look that was almost a smirk. And with all of these powerful people, for reasons I could not fathom, stood Logan Underbridge, trying his best to look important and dignified.

The King raised his hand as we drew near, and eventually the hall fell silent. Silent, at least, to anyone but me. The whispers of the Wyddin did not cease. Their voices filled the room—and the palace, and the city—so thoroughly that it was difficult to distinguish one source from the next, but when I focused on the King I could sense the silent screams flowing from him, a strong current in a vast ocean of noise.

"Bryndine Errynson and Scriber Dennon Lark," said King Syrid, and there was nothing in his words or manner of the shrewd, sharp-tongued King I had met before. The eyes that had once darted ceaselessly were still; his voice was cold and empty. "For giving aid to rebel criminals, for plotting against your King and his councillors, and for seeking forbidden Elovian sorceries, you and your companions stand accused of treason against the Kingsland."

"We have committed no treason," said Bryndine, holding her head high. "We have done our duty and kept our oaths."

"Lies from the mouth of a traitor," the King said coldly. He grasped something in his hand and held it up for all to see—a small scrap of paper. "You sent this message from Ryndport. It is full of vile, treasonous accusations against the High Commander. Prince Alyn will confirm that it was written by your hand."

In Ryndport, I had rarely seen Prince Alyn without a smile on his face; he was not smiling now. The Prince was lost to the Burnt, as his father was. Alyn had been a warm, kind man; this was not a man at all, just a thing wearing a man's skin. "She sent the letter with one of my birds, though I did not know what it said at the time," he said. "Moreover, when they came to Ryndport, they brought the rebels with them, and while the Burners gathered at our walls, my cousin and the Scriber were seeking books of magick. The same magick the rebels use."

Shocked murmurs and gasps rippled through the crowd with each accusation. When Uran Ord told of Bryndine's actions in Waymark, her supposed betrayal of the King's Army, the murmurs grew into outraged shouts; by the time Sister Olynna and Brother Cyril accused us of defiling the Old Garden in our search for "forbidden knowledge", the people were screaming for our heads. *It's the Forgetting come again,* I realized with horror. *We are going to hang for reading the wrong books.*

When Korus began to speak, my horror gave way to anger.

"Of course, the Council forbade Scriber Dennon's blasphemous pursuit," he said, and when he looked at me, his lips curled into a slight, self-satisfied smile. It was that smile that told me the truth of the matter: Korus was not one of the Burnt. *He is doing this out of spite.*

"But he rebelled against that ruling," Korus went on. "He was determined to find the power that destroyed Elovia—"

I could not stay silent any longer. "We are both sworn to uncover the past! Have you forgotten that oath? How can you condemn another Scriber for seeking the truth of our history?"

"He is condemning you for treason and dark magicks," said Uran Ord. He nodded to the guard holding me, and the man struck me hard in the stomach, stealing my voice and my breath away.

Korus looked down at me and wrinkled his nose in disgust, making a show of it. "As I said, Scriber Dennon was determined to find the magicks of the Sages. He has been looking into Elovian writings for years. It would not surprise me if he helped the rebels learn their sorcery."

"Thank you, Scriber Korus," the King said. He motioned

for Logan to step forward. "This man has known Scriber Dennon for five years, and was in Waymark during the rebel attack there. If you would, Master Underbridge."

Logan puffed his chest out proudly. "If it pleases yer Majesty, I got plenty to say 'bout the Scriber. And the Bloody—beggin yer pardon, uh, the Lady Bryndine." He paused, looking at the King with a stricken expression.

As though he cares what you call her, Underbridge. He's about to have her killed. I would have laughed, except that his stupidity proved he was not being controlled. He was the same Logan I had always known, and he was doing this of his own free will. Like Korus, like the crowd begging for blood behind us. *These are the people she wanted to save. This is how they reward her.*

"Go on, Underbridge." Syrid motioned for him to continue.

"Well, the Scriber was always a shifty sort, never much fer talkin', kept to his books. Don't surprise me none if he's been up to some godless business, all this sorcery and whatnot. Night afore the attack came, he met yer Majesty's niece, snuck her into his house. Next night, she comes back and the Burners come right after.

"We seen 'em doin' some ritual or such too, after the First saved us. Josia, she went to stop 'em and the Bloody Bride killed 'er on the spot. Josia's the one who seen 'em that first night they met too, I'd wager they wanted to stop her talkin'."

I did laugh then, but it was a rough sound, raw and bitter. "Mother below, this is a farce. Bryndine saved your *life*, Logan. All she has done is try to help you, all of you!"

The audience roared in outrage, and the guard struck me again, a vicious backhand across the face. My head snapped to the side. Spots floated before my eyes, and I could taste blood.

"I have heard enough," Syrid announced. "You are both guilty, that is clear. It breaks my heart to do this to my brother's only child, but I must sentence you to death. You will hang tonight, along with the other women who were captured."

It was no less than I expected, but the words still made my heart batter against my chest, trying to escape my doomed body. All the rage and defiance drained out of me in an instant.

Bryndine, though, showed no fear. She looked her uncle in

the eyes without shame and said, "Then I will die without regret, beside soldiers truer than any in this room."

The crowd jeered, but Bryndine ignored it. She turned to face the people, and though six men held her chains, all of them together could not hold her in place. "If there are any true Army men here," she said, "you will join Lieutenant Ralsten beyond the—"

"Silence her!" the King commanded, the voices of the Burnt screaming along with him.

Bryndine's voice cut off as one of the soldiers jabbed her in the gut with the butt of his spear. She gasped and bent forward over the haft of the weapon, and he struck her full across the face with a steel gauntleted hand.

But Bryndine Errynson was not so easily cowed. She straightened, spat the blood from her mouth, and spoke on in a clear, strong voice. "The people locked outside the gates have done nothing wrong. My uncle has left thousands to die. He has betrayed the people and broken the Promise. He has no right to the crown!"

"Take her away!" Syrid screamed, spittle flying from his lips. "*Death*," a thousand voices shrieked in my head.

The soldiers strained against her chains, tried to pull her away from the King, but Bryndine set her feet and stood firm. It would take more than six men to move her; it would take more men than there were in the entire King's Army, it seemed to me.

Insults and accusations filled the hall—Bryndine's words were falling on deaf ears. "*Bitch!*" they called her. "*Sorceress! Liar!*"

"It's a trap," one soldier declared. "We leave the city and her rebel friends are waiting to slit our throats."

Bryndine paid no heed to the vitriol they hurled at her; she just spoke louder to be heard above the noise. "Honor your oaths! Hold true to the Promise! This is not a time to hide within the walls; this is a time for courage!"

The big soldier who had struck her before the trial drew his sword and jammed the point against her back. "You best shut your mouth," he growled.

When she looked over her shoulder at him, he flinched

visibly, but she only said, "I have nothing more to say."

"That is truer than you know," the King said, staring at her with unconcealed hatred. "You speak with the voice of corruption. In the name of Erryn's Promise, I will not allow your Elovian magicks to curse my people!"

The people cheered at that, and most swept their fingers through the air in the sign of the Divide. Shouts of "*Long live the King*" and "*Mother shelter him*" and "*Father bless his rule*" roared through the throne room. It was sickening.

Syrid raised a hand to acknowledge the support of the crowd, then looked down at Bryndine and me with cold eyes and said, "Your sorcery will die with you." He motioned for the soldiers to remove us. "Take them to the gallows. If my niece tries anything, kill her."

The soldiers led us away from the throne, and this time Bryndine did not resist. *This is the end, then.* I thought of Illias, of what I would have said if I could have spoken to him one more time. Then, unexpectedly, I remembered the promise I had made to Deanyn that night in the Salt Mountains—to keep myself alive. I had not done a particularly good job of keeping it. *I won't see her again to apologize. But then, if I was alive to see her, I'd have nothing to apologize for.* It was a ridiculous thought; I wished I could have shared it with her. She would have seen the humor in it. *Still, maybe it is best to have it done swiftly. No time for fear.*

"I'm sorry, Scriber Dennon," Bryndine said softly.

"Don't be," I said. "You did all you could."

The citizens were quieter now, though they still pointed and spoke in low voices as the soldiers led us by. The sentence had been given, and these were the sort of people who liked to think themselves pious; it would not have been proper to cheer or gloat. So instead they pretended at solemnity, pretended that they had not come here with bloodlust in their hearts, praying to the Mother and the Father that they might see the Bloody Bride and her company hanged. I had preferred the insults. This false quiet reeked of hypocrisy.

We had not gone far when a voice shattered the silence.

"Your Majesty, wait!"

I could not believe my ears—it was Korus. *What is he doing?*

"What is it?" Syrid glared at his Royal Scriber.

For an instant, I entertained the mad hope that Korus had regained his senses, that his next words would save us somehow. I should have known better.

"If we wait until the morrow, we can make a better example of them," Korus said. "Let me spread the word, gather the entire city. We can burn them in the Commoncourt on a pyre made of their own vile books of sorcery, to show the people what happens to traitors. Give me one more day, Majesty, and I will see that they get what they deserve." He gave me a long look as he spoke those last words—savoring his victory, no doubt.

They have the books. Despair overpowered whatever comfort the prospect of surviving another day might have provided. If any of Bryndine's women remained free, they could have rallied the Scribers with Fyrril's journal. Without proof, though, the Council would never lend their aid. If the Burnt had the books, they had won.

The King smiled, though it did not reach his eyes. "Yes. Yes, that would please me. After sunset tomorrow, I think, so all can see the flames." He raised his voice to address the audience. "They will burn!"

Syrid's words rang throughout the throne room, echoing off the high ceiling as if spoken by a hundred voices at once. But only I heard the full extent of the echo—not a hundred voices, but a thousand, tens of thousands. The invisible voices all throughout the city and the surrounding countryside joined as one, hate-filled and savage, and chanted three words I had heard many times before: "*All will burn.*"

It was very likely true; there was no one left to stop them. Soon enough, they would feed all of us to the flames—not just me, not just Bryndine and her company, but the entire Kingsland. The memory of King Erryn watching a verdant forest burn black came to me then, and as I looked upon the faces of the mob, twisted with scorn and judgement, I could think only one thing:

We deserve it.

CHAPTER THIRTY-ONE

The sad truth is, we brought all of this upon ourselves.

— From the personal journals of Dennon Lark

Bryndine paced in her cell. "Why are they doing this, Scriber? Why hold trials and executions? Why not simply tear open the ground beneath our feet, or destroy the city with lightning? Do they lack the power?"

That would be too quick, I thought. *Too painless*. "What does it matter?" I asked. "There is nothing we can do to stop them now."

Bryndine ignored my answer. "And if their sorcery is not strong enough to do that, they could attack in force, lay siege to the baronies. They have the King and the Army in their grasp. They could overwhelm us in days if they attempted anything more than these raids. What stays their hand?"

From my own cell across the hall, I could see into hers. She marched by the door, disappeared from sight, then moments later marched by again. Everything above her shoulders was hidden from sight; she was taller than the doorway. The other cells I could see were empty, and as best I could tell we were alone. This was the upper level of the White Cells, where important prisoners were kept; common thieves and murderers would be on the lower floor. If there were others near us, they chose to stay silent while Bryndine mused endlessly on the motives of the Burnt.

I sighed. "You are thinking like a soldier, Bryndine. The Burnt are not soldiers. They aren't seeking some sort of strategic victory. They don't want to take the kingdom for themselves, or wipe it from the land, or anything so simple." What the Burnt did want was no mystery to me, not anymore. I had shared their memories, and felt their pain. It was not a subject I wished to dwell upon, not with my own death by fire fast approaching.

But Bryndine would not relent until she understood. "What do they want, then, Scriber?"

Rubbing at my temple, I said, "You must understand that they *hate* us. Not certain people, not only some of us—they hate every living person in the Kingsland." *And they should.* "They want to destroy us, yes, but they want it to be slow, and painful, and terrifying. They want us to see our loved ones turn against us, and to be so confused and afraid that we fight amongst ourselves. They want us to suffer, as they have suffered."

Ducking her head beneath the doorframe, Bryndine gripped the bars of her cell and stared across at me. "You have heard them speaking of this?"

"I saw… a vision. A memory. When Selvi and Elene burned their trees."

"Why? Why do they hate us?"

When I closed my eyes, I could see Erryn standing under emerald leaves, his crown shining red with reflected fire. "Because we burned them alive. Because we destroyed their forest, and it drove them mad."

"What do you—" Bryndine's voice cut off abruptly. Then, a moment later, "You mean the Burning."

"Of course I do. Why else call themselves the Burnt?"

"A thousand years have passed since then."

"They still remember. We burned only two trees today, and I felt it a thousand times over. I can't imagine what it would have been like when the whole forest burned, but a thousand years would not be nearly long enough to forget. They will never forgive us."

"You speak as though we brought this on ourselves,"

Bryndine said. "Even if Erryn burned their forest, should we die for the sins of our ancestors?"

"I don't know." Despite all the pain they had put me through, it was hard not to feel some pity for the Wyddin—there was no justice in what had been done to them. I could not say the same for my own kind, not after what I had seen at our trial. "Perhaps our own sins are enough. You saw the people today. They will watch us burn and love it. You tried to save them and they are going to let you die. As Fyrril's people let him die, let the Forgetting happen. The Burnt only gave them the excuse."

Bryndine shook her head. "No. They were afraid, confused, misled by their King. The Burnt have convinced them that enemies are everywhere. They do not all deserve to die. I am sorry for what was done to the Wyddin, but it does not excuse them." Anger flashed in her eyes. "It does not excuse what they did to Genna."

That was a difficult thing to argue against, and I did not try. "Deserved or not, the Kingsland will burn. The Army took Fyrril's books, and there is nothing we can do from these cells. The Burnt have already won."

"Ralsten knows the truth," she said stubbornly. "He may still be able to do something."

I did not want to debate with her any longer; I just wanted to be left alone with my despair. "Maybe," I said. "Either way, you and I will die tomorrow."

Bryndine opened her mouth to respond, but just then we both heard something—footsteps on the stairs. *The guards must have heard us.* The thought scared me, though I recognized how ridiculous that was. I was going to burn tomorrow, yet I was worried about being punished by an angry gaoler.

Bryndine raised a finger to her lips as the footsteps grew louder; in the hallway now, coming towards us. A figure came into view—a man draped in a long black cloak, his face obscured by a deep hood and deeper shadows cast by the torches lining the hall. He stopped in front of my cell and drew back his hood.

It was not a guard.

"Hello, Korus," I said. "Come to gloat?" I was not

surprised to see him; he had never been magnanimous in victory. He could hardly have let me die without some final comment.

Korus narrowed his eyes in annoyance. "Quiet, Lark."

"Please, tell me how much better… wait, what are you doing?"

He had pulled a ring of keys from his pocket, and now he took a long iron key in hand and inserted it into the lock. "What do you think? I'm freeing you." He scowled as though the very idea was distasteful to him.

"I can see that, but *why?*"

He actually looked insulted at that. "Do you really think that little of me? I remember my oaths. I don't intend to let another Forgetting happen."

"You spoke against us at the trial."

"Should I have taken your side and been thrown in here with you? A lot of good that would have done." He rolled his eyes. "This is why I never liked you, Lark. Illias handed you your sponsorship; you never understood the game I had to play to earn my pin. Sometimes you have to say what people want to hear. If you had ever learned that, you might have been more cooperative at the trial, instead of antagonizing the King. You would have been hung immediately if I hadn't suggested the public burning." Pulling open the cell door, he looked at me with a raised eyebrow. "Are you coming?"

"I suppose your company is preferable to burning to death," I said, but I peered down the hall in both directions before stepping out, half-suspecting to see a guard waiting just out of sight.

Korus snorted in amusement at my show of distrust. "This isn't a trap, Lark. Much as I would like to see you beaten for trying to escape, that isn't why I'm here." He turned away from me to unlock Bryndine's cell, and I stared at his back. It went against everything I thought I knew about the man, but I was starting to believe him. *We just may get out of here alive*, I realized.

Bryndine backed away from the bars and eyed Korus intently. "Where do you intend to take us?" she asked. "The guards will not let us walk out of here."

The lock clicked and Korus opened the door for her. "To Lord Elarryd," he answered. "The guards will not be a problem."

At the mention of her father, Bryndine's guard dropped, and she ducked out of the cell. "My father is well? Is my mother with him?"

"They are both safe, hidden in the Underground. We have been using the tunnels to get around the city." He gestured for us to follow. "Quickly. We still have to free your friends."

When we reached the stairs, Korus paused to pull his hood back over his face. "The others are on the lower level, but they are not the only prisoners there. Do not say my name where it might be heard. No one can know I was here." He started down the stairway.

"The guards must have seen you at the entrance, though," I said. "Won't it be obvious that you freed us?"

Korus shook his head. "They don't know I am here. I did not pass that way. Quiet now, Lark. The less attention we draw the better."

His response raised half a hundred more questions, but I followed him down the stairs in silence. When we reached the bottom, Korus led us into a small guard chamber just before the cells. It was little more than a place to sit for whoever was on duty, a bare white room with a small table and two chairs. A worn brown rug lay on the floor beneath the table, doing precisely nothing to make the chamber cosier.

"Wait here," Korus said. "I will get the others. Best no one sees you."

Bryndine frowned. "Where are the guards? There should be someone here."

Korus grinned. "I'm afraid I may have confused their schedule somewhat. There is a double shift of men upstairs, and this level has been sadly neglected. But they will sort things out before long."

"Go, then," I said, nudging him towards the door. "I'd very much like to not be here when they come."

When Korus was gone, Bryndine turned to me, and I recognized the worried lines around her eyes immediately. "Can we trust him, Scriber?"

I spread my hands. "I wouldn't have said so a few hours ago, but if this is a trick, I don't know what he could possibly gain from it."

She nodded. "I had the same thought. We have no choice but to go along with him and hope we are right, I suppose, but I would feel better if I had my sword."

"So would I," I said.

It felt like hours before Korus crept back into the room, though it must have been only minutes. Sylla was the first through the door behind him, surveying the room with a suspicious frown. Only when she saw Bryndine did she allow herself to relax, as though letting out a breath she had been holding for hours. "Bryn. They said… I thought…" She swallowed and looked away, wiping at her eyes with the heel of her hand. I did not often feel sympathy for Sylla, but I did then—it must have been torture for her, knowing Bryndine was in danger and being unable to help.

"Dennon!" A red-haired blur pushed by Sylla and leapt at me, pulling me into a tight embrace. Deanyn's voice caught in her throat as she whispered, "We thought you were dead."

I was unaccustomed to being greeted so affectionately, especially by women, and I tried to mask my awkwardness with humor. "I made you a promise. I was scared of what you might do to me if I didn't survive."

She laughed into my chest, and I hesitated only briefly before wrapping my arms around her. I had assumed I would never see her again; it surprised me just how pleased I was to be wrong.

After a moment, she released me and stepped back, looking me over to ensure that I was unharmed. Then, without any warning, she punched me hard in the shoulder. "I don't like worrying, Scriber. Don't do that again."

Rubbing my shoulder, I feigned an indignant scowl. "I assume you are speaking of my being taken against my will and sentenced to death?"

"Yes. That." She grinned, and I noticed for the first time how lovely she was when she did. Even in the dim torchlight her eyes sparkled with humor, bright and blue, striking in contrast against the red of her hair. I realized I was staring only when she quirked an eyebrow upward, and I yanked my gaze away, embarrassed.

Looking beyond Deanyn towards the door, I saw Orya and Wynne standing just inside; there was no one else behind them. Apparently the Burnt had not captured many—only the women who had been near when Bryndine and I were taken. Wynne smiled at me when my eyes landed upon her, and it was a relief to see that she was all right. I had worried that she or Deanyn might have been hurt defending me.

Orya tipped her head in the direction of the stairs. "Let's go. Glad to see you ain't dead and all, but if we don't move, we'll be back in those cells before long. I don't much like bein' locked up."

Bryndine stepped towards the door. "Orya is right. We have little time."

Korus raised a hand to stop her. "We leave through here."

Bryndine raised an eyebrow, but waited as he pushed aside the small table that sat in the middle of the room, then knelt and lifted the edge of the threadbare brown rug. Beneath, the outline of a wooden trapdoor was clearly visible. The confusion faded from Bryndine's eyes. "The Underground. That is how you got in without being seen."

"I have never heard of a passage under the White Cells," said Wynne.

Korus' mouth turned up into the smug smile I knew well, and he said, "You weren't meant to. It is used for prisoners who must be jailed in secret, for political reasons. Only the King and his chief advisors knew of it. And the Justices, of course. But the King remembers nothing of late, and the Justices have joined with Lord Elarryd. None of our enemies know it exists." He pushed back the rug and pulled the wooden door open. "Come—we don't want to be found here."

One by one, we descended into the subterranean darkness of the Underground.

* * *

Most of the Underground was a maze of half-ruined cellars and earthen tunnels, but eventually Korus led us into a different sort of chamber altogether. Clean and relatively intact, it was furnished with several wooden chairs and a number of Army cots, and lanterns in every corner provided ample light to see by. Crates and supplies were piled against the wall to my left, and a man with a Scriber's pin on his collar seemed to be taking an inventory. There were others too, more than a dozen men and women working at various tasks and speaking in low voices. Some wore Scriber's pins, others Army browns, and more than a few wore plain clothes, with no identifying color or sigil. A pair of Justices in their white cloaks stood before a door on the far right side of the room.

All eyes turned to us as we entered, and several hands went instinctively to sword hilts, but when they saw Korus, most returned to their work and their conversations.

"What is this place?" I asked.

"A black market hiding hole," said Korus. "The smugglers know the Underground better than anyone. They have been lending us their expertise."

Sylla raised an eyebrow. "You're working with criminals?"

"As it happens, I just now freed several." Korus glanced over his shoulder at her with a smirk. "We are working with whoever will help us. The black market, it seems, has suffered since King Syrid's isolation of the city." Nodding towards the door on the far side of the room, he resumed his stride. "This way."

The Justices at the door let us by with a bow, and Korus led us into the chamber where Elarryd Errynson waited.

This room too was well lit, and a round table sat at its center. Leaning over that table, the Lord Chancellor sat in close discussion with four others. I recognized his wife Branwyn immediately. Beside them sat the High Justice, a bald man with a craggy face who I knew only by his white cloak and the silver circlet around his forehead. A red-corded Army Lieutenant who I didn't know and a Scriber who I might have filled the other chairs; after a closer look I recognized the Scriber as Tenille's husband, Vance.

Korus cleared his throat to announce our presence, and Branwyn Errynson was the first to look up. When she saw Bryndine, her hand flew up to cover her mouth. "Bryndine—"

Her voice choked off and she rushed forward to embrace her daughter. She looked like some tiny elfin creature from the tales of the First Forest with Bryndine's huge arms folded around her, but it was a moving display all the same.

Lord Elarryd stepped around the table to join his family, clasping Bryndine's shoulder. "It is good to see you safe, Bryn," he said.

The High Justice ran a hand over his bald head and glowered at us. "We haven't time for pleasantries, my Lord."

"I am aware of our situation, Tevon," said the Lord Chancellor, casting an annoyed glance at the man. "I'm sorry, Bryn, but he is right; there are matters we must discuss before you can rest."

Bryndine nodded. "You wish to know what we have found about the Burnt."

"And how Ralsten fares outside the walls. I have sent men out to aid him, but it is harder for him to get information back—we must move constantly to avoid discovery."

"They are hard pressed, Father," said Bryndine. "Ralsten has too few men and too little supplies, and he was not trained to take on so much responsibility. An officer pinned in Warfare might be able to do more, but even then I do not think they could hold for much longer. A week, maybe, if the Burnt continue to toy with them. If they decide to bring their full strength to bear, the camp will fall in hours."

Elarryd pinched the bridge of his nose, reminding me for a moment of his brother. "I feared as much."

"How did all of this happen?" Bryndine asked. "When we left, it seemed Uran was going to be dismissed, and now he is the King's closest councillor."

"I know less than you do of the true reasons, I imagine, but the events themselves were simple enough. When Syrid told Uran of his dismissal, the lad asked to speak privately with him. After that, Syrid was not himself. Uran never left his side, and he would not hear my council." Elarryd gestured at Korus. "Scriber Korus was the one who first realized that it might be the same sorcery you left to investigate. I did not believe it at first, not until the rebels attacked and Syrid barred the gates."

The High Justice frowned, his face a mask of grim lines.

"We named him a Promise-breaker for that. He named us traitors and rebel sympathizers. Dozens of my men were executed."

"He kills all who oppose him, under the guise of executing traitors," said Elarryd. "Scribers too—he has not yet risked declaring them all rebels, for fear of the Academy's retribution, but any who speak against him…" Guilt twisted the Lord Chancellor's features, and his wife laid a gentle hand on his shoulder. "I tried to stop it, but Syrid would not listen. It was then that I knew he was no longer my brother. When he summoned me to his chambers to speak privately, I fled to avoid falling under the same spell. The Justices sought me out, and we have been opposing Syrid as best we can since."

"You did the right thing, Lord Elarryd," I said. "If you had gone to him, you would be a tool of the Burnt now."

"It is sorcery, then? What have you learned of it?"

"Some," I said. "Not enough." As briefly as I could without missing the important details, I related everything I had found in Fyrril's books, and Bryndine told of the attacks we had survived and the magicks we had seen on our journey.

There was a deep sorrow in Lord Elarryd's eyes when we finished our tale. "There is no saving Syrid, then?"

"I am afraid not," I said.

Lady Branwyn took her husband's hand. "You could not have stopped it, my love."

Vance had clearly been struggling to stay silent, but he could no longer hold his tongue. "What of Tenille?" he asked urgently. "She is not with you. Is she…"

"She was injured badly, but not mortally," said Bryndine. "She was in the infirmary when we were taken by the First Company. I hope that she escaped their notice, but I do not know."

"If they came for her, Tenille likely held them off with crutches and gauze," Deanyn said. "She's not one to give up easily."

"Ain't a man in the Army she couldn't outfight one-handed," Orya agreed. "She'll be waitin' for us."

Vance offered a weak smile, but the concern in his eyes did not fade.

"I hope your wife is well, Scriber Vance," said Elarryd, "but we serve her and the Kingsland best by finding a way to stop these Burnt."

"If these trees are their weakness, obviously we must put what men we have to burning as many as possible," said the High Justice.

It was the clear plan, but knowing what I now knew, it made me uneasy. "Burning their trees is what created this situation," I said. "Erryn burned them and they came back. Fyrril burned them and they came back again. Burning them does not solve the problem. It may take hundreds of years, but the trees always grow back, and when the Burnt return, they hate us all the more."

High Justice Tevon's face twisted as though I had offended him to his core. "My order is sworn to see the Promise kept, Scriber. If the King and the Army will not protect the people, we must. I cannot concern myself with what may happen centuries from now."

"Have you any better solution, Scriber Dennon?" Lord Elarryd asked.

"No," I admitted, but a wisp of a thought nagged at my mind, the memory of green fireleafs wreathed in flame.

"Then we send men to burn them," the High Justice said firmly.

"That is exactly what the Burnt expect, and they are not foolish enough to let us do it," said Bryndine. "It is a simple thing for them to protect the trees—they outnumber us badly, and they have us surrounded. The moment they think us a real danger, they need only have Syrid send the Army out behind us, and we will be trapped between two superior forces." She shook her head. "No, we cannot attack from here; we must take them by surprise."

Elarryd smiled at his daughter. "But you have a plan to do just that, I think."

"I do. My company will ride for the Academy tonight, before the Burnt know we are gone. With the aid of the Scribers, we can destroy thousands of fireleafs all over the Kingsland before the Burnt can stop us."

The High Justice rubbed his chin thoughtfully. "The

Scribers would be of great help to us, if you can win their support."

"They must already know we have escaped," I protested. "They will be waiting for us on the road."

"I doubt it," said Korus. "The King has Army men at the White Cells, not Justices—they are not accustomed to the work. They rarely stray from the guard rooms to check the cells, especially at night. Your absence will not be noted until morning."

"But we don't have the books," I said. "Even if we get to the Academy, the Council won't listen to us without proof."

The Lord Chancellor gave me a curious look, then turned to Korus. "Did you not tell them?"

"Tell us what?" I glared at Korus; it was just like him to withhold information to make me look a fool.

Korus waved his hand dismissively. "I was distracted with rescuing you, or I would have mentioned it earlier," he said. "I saved your books. The King believes me to be arranging your pyre; it was not difficult."

That gave us some chance, at least—even the Council could not be so stubborn as to dismiss our claims if we showed them Fyrril's journal. I shrugged. "Then there is nothing stopping us. The Academy is our best hope." And leaving Three Rivers would mean escaping the voices that assaulted me from every direction at all hours. I was almost becoming used to them now, and that was far more unsettling to me than hearing them to begin with.

"We should not delay, then," said Bryndine.

Elarryd sighed. "I had hoped you would not put yourself in danger again so soon, but you are right. Every moment we waste costs lives." He gestured to the young Lieutenant at the table, who had remained silent throughout the conversation. "Lieutenant Jeryn is joining Ralsten shortly with a dozen men and fresh supplies for the camp. They would be pleased, I think, if you would accompany them. Jeryn, tell my daughter what you told me earlier."

Jeryn saluted formally, though he seemed self-conscious in Bryndine's presence. "Captain Bryndine, I—I was at your trial, and, what you said… it rang true, for some of us. The Army should be protecting the people, not hiding behind the walls.

We sought Lord Elarryd out because of you."

Bryndine smiled and returned the salute. "I am honored, Lieutenant, but I cannot take credit for that. If you are here, it is because you are a good man, not because of anything I said."

The Lieutenant flushed and ducked his head, but I could see that he was smiling.

"I am coming with you as well," said Vance. "Someone has to lead you through the tunnels, and I want to see my wife."

"Very well," said Bryndine. "Let us gather the books and supplies. We must leave before daybreak." She embraced her mother and her father again. "We will ride with all haste. Promise me you will stay safe until we return."

Lady Branwyn held her daughter tightly, and I thought she might not let go. "Only if you promise the same."

"Do not worry for us, Bryndine," said Elarryd. "You heard the Lieutenant—Syrid's command over the people is not absolute. These creatures that control him are skilled at causing fear, but have no mind for intrigue or politics; I think we may even gain support, after your words at the trial. We may even be able to cause enough unrest in the ranks to delay the Army from attacking those outside."

The High Justice gave a firm nod. "There are still those who question the exile of the Justices. They can be swayed to our cause."

"And I am the King's trusted advisor," Korus said. "If he and Ord plan anything, we will know."

I looked at him in disbelief. "You are going back to Syrid? Sky and Earth, are you mad? He'll have you killed if he thinks you helped us escape." In a thousand years, I would never have thought Korus had it in him to risk his own life for the sake of the realm.

"I am an accomplished political Scriber," said Korus. "As long as they are still trying to control the city, they need me—as Lord Elarryd says, they have no mind for politics. I can convince the King to trust me. For a time." He attempted to sound haughty, but I saw the fear in his eyes. "Don't botch this, Lark. As idiotic as it is, we are depending on you."

* * *

When we entered Ralsten's tent, he and Tenille were studying a map of Three Rivers and the surrounding countryside. It was well into the night, and the light was dim, provided by a single lantern on the table, so they had to bend close to see. They did not immediately look up when we entered.

"Tenille!" Vance pushed past Bryndine and the other women and rushed to his wife's side.

The makeshift splints I had made for Tenille had been replaced and she wore a proper sling around her broken right arm. A wooden crutch helped her stand, but moving must still have been quite painful; I saw her wince as she turned. "Vance? What are you doing here? Where are the children?"

"Safe," he said. "With my mother in the Underground. The King is not terribly fond of Scribers at the moment. I thought it best to join Lord Elarryd before I was declared a rebel sympathizer." He hesitated before embracing her, eyeing her injuries. "Are you… in pain?"

Tenille laughed and pulled him close with her good arm. "I am not so fragile, love," she said, and leaned in to kiss him.

Ralsten coughed and looked away from the couple. "Captain Bryndine. Your women insisted you would find a way, but I did not expect to see you again, honestly. You have brought more men with you, I hope?"

Bryndine nodded. "A dozen men led by Lieutenant Jeryn. They are delivering the supplies my father sent."

"Good. We need them now more than ever."

Tenille released her husband and turned her eyes towards the rest of us. "By the Divide, it is good to see you all alive. I hoped you would escape, but I feared… well, it doesn't matter now. You survived." She hobbled to the back of the tent and unwrapped a large cloth bundle sitting on a table there. "We kept these safe for you. The soldiers left them when you surrendered." I recognized Bryndine's giant sword and shield right away. Several other pieces of equipment lay with them, and I assumed they belonged to the other women.

As they took up their arms, I couldn't help but smile; the women—especially Orya—seemed as excited to be reunited with their swords as with their comrades. But it was good to see the big blade and shield strapped to Bryndine's back once more. It made me feel safer, somehow.

While the others sheathed weapons and secured shields, Tenille explained the situation in the camp. "The Burnt have not relented since you were taken," she said. "We have been feinting attacks on their trees to keep them at bay. They devote much of their forces to protecting the fireleafs, and it lessens the number attacking us directly. But I do not know how long they will be fooled—we don't have the numbers to mount a real attack."

"We would have lost twice the men defending ourselves if not for Lieutenant Tenille's tactics," Ralsten said. "I never thought you lot knew what you were doing, but Father above, I wish we had more of you now. We might be able to get at those Dragon-damned trees."

"Even if you could, it would not help," I said. "The only reason they have not killed every one of you is because they do not think you a true threat. They like having so many trapped here—their own livestock pen. When they require new bodies, they only need slaughter a few. But they are on guard now. If any more of their trees are harmed, they will lay waste to the camp, and the city will not last much longer."

"What do we do, then?" Ralsten asked. "Wait to die of disease and starvation?"

"Nothing would delight the Burnt more, I'm sure," I replied.

Bryndine finished securing her shield on her back, and her hand went up to brush the hilt of her sword, as though reassuring herself that it was there. "You survive as long as you can, Lieutenant," she said. "My company rides for Highpass tonight; you only need hold until we can rally the Scribers to your aid."

"I will gather the women," said Tenille. "We'll need to prepare the horses."

"Orya will take care of that." Bryndine nodded at Orya, and she hurried out of the tent. Turning back to Tenille, Bryndine said, "You must remain here when we go."

"What? No. I'm coming with you. I know I am injured, but…"

"I would sooner have you fighting beside me injured than most men in perfect health. That is not why you must stay." Bryndine clasped Tenille's shoulder. "These people need you. You are the closest thing to a Warfare-pinned officer they have. It will not be an easy task to keep them safe until we can gather the Scribers, and I trust no one else to do it."

Ralsten grumbled at that, but he said, "She's right. Your strategies have already saved lives. We need you here."

Vance clasped his wife's hands. "Listen to them, Tenille. Our children need someone to protect them now, and there is no one else who can do that better. I will be here with you."

Tenille took a deep breath, looking from Vance to Bryndine, and then exhaled sharply. "Fine. I will stay. I cannot argue with anything you've said. But I hate it. If you are going to be in danger, I should be with you."

Sylla looked almost insulted, as though Tenille had questioned her ability to protect Bryndine. "I will not let anything happen to her. You are in more danger here than we will be on the road."

Deanyn grinned. "Of course. We only have to ride seventy leagues through rebel-infested territory." But her eyes were serious when she looked at Tenille. "Sylla is right, though—we should be worrying about you, not the other way around."

"Rylene will stay as well," said Bryndine. "It is best if you have an aide who knows you. She will want to stay; her family is here. And any others who wish to will be free to remain and protect the city. I only need sufficient escort to get safely to Highpass."

"None will stay if you do not order them to," Tenille said. "They are yours until the end, Bryn. We all are."

Bryndine smiled, but there was sadness in her eyes. "I know." Motioning for me and the others to follow, she turned to leave the tent. "Come, we ride within the hour."

CHAPTER THIRTY-TWO

Bryndine Errynson devoted her life to upholding Erryn's Promise. Others in the King's Army may have done the same, but none had to fight so hard simply to be allowed to protect the people of the Kingsland. Bryndine was faced with a kingdom that did everything it could to deny the help she sought to give.

It was fortunate, then, that Bryndine was a woman of deep stubbornness and conviction. Even in the face of ridicule and persecution, she did not abandon what she saw as her duty. She was determined to save her people in spite of themselves.

— From Dennon Lark's *Life of Bryndine Errynson*

"It's no good, Denn. They refuse to trust your findings." Illias looked exhausted—his body and face both sagged under the weight of defeat.

We had waited all day for this news, crowded into Illias' parlor in the School of History. The Master Historian's living quarters were not made to host so many. There was not enough furniture for eleven people, so most stood, or leaned against the walls. Even sitting, I was somewhat less than comfortable after so many hours. And now, after making us wait so long, the Council was going to refuse us. The Scribers were our best hope of victory, and they were going to let the realm burn.

Finally, Bryndine broke the silence, her eyes dark. "The

Kingsland is in dire need, and they would ignore it?"

"Worse than that," said Illias. "The Council will not approve of my sharing this, but you must know: the King has sent word to the Baron of your supposed treachery, and Ord is demanding you be given into his custody. Redmond wishes us to surrender you in order to prove the Council's loyalty to King Syrid. We have not yet come to an agreement, but Redmond and Ivynson are adamant, and they have swayed Mistress Evlyn. We reconvene in the morning, and by then I think they will have gained the last vote they need. The others are too afraid of disobeying the King to do anything but side against you."

Slouching in my chair, I laughed bitterly. "The King is *dead*. They are afraid of disobeying the thing that wears his skin." Even for the Council, this was appalling. I had known that Joryn Ivynson would support Redmond—the Master of Warfare had only been selected through Master Hantarin's efforts on his behalf. And Mistress Evlyn of the Arts had always been easily influenced. But I had always believed that Master Cerrol of the Sciences and Mistress Annala of Medicine respected their oaths, at least to some extent. Any yet, I couldn't find it in me to be surprised that the Scribers' Council did not trust me. *They never forget.*

Wynne frowned. "How can they hope to keep Syrid's favor? They must know he is already putting Scribers to death in Three Rivers."

"Scribers who opposed him," I said. "The Council, I'm sure, thinks that they can avoid being counted in that number."

Illias sighed. "And it is not only the King that concerns them. Nearly everyone thinks you traitors. The Children have condemned you, the people want your heads, and the Baron and his wife are all but breaking down the gates looking for you. And of course there is the support of the Schools to consider—you and Captain Bryndine are not popular at the Academy, Denn. The Council fears retribution from any number of sources if they do not turn you over."

"Idiots!" I slammed my hand against the arm of my chair, and winced at the impact. "Our treason is nothing more than finding the books Fyrril hid. We recovered a piece of history, and the King wants it lost again. The *purpose* of the Scribers is to stop that from happening!" Remembering all the times Tenille had scolded me over my oaths, I wished she was with us now—I imagined her marching into the Council chambers and killing the lot of them.

Bryndine rubbed a hand over her eyes in a rare show of fatigue, or perhaps frustration. "Is there any hope that this motion will not pass, Master Illias?"

The old man shook his head. "None," he said sadly. "I have sat in more than enough Council sessions to tell when I am losing, Captain Bryndine. They will give you to the Baron tomorrow. You must leave tonight."

"And go where?" Sylla asked with her customary glower. "Convincing the Scribers was our only chance."

"One of the other baronies, maybe," suggested Orya. "Might be they can send companies to Three Rivers."

"The other baronies will be of no help," said Illias. "You would not have heard all that has happened, I suppose. I had forgotten how long you have been travelling."

"Tell me," said Bryndine.

"The Burnt have taken pains to occupy as much of the Army as possible. They have been attacking the Crossing for the last week, and the brigade there is hard pressed to defend the city while keeping the barbarians from crossing the border. And yesterday we received word that King Syrid has declared Baron Hurryd a traitor for supposedly harbouring rebels. He has ordered the Ryndport and Timberhold Brigades to march on the Bridgefort. Highpass is the only barony left out of the fighting, and you will find no help here while Ord governs."

"It will not be long before Highpass is drawn in as well," I said. "The Burnt are fewer near the mountains, but that will not stop them from marching the Army up the Saltroad."

Bryndine's jaw clenched. "How can so many fail to see what is happening? When the Bridgefort falls, another barony will be accused of treason, and then another. The Burnt will have us kill each other until we are too weak to fight them."

"It is fear that keeps them from seeing," said Leste. "If they do not accept a thing, they think it will not be true."

Deanyn smirked. "We should be able to defeat the Burnt by closing our eyes and ignoring them, then. Has anyone thought to try that yet?"

"Every time we've come near them," I said. "It hasn't worked."

"Pity," said Deanyn. "It was my only idea."

Wynne looked hopefully at Bryndine. "What are we going to do, Captain? Where are we going to go?"

"I… do not know." With that simple admission, Bryndine silenced every voice in the room. All of us turned to her, waiting for something more; *needing* something more. But she could only hang her head, unable to meet so many disappointed eyes. "I thought the Scribers would join us."

The despair in the room was tangible—it seemed to thicken the air, make breathing more difficult. We had all, I think, counted on Bryndine to have an answer. Every crisis we had faced so far, she had met without doubt or hesitation. To see her confidence falter now was a grievous blow to the company's morale. And my own.

"I am sorry, Captain Bryndine." Illias' back was bent, his shoulders stooped; he looked fragile, diminished, far older than his fifty-some years. Absently, he touched the golden pin on his collar, then frowned when he realized what he was doing. "I was proud to wear this pin once. Not anymore." He curled his hand into a fist and dropped it to his side. "But you must make some decision. If you do not leave tonight, tomorrow the Council will send you to Ord in chains."

"Scriber Dennon." Bryndine turned to me, an almost pleading look in her eyes. "You must have some idea of where we might go, what else we might try. Something in what you have seen, or heard, or read."

Unbidden, I thought of King Erryn, and of leaves that looked like green flames. Rubbing two fingers against my temple, I shook my head. "No." I could not abide the thought of these women giving their lives for nothing. Without the Scribers, there were simply not enough of them. "There is nothing you can do, Bryndine. These people have proven that they don't want your help, and they don't deserve it. We should leave while we still can. We can follow the mountains to the coast and take shelter with the Clans, or perhaps find a ship to Raen. If we stay in the Kingsland, we'll be found and killed."

"How can we know who deserves to live and who deserves to die, Scriber?" Bryndine asked. "Not long ago, I thought Lieutenant Ralsten a small, foolish man, and you believed Scriber Korus to be selfish and petty. Both have put their lives at risk for the Kingsland. And what of our friends and loved ones?" She gestured at Illias. "Would you leave them behind?"

I pushed myself from my chair, too agitated to sit. "It doesn't matter! There is nothing we can do now!" I was yelling, and I knew she would not listen if I could not remain rational. Taking a deep breath, I tried to calm myself. "Illias can join us. We will send word to the others somehow, tell them to flee as well. But ten women cannot save the Kingsland, and you will be killed if you try. I would not see you die for people who hate you."

Sylla touched Bryndine's arm. "He is not wrong, Bryn. Most of them would happily watch you die." There was desperation in her eyes. "Please, you have to go. They don't deserve you, they never have."

Bryndine pulled away from Sylla's hand. "I will not flee. If any wish to make for the coast, I understand. But I cannot."

"I ain't goin' anywhere without you," Orya said, crossing her arms.

Debra grunted her agreement, and Selvi and Elene both nodded, though there was fear in their eyes. "You are our Captain," said Ivyla, as though it was all the reason she needed. The rest were quick to voice their agreement.

"My place is with you," Sylla said, but she could not hide the unhappiness in her voice.

Bryndine smiled at her company. "Thank you. All of you. I… it is my honor to serve with you." I thought I saw a glint of wetness in her eyes, but I may have only imagined it. When she blinked, it was gone. Clearing her throat, she said, "We will ride south and burn as many fireleafs as we can, unless the Scriber can offer us another course of action."

I had known from the start that I would never convince Bryndine to abandon the Kingsland, and that her women would not flee without her. Still, their willingness to give their lives infuriated me. "What can you possibly hope to accomplish?

The ten of you cannot burn every tree in the Kingsland. Even if you join with the men at Three Rivers, it will not be enough. Fyrril had five hundred, and he still died. You will not even stop the Burnt as he did—you will only die like him, for a kingdom that will not mourn you. They will not even *remember* you! Why are you so determined to help them?"

"Do you think that I have never asked those same questions, Scriber Dennon?" Bryndine spoke softly, and there was a sad look in her eyes. "I have. Every day I see how cruel and petty people can be, and I wonder if they are worth defending." She paused briefly, then set her jaw and said, "But I do not fight for the cruel and the petty. I fight for those hidden among them who are not so, like Korus and Ralsten. I fight for those who have the courage to fight beside me, and for those I love." If she had seemed discouraged earlier, it fled from her as she spoke; she stood taller with every word. "And I fight for myself. I swore to uphold the Promise because I believe in it. If I forsake that oath, I give truth to all the rumors. I become the woman they say I am, instead of the woman I wish to be."

"That is all very inspiring," I said, "but it won't keep you alive. You're mad if you think you can do any good with so few." Truthfully, though, I knew that she was right. It was not the pragmatic decision, but it was the moral one. I do not think Bryndine Errynson could have lived with herself if she had chosen any other path.

"Perhaps I am mad, but I suspect it is a madness you understand." Her mouth rose, just slightly, into what might have been the hint of a fond smile. "For all your complaints, I have never yet known you to break the oath you swore when you earned that pin. I do not think you will do so now. You are right that we are too few to defeat the Burnt by simply destroying their trees—you must find us another way."

I could accept them choosing to give their lives for the Kingsland, but I would not be the one responsible for it. "You can't ask that of me," I said. "The Council has Fyrril's books now. I have no resources. Even if I had some idea"—again, briefly, the memory of burning green leaves—"Even then, anything I said would only be conjecture, and if I am wrong… I have caused enough deaths already. Who am I to make this decision?"

"A friend," said Deanyn, and her clear blue eyes held none of their usual irony.

"And a teacher," offered Wynne.

"You're one of us, Scriber," said Orya. "Might as well accept it. You've proven yourself, this ain't just blind faith."

Rubbing at my temple, I looked from Deanyn's warm smile to Orya's wild grin, from the identical eyes of the twins to Sylla's ever-present glare. All were silent, waiting for me to speak. My throat was dry, like I had eaten a mouthful of sand. When I turned my gaze to Illias, he clasped my shoulder, but said nothing; he had no escape to offer.

And then I looked at Bryndine, and when she met my eyes, she gave a single, barely visible nod. It was the slightest of motions, but after travelling with her for so long, I recognized it for what it was: her way of showing support. She truly believed that I would honor the oaths I had made. In her eyes, I saw the steel resolve that I had followed this far, and I realized that I had already made my decision. After all we had been through, I would not let her down now—no matter how badly I wished to.

I swallowed, and in a hoarse voice, said, "There is something. A ghost of a chance, nothing more." Inside my head, King Erryn stood before a forest of flames. "When we burned the fireleafs at Three Rivers, I saw into the memories of the Burnt. I saw King Erryn setting fire to the First Forest. The leaves of all the fireleafs were green."

Sylla looked at me as if I was completely mad. "Fireleafs are red, Scriber. Do you not understand the name? And even if they weren't, what use could their color possibly be to us?"

"Some are green, where the First Forest still grows," Wynne said, though she looked as confused as the others. "But I don't—"

"The leaves were all green before the Burning, if what I saw was true," I said. "Only those destroyed in the Burning grew again with red leaves—like a scar of sorts. Which means that the Wyddin in what remains of the First Forest may not have been burned. They may not wish to see everyone in the Kingsland dead. And they may know of some way to stop the

Burnt."

"Then we must go to them," said Bryndine.

Sylla was quick to protest. "This is insane! You can't believe this, Bryn. You need to go someplace safe, not follow the Scriber's delusions across the Kingsland."

"It is the only chance we have left, Sylla," said Bryndine.

Sylla lapsed into angry silence, but her eyes spoke volumes, glaring accusation at me. Her scepticism was not unmerited. I wasn't at all sure of my conclusions myself.

"This is nothing more than a guess," I warned Bryndine. "It is possible that the Wyddin there will not have any answers for us, and they may hate Kingslanders as much as any. Unburned, they could be stronger than the others. I may be sending you to die." I took a deep breath, gathering my courage. "And myself, as well. I have to go with you. I am likely the only one who can speak with them." *Perhaps these Dragon-damned voices in my head will be of some use, for once.*

"Would that the Council were as brave." Bryndine's eyes seemed to say that she had expected no less of me. "You are a credit to your order, Scriber Dennon." The compliment made me wince; I hardly deserved it so soon after suggesting we abandon the kingdom entirely.

"Redmond and Ivynson expected me to warn you, no doubt," said Illias. "The Scribers at the gate will not let you by, and there may be men guarding your horses. I will see you off the campus. They cannot refuse a Master Scriber, not when the Council has yet to pass the vote to detain you."

"No," I said, shaking my head. "If you come, they will condemn you for sharing Council secrets and aiding us. I wouldn't be surprised if they gave you to Ord in our place. We must appear to have escaped on our own."

"There cannot be many guards," said Bryndine. "It would raise questions, with the vote not yet decided. We should have no trouble subduing them—they will underestimate our ability." She smiled ruefully. "That, at least, is an advantage I can always depend upon."

Illias exhaled through his nose and gave a cantankerous scowl, but said, "Fine. I may still be able to do some good if I retain my seat, I suppose. But be careful. And please, try not to harm anyone too grievously."

Bryndine nodded. "We will be gentle." Addressing her company in the commanding tone I had come to think of as her Captain's voice, she said, "Gather your things quickly and regroup in the entry hall. Selvi, Elene, scout the stables, see if the horses are being watched. Stay out of sight."

The parlor emptied quickly. Soon, only Illias and I remained—and Wynne, who approached me shyly as the others went to work. "Scriber Dennon?"

"What is it?"

"You said you would… I wondered if you might ask…" She glanced at Illias, then leaned closer to me and whispered, "If he would sponsor me?"

I could hardly believe she was still interested. "You would still be a Scriber? Even knowing what has become of the Council?"

Again her eyes shifted to Illias, but she nodded earnestly, and this time she did not lower her voice. "There is more to it than obeying the Council and wearing the pin, isn't there? The true Scribers are the ones who keep their vows. That is what I mean to be. If those who truly want to serve the Kingsland are scared away by those who don't, nothing will ever improve."

"That," I said, unable to keep the pride from my voice, "is a very good answer."

"It is indeed," said Illias, and I knew by the look in his eye that he was already intrigued. It never took him long to identify a kindred spirit. "You are… Wynne? I recall your face, from the Old Garden."

She nodded. "Yes, Master Illias."

"She is a fast learner, Illias," I said. "And she has already read more than most students have by their third year. I told her you would sponsor her, when this is all over. Assuming we are no longer wanted criminals."

Illias clasped her hand warmly. "It would be my honor. If only every student thought as you do, my dear." I had never doubted he would agree, but still it was good to hear him say it. Knowing that Wynne had a future here—that I had done something good for at least one of Bryndine's women—somehow made me feel better about whatever dangers we might face in the First Forest.

Wynne's smile was radiant. "I will make you both proud. I promise." She glanced over her shoulder, and looked slightly guilty when she saw that the others had all gone. "I should go help, though."

"Do not let us stop you," said Illias. "We can speak more when you return." He waved her on, and she hurried from the room.

"I'll have to go soon as well," I said. "They won't take long to prepare."

"Wait." Illias clasped my arm as if to hold me back, and his face was drawn with worry. "Denn, I hope you are not doing this because you think that I… I only wanted you doing real Scriber's work again. I never intended for you put your life at risk."

"It is not your fault Illias. I have no choice. If they cannot speak to the Wyddin, there is no use in their going at all. And besides that, if anyone dies, it is because of me. I should be with them."

"Every death is not on your shoulders, my boy. I wish you would not hold yourself responsible for so much. You pitied Prince Fyrril for doing the same, did you not?"

"It is *not* the same. Fyrril saved the Kingsland. I have only ever gotten people killed."

"And recovered more of our history than any Scriber ever has. We found a book on glasswork in the chests from Three Rivers, you know. Some in the School of Arts think the techniques it mentions will allow them to repair the stained glass at the Old Garden."

The destruction of the Mother and Father at the Old Garden had long weighed on my mind, and knowing that they might be fixed meant a great deal. It would be one of my worst mistakes undone. But it changed nothing. "Perhaps you are right. But it doesn't matter. I must go with them."

"Yes, I suppose you must," he said with a sigh. "I would sooner have you seek safety, but it seems you have more courage than even I suspected, my boy." With outstretched arms, he drew me into an embrace.

I hugged him fiercely in return, his rough beard scratching

against my cheek. For just a moment, I was a boy again, clinging to the only man who had ever truly been a father to me. *I might not see him again*, I realized, and tears welled in my eyes. I wanted to tell him what he meant to me, that he had made my life better in a hundred different ways, but I could not find the words. Instead, I whispered, "Thank you, Illias. For… everything."

"You can thank me by coming back safely," he said. "Now go. They will be waiting."

Sylla met me as I left Illias' quarters. "Scriber," she said. "I was looking for you." In the poor light of the hall, her already severe features were draped with shadow, giving her face an absolutely sinister cast.

I eyed her nervously. "What do you want?"

"Everything they said before, about trusting you. About you being one of us. I want you to know that I don't believe it."

"Excellent. I'm glad you told me. Shall we go?" I had little patience for her bluster, and being alone with her made me nervous. I tried to move by her towards the stairs.

She grabbed me by the wrist and pulled me to her. "There is nothing in the forest. You're leading Bryndine back into danger over some half-remembered trees you saw in a dream."

She is going to kill me. My heart pounded, but my blood went cold. "I'm not—"

"Shut up." She twisted my wrist, and I squeaked in pain. Then, leaning in so that her mouth was only inches from my ear, she whispered, "You should have convinced her to run, Scriber. If she dies, you die."

CHAPTER THIRTY-THREE

It should have been me.

— From the personal journals of Dennon Lark

"Riders behind us, Captain," said Selvi, pulling her horse alongside Bryndine's and pointing behind us and to the west. "Ten of them, just over the rise there, no more than five hundred yards back. Scouts from the Timberhold, I think."

Bryndine frowned. "Did they see you?"

"No, but they are riding in our direction. We'll be impossible to miss when they top the hill."

Ahead of us, the First Forest was visible, a dark green-brown line stretching across the horizon. We were nearly there. "Another hour, that is all we needed," I muttered. "The forest would have hidden us from sight. Father above, would a bit of good luck have been too much to ask?"

"I mistrust good luck," said Bryndine. "And we have had too much of it since leaving Highpass."

It was true; so far it had been an easy ride. After the Burnt attacks, the countryside was nearly deserted. If anyone still lingered, they were not like to show themselves to a band of armed riders. And with the Crossing under siege and Timberhold's forces marching on the Bridgefort, the lands east of Three Rivers lacked any meaningful military presence to hinder us.

I scowled at her. "So you are glad, then? I would prefer not to be captured, personally."

"We don't know who they are or why they are here. They may not give chase at all. If they do, we have a good chance of reaching the forest."

"If?" I asked incredulously. "Of course they will chase us. We are enemies of the King."

"They may not know that on sight."

"Bryndine," I said, "you are larger than most horses. I think they may recognize you."

Riding beside me, Deanyn could not help but snicker. "He has you there, Captain."

"I suppose he does, at that." Bryndine looked somewhat amused herself, but she quickly hid her half-smile. "Scriber, you do not hear any of your voices, do you?"

"Nothing." I had heard few voices during the trip, save for a brief period when we strayed within the range of Three Rivers. "I don't think they are Burnt, but that does not mean they are friendly."

"Good," said Bryndine. "Then they cannot share thoughts, or whatever else the Wyddin do. If we outrun them, it will take at least a day for them to return to Timberhold and report our location." Cupping a hand around her mouth, she called out, "We have guests! Make for the forest!"

The company surged into a gallop, and I clumsily followed along, clinging tightly to the reins of my horse. Looking back, I saw the scouting party just cresting the hill. They could not possibly have failed to notice us—there was nothing but open ground right up to the forest's edge. Without pause, they spurred their mounts into pursuit.

They gained on us rapidly. Our horses were tired, ridden hard for almost a week; theirs were fresh from Timberhold, a day's ride to the west at most. The five hundred yards between us fell to four hundred, then three hundred. As the men drew closer, I could see that several of them were readying bows. We would be within their range before long.

"Captain!" Elene shouted over the thunder of hooves, holding her shortbow up with a clear question on her face.

Bryndine shook her head vehemently. "No! They think they are doing their duty, we will not harm them."

"They will harm *us* if they can," Sylla yelled, but Bryndine only shook her head again.

The women were experienced riders; I was not. Despite all my practice in the last months, it was all I could do to keep up, and even then I was the slowest among them. Riding at the back of the company, I was utterly exposed to the archers behind us, and I ducked low in the saddle as the first volley came. But the scouts had loosed their arrows too soon—the shafts struck the grass some thirty yards away.

Deanyn and Wynne lagged from the others to match my speed, making sure I was not left behind. "Faster!" I called to them. "Don't worry about me!"

"I'll go faster when you do," Deanyn answered with a grin.

"We won't leave you, Scriber Dennon," said Wynne.

I urged my horse forward, trying to coax some hidden speed from the animal, but it did little good. I looked back over my shoulder at our pursuers; they were close enough now that I could see the crimson spot on their chests where the burning tree would be.

That was when I saw the arrow that should have killed me.

It flew through the air in a perfect arc, and somehow I knew, without doubt, that it would strike true. I tried to guide my horse out of the way, but it did no good. The idiot beast responded too slowly, and what movement it did make only seemed to put me more firmly in the arrow's path. Time slowed, and I could only watch as death hurtled down from the sky.

Following my eyes, Wynne turned in her saddle and saw the arrow coming. "Scriber Dennon!" She yanked at her reins, and her mount veered left, colliding hard with mine. My horse staggered sideways, out of the arrow's path.

An instant later, the feathered shaft buried itself between Wynne's ribs.

"No!" I cried.

At the same time, Deanyn shouted, "Wynne!"

Wynne forced herself upright in the saddle, clutching her left side where the arrow protruded. The agony was plain on her face. "Keep… going. I… I can still ride." It was not convincing—the shaft had struck deep. But she kept pace with us, and I could not help her, so I did as she said.

Bryndine heard our cries and looked back. When she saw Wynne, fury flashed in her eyes. "Selvi! Elene!" She nodded to the twins.

They understood. Both women twisted in the saddle, drew back their bows, and loosed. Two of the scouts fell with arrows jutting from their chests.

More arrows flew at us; one clattered off the shield at Bryndine's back, and another lodged itself in the leather of Ivyla's saddle, just missing horse and rider. The twins shot again, and a third man pitched off his horse. Before the scouts could even respond with another volley of their own, Selvi and Elene released two more arrows. One of the horses chasing us staggered and collapsed. I had known the twins were skilled archers, but now, watching them shoot backwards from horseback and hit their targets more often than they did not, I realized I had underestimated them greatly.

Our pursuers, apparently, had a similar revelation. The six remaining men fell back and changed their course, fleeing west towards Timberhold. When Selvi and Elene made to shoot again, Bryndine stopped them. "Let them go."

"They will tell others that they saw us," said Elene.

"They have proven they have the faster horses," Bryndine replied. "You cannot shoot them all before they are beyond reach." She was right—they would report seeing us here, but there was little we could do to stop it.

With a raised hand, Bryndine brought the company to a halt and drew her horse close to Wynne's. When her eyes fell on the arrow, a shadow passed over her face. I saw it only for an instant before she composed herself, but it looked like guilt. The others were silent, watching with fear and concern. Wynne was their youngest, little sister to every woman in the company, and I knew that any one of them would gladly have taken that arrow in her place. *But it was meant for me.*

Wynne saw the look on Bryndine's face, and said, "I will… be fine, Captain." She tried to smile.

Bryndine looked at the young soldier with surprising

tenderness. "Yes. You will. Do not forget it." She turned to me. "Can she ride, Scriber Dennon? We must find cover in the forest. If those scouts were part of a larger force, they may return with others."

I shook my head. "Absolutely not. Mother below, she has an arrow in her side. No, we must stop." I could not keep my eyes from the wooden shaft. *You should have let it hit me, you stupid girl.*

Wynne's face was pale and her breathing labored, but she waved us forward determinedly. "Too dangerous… to stay here. I can ride."

"I need to examine her right away," I insisted, though I could likely do very little. If the arrow had pierced any vital organs—and I did not see how it could have missed them—my limited medical training would be meaningless. But I had to try. "Please, Bryndine. She saved my life."

Bryndine stared at Wynne for a long while, then said, "She is right, Scriber. We are all at risk here. As soon as we are out of sight, you can see to her wound." She laid a gentle hand on Wynne's arm. "You will get through this, Wynne. I promise." Wheeling her horse around to face the others, she said, "We ride for the forest, with all haste."

At her command, the company galloped on. I did not stray from Wynne's side as we rode.

A quarter-hour later, we passed the first scattered young maples and birches of the outer forest—mere heralds of the thicker, older growth that lay beyond. A single fireleaf with rich green leaves grew nearby, and I was surprised when I heard no voices creeping through my mind. *Perhaps further in, where the trees are older.* At the heart of the woods, I had read, the trees had trunks as thick as guard towers. We would find the Wyddin there, I was certain of that. Whether or not we *wanted* to find them, I was less sure.

We were not far past the forest's edge when Wynne fell. Swaying in her saddle, she sagged abruptly to one side, and then, before I could do anything to stop it, plummeted to the ground. Her foot caught in the stirrup, and her confused mount dragged her a step before I grabbed its reins.

"Stop!" I shouted to the others, leaping from my horse.

After freeing her trapped leg, I knelt beside her.

She looked at me with glassy eyes. "Scriber Dennon… it hurts…"

"I know," I said. "Be still. I can help you." My hands went to the arrow. It entered her left side through the unprotected area just beneath the arm, and angled towards the center of her back. As far as I could tell it had not pierced all the way through; I had not seen the arrowhead come out the other side.

The women were gathering around us now, and I pointed at the nearest two: Deanyn and Ivyla. "Sit her up and get her armor off."

They followed my instructions without hesitation, lifting Wynne into a sitting position and stripping off her boiled leather plates so that I could probe her back with my fingers. As I had thought, the arrow had not penetrated completely—the head was lodged somewhere in her body. "I need to see what the arrowhead looks like. Do we have any others?"

"Got one here." Debra yanked free the arrow that had struck Ivyla's saddle and handed it to me. As I had feared, it had a viciously barbed head.

Bryndine knelt at my side. "What will you do, Scriber?"

"It didn't go through. We need to"—I swallowed and wiped my brow—"push it through her to safely remove it."

Bryndine frowned. "That seems dangerous."

"Less so than pulling it out—the barbs would do too much damage. But yes, it is dangerous. I do not know how badly injured she is inside. Removing the arrow may…" I glanced at Wynne, but she hardly seemed aware of my voice. I lowered it anyway. "It may cause too much bleeding. It could kill her. But if I leave it she will die for certain before we can find help."

"Take it out… please…" Wynne gasped. I had not thought she was listening, and I cursed myself for not being more careful. I didn't want her to be afraid.

Bryndine reached out to brush a strand of damp brown hair from Wynne's face, and I had never seen her look so sad. "He will, Wynne. He is going to save you." She looked back at me. "What can we do to help, Scriber?"

"I need a knife, and alcohol. A needle and thread, and

bandages from my bags."

Bryndine pulled a dagger from her belt and handed it to me, and Sylla rushed to my horse to fetch my supplies. Orya rummaged in her saddlebag for a moment and pulled out a small flask. "This good enough, Scriber?"

"It's fine. Bring it here." Taking the flask from Orya, I cut Wynne's tunic open around the arrow and doused the shaft and the wound with alcohol. "You are stronger than I am," I said to Bryndine. "I need you to break off the fletching."

Bryndine grasped the arrow in one giant hand, snapping the feathered end off with the other in a single motion. "What next?"

"When I say, push it through. Carefully, at the same angle it entered by." I moved around behind Wynne and lifted her shirt to expose her back, where the arrow would emerge. "Wynne, this will hurt, but you must remain still."

"I'm ready," Wynne whispered.

"Now," I said to Bryndine.

Inhaling deeply, Bryndine gripped the broken shaft and began to push. Wynne screamed, but Deanyn and Ivyla held her tight and kept her from thrashing. A moment later, the bloody arrowhead split the flesh of her back, just to the left of her spine.

"It's through," I said. Grabbing the shaft, I slowly drew it the rest of the way out. After pouring the last of the alcohol over the new wound, I took up my needle and thread. "Hold a handful of bandages over the entry wound," I instructed Bryndine. "You'll have to keep pressure while I sew this side."

Blood poured from the hole in Wynne's back. Too much blood. I stitched the wound shut as quickly as I could, then packed cotton bandages over top and wrapped them tightly against her. "The other wound now," I said. "Lay her down." Deanyn and Ivyla lowered her gently to the ground.

When Bryndine removed the wadded bandages from Wynne's side, they were soaked crimson, and still blood rushed forth from the wound. *There is too much bleeding inside*. But I could not simply let her go—she had taken the arrow in my place. Threading my needle, I put it against her skin and began to stitch.

"Scriber," said Bryndine. When I glanced up, she was looking at Wynne's face.

There was blood on Wynne's lips, and a thin red trickle ran from the corner of her mouth when she spoke. "It doesn't… hurt anymore." She met my eyes. "Am I going to die?"

"No," I said, but we both knew it was a lie. "No, I can still—"

"It's... it's all right, Scriber Dennon." She patted my arm, and her eyes seemed to focus on something very far away.

"Wynne?" Bryndine took Wynne's hand in her much larger one, squeezing it tightly. "Wynne, look at me."

As if from a dream, Wynne said, "I was going to be a Scriber."

My eyes blurred with tears. "You are, Wynne." Fumbling at my neck, I unclasped my Scriber's pin. "It's as you said. Being a Scriber is about serving the Kingsland. Seeking knowledge and keeping oaths. You *are* a Scriber."

Her voice was barely more than a whisper. "I am?"

"One of the best." With trembling hands, I attached the golden inkwell to the collar of her tunic.

She smiled before she died.

A sob tore itself from my lungs, and the world lost focus. I was aware only distantly of women crying, comforting one another. Deanyn, I think, was kneeling beside me, holding me, saying my name. Bryndine, still holding Wynne's hand, called for something to wrap the body. None of it mattered; I was barely conscious of any of them. Their voices were dull murmurs, their faces featureless blurs. All that mattered was Wynne. She was dead, and all my hopes for redemption had died with her. That I had found her a sponsorship meant nothing anymore—I had still gotten her killed. Like all the others.

It should have been me, I thought, reaching out a hand to close her empty, staring eyes.

And then she blinked.

CHAPTER THIRTY-FOUR

We know the truth now. We may even have a chance to stop the Burnt.

If I were a pious man, I would pray to the Mother and the Father not to let me fail Bryndine and her company. But I have never been pious. When I close my eyes, I don't commune with the gods. I just hear Korus saying, "Don't botch this, Lark."

— From the personal journals of Dennon Lark

Bryndine's dagger still lay by my side, and I had it at Wynne's neck before she could move. "Get out," I hissed through gritted teeth. "Get out of her."

"We are not your enemy." It was Wynne's voice, but at the same time it was not.

Beside me, Deanyn started at the sound. "Dennon, what…"

"The Burnt." They had fooled me with Uran Ord, and with Genna I had let hope cloud my judgement, but I had *seen* the life leave Wynne's eyes. I had already let her die; I would not let the Burnt have her body. "Get *out*."

Deanyn and Bryndine were on their feet instantly. The women drew their weapons, making ready for battle. "Are there others coming, Scriber?" Bryndine asked urgently. "Do you hear them?"

I frowned. I could hear nothing, not a single whisper since we entered the forest. I let the dagger stray from Wynne's neck as I glanced down at the half-stitched wound in her side. The bleeding had stopped. I looked up at Bryndine, confused. "The Burnt have her, but… there are no voices." It made no sense. If the Burnt could hide their voices from me, why had they not done so before?

"We are not of the Burnt," said the thing inside Wynne. "We have come to help you."

Bryndine's eyes were hard and her voice was cold. "We will not hear you while you desecrate our friend's body."

"We are sorry. This is not our way, but we had no other choice. You must listen."

I did not remove the dagger. "You are one of the Wyddin?" I asked.

"We are of the Wyd," it said, which I took to be an affirmative answer.

"Then why can I not hear you? Why don't you speak into my mind?"

"We are of the Wyd, but we can no longer touch it, human. The madness of the Burnt consumes it. We would become as they are." It gestured at Wynne's body. "This is the only means by which we could speak with you, though it is sacrilege of the worst kind to use a human body in this way."

The Wyd. I knew that word. Fyrril's books had spoken of it, but its meaning had never been clear. "What is the Wyd?" I demanded.

"You do not know? The Wyd is everything. It is the Earth and the Sky. It is the voice of the world."

The books had said that the Wyd gave the Sages their power. I wanted the Wyddin to leave Wynne's body, but I could not let this opportunity pass—I was very close to the answers I had been seeking for months. "Why can I hear it?"

"Some humans are born with the Gift of the Sages, as it was called in Elovia. Many were blessed in those days. Now, perhaps one in a thousand."

A question formed in my mind, one I could not think how to ask without sounding foolish. "Am I…" I hesitated, glancing self-consciously at the women around me. But I had to know.

"Am I a Sage?"

It chuckled in a way Wynne never had, with a mild, patronizing sort of amusement. "Is a rock a mountain? Is a pond the ocean? No, human, you are no Sage. Their power rivalled our own. We can feel the Gift in you, but it is very weak, as it is in all humans born after Elovia fell."

I had not been prepared for such a flat dismissal. All this time I had been expecting some great revelation that would give meaning to everything I had been through, but apparently the voices were little more than a random fluke of birth, so meaningless and unimpressive that this creature barely cared. I had never asked for this "gift", but after all the pain it had caused me, I felt an absurd need to defend it. "I stopped the snow in the Salt Mountains," I said. "The Burnt called it down and I stopped it."

"The Salt Mountains belong to the Dragon," it said, as though it was the most obvious thing in the world. "The Burnt strayed far from their birthtrees to follow you there. Even without your intervention, their power might have failed. But we do not mean to insult you, human—your gift is necessary to put the Burnt to rest. We are here to tell you how."

I do not think the Wyddin intended arrogance. It simply took for granted many things that I did not know, and was not used to having to explain them. But hearing that slight condescension in Wynne's voice—Wynne, who had never been anything but completely earnest—made my hand shake with anger. The dagger's blade nicked her skin, opening a small wound that did not bleed. "Tell us then."

"You will need to release this body, human. There is a place we must bring you."

"Not while you have Wynne." I would not risk the Wyddin fleeing with her body. "Tell us what you have to say and go."

Bryndine laid a hand on my shoulder. "Let the creature stand, Scriber Dennon."

"But—"

"I do not like it any more than you do, but this is why we came." She looked down at the Wyddin without expression. "You say 'we' instead of 'I'. Do you speak for all your people?"

"All who were not burned."

"Then we will listen. Say what you have come to say, and take us where you must take us, and then leave Wynne in peace."

It nodded Wynne's head. "As you wish."

Shaking my head, I kept the dagger against Wynne's throat. I knew that Bryndine was right, that we had come to speak with the Wyddin, but I was not entirely certain whether I cared anymore. Releasing the creature felt like letting Wynne go.

"Please, Scriber Dennon," said Bryndine. "Wynne died for this. Do not rob that of meaning."

She was wrong. Wynne had died for *me*. Nothing we found would make that a worthwhile trade. But I handed Bryndine the dagger with a wordless grunt of frustration, and stood.

The Wyddin climbed awkwardly to its feet, then stumbled, as though it did not understand how to balance on two legs. Bryndine grabbed Wynne's arm and helped the creature find its footing.

"You are free," she said. "Take it as a gesture of good faith. Now tell us how we can stop the Burnt."

"We will tell you how you might," the Wyddin answered. "There is no certainty in this."

Sylla stood inches from Bryndine with her sword in hand, watching the Wyddin with a level of distrust she usually reserved for me. "Why would you help us kill your own kind?"

"You misunderstand," it said. "We will not help you slay the Burnt, nor could we. We wish to give them peace."

"Doesn't seem to me like they much want peace," said Orya.

"They want it badly, but do not know how to achieve it. They live in constant, unending anguish. In their madness, they think that vengeance will end their suffering. It will not." It described the fate of the Burnt in a flat, factual tone that I found unsettling, though it made sense—the Wyddin were accustomed to sharing thought and feeling directly, not showing them in ways humans could understand. "Our trees had never been harmed on such a scale before your Burning. When the forest was set aflame, the pain of it echoed and grew with each birthtree that burned. As long as the Burnt remember, it will never stop. But if you do as we say, you can give them sleep, for as long as the life of the world, and without dream. It is all that can be done."

"Why do you need us?" asked Bryndine. "Why have you not done it before now?"

"We cannot. When your people burned our forest, we whose trees were spared removed ourselves from the Wyd so that we would not share in the madness of the others. If we open ourselves to it again, we will become as the Burnt, or be destroyed. It must be a human with the Gift." It pointed Wynne's hand at me. "We have waited many years for one like this to come to us."

"If I am so weak," I asked with a scowl, "how can I possibly be of any use?"

"You must wake the Eldest."

"The Eldest?" Orya sounded as puzzled as I felt. "They'd let the Dragon bugger every one of us and not lift a finger to help. And what've the Children got to do with it anyway?"

"Do you think that your people were the first to worship the Mother and the Father?" Again, that slight almost-arrogance colored its voice. "The humans who call themselves Eldest learned the name from us, centuries ago. We do not speak of them. We speak of the true Eldest, the first of our kind."

Deanyn raised an eyebrow. "You want us to fetch your parents? What will they do, scold the Burnt and send them to their beds without dinner?"

The Wyddin actually seemed affronted by the question. "The Eldest have great power, human. The Wyd is theirs to command, and only they can resist the agony that corrupts it. Their word binds us all. They will command the Burnt to join their slumber, and the Burnt will obey." It shifted Wynne's feet in a surprisingly human show of impatience. "Come, mount your horses. We will take you to the First Tree, where the Eldest sleep. Any questions you have, we will answer on the way."

Sylla objected before the Wyddin even finished speaking. "It could be a trap, Bryn."

Elene nodded. "Let Selvi and me scout ahead first,

Captain."

But Bryndine's face hardened with resolve, and she shook her head. "No. We must not delay. We are not well hidden here; those scouts may still lead others back to us. And the Kingsland suffers more with every hour that passes. We came here to speak with the Wyddin—if it is a trap, so be it. Without their help, we are doomed regardless." She strode to her horse and mounted gracefully, then looked down at the Wyddin that bore Wynne's face. "Lead us."

It did not take long for us to mount once more, and soon we were following our Wyddin guide into the trees. It sat astride Wynne's mount with a stiff, unnatural posture, but had no apparent difficulty directing the animal towards the heart of the First Forest. I rode at the head of the company, alongside Bryndine and the Wyddin, unwilling to let Wynne's body out of my sight.

The smaller maples and birches of the outer forest gave way to great oaks and towering firs, and more and more often, broad-trunked fireleafs bursting with green leaves. The air was thick with the earthy smells of the forest: old soil and sap and decaying leaves, laced with the sharp scent of evergreens. Overhead, the canopy thickened as we made our way deeper, and sunlight penetrated only in scattered patches, breaking the shadows with thin shafts of brightness. We picked our way through heavy undergrowth—undisturbed for centuries, it was so tangled in places that passage was impossible—and around huge trees that often grew too closely together for our mounts to fit between. At times it seemed the forest had blocked our way altogether, but our guide always found some path that the horses could manage.

As we wended our way through the woods, I thought back to what the Wyddin had said earlier. *You must wake the Eldest.* Whatever I was meant to do, I was quite certain I could not. I had no more control over the voices I heard than I did over the beating of my heart. I glanced sidelong at the creature riding beside me. Even looking at the thing while it was wearing Wynne's form made me sick to my stomach, and I certainly did not want to hear it speak with her voice again, but I could not deny my curiosity. Finally, I blurted, "How am I supposed to wake these Eldest? I know nothing about them."

"You must speak to them through the Wyd, and convince them of your need," it replied. "We cannot tell you what words will suffice, only that they will not wake easily."

"Why? Why do they sleep at all?"

It looked at me for a long while, and I thought I saw a glimmer of sorrow in Wynne's green eyes. "What short lives you humans live. To have forgotten the Eldest already… you remember so little."

"Tell us of them," Bryndine said. "It may be useful."

It gave a single nod of Wynne's head. "The Eldest were the first of the Wyddin," it began, "created by the Mother and the Father in the time before the Divide. When the Earth and Sky were separated to make the world, the Mother and the Father charged the Eldest with watching over mankind, and they swore to do so gladly. And from the Eldest we were born, the lesser Wyddin, to aid them in their task."

"I always heard the Wyddin hated us," Orya interrupted from behind. "For takin' their place as the favorite children."

"Those lies came later. No, we treasured mankind. How not? Humans were our beloved younger brothers and sisters, clever and creative and always curious. But some viewed us with distrust—your kind has always been given to superstition, and our… intangible nature confounded them. They fled from our forests to the plains. Those who remained, though, lived their lives in the presence of the Eldest, and the strength of the Wyd seeped into them. The Eldest taught them of the Mother and the Father, and showed them how to open their hearts to the Wyd and harness the Gift of the Sages—but only for peaceful means."

"The Elovians," I guessed, hating myself for the eagerness I heard in my voice. I could not forgive the creature for possessing Wynne, but there was no denying the draw this tale held for me. I had never dreamed that I might hear the story of Elovia from one who had lived during the fabled kingdom's golden age.

"Yes. Those humans founded Elovia, and it was a peaceful kingdom. Our two races lived in harmony for many years. Using the Wyd, they erected great cities and palaces, and coaxed endless crops from the land. But in time, the tribes of the plains grew jealous of Elovia's prosperity. War began.

"The Elovians had their Sages, but the people of the tribes were born warriors, unmatched throughout history. Humans were greater and more powerful then—the divine might that created them still lingered within. Imagine an army of men and women, all as tall and strong as this one." It pointed at Bryndine, and I imagined tens of thousands of her charging towards me with swords drawn. The image was terrifying. "The war lasted generations. Hundreds of thousands died. Each side made demons of the other, and their hate grew with every battle.

"It might have gone on for centuries more, but for Alistan, the last king of Elovia. After his wife and son were killed by the tribesmen, Alistan begged the Eldest to teach him and his Sages how to use the Wyd as a weapon. To turn the Earth and Sky against their enemies. He claimed it would be used only in defense, and eventually the Eldest relented, trusting the humans to use their power wisely.

"In truth, King Alistan meant to use this knowledge to seek vengeance, to destroy the tribes entirely. He had the Sages summon the fire that burns in the belly of the world. But the Wyd is only a language, at its heart—it can make requests of nature, but not truly command it. The Earth's fire was too mighty to be controlled. It rose up and swallowed Elovia whole, leaving nothing but smoke and ash.

"The Eldest were heartbroken. It was their duty to protect and guide mankind, and they had failed. Swearing to remove their power from the world so that such a thing could not happen again, they entered a deep sleep, leaving us to watch over your kind in their place. And with their absence, the strength of the Gift dwindled in humankind, and was forgotten."

There it was. The history of Elovia laid bare in a way it had not been for a thousand years. Yet something was missing from the tale, and a terrible suspicion gnawed at the back of my mind. "All of our stories tell of how the Wyddin hate mankind," I said. "How they destroyed Elovia. But if your story is true, the King and the Sages were at fault."

"No more than we were, human. It was our duty to teach

and guide them. If they misused the Wyd, we led them to it."

I waved a hand dismissively. "Share the blame if you like; that is not the issue. My question is this: our first queen, Aliana, was supposed to have been the last princess of Elovia. She would have been King Alistan's daughter?"

The Wyddin nodded, but did not speak.

"Then she could not have been ignorant of her father's role in the cataclysm. She chose to hide his mistake, to blame you instead. Erryn would not have been difficult to convince; he was of barbarian stock, and his people never trusted yours. And Aliana must have known what the Burning would do to you—she grew up in Elovia, alongside the Wyddin." The pieces fell together in my mind, but it brought no exhilaration, no excitement. I did not want it to be true, though I was certain that it was. "It was not done simply to clear the land—it was an attack. They meant to destroy you."

It held its silence for a time, then quietly said, "Yes."

Disgust and anger welled up inside me. I had once told Bryndine that we had brought this upon ourselves, but I had assumed it was accidental, an ignorant mistake. If Erryn and Aliana had wrought such suffering on the Wyddin out of petty vengeance, it tainted the entire past of the Kingsland. "They rewrote history." It was not the worst of their crimes, but to me—to any Scriber—it came close. "That is where the lies came from. False tales, told to make sure every generation to follow them would hate the Wyddin. They *knew* the blame was not yours, at least not entirely, and they still burned your trees." I had never felt such shame—shame for my kingdom, for my history, for my very species. "How can you… After what was done to you, why in the depths would you want to help us now?"

"The Mother and the Father gave us life and purpose," the Wyddin said, and though its voice was hollow, conviction burned behind Wynne's eyes. "They charged us with the protection of mankind. Your people will not fall at the hands of our brothers and sisters if we can prevent it."

Bryndine looked at the creature with something approaching respect. "You are keeping your oath."

"Putting the Burnt to rest will bring peace to the Wyd.

Our exile will finally end. Once again, we will be free to give mankind our aid and protection, as we promised long ago."

Such pious devotion was unfathomable to me—I had never so much as sat through an entire Garden sermon. Had I been in the same position, I do not think I would have had the strength to spare a kingdom that had caused me so much pain, gods or no. "Is it all true, then?" I asked. "The Mother and the Father, the Divide, everything the Children preach?"

"We cannot answer that, human. We have only our faith, and that is as it should be. None but the Eldest can claim to truly know how the world was born." Urging Wynne's horse forward through a narrow gap between two massive firs, the Wyddin looked back at me and said, "Perhaps when you wake them, you can ask."

* * *

Evening had enveloped the forest by the time we emerged into the moonlit clearing where the First Tree grew.

Fireleafs surrounded the clearing, standing so close together that I could not see between their trunks, their roots and branches so tightly interwoven that nothing larger than a mouse could have fit through the gaps. The result was something like a large box canyon, with great cliff walls of wood and bark and leaves. The only point of entry was from the north, a space of perhaps ten feet in a circle that must have been more than three hundred yards around, and riding through that opening was like riding between the legs of a giant. The trees rose hundreds of feet into the air, higher than any man-made structure I had ever seen, higher than the Kingshome itself. When Elovia fell they had been old already; they were ancient now, possibly the oldest of all living things.

All living things save one.

How to describe the First Tree? It was like nothing I had ever seen. Just looking at it, I could tell that it was as old as the world—nothing could have reached such a size without millennia of growth. It was nearly as wide as the fireleafs around it were tall, and taller than them by half their height again. Its massive trunk grew gnarled and crooked, bent under the weight of the ages. Bark like an old man's skin covered every inch of its surface, so pale that it was almost white, and creased by knots and cords and wrinkle-like folds. Far overhead, its huge, nearly bald branches were silhouetted against the starry sky, bearing no more than a few scattered tufts of leaves that glinted silver in the moonlight. Twisting and weaving around one another, the branches bowed under their own weight to form a great latticed dome that ended just above the canopy of the surrounding forest.

We were all silent as we rode across the lush, perfect grass that carpeted the clearing, towards that impossible tree. It was a silence I knew well, the quiet of the library in Delwyn's Hall, or the Old Garden before the accident. A reverent hush, as though even the air itself knew to hold its breath in the presence of something so old and so precious.

Orya, of course, was the first to break the spell. "Mother's teats, that's a big Dragon-damned tree."

Deanyn snickered. "Eloquently put, as always." But then she glanced at the Wyddin, riding ahead of us, and a look of guilt replaced her grin. I understood. When the creature was not speaking, it was easy to see Wynne in its place, to forget that she was really gone. Every smile—every moment not spent mourning her—felt like betraying her memory.

We dismounted at the foot of the First Tree, hitching our horses among the huge twisted roots. Looking up the massive trunk, it occurred to me how unlikely it was that something so huge had been undiscovered so long. Nothing was written of the First Tree in any book I had ever read. Certainly the Kingsland was rife with superstition about the First Forest, and we were in the deepest part of the woods now, where even the woodcutters of Timberhold dared not tread. But still, someone should have noticed a tree taller than anything ever built by human hands. Curious, I asked, "Why would the First Tree be here? Shouldn't it have grown somewhere in Elovia?"

"It is here now," the Wyddin answered cryptically.

"Yes, but how? It would have been destroyed in the cataclysm, wouldn't it?"

"No birthtree can be truly destroyed, human. When one is burned or cut down, the Wyddin born of it are not slain, but drawn back to the Wyd to give the tree new life and to be reborn from it in turn. This is why the Burnt will always return, no matter how many times you burn them. But even so, we would never risk allowing the First Tree to be harmed in that way. It was gone from Elovia before the cataclysm could take it."

"So it can move."

"Not as you would understand it. It is where it must be."

I could tell that I would get no better answer, so I moved on. "What must I do to speak to the Eldest? I don't know how to use the Wyd. I just… hear voices."

"Hearing the Wyd and touching it are not the same. To touch the Wyd is to feel all that courses through it—only then can you make yourself heard by the Earth and Sky. You have done so before. You spoke of ending the snow in the mountains."

"The only time I have felt anything is when the voices made me burn." Even in the Salt Mountains, where they had been too weak to burn me, the clarity had come only after they had tried. "I don't control it. It only happens when I'm afraid."

"Yes. The Wyd is a thing of…" It tapped Wynne's chest and seemed to struggle for a way to explain. "…Of spirit. Of heart, humans might say. Where the Gift is weak, it may take moments of vulnerability to touch it. Your kind often experiences it only in dreams."

"I have dreamed of the Burnt more often than I would like." It made a strange sort of sense. Everything I had experienced through the Wyd had been based strongly on emotions and feelings—pain and anger, sorrow and fear. "But I don't know what you expect me to do. I can't scare myself on command."

"We can scare you plenty, Scriber," Orya said, cracking her knuckles and grinning her wild grin. Though I knew it was a jest, I could not help glancing at Sylla. If there was one woman in the company who truly frightened me, it was her. For once, though, she was not glaring back at me; her eyes were on Bryndine.

Wynne's voice brought my attention back to the Wyddin. "You must find your own way to touch the Wyd. You know your spirit best. When the time comes, lay your hands upon the First Tree. Your Gift is weak, but the Tree is strong. It will help you reach the Eldest."

"When the time comes? Why not now?" I wanted it done with. I reached towards a nearby root.

Wynne's hand seized my wrist. "No!" The Wyddin's vehemence startled me, and I pulled my arm back.

Bryndine gave the creature a sharp look. "Why stop him? What have you not told us?"

"We… thought you might not come if you knew." The Wyddin's usually flat voice sounded almost abashed. "It seemed best to bring you here first."

Bryndine's eyes hardened into steel. "Tell us. Now."

"The First Tree is a beacon within the Wyd. The Burnt will be aware of your efforts as soon as you begin, and they will not let you rob them of their vengeance. They will come for you the moment they feel you touch the Tree, with your hand or your mind. Your lives will depend on how quickly you can reach the Eldest."

"We're leagues away from the nearest city," Deanyn said. "Unless they can fly, they won't reach us in time."

"You do not understand. If they cannot reach you in their current bodies, they will leave them. The forest is full of animals for them to use. They will come as wolves and stags and any other creature they can find, and nothing will stop them but your deaths. Your deaths, or the sleep only the Eldest can grant."

"Sky and Earth," I swore, rubbing at my temple in agitation. When the Burnt came, our lives would be in my hands. Every woman there would die if I could not find a way to communicate with a tree full of ancient forest spirits. They might as well have asked me to reunite the Mother and the Father. "I have never touched the Wyd on my own. I don't even know where to begin, and if I take too long, we all die. I can't—"

"I am sorry, Scriber Dennon, but you must." There was sympathy in Bryndine's voice, but the steel in her gaze did not falter. "We cannot do this without you."

Deanyn squeezed my shoulder, and I thought she might

make some joke. But she only smiled, and I could see the trust in her eyes.

Orya stepped up, clapped me on the back, and said, "Don't worry, Scriber. We ain't about to let you get hurt."

The others looked less certain—I saw the twins exchange worried looks—but they nodded, or half-heartedly voiced their agreement. All save Sylla. One look at her dark eyes told me everything I needed to know: *if she dies, you die*, they said.

Their reassurance would have done little to calm me even without the menace of Sylla's glare. It was not my own safety I worried for. But there was no way out now—I was the only one who could speak to the Eldest. That was why I had come. I nodded slowly, and managed to croak, "I will try."

"Will the Wyddin stand with us?" asked Bryndine.

It lowered Wynne's eyes. "We cannot. We are still of the Wyd—it is our very nature. Holding ourselves apart from it is… difficult. If we were to fight the Burnt, it would be far too easy for us to succumb to their pain and anger, and become as they are. No, you must stand against them on your own, if you cannot wake the Eldest before they come."

It was so absurd that I almost laughed. *Nine women and an historian against the Burnt. The Kingsland is doomed.*

Sylla snorted with scorn. "So you brought us here to risk our lives while you run away. Is this your idea of honoring your oaths?"

"We cannot ask for what they cannot give," said Bryndine. "The Wyddin have offered us a chance we did not have a day ago."

"They offer us a chance to die," Sylla said bitterly. "The Burnt outnumber us, and they have sorcery. What can we do against that?"

"That is… a concern." Bryndine turned back to the Wyddin. "Will they not simply use their magick to defeat us?"

It shook Wynne's head. "Their communion with the Wyd is not precise. The madness that consumes them hinders their control. Any force powerful enough to destroy you would harm the birthtrees, and the First Tree itself. The Burnt are difficult to predict, but we do not believe even they would go so far. There are many things that they might turn the Wyd towards, but they will not call down lightning, or open the earth."

"Still," said Bryndine, "you expect a great deal of us."

"We are not unaware of that. But there is one more thing we must ask."

Bryndine inclined her head. "Ask it, then."

"If you should survive, you must tell your people the truth of the Burning. Tell them that we mean them no harm; that we never have. There is much that we can do for humanity, if only they would let us. But if the past remains obscured with lies, someday all of this will repeat itself again."

The Scriber in me could not refuse that request. The Burning, the Forgetting, and now this—all of it had happened because we had forgotten our history. The cycle had gone on long enough. "I will tell the Scribers, if I can make them listen," I said. "It is time for this to end."

"Then we are in your debt, human." It offered a thin smile, an attempt to show some kind of human emotion. "Now we must go. A final word of advice: wait for the sun to rise. Darkness does not hinder our eyes as it does yours, and there is no reason to give the Burnt any more advantage."

"We will rest tonight," Bryndine said. "Thank you, for all you have done."

"It is we who should thank you. We will leave your friend, as promised."

"Wait." I had one more question to ask. A question I had been avoiding, because I dreaded the answer. "I have seen others like me… others with the Gift. I have seen them burn and die from hearing these voices, but I still live. Why?"

"The pain of the Burnt is enough to destroy those who do not guard their hearts. They will feel the suffering more keenly, and succumb to it more quickly. A guarded spirit, though, may retreat before it burns away."

"I have always fainted when they burn me."

"Your spirit protects you from their attacks. You ward yourself well to have lived this long."

Josia had always kept her feelings in plain sight, and had no qualms about listening to the problems of others. No one would ever accuse me of the same. I had hidden in Waymark for years rather than face my shame, and avoided anything resembling friendship for longer still. My cowardice, it seemed, might have been good for something after all. "Am I safe, then?"

"Perhaps. Perhaps not. We will not hide the truth from you—there is great risk. If you allow your spirit to pull away from the Wyd before reaching the Eldest, all is lost. But every moment you use your Gift, you are vulnerable to the Burnt. Even if your spirit is armored well, swiftness is the only thing that will ensure your safety."

It was not the reassurance I had hoped for, but I tried not to show my disappointment. "Then I suppose I will do my best to be swift."

"May the Mother and the Father protect you," it said. "Farewell." I could almost imagine it was Wynne saying goodbye, and a wave of grief washed over me.

Wynne's body went limp as the Wyddin left it, and I caught her as she fell, sinking to my knees on the cold grass. For the second time that day, I looked upon her lifeless face, and felt my throat constrict. All around me, the women gathered to salute their fallen friend, the sweet young girl who should have been a Scriber, not a soldier.

I realized something then, as I cradled Wynne in my arms: I cared more about these women than anyone I had met since Illias. I could not bear to see any of them harmed. Not Selvi and Elene, whose only fear was that they would lose one another; not fearless, foul-mouthed Orya; certainly not Deanyn, with her quick wit and her smile that made my heart race. And Bryndine, with all her infuriating nobility and stubbornness; Bryndine, who I think I would have followed into the Dragon's depths if she had asked it of me—her least of all. All my life, I had kept my distance from the people around me, tried not to get involved in their lives. It was, apparently, what had saved me from the Burnt. But I was not that man anymore.

Control yourself, Lark. Sentimentality was something I could not afford, not now, not when it would make me vulnerable to the Burnt. If I died tomorrow before I could wake the Eldest, the others would die with me, and I could not allow that to happen.

But the tears flowed all the same.

CHAPTER THIRTY-FIVE

I have lived more in these last months than in my entire life before them, I think. I have found true friends, and realized a childhood dream. I have travelled with women who I am honored to have known, women who are heroes by any standard. I met Deanyn, and I would not give that up for anything. I think that I may even have become a man who Illias can truly be proud of. And I owe all of it to Bryndine.

— From the personal journals of Dennon Lark

"I never understood half what she was sayin'," Orya said. "I remember, she was tryin' to explain that theory of yours to me, comin' out of Highpass a few months back, Scriber. Thought she might knock me off my horse, all that arm wavin'."

A ripple of gentle laughter circled our small fire at the foot of the First Tree. It was past midnight, and considering what was coming in the morning, all of us should have been sleeping. Instead, we sat together around the fire and shared stories of those we had lost.

I forced a smile. I was preoccupied with everything the Wyddin had told us, and talking about Wynne made my chest ache, but if this was what the company needed, I would not deny them. "She was more excited than I was," I said. "And it was my idea."

"She would have been a fine Scriber," Bryndine said softly, and Sylla squeezed her shoulder with surprising gentleness.

There was a quiet moment then, and my hand wandered to my collar. The pin that I had worked most of my life to earn was absent. It was somewhere in the ashes of Wynne's pyre now, a melted lump of gold and bronze.

Eventually, Leste broke the silence. "We might learn from her. She was never forgetting her dream to be a Scriber. When this is done, I have it in my mind to sail again."

"If we survive," said Deanyn, and there was an unfamiliar edge to her voice. She had been sitting beside me for some time, but had taken little part in the conversation until now. I glanced at her with concern, but she just stared into the fire.

Orya ignored the comment and looked at Leste with a raised eyebrow. "Leavin' us, are you?"

"When we sailed to the mountains, it was good to be having the sea under my feet again. Life is very short, my friend."

"Elene and I might get out too." Selvi looked at the others apologetically. "If we make it through this, I think we'll have about used up all our luck. And we've been saving to buy some land."

"For breeding horses," added Elene. "It's something we've always wanted to do."

Ivyla crossed her arms and said, "I don't know how anyone could leave the Captain after all she has done for us."

Bryndine smiled faintly at the girl's loyalty, but her eyes were solemn. "You owe me nothing, Ivyla. All of you are free to live lives of your choosing; that is what the Promise is for. I did not blame Wynne for seeking to enrol at the Academy, and I would not blame anyone for leaving after this is over. You have all earned your rest."

"Rest sounds dull," said Orya. "I ain't goin' nowhere."

Debra nodded her agreement. "Not much else I'm good at."

"What of you, Scriber Dennon?" Bryndine asked. "We have taken you from your life for a long time now. What will you do with yourself when this is done?"

What will *I do?* I had not thought about it until now, but I would be no use to the company when the Burnt were gone. And what other options did I have? I was still unwelcome at the Academy, and most of the small towns I might have sought work in had been razed to the ground. I had no life to return to. "I honestly don't know," I said, attempting a nonchalant shrug. *I can think about it later*, I told myself. *I have to keep everyone alive tomorrow first.*

"Might be I know someone who has suggestions," said Orya, waggling her eyebrows at Deanyn. "Way she grabbed you when Korus got us out of the dungeons, I thought you two might be needin' a private cell."

I flushed and glanced sidelong at Deanyn, more than a little bit interested in her reaction. I expected some clever retort or the like, but instead she surveyed the women around her with a pained expression, and then stood abruptly. "I have to… excuse me for a moment." She strode away from the fire without looking back, and soon passed through the gap between the trees to the north and disappeared from sight.

Orya looked stricken. "I wasn't tryin' to…" She started to stand, ready to go after the other woman.

I held up a hand and got to my feet. "Let me." I was startled by my own willingness. This was exactly the sort of personal situation I had always avoided. But it was different with Deanyn; I actually wanted to know what was wrong. I hoped—quite fervently—that it wasn't the implication that there was something between us. Given the dangers we would face tomorrow, I felt terribly selfish for worrying over something so… adolescent, but I could not seem to help myself.

Beyond the wall of fireleafs that ringed the clearing, the forest was dark. I regretted stepping outside the reach of the firelight almost immediately. "Deanyn?" I called softly, trying not to alert the dozens of hungry animals I felt certain were waiting just outside the reach of my vision.

"Here," she answered.

I turned in the direction of her voice, and saw a faint silhouette sitting on a log nearby. I stumbled towards her, scraping my shin against a rock in the dark. "Why did you leave?" I asked, sitting down beside her. "Orya shouldn't have said… Obviously it was embarrassing but… She didn't mean anything by it. You know how she is."

"Her mouth gets ahead of her mind. I know. It wasn't that." Deanyn touched my hand lightly in the dark. "And it wasn't you. I wasn't embarrassed."

I allowed myself a moment of relief at that, despite everything else that I had to worry about. "What then?"

She gave a self-deprecating snort. "Would it surprise you if I said that I'm afraid?"

"A little bit, yes. I've seen you fight hordes of the Burnt. You didn't seem afraid then."

"This isn't the same. It's the waiting. All this talk of what we'll do after, and nobody adding the 'if we survive' at the end. It just makes me think how much I don't want to die here."

I probably shouldn't have, but I laughed. "That is what you're worried about? Sky and Earth, Deanyn, I've felt that way for months. Nobody wants to die."

I couldn't see her face in the dark, but I could sense her annoyance. "You don't understand," she said. "I… I told you once that I followed Bryndine for the excitement, and that's partly true, but… what I really wanted was to prove I wasn't like my parents. That I cared about something beyond myself. And now people are dead and everything is at stake and all I can think to do is make stupid jokes and worry about my own safety." She hung her head. "Perhaps I'm not so different from them after all."

"You are," I said firmly.

"How do you know?"

"Because you're *here*." I was not entirely confident about what to say or do, but I clasped her hand and squeezed it and barrelled onwards. "Because I know you. You're brave and you're intelligent, and without your jokes I think everyone here would have gone mad a long time ago."

"That is… sweet, Dennon, but I think you're just trying to make me feel better."

"I am quite serious," I said. "I remember the first time we met, Orya said something that embarrassed me, and I didn't know what to say—I never do. You made some clever comment and saved me. You didn't know me, and you had no reason to help, but you did it anyway. That's who you are." I smiled at her. "In any event, if you are being this hard on yourself for a moment of fear, what about me? I can't remember the last time I *wasn't* afraid."

Deanyn was silent for a long time, and I could feel her eyes on me. I squirmed uncomfortably. *Did I say something wrong?* I had little experience with these sorts of situations, and choosing the right words had never been a strength of mine.

And then, to my great surprise, she said, "You are a better man than you think you are, Dennon Lark," and her hand gripped my collar and pulled me close, and she kissed me full on the mouth.

When I was younger, the occasional woman had thought it might be interesting to pursue one of the Academy's so-called prodigies, and I had gone along with it from time to time, out of curiosity more than anything. These relationships had not been plentiful and had never lasted long—I always said just the wrong thing at just the wrong time—but it was fair to say I had *some* experience with romance. And yet, when Deanyn's lips touched mine, my heart began to beat wildly against my chest, and I couldn't decide what to do with my hands. When she pulled back, I could only stammer. "I… I wasn't expecting… That was—"

She cut me off, with some amusement. "Don't strain yourself, Dennon. You don't have to say anything. Just… you promised me once you'd keep yourself safe. Do that, and we'll see what happens after this is all finished." Despite the darkness, I could tell she was smirking when she said, "If we survive."

I felt like I should say something meaningful, or romantic, but nothing leapt to mind. What came out of my mouth was, "I could ask you to make the same promise."

"What, to keep myself safe?"

"No," I said. "To keep *me* safe. You're the one with the sword."

She laughed and drew me close again, and this time I found the confidence to fold my arms around her and kiss her back.

* * *

When we returned to the First Tree, most of the women had retired for the night. Bryndine and Sylla waited for us by the fire.

"There you are," said Bryndine. "I was about to send Sylla for you. You will need your rest for tomorrow. I have the first watch."

"I'm sorry if we worried you, Captain," Deanyn said.

"There is no need to apologize. The others have their bedrolls on the other side of the tree." Bryndine gestured in that direction. "Scriber Dennon, please stay a moment. I would like to speak with you."

"Don't keep him too late." Deanyn grinned. "He gets terribly cranky." She gave me a quick peck on the cheek before she left.

Bryndine gave me a knowing look as I seated myself by the fire. "She is very fond of you," she said.

Sylla snorted derisively. "Shows how good her judgement is."

I did not reply to either of them. I didn't know what to say. Wynne was dead, and the lives of every woman in the company depended on me doing something I hadn't any idea how to do, and yet… for the first time in years, I could almost believe that I might have some chance at happiness. The guilt of it was unbearable. How could I sit there and imagine a future with Deanyn when Wynne would have no future at all? *And more will die still, if I don't succeed tomorrow.*

After a moment, Bryndine said, "Sylla, you should rest as well."

"I'm fine," Sylla said stubbornly.

"Please, Sylla. I wish to speak privately with the Scriber. I will wake you when it is time to relieve me."

Reluctantly, Sylla nodded and stood. "Make sure you do. You need to get some sleep too, Bryn." Then, with a suspicious glance in my direction, she strode away.

"I will not keep you long, Scriber," said Bryndine.

"What did you want to speak to me about?"

"You believe that Wynne's death was your fault."

The bluntness of the statement took me aback, and I struggled for a response. "It… certainly feels like it was."

"You could as easily blame me. If I had let Selvi and Elene defend us sooner, or allowed you to begin your treatment earlier…"

"It wasn't you that she died to save."

"I thought you would say that." She gave me a long, thoughtful look. "Millum Wren told me something about guilt once. Do you know why they call me the Bloody Bride?"

I couldn't imagine the relevance, but I nodded. "Herryk Rafynson's death." It was a well known story. When Bryndine was younger, she had been engaged to the son of Baron Hurryd of the Bridgefort, until the boy had been slain trying to fight off bandits while they were riding together in the countryside. "The rumor was that you killed him. Nonsense, of course."

A small, sad smile crossed her face. "Actually, it is not so far from the truth. Our families saw fit to withhold certain details from the public story. It was not Herryk who tried to fight the bandits. It was me. I might have waited for our escort—we had only ridden a short way ahead, and they would have come before long. But I was young, and eager to be a soldier. They killed Herryk because I fought back." She lowered her eyes to stare into the fire. "I blamed myself, of course. As much as those spreading the rumors did. I had wished to prove myself a warrior, and it cost a man his life. For a time, I abandoned my hopes of joining the Army.

"But a year later, I met Master Millum at the Academy, and he was never one to accept excuses. I will never forget what he said to me: 'If you think you are responsible for his death, then *take* responsibility for it.' I began my Warfare training the next day." Bryndine fixed me with an intent stare. "Do you understand, Scriber Dennon? We owe it to those who died to do more with our lives. If you wish to hold yourself responsible for Wynne's death, I cannot stop you. But you must *use* that guilt."

Finally, I understood what she was saying. "To speak with the Eldest." According to the Wyddin, emotion was key to touching the Wyd. I expected fear would serve well enough when the Burnt came, but a healthy amount of remorse could not hurt.

"Yes. Can we rely on you?"

I sighed. "I hope so. I don't want anyone else to die."

"We need more than hope, Scriber."

This woman had saved my life more than once. She had risked everything to protect the Kingsland. I owed her this. I owed it to all the women who followed her, and all those who had died. I owed it to the history of the Kingsland itself, a history that I had studied all my life, that would forever remain distorted by lies if we did not survive.

I looked her in the eye. "Bryndine," I said, "I will not fail you." I didn't know if it was a promise I could keep, but I meant to try.

She smiled. "I do not think you will at that, Scriber Dennon. Now get some sleep."

I stood, and was about to walk away, but I hesitated. *Who knows what will happen tomorrow?* There were things I had to say. "I am only here because of you, you know."

She looked up at me with a frown. "I am sorry, Scriber. I never meant for your involvement to go so far, but we need you."

"I didn't mean it that way." I couldn't blame her for assuming it was a complaint; she had heard enough of those from me. "I would be dead a hundred times over without you, and even if I wasn't, I would be wasting my life somewhere. You took me out of Waymark and forced me to do something of worth, and… you gave me a place to belong. That is something I have not had in a long time. Deanyn told me that I was a good man tonight, and I don't know if that is true, but if it is, I think it is because of you."

Bryndine Errynson could stare down snowcats and fight armies, but she did not know how to deal with praise. I had never seen her blush, but she blushed now. "I don't… surely you owe more to Master Illias than to me."

I shook my head. "No. I owe Illias a great deal, but not in this. He tried to convince me to return to the Academy for years, but he was part of the reason I could not. When I failed, I was failing him as much as myself. Imagine if you had done something to shame Millum Wren—would you have believed him when he told you it didn't matter?"

"I take your point," Bryndine said. "But I will not take credit for another's deeds. You *are* a good man, Scriber Dennon. I suspect you always were."

"Perhaps, but without you I would never have known it. I would never have left Waymark." I grinned. "I spent so much time annoyed with you that I didn't realize what was happening until it was too late."

She laughed at that, a rare thing for her. "I spent a great deal of time annoyed with you as well," she said. "Let us say that we owe each other."

I chuckled along with her. "If you insist." I looked over my shoulder, to where the others were sleeping, though the First Tree sat between us and them. "I suppose I should rest."

"Go," she said. "And sleep well. We will need you at your best tomorrow."

I nodded and turned away, but her voice stopped me after only a few steps. "Scriber, wait." When I glanced back, the glow of the fire seemed to cast a shadow of uncertainty across her eyes. "Do you truly believe we can succeed?"

Not really, I thought. *Not if it depends on me*. But I couldn't say that aloud; I had promised her that she could rely on me.

I was going to give a glib answer to cover my doubt, but when I looked at her face, something stopped me. There was such strength there, such dignity, even with doubt lining her features. I could see all of her legendary ancestors in those steel grey eyes, in that determined jaw and golden hair, and I wondered how I had ever thought her plain.

This is what the blood of kings and heroes looks like. In her veins ran the blood of Elovians and tribesmen going back to the beginning of time. The blood of King Erryn and Queen Aliana, who had, despite all their sins, forged a kingdom and a peace and a Promise. The blood of Rynd the Explorer, and of Delwyn the Scriber King, and of poor, brave Prince Fyrril. All of them were there in her face, in her broad shoulders and her impossible height, in her stubbornness and her strength and her grace. Looking at her now, I could almost believe that she would save us all. The fate of the Kingsland was not in my hands alone—Bryndine would be there with me, and she would not let me fail.

"Yes," I finally said, and I was surprised to find that I believed it. "Yes, I think we just might."

CHAPTER THIRTY-SIX

The battle in the First Forest was the most incredible, terrible thing I imagine I will ever experience. It was at the same time both the worst and the proudest moment of my life. The worst because of the friends that I lost there; the proudest because it was likely the most important thing I will ever do. Because there are only a half-dozen people left in the world who can say that they stood with Bryndine Errynson that day, in defense of the Kingsland and the Promise.

And she was glorious.

— From the personal journals of Dennon Lark

Dawn came too soon.

Sunlight made it to the floor of the clearing in patches, wherever it could avoid being tangled up in the web of shadows cast by the branches of the First Tree. Where the light reached the ground, it sparkled off the dew and scattered rainbows across the rich green grass. On the whole, the effect was far too idyllic. I found myself wishing for clouds.

In the brightness of the morning, the task ahead seemed too real, too immediate. I wanted to close my eyes and pretend it was all a dream, but I could not. The women had already donned their armor, strapped on their shields, readied their weapons. The horses had been taken as far from us as Selvi and Elene could lead them in an hour and secured there, so that the

Burnt could not turn our own mounts against us. Everything was prepared.

The time had come.

Standing before the First Tree with the sun reflecting off her golden hair, Bryndine Errynson silently swept her gaze over her company. Only nine sets of eyes looked back at her—mine, and eight others. Eight, of what had been near twenty when they had first come to Waymark. Too many women lost, and I knew Bryndine felt their absence. I could see it in the tightness of her lips, the slight wrinkling around her eyes. But she could not show any weakness now, not with those who remained depending on her. No, she would be strong for them. She would be strong right down to her last breath, I suspected.

She would have to be. The women seemed to dread what was to come as much as I did. The Kingsland had never given them reason to sacrifice their lives eagerly.

"I will not lie to you," Bryndine said at last. "If we make our stand here, we fight for a kingdom that would not grieve to see us slain. The Army does not want us. The Scribers have abandoned us. The people have turned against us. They think that we are blasphemers, or traitors, or worse." She drew herself up to her full height then, and held her head high, and her voice rang out like a hammer on steel. "But they also need us!

"All of us here have sworn oaths. We may not all have said the same words"—she looked in my direction at that—"but in the end, all of us have vowed to do the same thing: to serve and protect the people of the Kingsland. *All* of the people of the Kingsland. Not only those who we approve of, and not only when we wish to do it. Keeping an oath when it is easy to keep means nothing—it is what we do when those oaths become difficult that defines us.

"Let others break their vows. Let them bicker, and blame, and fight amongst one another. Let them ignore the truth that stands before them. But not us!" And now she set her jaw, and her eyes shone like polished steel as she said, "We *will* stay true. We *will* honor the oaths that we swore. The people may not want our protection, but they *will* have it!" She drew her sword and held it high, and its blade was gilded by the morning light. "For the Promise!"

Her women did not disappoint her. As one, they lifted their weapons and took up the cry. For what must have been the first time in more than a thousand years, the First Forest echoed with the sound of human voices.

I did not join in. It would have been a lie. Bryndine's words were stirring, but I was not risking my life for some ancient ideal. I had sworn an oath, and I would keep it, but not for the Promise. This was no longer about the good of the many for me—it was about the lives of the few I cared about, and the memory of those who were gone. It was about setting right the crimes that had distorted our history for so long, that had led us to this point. If the citizens of the Kingsland were saved too, it was lucky for them, but honestly, I couldn't have cared less.

As the women organized themselves, I moved into position at the eastern side of the First Tree, nestled in the cleft between two enormous roots. The spot provided some amount of cover, but left me with a clear view of the gap in the trees to the north, where Bryndine and the others were forming their line. Where they would mount their defense.

The plan, as Bryndine had explained it, was a simple one. We had a certain advantage here, she had said. The thick wall of trees around us made the clearing defensible. The narrow gap to the north was the only way in, and it would limit the numbers the Burnt could bring against Bryndine and the others. Nine women could hold such a spot. For a time. Not forever. It fell to me to ensure that it was a short fight.

Of course, if things went badly, the single point of entry also meant there was no escape. But I preferred not to think about that.

"Isn't this cozy." Deanyn's voice cut through my thoughts as she slipped into the gap in the roots that sheltered me.

"Shouldn't you be with the others?"

"I know where I'm supposed to stand, and I don't think they will start without me. I just… wanted to see how you were."

"Anxious. Frightened. Several thousand leagues from prepared."

She smiled. "That may be a good thing, if what the

Wyddin said is true. Perhaps you'll reach the Eldest on your first attempt, and we'll look like fools for being so worried."

"Perhaps," I said. "But I don't think it very likely." I looked down at my feet. "Deanyn… If I can't make them listen, you should know…" But I could only gesture vaguely, unable to come up with the words I wanted.

She touched my cheek, gently, and lifted my chin until I was looking her in the eyes. "You can tell me after," she said. "They'll listen. I trust you." Then, she pulled me into her arms, pressed her body against mine, and whispered into my ear, "Be careful, Dennon. Remember your promise."

"You're the one who will be in danger, trying to protect me. I…"

She clubbed a hand against my back. "Shut up, Scriber."

Laughing despite myself, I closed my mouth and held her.

And then, over her shoulder, I saw Bryndine approaching, with Sylla at her side, and I knew it was time. My throat went dry, and I pulled away from Deanyn's arms.

"We are ready, Scriber," said Bryndine. "Deanyn, you should take your position."

"Yes, Captain." Deanyn gave my hand a final squeeze, and departed.

"Are you certain this is the best place for you, Scriber?" Bryndine asked. "I would sooner have you out of sight behind the tree."

I shook my head. "No. I need to be able to see when the Burnt come. I need to be afraid. Fear is the only thing I know that works."

"Very well." She gave me a very solemn look, and she said, "The Kingsland owes you a great debt, Scriber Dennon." Then, to my surprise, she saluted me before turning away.

An unexpected sense of pride rose in my breast as I watched her go. I knew what that salute meant. To Bryndine, who had devoted her life to the King's Army and everything it represented, it was the highest honor she could give.

Strangely enough, Sylla did not immediately follow her Captain. With a worried glance over her shoulder at Bryndine, she stepped towards me, and my stomach clenched with dread. But there was only supplication in her dark eyes, and her voice was soft and plaintive as she said, "Please, Scriber. Be swift. Do not let her die for you."

"No harm will come to her," I promised, and prayed that it was true. Looking at Sylla's face right then, I could not bring myself to tell her anything else.

Sylla looked at me in silence for a moment, then nodded brusquely and hurried back to Bryndine's side.

I was alone beside the First Tree.

I looked up at the giant, crooked trunk and the maze of twisted branches high above. The leaves I had seen reflecting the moonlight the night before were nothing but tiny spots of green among the distant boughs. There couldn't have been more than a hundred. If each leaf was the spirit of one of the Eldest, there were not many ears for my voice to reach.

Please listen. Wake up. I tried to direct my thoughts towards the tree, but there was no response. I had not expected one. It would have been too easy. No, I had to use a Gift that had been lost to mankind for a thousand years. I had to somehow find an emotion powerful enough to reach the Wyd, while at the same time staying distant enough to protect myself against the Burnt. It was ludicrous, and insane, and impossible; it was a thousand things, but easy was not one of them.

Taking a deep breath, I laid my hands against the pale bark of the First Tree.

A prickling sensation began in my palms, then swept up my arms and spread throughout my body. Gooseflesh rose on my skin. There was power here, woven into the very wood of this ancient tree, and something inside me responded to it.

And the Burnt responded as well. In the back of my mind, I heard a distant voice.

"*All will burn.*"

They were coming.

Fear lanced through my heart, but it was not enough. There was no moment of clarity, nor did I feel the awareness of the Burnt sweep over me. I could hear their whispers, low at first, then growing louder. "*We will have vengeance,*" they hissed. "*We will not be robbed.*" But they did not command me to burn.

"There!" I heard Selvi cry, and I looked towards the sound.

The twins' hands blurred as they drew and released their bow strings, sending arrow after arrow into the trees. The women blocked my view, but I knew what they must be seeing—the animals of the forest gathering to attack. Distance was no obstacle to the Burnt; they were already here, in whatever bodies they could take.

"*Death*," they shrieked into the Wyd. And then they attacked.

Ivyla fell to the ground as a lithe grey form leapt upon her. The wolf snarled and went for her throat, but Debra kicked it aside and wrenched the other woman back to her feet as Deanyn brought her blade down on the creature's spine.

Over their heads, I saw a set of antlers emerge from the trees. A large stag lowered its head and charged at Leste. Bryndine stepped into its path. There was a loud screech as the antlers scraped against the steel of her shield, and she staggered back. Sylla darted forward, slicing low at the stag's leg. Its knee gave way, and Bryndine cleaved downward with a heavy stroke that severed an antler and bit deep into the animal's skull.

The battle became a blur of fur and steel, growls and cries. The women held their line, but they were being slowly forced back, step by step. Terror pulsed in my veins, for the company and for myself, but I could not find the tipping point that had always come naturally before. It was as though reaching for the Wyd only made it retreat further. "Please!" I yelled at the tree, pushing my hands against the bark until my skin was raw. "Help them!"

The only answer was the voices of the Burnt. "*Pain. Fire. Death.*"

And then I heard something else: a dull roar, like hundreds of banners flapping in a heavy wind. A shadow fell over the clearing. I looked up.

Birds. Birds of all sizes and colors and kinds flew together, crows and sparrows and falcons and more. A thousand pairs of wings blocked out the sun.

They dove.

The birds threw themselves through the boughs of the First Tree with no regard for their own lives. Hundreds collided with the branches and plummeted to the ground, but hundreds more slipped through the gaps. And many of them were coming directly at me.

I didn't know what to do. There was nowhere to hide, and still the Wyd would not open to me. No matter how afraid I was, I could not find a way to do intentionally what I had done so many times by instinct. "Wake up," I whispered, over and over again, as I pressed my bloody hands against the First Tree. But no one was listening. I hunched against the tree and closed my eyes as the birds descended.

"Down, Scriber!" I recognized Bryndine's voice, felt her big hands push me lower. I looked up to see her standing over me with her shield held high, just as I had seen her the night she had first saved me in Waymark. The birds hurled themselves against her shield, against her body. Their talons and beaks tore at her leather armor, and at her skin wherever they could find it. Hundreds collided with the ground around us, and against the trunk of the First Tree. The sound was deafening.

Peeking through a gap in the roots around me, I watched the others trying to defend themselves. The line had scattered. The sheer number of the birds had driven the women apart, and the other animals were using it to their advantage. Debra knocked a falcon aside with her axe as it dived for her face, but a wolf bit into her leg and pulled her down, then leapt atop her and tore out her throat. I turned my eyes away, pressed my face against the First Tree and screamed. "Listen to me! You have to help us!" There was no response.

Finally, Bryndine stepped away from me, bleeding from a long wound across her brow. There were few birds left now—most had shattered themselves against the ground and the trees. Those that were left flapped about the heads of the women, clawing and screeching, distracting them as the more dangerous animals attacked. The gap that led into the clearing was open and undefended, and more creatures entered every moment.

"To me! Protect the Scriber!" Bryndine's voice cut through the noise of battle, and her women responded. They fell back towards us, forming a half-circle around my niche in the roots of the First Tree.

The Burnt followed, in the bodies of badgers, wolves, deer, even various vermin; every kind of animal I could imagine.

Their voices howled through my mind, the same insane litany I had heard so many times before.

Elene screamed as a boar impaled her leg with a huge curled tusk, and her sister came to her aid, plunging her sword into the creature's skull until it ceased moving. Wolves bit at the women's ankles and birds clawed at their eyes. And Bryndine and her company held. Against an unceasing horde of beasts, they held.

I noticed then that only seven of them remained. In a panic, I swept my eyes over their faces. Ivyla was missing. Debra was not the only one who had fallen.

I am letting them die, I realized with horror. *I have to do something.* Climbing to my feet, I placed my back against the tree and held my palms against it. I pictured the men who had died at the Old Garden. I thought of Janelyn and Genna and Varrie and Wynne. I gathered all my fear and sorrow, all my guilt over every death I had ever caused. I could still feel the power of the First Tree tingling in my palms, and I poured everything I had into grasping it.

"Let me burn, let me die, just *hear me*," I begged.

The Eldest remained silent. Fear had always sufficed before; now, nothing seemed to be enough.

In the corner of my eye, I saw a blur of brown and crimson, and I turned my head to see a dozen men of the King's Army enter the clearing. For just a moment I hoped that they had come to help. Until I saw their wounds.

Where the men had come from, I could not say—perhaps they had been looking for us, sent by the scouts from the Timberhold. But one thing was certain: the Burnt had found them first. One man's stomach had been rent open and his intestines dangled free; another had a ragged red hole in his throat. Every one of them bore horrible wounds that did not bleed. These were dead men, kept on their feet only by the spirits possessing them.

And behind them came the Beast.

That was the name that came to me, the moment I saw it. I might have called it a bear, but the word simply didn't suffice—there was a sheer primal presence to the animal that defied classification. It reared up on its hind legs behind the men, monstrous and powerful, more than twelve feet of muscle and claws and teeth. Its forelegs were as thick as my torso; its claws were longer than knives, and undoubtedly deadlier. Huge puckered scars like mountain ridges rose from the forest of matted fur all over its body, and a great gash across its face had taken one eye. I had the distinct impression that this creature had survived battles I could not have dreamed of, that it was a warrior from the dawn of the world, full of the might of Earth and Sky.

The Beast loped forward, and the men parted to let it by. They advanced together, the men flanking the monster as though following their commander into battle. And as they came, two more figures joined their ranks. *No. Mother below, please not this.*

Debra and Ivyla walked with the Burnt. Their wounds did not bleed.

Despair gripped me. Bryndine and her women could have held back the animals, even the possessed men for a time. But not the Beast. Not with every woman who fell turning against us. It was hopeless.

A thick mist rose from nowhere, filling the clearing and thickening with unnatural speed. In moments, everything further than a few yards from me was gone. Of the women, I could see only Orya and Deanyn nearby, and only as ghostly forms moving through the grey. I remembered the words of the Wyddin: *There are many things that they might turn the Wyd towards.*

The Burnt were doing this. And somewhere in the mist, they were still coming. I felt the footsteps of the Beast shaking the ground beneath my feet, and the sound of steel on steel rang from somewhere to my right as the dead crossed swords with the living.

"What in the ruttin' depths?" I heard Orya curse, looked, and saw a giant shadow forming before her in the fog.

The Beast struck.

With astonishing speed, Orya ducked under the massive blow. She was pitifully small next to the Beast, but she did not retreat, did not even take a step back. Fearless as ever, she lunged forward, and her sword pierced the monster's hide.

An instant later, a huge foreleg caught her in the chest and flung her against the First Tree. She slumped to the ground and moved no more.

Deanyn leapt at the Beast's side with a two-handed strike that bit deep, but the creature hardly seemed to notice. She rolled under a sweep of its claws and came to her feet behind its back, swinging at its hind leg. Her blade struck flesh, but if it hurt, the Beast gave no indication. It turned and swung; she dodged to the side. She was too slow. The Beast's claws tore into her calf, flaying down to the bone. Deanyn screamed, and I shouted her name, certain that I was about to watch her die.

But the circle was broken now. No one stood between me and the Beast, and I was the one it had come for. It turned to face me, bared its teeth, and charged.

Out of the mist, Bryndine Errynson stepped forward to meet it.

She swung her sword in a vicious arc, and the Beast halted and reared back just in time. The blade cleaved the air inches from its chest. The monster swung back. Bryndine caught the blow on her shield, and the Beast's claws tore deep gouges in the metal, with all the force that had sent Orya flying through the air.

Bryndine kept her feet, undaunted and unmoved.

I looked at her, standing firm before that impossible creature like a hero out of legend, and for just an instant, everything else dropped away. All my life I had dreamed of moments like this. When I was a boy, discouraged by a world that seemed to celebrate mediocrity over all else, Illias' stories had taken me to those moments in time when extraordinary people had done incredible things. The moments that were never forgotten. The moments that history was made of. And watching Bryndine stand before the Beast, I knew that this was one of those moments. Like Erryn and Rynd and Delwyn before her, Bryndine Errynson was forging history. And I was there to see it happen.

Something opened up inside of me then, and the power of the First Tree coursed through my veins. I felt the invisible eyes of the Burnt turn towards me, and heard their voices wailing through my mind, joining as one to speak that single, terrible word.

"*BURN,*" the voices ordered. And I did.

Fire danced across my flesh, and pain came with it. But I had found the Wyd, and I could not let this chance pass. I forced myself to push past the agony of melting flesh, to look beyond the flames. And there, I found something more. Something pure. Everything slowed, became sharp and clear. I could see *between* the mist in the air. I could see every creature, every movement in the clearing.

Then, suddenly, I was somewhere else.

A deep green forest, and in it stand two groups of humans dressed in crude clothing, tall and broad of shoulder, filled with the power of the Earth and Sky. They argue. We watch as one group leaves in anger, and we are saddened. We wanted only to give them guidance.

My senses returned to me, and I looked around, disoriented. I still stood before the First Tree; the fighting had not stopped. Flames devoured my body, but I ignored them, shoved the agony into the deepest recesses of my mind. The Eldest slept, but I could feel their dreams floating through the air around me. I just had to find the right words to wake them.

"We need you," I called. "The Burnt need peace. Please!" But there was no power in the words.

The Beast struck again and again at Bryndine; her shield was a ragged mess of holes and claw marks. Sylla fought beside her now, holding back two men in Army browns who sought to reach her Captain. Deanyn limped on her ruined leg, but still managed to cleave through the skull of a boar as it lunged towards Bryndine.

The women closed in around me, surrounded on all sides by beasts and the dead. Ducking low, Leste avoided a wild stroke of Debra's axe, then jabbed her saber up through the open mouth of the wildcat that leapt at her out of the fog. Selvi caught Ivyla's sword on hers, and Elene stabbed their former comrade in the chest. Ivyla did not fall. She was already dead. It would take a worse wound than that to stop her.

Back to back and shoulder to shoulder, vision clouded by the mist, what was left of Bryndine's company fought desperately for survival. If I did not reach the Eldest soon, it would be too late.

A shining city of arches and spires and gardens, but beyond the walls, war rages. A man with a crown atop his golden hair begs us for the power to defend his kingdom. We cannot refuse. We love these humans as our brothers and sisters. We tell the King of secrets we have hidden from humanity for thousands of years.

Fire and pain pulled me back to reality. It was not just my body burning; I could feel the flames eating at my mind. This was what the Wyddin had warned me of—I could not pull away, and soon my spirit would be consumed.

But I had seen what the Eldest dreamed of: Elovia. If the Plainstongue could not reach them, perhaps Old Elovian would. "*Evea!*" I cried. "*Ael!*" *Wake! Please!* It did no good; the words felt dead on my tongue.

Bryndine caught the Beast's claws on her shield once more, then leaned away from a second blow and swung her sword. The huge blade cleaved into the Beast's shoulder and caught there. Bryndine tried to pull it free, but the Beast jerked back and reared up to its full height. The violent motion sent the blade flying free of both the Beast's body and Bryndine's hand, and it fell to the ground several feet away.

A kingdom burning. Ash fills the Sky; molten rock spews from the Earth. The arches and spires and gardens are gone, burned away by a power we should have kept hidden. Bodies fill the streets, charred and black. Our brothers and sisters are dead. And it is because of us.

The vision faded, but the guilt remained, deep and eternal. The Eldest could not forgive themselves, and all those who might have given them forgiveness were dead and gone. In that moment, I knew exactly what they needed—the same thing I did. I opened my mouth to speak the word that would wake the Eldest.

But the word did not come.

Fire ate at my mind, reducing everything I had ever known to ash. My vision burned down until all I could see was Bryndine and the Beast, surrounded by flames. I heard a cry somewhere beyond sight, but I could not place the woman's voice, and then a man's scream that I faintly recognized as my own. I felt all that I was burning away, and could do nothing to stop it.

I watched helplessly as the Beast lashed out at Bryndine with both paws. She raised her shield, and claws like scythe blades lodged in the metal. With a violent heave, the Beast wrested the battered metal disc from her arm and threw it from her reach.

"Bryn!" Sylla threw herself in front of Bryndine, and her blade lashed out. The Beast knocked her aside with a single blow.

And still Bryndine stood. She had nothing left, no way to defend herself, but she stood between me and the Beast, and she did not flinch as it came for her.

"*Vengeance*," the Burnt screamed, and with devastating strength, the Beast rammed five foot-long claws into Bryndine's chest. Five claws pierced her armor and the flesh beneath. Five claws, red and dripping, erupted from her back.

"No!" Through the fire and pain that consumed me, some last spark of consciousness fought for control. *I can still save her!* Desperately, I shouted every Elovian word my fire-blackened mind had left. None of them were right. None of them were the word I wanted, the one that would echo through the Wyd to reach the ears of the Eldest.

The Beast's claws ripped upwards through flesh and bone, lifting Bryndine from her feet. She struggled, gripped the monster's foreleg, tried to pull herself free. The Beast obliged. With a savage jerk, it tore its claws from her chest. Thick ribbons of crimson colored the mist as she fell. She crumpled to the ground in front of me, still as death.

And now it was too late. There was no one left who could stop the Beast. It loomed over me, so close that I could smell the rank odor of its hide, see the tiny insects crawling in its fur. Its claws descended towards me, streaked with Bryndine's blood.

And then something impossible happened.

Somehow, Bryndine pushed herself to her knees, and with one hand, she *caught* the Beast's foreleg inches above my head. The Beast struck with its free claw, tearing deep furrows in her side; she grappled the limb under her arm, and held it there.

"No," she said. "You will not have him."

Somehow, bleeding and broken, she stood. With all her might, the might I had seen move boulders, she surged forward. The Beast towered over her by half her height again, and must have outweighed her by thousands of pounds, but when Bryndine pushed, it stumbled back.

Somehow, she found the strength to move. She took a staggering step, and another, leaving a crimson trail in the grass as she lurched towards her sword. The Beast fell forward onto four legs, found its footing once more, and lunged. A maw full of jagged yellow teeth gnashed towards my head.

Somehow, with her life's blood flowing from a dozen wounds, Bryndine Errynson lifted her giant blade with both hands, and she brought it down on the Beast's neck.

It was the last thing I saw. My sight dissolved into fire and blackness. My mind was nearly gone. But Bryndine had defied death itself to give me this last attempt; I could not waste it. As my spirit burned into nothingness, a single word rose in the dark, and I knew that it was right. I felt its power on my tongue as I threw back my head and shouted it into the Wyd for the Eldest to hear.

"*Caravei!*"

I forgive.

In my last moments of awareness, I heard a voice, full of power and wisdom and sorrow.

"*Revea,*" it commanded. *Sleep.*

And I did.

CHAPTER THIRTY-SEVEN

Though most shunned Bryndine Errynson when she sought their aid to fight the Burnt, there were those who answered the call. Master Illias Bront helped her to find Prince Fyrril's journals. Korus Creven and Lieutenant Ralsten Torrylson preserved the capital under the leadership of Bryndine's father, Lord Elarryd Errynson, who would later be crowned King. And the women of Bryndine's company followed their Captain to the very end, though many of them died along the way. Without any one of these people, the realm might have been lost.

But it was Bryndine Errynson who sought the truth when no one else would. It was she who refused to surrender when the Army, and the Scribers, and the people themselves deserted her. It was she who led her company to the First Forest when all other options failed.

In the end, it was Bryndine Errynson who saved the Kingsland.

— From Dennon Lark's *Life of Bryndine Errynson*

"Dennon?"

Deanyn's voice ushered me back into the world, aching and disoriented. But alive.

I was lying with my back against the First Tree, and the first thing I saw when I opened my eyes was green. The boughs of the First Tree were laden with foliage, so thick that the entire clearing was cast into shade. Where there had once been little more than a hundred leaves, now there were hundreds of thousands. The spirits of the Burnt.

There were no voices in my head. The Wyd was silent. It was over.

The second thing I saw was Deanyn's worried face leaning over me. "Thank the Mother and the Father," she breathed, and pressed her lips against mine. For a moment, I let my muddled mind stop working and lost myself in the feel of her, pulling her close, twining my fingers in her hair. Finally, she drew back, and laid her hand against my chest, as though to check that my heart was still beating. "I… thought I'd lost you. Are you hurt?"

Confusion came rushing back. "I don't know." I remembered the voice of the Eldest, and then nothing. I blinked to clear my eyes, and looked around.

Though it felt like I had slept for years, I could not have been unconscious for more than a moment. The clearing was still littered with bodies; none had been moved from where they had fallen. Men of the King's Army sprawled beside the creatures of the forest. Debra and Ivyla had fallen beside one another, their weapons still in hand. Elene held her sister's still form in her arms, sobbing. I was shocked to see Orya getting shakily to her feet—I had believed her dead.

And just beyond me, mere feet away, lay the great heap of fur and scars that had been the Beast. Its head had been severed from its neck in a single clean stroke.

I could not see Bryndine.

"Where is she?"

Deanyn knew what I meant instantly. "Dennon, she… I don't know if…" She glanced over her shoulder, and I saw the pain on her face.

"No." I forced myself to my feet. My legs trembled beneath me.

There, beyond Deanyn, I saw her. She lay on her back in the grass, her head cradled in Sylla's lap. Leste stood beside them, a helpless look on her face.

"No." I stumbled towards her and fell to my knees in the grass at her side. The others gathered around us—all save Elene, who would not leave Selvi's body.

She was still alive. Her skin was pale, nearly white; her

breathing was shallow and ragged. Her chest was soaked with blood. There was something innately *wrong* about the sight of her so prone and still; it was like seeing the First Tree itself toppled to the ground. Though I had seen what the Beast had done to her, I had believed, somehow, that she would endure. That she was as invincible as she had always seemed to be.

Sylla's eyes were wet, but she fought to control her voice. "Help her, Scriber."

But Bryndine's wounds were too great. The Beast's claws had shredded skin and bone and organs. That she still lived at all was a miracle. She had given me so much, saved me so many times, and now, when she needed me, I was useless.

"There is nothing he can do." Bryndine's voice was a hoarse whisper, but there was still steel in her eyes; even in the face of death, she was braver than she had any right to be.

"I'm sorry," I said. "Bryndine, I'm so sorry."

"Do not be, Scriber Dennon. You did as you promised. You did not fail." Her fingers flexed, and she tilted her head to search the grass beside her. I knew immediately what she was looking for—she wanted her sword in her hand, at the end. It lay just out of her reach, and I dragged it closer and pressed the hilt into her palm. Her fingers closed around it. She smiled weakly.

"Don't," I begged, as though she could stay through sheer strength of will. "Please don't."

"Tell them… that I kept my oath." And then Bryndine Errynson closed her eyes, and breathed her last.

I could not even cry. I was too empty. It was too much.

Tell them that I kept my oath. In her last moments, despite all of her strength, after all she had done, she had still been the girl in the ill-fitting dress, out of her element at her aunt's table, looking for approval from the people who had denied it to her all her life. They had never deserved her. And right then, if I could have, I would have traded all of their lives to bring her back.

But I could not. "I will tell them," I said softly, clasping her hand.

"Take your hands off her." Sylla's voice was flat, but when I looked up, her face was twisted with barely contained fury.

"Sylla, I…"

"*Do not touch her.*" Sylla's hand darted out, and grasped the hilt of Bryndine's sword. She was on her feet in an instant, holding the point of the blade against my neck. The sword was too big for her; it took both of her hands to hold it steady, and the tip shook dangerously, a quarter-inch from my skin. "I told you what would happen, Scriber. I told you what would happen if you let her die."

"Sylla!" Deanyn put her hand on the other woman's shoulder, but Sylla jerked away. "Don't do this. This isn't what Bryndine would want."

"What she would *want?* She is dead, she doesn't *want* anything!" She glared down at me with red-rimmed eyes. "Why should you live if she doesn't, Scriber?"

Strangely, I was not afraid. Not because I didn't think Sylla would harm me, but because at that moment, it didn't seem to matter much if she did. "I don't know," I said. "It isn't fair." A world where I was dead and Bryndine lived would be a far better world than this.

Elene still cradled Selvi in her arms, but she looked up from her sister's face, and in a quavering voice, she asked, "Haven't enough people died already, Sylla?"

"They died because of him!" Sylla shouted. She was not wrong. *How many would still live if I had found the Wyd sooner?*

"You're forgettin' that the rest of us lived because of him," Orya said. Her sword was in her hand. "We ain't just going to let you kill him."

The last thing I wanted was more bloodshed. "Don't," I said. "Don't hurt her. She's right. I… should have been better. Faster."

"And you should die because of that?" Deanyn shook her head. "No. You did as much as anyone could have asked." She stepped towards Sylla again. "Please, give me the sword. It doesn't have to be like this."

"No further!" Sylla warned, her hands trembling. The tip of the sword touched my neck, and I felt a sharp pain as it drew blood. Deanyn held up her hands and backed away.

"This is not the way, Sylla," said Leste. "Tenille waits in Three Rivers. There is a place for you still. But if you are doing this, you cannot go back."

"Do you think I am just looking for someone else to *follow?* Bryndine was more than just... She saved me, when she had no reason to. She trusted me when no one else would." Tears fell down Sylla's cheeks, tracing lines through the blood and dirt there. "I *loved* her."

And hearing her say that, I realized something so simple I couldn't believe I had not known it until now. Looking up at Sylla along the length of that massive blade, I said, "So did I."

For a moment, Sylla stared back at me, her eyes dark pools of despair. And then, with a wordless scream of anguish, she swung Bryndine's sword.

But not at me.

With all of her rage and all of her sorrow, Sylla drove the huge blade into the First Tree, and it sank into the ancient trunk as though cleaving through air.

She had expected that no more than I had; she had done it, I think, only because she needed to strike *something.* She stared in disbelief as the wood parted to accept the sword and knit together again as it passed. No wound was left behind. Only a foot of blade still jutted from the tree, and a plain steel hilt, too long in Sylla's hands. As big as it was, the sword should have looked tiny buried in that vast trunk, but somehow it did not. It looked like something from a story—a hero's weapon, waiting to be pulled free.

A sudden wind stirred the boughs of the First Tree, and a voice that only I could hear, calm and strong and sad, whispered, "*We will not forget her.*" The sun reached a single golden finger through the parted leaves, and for a moment, Bryndine Errynson was bathed in light.

And then I understood. It was a memorial. The Wyddin were honoring her sacrifice.

And though she could not hear the voices, I think Sylla understood as well. She stood in silence for a long time, her hand lingering on the hilt of the sword, and then she sank to her knees, and wept.

CHAPTER THIRTY-EIGHT

I didn't know how much Bryndine meant to me until she was gone. I will remember her for the rest of my life.

— From the personal journals of Dennon Lark

We commended Bryndine Errynson to the Father that night, before the First Tree, with the women who had died beside her. And as the pyre burned, we stood vigil, just as Bryndine had done so many times before for so many others.

Standing with the few survivors of Bryndine's company, I watched as the flames consumed the bodies. Deanyn leaned against me to keep the weight off her injured leg, and I held her hand tightly in my own. Elene and Leste and Orya clustered beside us. Sylla stood alone a short distance away, solemn and quiet.

Bryndine had always given a short farewell to her fallen women, but we stood in silence. No one wanted to take her place. She deserved something though—they all did. Some words that might honor what they had done. After a long while, I swallowed nervously, and I said, "People will know their story. They… won't be forgotten."

Sylla laughed bitterly. "Do you really believe that, Scriber? No one will remember them. No one will remember *her*. Look where we are. No one saw what she did, no one but us. Do you think they will listen when you tell them what happened here?"

"Her father will be King. He…"

"The King doesn't write history. People remember what they want to remember, and they have never loved Bryndine. They will say Lord Elarryd saved them, or Ralsten, or Korus, someone who was *there*, in the capital. Even Tenille, if they must." She looked at me, and her mouth rose into a cynical smirk that couldn't quite mask the anguish in her eyes. "Or perhaps they will hear your story, and call you their hero, Scriber. They have done it before, after Waymark. But whoever it is, it will not be her."

Silence fell again. I could not find the words to counter Sylla's argument; she was very likely right. The people of the Kingsland had always been blind when it came to Bryndine. I could see the outline of her body in the flames, and I gazed at her, and wondered. Would it be like Waymark again, citizens insisting they owed their lives to anyone but her? Was that Bryndine's legacy, to be remembered only by the spirits of the forest, reviled and then forgotten by her own people? It would have been all too easy to accept. So much of the Kingsland's past was already lies, why not this? It would have been easy to blame myself for her death, and retreat into the guilt, and let Bryndine fade from history.

But I could still hear her words from the night before: *we owe it to those who died to do more with our lives*. She was gone, and I owed it to her to stop running away. I could not ride a horse, or shoot a bow, or wield a sword; I had not been fast enough or strong enough to save her when she needed me. But I could do this. I could do this for her, if nothing else. She would not be another Fyrril. While I lived, she would not be forgotten.

"No," I said. There had been enough lies already; it was time for the Kingsland to know the truth. "She died for them. They *will* remember her."

"I wish that was true, Scriber. I truly do." There was only hopelessness left in Sylla's voice. "But whatever you say, they will ignore it."

"They won't. Because you were right before: the King doesn't write history. But neither do the people. *I do*." Something burned inside me, a determination like nothing I had ever felt before—the determination I had learned from Bryndine. "If Erryn and Aliana could turn the past into a lie with their stories, I can turn it into truth with mine. I will write of what she did here today until my fingers cannot hold a quill. I will speak of her courage until my voice is gone. And *they will remember*."

I swept my eyes over the faces of the women around me, and when I spoke again my voice was so strong that I could hardly believe it was mine. "You do not have to stand by while they forget. Help me. Tell them of what happened here, and of the women who died to save them. Tell them of Bryndine, and of Selvi, and Genna, and Wynne. Tell them of the Wyddin and the Burning, so that it can never happen again. Tell them the *truth*. *Make* them remember."

Deanyn smiled at me, pride shining in her eyes, and she said, "I am with you, Dennon."

"And I," said Leste. Beside her, Elene nodded without speaking, never looking away from Selvi's body.

Orya flashed her wild grin. "Never could keep my mouth shut anyway."

Only Sylla gave no reply, staring at Bryndine through the flames of the pyre. And then she turned, and met my eyes, and nodded, just once. "We will not let them forget," she said softly.

We stayed there for a long time after that, until the last of the flames died. Until all that was left of Bryndine Errynson burned away.

You will be remembered, I promised, as the last embers smouldered into ash.

A Scriber never forgets.

EPILOGUE

Scriber Elyse closed the journal and looked over her shoulder at the statue. Not for the first time, she wondered what she had done to earn this opportunity.

Reading Scriber Dennon's words always made her ask the same question. There were other artists, better known and more prestigious than she, more suited to sculpt such a beloved figure. Indeed, when the Children had come to Elyse with the commission, she had thought it a joke. She had been pinned in the School of Arts only two years before, and one needed decades of experience, she had been told time and time again, to truly become an artist of worth.

She had impressed her teachers at the Academy with her statue of the renowned High Commander Tenille, that much was true. She had resisted the urge to make the woman young and strong, as was so often done with heroes. Instead, Elyse had sculpted her with a lined, weathered face, full of cunning and experience. When the ninth Barbarian Incursion had begun, Tenille had already been a grandmother, but still she had led the Army with a firm and wise hand. Remembering her for that had seemed more important to Elyse than making her beautiful. But a single statue hidden away at the Academy hardly merited the attention of the Children.

Her second commission was perhaps better known, a statue of King Elarryd the Golden, for a small park in the Kingscourt. It was good work, certainly, but there were many statues of the man. Of course there were. He was the King who had rebuilt the Kingsland after the dark final year of King Syrid's reign, and allied with the Wyddin to bring life back to the realm's wasted fields and farms. He had named Tenille his High Commander, and with her guided the realm to victory in the eighth and ninth Incursions. He was among the most beloved Kings in history. The statue would have been liked no matter its quality.

No, the statues of Elarryd and Tenille had not earned Elyse a place among the most respected Scribers of the Arts. They were well made, but there were many others. So when the request had come for her to create a piece for the newly rebuilt Old Garden, she had thought her friends from the Academy were playing a trick on her. She had been even more certain of it when she read the name of the statue's subject—far too ironic a choice for the normally humourless Children, if it was to stand in the Old Garden of all places.

But some weeks after she had dismissed it as a jest, the Eldest Brother and Sister had come to her themselves. The Children liked her work on other figures from the period, they had said, and felt it fitting, given those other pieces, that she be the one to sculpt this statue for them. When Elyse asked about their choice of subject, the Eldest Sister had only said, "The Mother is as wise as she is forgiving," and the Eldest Brother had followed with, "And the Father blesses all those who protect his children." They were adamant that this was what they wanted for the Old Garden's antechamber.

Elyse had accepted, of course. Not for the prestige or the extremely generous pay—or not *only* for those things—but for the chance to sculpt a childhood idol, a near mythical figure in the Kingsland's history.

Research was always her first step, to truly get to know the subject before she ever set chisel to stone, and so Elyse had read every word Dennon Lark had ever written. The breadth of the man's work was staggering. He wrote with confidence and authority on nearly every subject imaginable, every period of history. And if sometimes he was not as impartial as an historian ought to be, if he made the occasional caustic remark, or at times scolded the world for not remembering certain things he thought it should, what did it matter? He had lived through and recovered more of the Kingsland's history than any Scriber before or since. He had earned the right to make his opinions known. It made it easier for her, actually, that he let his personality saturate his work.

Few had lived as eventful a life as Scriber Dennon, or done so much for the realm. He had married one of the wealthiest women in the Kingsland, and he and his wife had put much of their fortune into charitable works. One fund they had started, known as Wynne's Trust, still paid admission to the Academy for any who desired it. It was this fund, in fact, that had paid Elyse's own entry to the School of Arts. That was another reason she had taken the commission—to show her gratitude. She liked to think it was what Scriber Dennon would have wanted.

It was not works of charity that Dennon Lark was best remembered for, though. This was a man who had counted kings among his closest friends; who had been named an honorary Storyteller by the Salt Mountain clans; who had travelled over the Dragon's Sea to the lands beyond, and across the Wasted Plains to the ruins of Old Elovia. He was the Kingsland's first emissary to the Wyddin, and after the death of his mentor, the respected Master Illias Bront, he became the Academy's first unanimously chosen Master of History.

And most importantly, Dennon Lark had saved the Kingsland in its time of greatest need, from the mad Wyddin known as the Burnt. It was this part of his life that interested Elyse more than anything, that gave her the truest insight into her subject. She had read the journals from the period over and over again as she worked, dozens of times.

And now she was almost done. It was very close to perfect, she thought, standing from her desk and crossing the room to survey her work.

The statue was tall—the journals had been clear on that. Elyse had to clamber up a ladder to reach the head so she could chip slightly at the hair, making sure it looked as it should: short and efficient. Moving down, she set her chisel against the jaw. It had to be firm, determined; a small scrape there, and then the line was right. Leaning against a broad stone shoulder, she examined the eyes. There was a power in them that she hoped others would see; it influenced the entire face. Not a beautiful face, true, but one that suggested deep strength.

Finally, she stepped down and returned to the books, checking one last time. The writings were the best way for her to measure her work, to ensure she had captured her subject correctly.

And Dennon Lark had written many, many things about the subject of this statue.

Elyse knew his words almost by heart; she could almost see through his eyes. And when she looked at the statue now, looked with Dennon Lark's eyes, she knew that it was done.

She had always attempted to sculpt her subjects as they had been in life—as people rather than figures of legend—but the statue looked like legend all the same: a woman nearly eight feet tall, broad-shouldered and powerful, holding aloft in one hand a sword that most could not have lifted with two. She might have been a giant from the dawn of the world, with the strength of kings and heroes behind her eyes.

The statue looked like legend because this woman had never been anything less. She had battled monsters and inspired heroes. Those she had led went on to command armies and advise rulers and sail uncharted seas, taking her story with them wherever they travelled. Ballads of her sacrifice were still sung in taverns and before kings and queens; tales of her valor were still told to children before bedtime even now, more than a hundred years after her death.

She was known as the Soldier Princess, though she had not, in truth, lived to be a princess; some—very few—named her the Bloody Bride. She was called the Seeker of Truth and the Sword in the Forest, Beastslayer and Promisekeeper, martyr and savior and saint. She was called all these things, and many others.

Her name was Bryndine Errynson.

And she would never be forgotten.

ABOUT THE AUTHOR

Ben Dobson is a Canadian fantasy author from the beautiful province of British Columbia. When he isn't writing to indulge his lifelong passion for epic tales, he can probably be found playing Dungeons and Dragons or watching a Joss Whedon show or something similarly awesome and stereotypical.

For more information, check one of these places:

Website: www.bensdobson.com
Facebook: www.facebook.com/bensdobson
Twitter: www.twitter.com/bensdobson
Email: benificus@gmail.com

Made in the USA
Coppell, TX
25 October 2019

10477829R00217